"Ho

Kiss me, Farr—"

✳

His lips trailed down the side of her face to her throat. His heart was pounding violently against her soft breasts. He hadn't meant for this to happen tonight. She was tired and sore after her ordeal today; but when she turned to him and touched him, he hadn't been able to help himself. Even as he was kissing her, a small voice in his head told him to stop . . . that he would hurt her.

"Liberty . . . I've got to know. I want you, but not unless you want me too. Do you . . . want me to leave you?" he whispered the words against her ear.

"Oh, please! Don't leave me now!" Whatever comes, this night was hers. The thought that followed her words was so tangible in her mind that she didn't know or care if she had voiced it. "Hold me, Farr. Hold me as if . . . you love me—just for tonight."

His kisses came upon her mouth, warm, devouring, fierce with passion . . .

✳   ✳   ✳   ✳   ✳

"Dorothy Garlock writes about love in such a way that one would almost believe she coined the word."
—*Affaire de Coeur*

"You'll find yourself actually there, right in the picture. You can feel the heat of the campfire, you can hear the wagon creaking and the slice and snap of the bullwhip. . . . There's good reason why Dorothy has been called the 'Louis L'Amour of the romance novelists.'"
—*Beverly Hills California Courier*

Also by Dorothy Garlock

Annie Lash
Restless Wind
Wayward Wind
Wild Sweet Wilderness
Wind of Promise

Published by
POPULAR LIBRARY

LONESOME RIVER

Dorothy Garlock

POPULAR LIBRARY

An Imprint of Warner Books, Inc.

A Warner Communications Company

POPULAR LIBRARY EDITION

Popular Library® and the fanciful P design are registered
trademarks of Warner Books, Inc.

Cover art by Sharon Spiak

Popular Library books are published by
Warner Books, Inc.
666 Fifth Avenue
New York, N.Y. 10103

 A Warner Communications Company

Printed in the United States of America

First Printing: August, 1987

10 9 8 7 6 5 4 3 2 1

Dedicated to
my son Herb
and
his wife Jacky,
who give me
luck and logic,
laughter and love

1. Quill's Station
2. Fawnella's Grave
3. Shellenberger Place (taken over by Stith)
4. Maude Perkins' Homestead
5. Luscomb's
6. Palmer Homestead
7. George Thompson's
8. Sufferites' Homestead
9. Mr. Washington's Ferry
10. Edward Brown Homestead
11. Where Liberty Rescued the Indian Woman
12. Sawyer Camp

Chapter
One

"We are not turning back!" The girl's gaze was as direct as a saber thrust, and her voice was as cold as its steel blade.

Elija Carroll looked at his daughter for a full minute before he spoke. "I jist said 1811 ain't a good year fer movin'. The whole country's in a hell of a mess. It's agoin' broke, is what it is. We ain't ort a left Middlecrossin' 'n come out here where there ain't no towns, no folks, no nothin'. But if'n ya had to go, why clear to the Indiana? Ya could've stayed in the Ohio. Folks is pouring in thar. But ya jist want to roam around and see country, don't ya? Why, there's places at home that's wilder'n all get out, if'n it was backwoods ya was seekin'."

"Any year that you have to work is a bad year for you, Papa. You didn't have to come along, but you did. You know why we came. Jubal and I couldn't stay in Middlecrossing. Stith Lenning would have killed him. Jubal wanted to come, and I go where my husband goes. And you'll go with me because you have no one but me and Amy, and you're afraid you'll die alone."

"Yo're hard, Libby. Hard. That school learnin' yore ma give ya has dang near ruint ya. Ya ain't never learned a woman's place. Them fancy notions has made ya hard as any man I ever knowed."

"You have to be hard to get through this life, Papa. You can call it hard and stubborn if you want to. If you'd had your way I'd be nothing but a drudge during the day and a whore at night. That's what Stith Lenning wanted. He wanted me to cook his meals, keep his house, milk his cows, raise a house full of younguns to grow up to work his fields. He wanted me to do all that and fornicate all night long!"

"Hush yore mouth! It ain't fittin' fer a woman to be talkin' such as that. A woman ort ta keep to her place—"

"What place is that? You expect me to work for my keep like a dumb milch cow, is that it? Work, service a man, and keep my mouth shut? I'll be damned if I will! I'll be his helpmate, but not his servant." Liberty looked at her father's bent, thin shoulders when he turned his back on her, as he always turned it against trouble. Her voice softened with resignation. "Oh, get some sleep. I'll sit up with Jubal."

Elija didn't reply. There was plenty of argument left in him, but he knew he didn't stand a chance to win. The only woman he had ever known who was like his daughter had been her mother, and during their entire married life he hadn't won an argument with her. He had not been able to put an end to her independent ways, either, and the nonsense had been passed on to the daughter who was the spitting image of her.

For the past few days, Liberty had spent most of her waking hours tending her sick husband in the Dearborn wagon in which they were making the journey cross-country to Vincennes. Their two oxen and two horses were picketed nearby, and in the quiet she could hear the comforting sound of their stamping and cropping the grass. After leaving the boat at Louisville, they had joined four other families for the journey cross-country to the Wabash River. Now, because the settlers feared Jubal had the flux, Liberty's family was forced to travel far behind the other wagons.

"Come on out and go to bed, Amy." Liberty stood at the end of the wagon and helped her sister as she climbed over the tailgate. Twelve-year-old Amy was a slim, wiry girl with brown eyes and curly brown hair. She had been born to Elija's second wife to whom he had been married a scant year when she died in childbirth.

"Jubal's hot, Libby, awful hot. I kept the wet cloth on him like you said."

"I'll take over, now. Get under the wagon and get some sleep." Amy crawled into the nest of blankets and Liberty dropped a sheet of canvas over her to shield her from the wind. She and Amy were forced to sleep under the wagon with Elija since their belongings and Liberty's sick husband occupied all available space inside.

From inside the wagon Jubal Perry's hacking cough became stronger, ending finally in a choked gurgle. Liberty climbed into the wagon and moved the copper dish containing the burning black gunpowder closer to the pallet of folded blankets. So far the acrid fumes had done little to clear the strangling phlegm from Jubal's throat. His skin was stretched tightly over the bones of his face, and she could see the large veins throbbing at his temples. He had lost so much weight since they had started this journey that she doubted if his weight even equalled hers now.

Liberty didn't know what else to do for him, and because of that, she felt a strong sense of guilt, a conviction that she was failing this man when he needed her most. He had stepped in and married her, giving her his protection and his name, and by doing so had snatched her from the clutches of Stith Lenning, who had been determined to have her.

A severe fit of coughing seized Jubal, and when it subsided he lay breathing heavily.

"You came out here more for me than for yourself, didn't you, Jubal?" Liberty's fingertips smoothed the sparse hair back from his dry, hot forehead. "You knew that if we stayed Stith would have found a way to have me even if he had to kill you. You gave up everything you had worked for to come to this new land. You're such a gentle man, Jubal. All you ever wanted was to make your pots and jugs. But you insisted on coming—saying you wanted to go to your brother so I wouldn't feel bad about you giving up so much. I guess in your own way, you're as stubborn as I am."

Jubal lay with his eyes closed. He had said very little all day. He had just lain there, not complaining as her father would have done. Liberty didn't know if he had gone to sleep or not. Yet she talked, wanting him to know that she cared for him, in a way. He had not asked anything for himself, not even the consummation of the marriage. Jubal Perry was not the kind of man who fought for what he wanted. Small of stature and weak of body, he had made his pots, seemingly content to stand on the sidelines and watch life pass him by. The only daring thing he had ever done in his entire life was to marry Liberty Carroll, knowing a younger, stronger man wanted her desperately, and also knowing Stith was capable of killing to get her.

Stith Lenning, a storekeeper in Middlecrossing, had watched Liberty grow from a child, younger than her sister Amy was now, into a lovely young woman. He had planned for years to ask Elija for her hand in marriage. It wasn't her comely features that attracted Stith so much as her strong, proud body, made for rutting and childbearing, and his desire to squelch her independent spirit. She also would have brought to the marriage her father's hands to labor in the fields behind his store. In spite of Elija's hangdog attitude and complaints of ill health, he had a good ten years of work left in him. Amy would have helped with chores in the barn and they would have brought oxen, horses, and a houseful of furniture Liberty's grandfather, an excellent craftsman, had made. He would have beaten her when she was rebellious and scolded her for her foolish dreams. He would have made her old and worn out before she was thirty.

Jubal realized this. He married Liberty when she asked him, because her father wanted Liberty to marry Stith, and the law said a father had the right to give his daughter in marriage to a man of his choice. Stith was considered a rich man, and Elija saw years of easy living if his daughter married such a man. Jubal pampered her, provided for her father and sister, and when she wanted to leave Middlecrossing in upper New York State because she feared for his life, and because it would fulfill her dream of building a home in a new land, he sold his pottery shop and purchased supplies for the journey. During their year of marriage he had made no attempt to drive the laughter and ambition from her as Stith Lenning would have done. And now she felt a touch of shame, for she had only affection to give him, affection much like that a woman would give an older brother.

All through the long night hours Liberty applied warm cloths to Jubal's chest, trying to relieve the congestion that was slowly strangling him. An hour before dawn she dozed, and when morning came, she looked out of the wagon and into a steady rain. The wagon was sitting on a small rise in the middle of a shallow pond.

"Libby! Come on out here. I ain't likin' what's agoin' on a'tall." Elija stood at the end of the wagon with his shoulders hunched and spoke in a tired, fatalistic voice.

Liberty lifted her long skirts and climbed out over the tailgate. She could tell by the tone of her father's voice and the way his head was sunk between his shoulders that he was unable to cope with whatever was wrong.

"What do you mean?"

"Jist that." Elija waved his hand at the water standing in the trail and around the wagon. "The confounded rain is washin' us away. Can't nobody travel in sich weather as this here. We ain't never agoin' to get out of here. I said we ain't ort a come," he murmured in a tone that said he'd walked with trouble for a long time. "I told ya, and I told Jubal. We ain't ort a come. But ya jist wouldn't listen."

Anger blazed into a sudden flame in Liberty's mind, but she doused it with logical reasoning. There was nothing she could say that would change her father's attitude. She gave him a quelling look, and he stopped talking.

"If the wagons up ahead can travel, so can we. We'll hitch up and go on. Jubal needs medicine." She bit her lower lip so she could speak without anger. "He needs medicine or he'll die." She said the words slowly as if her father didn't understand.

"Where'll ya find medicine? That a way?" He flung his hand toward the thick forest.

Fury reddened Liberty's face and narrowed her eyes. She clenched her fists in frustration. "You don't care if he dies!

If he does you think we'll turn back. We are not turning back. We're going on until we reach the Wabash and follow it to Vincennes."

"Oh, Lordy! Oh, Lordy, mercy me!" he wailed.

"Papa?" Amy crawled out of her nest under the wagon and went to him.

"I'm all right, sister. Get in the wagon outta the way."

Amy ran to the back of the wagon and climbed in. Elija, moving slowly, sloshed through the water to where the oxen were tied and led them to the wagon.

Watching her father's slow, ponderous movements, Liberty felt tears of rage run down her face, already wet with rain. There were times when she wished, truly wished, her father had remained in Middlecrossing. He was against every decision she made. Now there was the chance Jubal would die. The dampness and the jolting of the wagon might kill him, but what else could she do? They had to get to dryer ground before the water rose any higher.

As she worked, she thought of the words wheezed in her ear by Hull Dexter, the leader of the party that had moved on without them.

"Ya don't hafta stay with 'em. Ya be a purty bit a fluff, even if'n ya are skinny as a starved rabbit. Ya 'n the gal can come with me. I'll bed ya gentle like."

"You buzzard bait!" she had replied. "I'd as soon bed down with a nest of rattlesnakes. Get your filthy hands off me."

"Yore old man stinks like the flux. When he goes, bury 'em deep or the wolves'll get 'em. If'n ya don't come down with it, ya can c'mon 'n catch up. I'll be waitin' fer ya up ahead."

"I'll come on all right. I'll get you, you rotgut, flea-bitten, son of a jackass! You took our money to lead us to Vincennes. You give it back or I'll have the law on you. My brother-in-law is with the militia at Vincennes. He'll—"

"Ya figgered he was at Limestone, then at Louisville." Hull Dexter laughed. "If'n I warn't sure yore old man's got the catchin' sickness, I'd not leave ya. Ya'd not be so feisty if'n ya had a real man atween yore legs 'stead a that puny thin' ya got."

"You're not a man, Hull Dexter. You're a . . . a lily-livered, bush-bottom warthog, is what you are." She had shouted the words as he mounted his horse and told the others to move out. "Every blasted one of you put together wouldn't make the man Jubal Perry is. You wait till Hammond Perry hears what you've done." Liberty was so angry, unguarded words spewed from her mouth. "I'll blacken your name all over this territory, you . . . louse! Hog! Rotten river trash! I'll have you arrested and put in the stocks, and I'll throw cow dung in your face! By jinks damn! I . . . I hope you *all* get scalped!"

Hull Dexter laughed heartily. "I'll be back to get them fine horses, if'n the Injuns don't steal 'em."

The women from the other wagons were appalled by her outburst and turned their backs. Those riding climbed into the wagons, the ones walking switched the oxen, and the wagons moved away. Liberty had tried to make friends with them. They had tolerated her but made no overtures themselves. Deeply religious and subservient to their husbands' wishes, they had been shocked to discover she was not properly submissive, that she argued with her father, spoke with the men as if she were their equal, left her hair uncovered at times, and was the one in charge of the family.

Liberty shook her fist at the departing wagons. Angry tears filled in her eyes.

"I'd prefer the Indians to have them rather than you, Hull Dexter. You're a coward, a blackguard—"

"Hush up yore hollerin', Liberty. Yo're makin' a plumb fool a yoreself. Ya ain't gonna say nothin' that'll hurt 'em, 'n they ain't carin' what happens to us. Oh, Lordy! I don't know what's to become of us way out here in the wilderness all by ourselves."

That was two days ago, and Elija's voice of doom had droned continually since then.

"I jist knowed it'd turn out like this. I jist knowed we hadn't ort a come. They ain't even a track a them folks, we done dropped so fer behind. Ya jist wouldn't listen, would ya? We had us a place, but ya had to go 'n get Jubal all riled up to leave it, atellin' him tall tales 'bout Stith agoin' to kill him. Ya just go a root-hoggin' to get yore own way. Now see what ya've gone and done? Ya got me 'n Amy stuck off a way out here, 'n Jubal is dyin'—"

Liberty turned on him. "Hush up, Papa!" She lifted her skirts and pushed her way through the wet grass toward the horses. "Stop feeling sorry for yourself for a change! We had a place all right. It was Jubal's place and right next to the Bloody Red Ox. That was right handy for you, wasn't it, Papa? How long do you think we'd have stayed there? Another week? Month? Can't you get it through your head that Stith was going to kill Jubal? He bragged about it to me and to Jubal. Jubal and I decided this together, Papa. I preferred to take my chances out here in the wilderness, and Jubal did too. He had rather come than stay there and face sure death." Her last words were shouted angrily.

"Stith was a workin' man. He warn't agoin' to kill nobody a'tall. I told ya when ya married Jubal that a dog what follows anybody what comes along ain't worth a hoot. Beats me all hollow how two men can be so different. Stith had a good place, woulda give us a home. All Jubal done was fiddle around with them pots, atryin' to make 'em pretty. But ya wouldn't listen. Ya tied up with a man who pandered to yore foolish notions. I told Jubal a dozen times to look afore he jumped up 'n sold ever'thin'. He paid no more heed than ya did. To hear him tell it, *ya* knowed all that was fit to be knowed."

Liberty took several deep gulps of air into her lungs, then said calmly but firmly, "Don't ever say another bad thing about Jubal. If you do—I'll take Amy and the wagon and leave you sitting right here. Do you understand, Papa?"

Elija snorted. "Back to that, are ya? Well, there ain't no use arguin' with a woman like ya are." He shook his head. "Ya sure like shootin' off yore mouth, but ya never listen to a word a body says. I might jist as well hush my mouth 'n save my breath." He tied one of the horses behind the wagon and moved the oxen up in front and hitched them.

"Yes. Save it and use it to help me get this wagon someplace where we can build a fire, if not for Jubal's sake, then for yours and Amy's." She picked up a stick and struck the patient ox on the rump. "Get to humping, Molly. Move on out, Sally." The oxen strained at the yoke and slowly pulled the heavy wagon out of the mud and onto a trail that ran between trees so thick one could scarcely see twenty feet into their depth. "Amy," Liberty called once they were moving, "how is Jubal?"

Amy came out of the wagon and climbed onto the seat. "He's sleepin', but he makes a awful racket."

Liberty looked at her shivering sister. There was a scared, peaked look on her freckled face. Good heavens! She had forgotten how it upset Amy for her to argue with their father. Oh, God, she prayed. Please don't let Amy get sick. Liberty's greatest fear was that something would happen to Amy. Next was the fear that Stith Lenning would follow them into the wilderness.

"You're all wet, love. Get back in there, put on something dry, and stay out of the rain. You don't have to be afraid you'll catch what Jubal has. Those ignorant louts that left us here wouldn't know lung sickness from the pox."

"Aren't you hungry, Libby?"

"Sure, I am. We'll be out of this bog soon. There's a rise up ahead where I think we can stop. Papa should be able to find some dry wood for a fire under that thick stand of trees and I'll fix us something hot. We'll spend the day there. The wagons up ahead can't make time in weather like this either."

Liberty walked beside the oxen. Her long homespun dress was wet. It molded her shoulders and high pert breasts and clung to her slender thighs as she walked. She was not a tall girl, but her erectness and the proud way she carried her head made her seem tall. Her face was smooth and slightly tanned, a perfect oval frame for her straight, golden brown brows and large, clear, deep set eyes that were as blue as the feathers on a young bluejaw. Her slightly tilted nose and soft, red mouth were just there in her face, because it was her curly blond hair, a legacy from her Swedish mother, that drew one's attention. She wore it parted in the middle, and now it hung to her hips in two long, soggy braids that were secured at the ends by a heavy linen string. In the rain the short hair about her face curled in ringlets so tight they resembled small corkscrews plastered to her forehead.

Back in Middlecrossing no one paid much attention to the color of her hair because there were so many blonds among the Dutch and Swedish families in the area. But the farther west they came, the more it was noticed, and in Louisville the rivermen had hooted and whistled when the string broke and her bonnet went sailing in the wind.

Liberty guided the oxen to a place where the branches of two huge oaks intermingled, making a canopy under which they could park the wagon. She could see where another wagon had parked in this place and where the traveler had left a circle of stones, made to enclose a cookfire.

She hoisted her skirts and climbed into the wagon as soon as she picketed the extra horse. Amy had changed her clothes and put on one of their father's old buckskin shirts that hung below her knees. She climbed out onto the wagon seat and down the wheel to the ground.

"Jubal, are you awake?" Liberty knelt down and peered into his face.

"Libby?" he said weakly and groped for her hand. He held it to his feverish cheek. "I'm sorry I'm no help to you."

"You will be when you're feeling better. We'll get a fire going and I'll make you some hot switchel."

"I don't know, Libby. I don't know if I can drink it." His voice rasped and a severe fit of coughing seized him.

"Of course you can. I'll put in a dab of rum." She spoke gently when his coughing subsided. "You'll get well, and we'll build us a place near the river where you can get the finest clay to make your pots. People need jugs out here, too. Maybe we can send them downriver to New Orleans.

I'll do the farming and we'll have milk and butter and eggs to make the nog you like so much."

"I'm not much good to you, Libby." His voice was so much like her father's defeated voice that it frightened her.

"Yes, you are. You're going to get well, or I'll . . . or I'll snatch you plumb bald, Jubal Perry. That's what I'll do," she threatened with a catch in her voice, hoping he would smile.

He didn't.

"We're going to have that place we dreamed about, away from Stith Lenning, away from all of those pissants back in Middlecrossing who thought a jug was a jug as long as it held their corn liquor." She brought his thin hand to her cheek, one of the few gestures of affection she had ever shown him.

"Is it still raining, Libby? I don't know as I ever felt the cold and damp so much. I don't know how Hammond has stood this country."

"It's only a puny little old drizzle now. Tomorrow the sun will be out and will dry things off. Try to sleep, Jubal. Are you warm enough?"

"I guess so. Are we keeping up? It seems like we go so slow and stop a lot."

"We're keeping up. We're all stopping today because of the weather. It won't be long, Jubal, and you'll see Hammond." Liberty felt not a twinge of guilt for the lie she was telling. She would tell a hundred lies, she vowed, if it would ease Jubal's mind.

"I hope so. You'd better get out of those wet clothes or you'll come down with the fever." He wearily closed his eyes.

Liberty looked at him for a moment. His mouth was agape as he struggled to get air to his lungs. The daylight that filtered through the thick forest made the interior of the wagon dark and gloomy and gave a yellowish cast to his face. She could not remember feeling more helpless or more alone. It was her fault they were there. Jubal had given up everything to try to keep her out of Stith's clutches. She knew it wasn't fear for his life that prompted him to leave

Middlecrossing. He had taken a fatalistic attitude about Stith killing him. Now he would die and be left in this lonely place.

She stroked his hot, dry brow and thought back to the day she had married Jubal. She had been sure Stith would back off and leave her alone, but that wasn't the case. He seemed to be all the more determined. As the days, weeks and months passed, she was afraid to be alone even long enough to go to the outhouse. She talked it over with Jubal and they had decided to move West. Together they had reread the letters he had received over the last few years from his brother, Hammond, telling about the free land in the Illinois and Indiana country. He was a militiaman, and when Ohio became a state in 1803, he had been sent further west to posts along the Ohio River. At Limestone they were told he was at Louisville, and there they were told he was at Vincennes, so they had joined the party led by Hull Dexter, who promised to take them to the village on the Wabash River.

Liberty allowed herself one brief moment of regret for the pain she had caused her gentle husband, then she squared her shoulders and climbed out of the wagon. She unhitched the oxen and staked them beneath the tree where they could reach the long, green grass. Elija and Amy searched for dry wood. They found some and piled it beside the wagon. Liberty dug punk from a rotten log, poured on a small amount of black powder, then struck steel against flint to make a spark. It caught suddenly, and she fed in small twigs until it blazed brightly.

"How's Jubal?" Elija asked without looking at her. It would take the rest of the day for him to end his pouting.

"His cough is worse."

"He'll choke is what he'll do. Lung fever's bad. Mighty bad. It dang near killed off the army at the Potomac. General Washington was in a fine kettle a fish, I tell you. Why, when I was a boy, my papa said—"

"Get some more wood, Papa. Then we've got to build

some sort of shelter so I can cook something hot for Jubal and Amy."

"Papa do this, Papa do that," he grumbled. "Papa's good enuff ta work, but he ain't good enuff to listen to. And his advice ain't worth a flitter."

"Advice is like croton oil. It's easy to give to someone else." Liberty tried to take the sting from her words by smiling at her sister as she took a load of wood from her arms. "Are you warm now?"

"Uh huh. But I'm hungry."

"I'll make some pap and lace it with molasses. It'll be good for Jubal too."

"Won't do no good. Won't do no good a'tall." Elija fed wood to the growing fire. "I told him it was foolhardy to come out here. I told him he ain't the buildin' kind a man. But it's too late now." He shook his head sadly. "Way too late."

Liberty suspended the kettle over the fire, boiled the water, and sifted in finely ground cornmeal. While it bubbled, she filled the copper pot with water to make tea and the switchel for Jubal. She went to the wagon to feed him before she ate, but he was asleep and didn't respond when she called his name.

They spent the rest of the morning looking for dry firewood, and most of the afternoon erecting a shelter. Elija complained about his back, and finally, with Liberty and Amy doing most of the work, the poles were set and a canvas that reached from the end of the wagon was stretched over them and tied down. The end of the canvas overhung the fire and helped throw the heat inside, dispelling the dampness inside the wagon.

"There's gotta be a town here somewhere." Elija had thrown himself down by the fire and hadn't moved for an hour. "Them tracks is rutted. Wagons aplenty has been headin' fer somewhere. Hull Dexter might not a been tryin' to hornswaggle us, Libby. He could a knowed we be 'bout there."

"Fiddle faddle! Of course those tracks are heading somewhere or else he wouldn't be following them. And we're not about there. Hull Dexter cheated us. He's not scouting for us, hunting, protecting us from the savages. He left us to fend for ourselves because those ignorant louts thought Jubal had the flux. He refused to give any of our money back. He's a rotten skunk, not fit for crow bait!"

Liberty was bone-tired, her mind not on what she was saying. Her gaze fixed abstractedly on the dim trail that disappeared into the thick forest. She was feeling lower and more frightened than she had in all her life. They were in a dense forest with a coach pistol and a rifle to defend themselves. And Jubal was dying. He hadn't wanted to eat. He had swallowed barely a spoonful of food. When she tried to force it into his mouth he had choked. Late in the afternoon he had become delirious and had messed on the bedclothes. She had changed them, taken the soiled covers back down to the rain pond and washed them. Now darkness was drawing near, and she stood shivering, not wanting to listen to her father's dire predictions.

"Bake your back for a while, Papa," she said crossly. "I've got to get out of these wet clothes."

Elija grunted and turned his back to her. "Ya want that I whittle ya a whistle, Amy?"

"If you want to." Amy looked up at her sister and grinned. "He thinks I'm still a baby."

Liberty loosened Amy's braids and spread her hair over her shoulders so it would dry. "If it makes him happy, let him do it," she whispered. "It gives him something to do."

Darkness grew thicker. Elija rolled up in a blanket with his back to the fire. Liberty stood shivering in her shift and pantaloons. She had peeled off her dress and her petticoats, hanging them over two saplings she had thrust in the ground with the tops tied together.

The firelight flickered against her white skin and the heat dried her undergarments. Turning often to keep from burning on one side, she unbraided her hair and ran her fingers into it, lifting it to shake it. In this pose of arrested motion she saw the tall man standing on the fringe of light made by their fire.

"Oh! My heavens!"

The shock was so acute, she was stunned motionless for a few seconds. Then she dived for the heavy coach pistol she had kept nearby.

Chapter
Two

Liberty cocked the gun and pointed it at the man who stood just inside the circle of light. He wore a buckskin shirt with the tail outside and belted about the waist. Fringed leather pants were tucked inside his knee-high fringed moccasins. He was taller than average with wide shoulders and chest, but with a lean trimness. His flat-crowned, round-brimmed hat sat low on his forehead so that Liberty couldn't see his eyes, but she saw a narrow nose, prominent cheekbones and wide mouth with a white scar at the corner. His free hand held the barrel of a long rifle, the stock resting on the ground beside his foot. In his other arm he held a sleeping child.

"What do you mean sneaking up on us? What do you want?" Fright made her voice shrill.

Elija rolled from the blanket and got to his feet. "What, what . . . Who're you?"

The stranger stood quietly and Elija's eyes went to Liberty, standing in her underdrawers, holding the pistol in both hands.

"Libby! Ya ain't decent. Get some clothes on. Gimme that pistol." He snatched it from her hand and stood in front of her.

"I saw your fire," the man said. "I've come from the river." He took several steps before Liberty's words stopped him.

"What river? Don't come any closer. Lean that gun against a tree and stay right there." She peered out from behind Elija. When the man did as he was told, she snatched up her dress, slipped it over her head, and pulled the draw-strings at the neck and waist. She pulled her hair free and let it hang down her back. When she was decently covered she stepped out from behind her father. "Now, who are you and what do you want?"

"The name's Farrway Quill, ma'am. As to *wanting* some-thing, well, I saw your fire and thought a visit with folks and a cup of tea would be comforting. The river I come from is the Ohio. It runs a few miles south of here." His voice carried a slight flavor of the south, and yet he bit off his words sharply. "But I'll not force my company on you. I'll take my leave."

"Hold on," Elija said. "Liberty, my daughter, is edgy. Come on in. Come right on in. Sister," he said to Amy, "get a cup and pour Mr. Quill some tea." He shoved the pistol into Liberty's hands. "Put that thing away."

Elija's commanding tone riled Liberty, but she bit back the retort that came to her mind. He liked people to think he was in control. If he would really take control, she wouldn't mind, but this playacting always irritated her.

Elija stepped out and offered the man his hand. "Elija Carroll, of the Virginia Carrolls, late of New York State. Ya gotta excuse our manners. We jist ain't used to bein' out here in the wilderness all by our ownselves this way. I'll be dodfetched if'n we meant ta be standoffish."

"No offense. It pays to be careful."

When the stranger came forward Liberty could see that he had a huge pack on his back, and that the child sleeping on his shoulder was a little girl. Her long blond hair had been tied at the nape of her neck and in several more places down the long rope. She was covered with a piece of soft doeskin. Liberty took a quilt from the back of the wagon and spread it on the ground sheet Amy had been sitting on. She indicated with a nod of her head that the man could place the child on it. He knelt down and with a large hand on the back of her head, placed her on the quilt and covered her with the doe-skin. The child's feet were bare, and she wore what appeared to be a man's ragged homespun shirt.

Still kneeling, Farrway Quill looked up at Liberty and she saw eyes as green as new oak leaves in the spring—eyes of a man in his middle or late twenties, eyes that revealed nothing but saw everything. They looked into hers for as long as it took him to get to his feet. Then they passed out of her line of vision, and she stared at his brown throat and the patch of chest hair that showed between the lacing of his shirt.

She studied him while he shrugged the pack from his broad shoulders and slipped it beneath the wagon. He was not a handsome man, but he was far from being an ugly one. He had a scar on his chin and one on the side of his mouth that drew it slightly toward his cheekbone. The stubble of beard on his face was as black as his lashes and brows. His hair was long and clubbed in the back.

Amy smiled broadly at the little girl. She loved any child younger than herself. "Isn't she pretty, Libby?" She sank down onto the pallet beside the child. "I'll sit by her in case she wakes up. What's her name?" Amy had to tilt her head far back to look up at the stranger.

The man squatted down on his haunches, and a smile spread over his face, changing it magically. "I don't know. I found her a couple of days ago. She doesn't say much. I've called her girl, but she should have a name of her own. Could you give her one?"

"Can I? Really and truly?" Amy's eyes shone, and her smile displayed even white teeth. "I've never given a name to anything except a dog we had back home. I named him Zeke after a mean old man, cause he was a mean pup." She put her hand over her mouth and giggled.

"Zeke doesn't quite fit her."

Amy giggled again. "I know. How old is she?"

"You'll have to ask your—" His dark brows drew together and guarded green eyes looked up at Liberty.

"She's my sister. How old do you think she is, Libby?"

"Two, maybe. She isn't as big as the little Swenson girl back home."

"I'm going to call her Mercy. Is that all right?" Amy's shining eyes went from the sleeping child to the man's face.

"Mercy. That sounds just right for her." He stood, and for an instant his big hand rested on Amy's head before he turned his back to Liberty and went to the fire.

"We'd be glad fer ya to eat." Elija moved briskly around the fire to where the teakettle sat in the coals and filled a pewter mug. "We got plenty a pap left over."

"Sounds mighty tempting, but I had a bait of river trout. I'd be beholdin' if you'd spare some for the child when she wakes up. Be glad to pay for it."

"Why . . . I'd not hear of it." Elija sputtered.

"We're not so short that we can't feed a hungry child, Mr. Quill," Liberty snapped.

The sound of a severe fit of coughing came from the wagon and Liberty hoisted her skirts and climbed into the back to kneel down beside Jubal. His eyes were closed and he was breathing heavily. She could hear her father talking to the stranger. Not a trace of a whine was in his voice now.

"Her man's got the lung fever. We been aworkin' over him day 'n night. Bad off he is, real bad off. We jist done all we could fer him, but it's no use."

"Yes, *we* sure have," Liberty muttered angrily and wiped the back of her hand across her eyes. "You haven't sat up with him one time, Papa. You'd have liked it if he'd died back home. Jubal was good to you. He never asked you to lift a hand. I had to do all the asking, or you'd have sat on your bottom all day long in the Bloody Red Ox." Liberty bowed her head and covered her face with her hands. She hurt inside because Jubal was dying and there was no one to care but her.

"He warn't a strong man no ways. Ain't like us men what can make do with what's at hand. It's certain his time is come to stand at the Pearly Gates." Elija's voice took on a dreary note and droned on. "Pot maker is what he was.

Goodun, too. But didn't turn 'em out fast a'tall. All the time behind with orders. Had to be paintin' rings round 'em 'n fancyin' 'em up. We had us a good place thar in Middlecrossin', but that girl a mine is got the wanderin's."

"Papa! Mr. Quill isn't interested in our personal affairs." Liberty climbed down from the wagon.

Farrway Quill was sitting on his haunches beside the fire. The flickering light shone on his still, sharply chiseled features. The brim of his hat covered his eyes, but Liberty could feel them on her and suddenly became aware that her hair was hanging down about her shoulders.

No decent woman back in Middlecrossing would have allowed a stranger to see her hair hanging down her back—or up for that matter. She wore her day cap or was classified as a fallen woman.

Liberty wondered if the strain of the journey and Jubal's sickness had muddled her mind. Back home she'd always remembered to do the conventional, respectable things. Oh, fiddle with being respectable! In an act of pure defiance for all the misery she had suffered in that blasted village and since leaving it, she reached into the back of the wagon and brought out one of her most precious possessions, the ivory handled hairbrush Jubal had given her just after they married. She turned her back to the men and began to brush her hair. After the snarls were out she started the plaiting process, fully expecting her father to chastise her. He was too busy, she realized a moment later, bragging to the stranger about how *he* had brought them this far, and how *he* had told Hull Dexter he wasn't forgetting the wrong he'd done them.

When she turned, the stranger had pushed his hat back on his forehead and his green eyes were looking directly into hers. He had been watching her swift, deft movements as she twisted and overlapped the individual hanks into one long braid that hung past her waist.

"If you want to keep that hair, ma'am, keep it covered."

"We were told the Shawnee were friendly."

"Some of them are, but not all. Tecumseh is friendly, but he's not liking the whites coming in and taking up the land."

"See thar. I tole ya we'd done a foolhardy thin' comin' out here. Yore stubbornness will get us all kilt, is what it'll do," Elija moaned, his boastfulness suddenly gone.

"We were told the militia had built forts on the Wabash."

"The only one I know of is at Vincennes. There's one at Cairo and at Illinois town, and Fort Dearborn is up north. Folks don't usually come into this country unless they've got a force of six or eight armed men."

"What about yourself? You're traveling alone."

"I always do."

Liberty waited to see if Farrway Quill would say any more about himself. When he didn't, she said, "We're with four other wagons. They're up ahead."

"Why is that?"

"They moved out ahead of us when my husband became sick. The dunces think he's got the flux and refused to let us continue on with them. That's why we're sitting out here by ourselves."

"Does he have the flux?"

"He's got the lung sickness. Any fool would know it if they would listen to his chest."

Farrway Quill shrugged his shoulders and drained the tea from the pewter cup.

Elija refilled it. "Is we far from the Wabash? The guide said we could get a boat to take us to Vincennes."

"You may find a boat to take you up the Wabash, but you'll have to wait a while. It would be dangerous to do so now. This track will take you to Shawneetown. There's a ferry at the river to take you across if you can afford to pay. Hull Dexter knows this isn't the way to Vincennes."

"That dirty, low-down, bush-bottom warthog!" Liberty's eyes dared him to contradict her. He ignored her outburst and looked away from her. Suddenly she disliked him intensely. "Is he a friend of yours?" she asked bitingly.

"I know him."

"My brother-in-law, Hammond Perry, will settle with him. He's expecting us."

"Libby! He ain't doin' no such thing."

Liberty's face turned a fiery red, but she held her head proudly and faced her father.

"Yes, he is, Papa. I sent word ahead with a regiment going cross-country."

"There ain't no reason fer us to go on now, what with Jubal dyin' 'n all. We can go back home where we belong 'n stop this here slitherin' 'round. I jist knowed it would end up like this. I jist knowed me 'n Jubal'd die fightin' the heathens 'n you 'n Amy'd be carried off. Ya ain't ort a made me 'n Amy come, Libby. We ain't ort a be wanderin' round out here in the wilds like a chicken with its head cut off. The man said we're just a few miles from the Ohio. We can get a boat 'n go back upriver. We can go home—"

"We're here, Papa. It's too late to be placing blame, and I don't have money to take us back upriver by boat. You didn't have to come, and you can go back anytime you want to. You can work your way back home." Liberty tried to keep the bitterness out of her voice and speak patiently, not daring to look at Farrway Quill lest he see her anger and embarrassment.

"You'd like that, wouldn't ya? You'd not have nobody to buck ya, nobody to remind ya of yore shortcomings. Ya could go fiddle faddlin' all over, havin' yore own sweet way till ya got yoreself 'n Amy took by the savages."

Liberty turned her back on the two men and stooped down to put another cover over Amy and the sleeping child. It bothered her, even after all these years, when her father whined and complained while in the company of others. It was, she supposed, an affront to his imagined manly superiority, that she, and her mother before her, were more capable of coping with the trials of everyday living than he was.

"Guess ya ain't no stranger to these woods." Elija was talking again. "We'd sure be obliged if ya'd trail along with us. It'd beat walkin' 'n carryin' the youngun."

"I'm not going to Vincennes, or to Shawneetown."

Liberty turned and looked down at the man who had removed his hat and placed it on the ground beside him. His thick hair was lighter than she had at first thought it was—a light brown, and pulled straight back from a broad forehead.

"How far are we from Shawneetown? My husband will die if he doesn't get help soon." Her blue eyes looked directly into his.

"Do you mind if I take a look at him?" He got to his feet and waited. Liberty felt dwarfed beside him. He was extremely tall. His fringed buckskin shirt came down over his hips and was belted. There was a knife at his waist and a small ax was tucked into the back of his belt. His buckskins were clean, but smelled strongly of woodsmoke.

"I'd be grateful for your help."

Farrway grasped the end of the wagon and hauled himself up. Liberty took a burning stick from the fire, brought it to the end of the wagon and held it aloft so he could see. He knelt down beside the pallet. The man's breathing was an agonized sawing for breath. His eyes were deep sockets and his gray whiskered cheeks were sunken. He was small, and the thin hands that lay on his chest were slender, like a girl's. What surprised Farrway was that Hammond Perry's brother, this girl's husband, looked as old, or older than her father.

"Ma'am, he's in a bad way," he said gently. "The only thing I know to do is something I learned from the Indians. We can put him in a steam tent. It might help, but it might kill him, too. It's a chance, if you want to take it."

"He's going to die anyway, isn't he?"

"Yes, ma'am. I'm afraid so."

"Then let's do it. Let's take the chance it might help." She turned and poked the burning stick back into the fire. "Papa, help me take the canvas off these poles and build a tent. What else do we need to do, Mr. Quill?"

"We'll need a lot of firewood." He stepped from the wagon and walked off into the darkness.

"Ya know this ain't goin' to do no good, Libby. Why don't ya let the poor man die in peace? If'n ya'd only listen—" Elija put his hand to the small of his back and bent over several times. "My back's killin' me."

Liberty ignored him, folded blankets and placed them under the wagon before she shook Amy's shoulder to waken her.

"I've fixed you and the little girl a pallet under the wagon. You can snuggle up together and keep warm."

"Her name's . . . Mercy."

"All right. Crawl under and I'll put Mercy beside you."

"I jist never heard of rousin' a dyin' man out of his bed on a night so cold." Elija grumbled as his fingers worked at the knot holding the canvas to the poles. "Yo're determined to keep us all stirred up, ain't ya, Libby? Stith don't know how lucky he was that Jubal got ya, but then, he'd a not took yore sass like me 'n Jubal's done."

Liberty straightened after she placed the child beside Amy and covered them. Her mouth was set and her eyes held shards of anger.

"Hush your complaining! If you don't want to help, get out of the way."

"Ya ain't ort a talk to yore pa like that. Yo're hard, Libby. My back—"

"There's nothing wrong with your back except that it's weak!" she hissed.

"By Jehoshaphat! Ya ain't got no feelin' a'tall. Now, if'n I jist had a tot of Bald Face—"

She elbowed him out of the way and unfastened the ropes. Farrway returned carrying a flat stone and an armful of wood. He set them down and began to feed the fire with heavy chunks of wood.

"I was jist atellin' Libby that I hurt my back somethin' awful during the runkus I had with them rivermen in Louisville. Guess I never knowed it at the time; I was so dang bustit mad when they sung out at my girl here. I ort a knowed better than to take on more'n one at a time."

Liberty saw Farrway glance at Elija, then away. Oh, Papa, she thought, why didn't he shut up? She loved him in spite of his complaining, and she hated seeing him make a complete fool of himself. She yanked the canvas off the poles and went to pull up more wood for the fire.

"What else do we need, Mr. Quill?"

"A couple buckets of water to start."

"I've been catching rain water in a barrel." Liberty looked pointedly at her father.

"I reckon I could get it, if'n ya ain't wantin' a full bucket. My poor back—"

"The water can wait until after we get the tent up." Farrway took a small axe from his pack.

"Well, if'n yo're sure. I'm plumb willin' to do what I can." Elija sank slowly down on the wagon gate, his hand pressing into the small of his back.

Farrway placed the rock in the flames at one end of the fire, waited until it was blazing hot, then filled the iron tea-kettle from the water bucket and set it on the rock. He took the axe, and with a few well-placed strokes slimmed down two forked poles and stuck them into the ground. After placing another pole in the forks he swiftly threw the canvas over and pegged it down, leaving a side open to the fire, then picked up the oak water bucket and dipped it into the barrel.

"As soon as the water is boiling, we'll bring him out here. The steam should go into the tent. Heat another pan of water too, Mrs. Perry, so you can lay a warm, wet cloth over his face. The moisture may help loosen what's in his chest."

"All that wet? I heard tell that'd kill a man," Elija said with a sad shake of his head.

Farrway walked away to fetch more wood, and Liberty gritted her teeth to keep from saying something to her father that she would regret later.

It was Farrway who lifted Jubal out of the wagon and gently placed him on the pallet Liberty had made inside the low tent. He roused and his eyes sought Liberty's.

"It's all right. He's helping us, Jubal." She covered him and gently turned his face toward the fire.

"Libby . . . I'm sorry," he gasped. "Don't go back. Go on and find Hammond."

"We're going to stay right here until you're better. Then we'll go to Hammond together." She stroked his hot, dry forehead as if he were a sick child. He closed his eyes wearily.

Farrway fashioned a curved piece of bark to funnel the plume of steam coming from the teakettle into the tent over Jubal's face. He kept the fire built up and the teakettle filled while Liberty placed warm wet cloths over Jubal's face at intervals so he could breathe in the warm dampness. Elija, grumbling that what they were doing was useless, crawled into the wagon and went to bed.

At first it seemed Jubal was able to breathe easier. It was almost as though he were sleeping peacefully. Then he roused and Liberty knew he was delirious when he started babbling about his mother who died when Hammond was born and his father who despised him because all he wanted to do was make pots and jugs.

"Don't . . . Pa! Don't break 'em. I done my chores! Please, Pa. I'll work hard—" The words came from his cracked lips in gasps. "Libby asked me to marry her. Me, old Jubal Perry can have pretty Liberty Carroll for my wife. I'm old . . . I don't know what to do. It hadn't ought to be like this—Stith'll crush her, make her old . . . worn out! I'll kill him . . . oh, I wish I could kill him. We'd not have to go if I did."

"Jubal, dear, don't worry about Stith. Shhh. . . . " He tried to raise up and Liberty gently pushed him down.

"He'll put out my eyes! He said he'd put out my eyes so I couldn't see Libby!" His eyes rolled back in their sockets and he struggled for breath through quivering lips. "She's . . . sweet, and I can't let him hurt her . . . If I was big and strong, I'd fight him . . . I want to, but I'm afraid—"

"It's all right, Jubal. You don't have to fight anyone." Liberty spoke soothingly and stroked the hair back from his face with her fingertips. "Don't think about Stith. He can't hurt us now. I'm here with you. I don't care if you're not a big, strong man. You're a good man and the best potter in all New York State and this vast territory. You make beautiful, lasting things, and that's more important than being able to fight. I've got your best pieces packed in my trunk. No one will ever have them. I'll keep them forever and . . . ever—" A sob came up in her throat, and she choked it back. "Think about that clay dye you were going to make, Jubal. You said the madder plant would make strong red to go with your blue. Your jugs will be so pretty with blue and red stripes around them."

Liberty looked up at the tall stranger with tears clouding her eyes. "He dying," she whispered.

Farrway squatted down on his haunches. "Yes, ma'am."

She gazed at him blankly as if she had not heard clearly what he had said. She shivered.

Farrway sat back on his haunches and studied the woman. The shock at seeing her standing in the firelight in her pantaloons, with hair as white as a cloud floating down about her shoulders and over her breasts had stopped him in his tracks. He had just come from the Shawnee village where he had visited his friend, John Spotted Elk, and the light-haired woman had been a sight to stop any man. He had been dumbfounded to see the lone wagon with a fire blazing. The road from Louisville to Shawneetown had almost been taken over by roving bands of cutthroats and robbers, not like a few years before when all one had to worry about was Indians. It had been his intention to give these people a warning and move on. He could have been almost home by another day. But to his experienced eye it would have been like giving sheep to the wolves.

"If you want to get some sleep, Mrs. Perry, I'll sit with him."

"Thank you, but I'll stay. He might open his eyes again, and I want him to know that I'm here. He gave up a lot for me. I'll not leave him now."

"We should let this fire go down. The steam has done all it's going to." He considered telling her that the light of a single campfire was like a beacon to Indians as well as to river pirates who plundered along this track, but she looked like a small, weary child, and he decided not to worry her more.

"I know. I thank you for what you've done."

Farr got to his feet and smothered part of the fire with several scoops of loose earth. With the loss of part of the cheery flame, the campsite took on a ghostly atmosphere. Liberty tucked the covers around Jubal's thin shoulders. In the silence she could hear the forest begin to crackle and pop, and she wondered how she could have ever thought the wilderness a silent and peaceful place.

They sat silently. Liberty was tired but not as frightened as she had been other nights. Sitting with this man beside the fire, a feeling of safety engulfed her, but her eyes, out of habit, continued to look beyond the small circle of light. Caution had become a part of her since she first became aware that Stith Lenning wanted her in the ways a man wanted a woman. She had learned to watch and listen, to not let herself get cornered, and always to have a weapon handy. Those watchful habits had intensified during the journey.

"Where did you get the little girl?" she asked suddenly, needing to talk.

"Down on the Green in Kentucky. I found her in the cellar of a burned-out cabin. I suspect her folks put her there when they feared trouble."

"Indians?"

"River pirates. They tried to make it look like Indians. Scalped a man, woman, and a boy. But no Indians I ever heard of spoiled sacks of grain and killed horses."

"Poor little girl."

"She was scared to death of me at first. That, too, makes me think white men did it."

"Are you taking her to your wife?"

"I don't have a wife. If I can't find someone to take her here, I'll have to take her to some friends up the Ohio at Carrolltown."

"We passed Carrolltown coming downriver. My father's name is Carroll."

"Any kin to Sloan Benedict Carroll?"

"Not that I know of. Papa has lived in New York State all his life. I don't know where he got the idea he was from the Virginia Carrolls. You don't have to sit up with me, Mr. Quill."

He wondered what she would think if she knew that there were five hundred men in the territory who would give anything in the world to be sitting with her, talking to her. Pretty women were scarce in the territory. Why had this one come into the wilderness with two such men as her pa and Jubal Perry? He suspected she had more courage than brains. He would be surprised if they made it to Shawneetown without her being raped by the riffraff that roamed the river. In this country women like her were almost like a crust of bread to a starving man.

"Do you live near here?" Liberty decided it was very peaceful sitting there with this strange man. She liked hearing him talk. His voice was low and soft, and his manner of speaking suggested that he was educated.

"I have a place up on the Wabash, on the Illinois side."

Liberty drew her legs up, wrapped her arms around them, and rested her chin on her knees. She pulled her shawl tightly around her shoulders and stared into the fire.

Silence stretched between them. Finally she said, "Please talk to me." Tears sprang to her eyes, stinging, unshed tears, and such a feeling of helplessness sliced through her that she winced. She and Jubal had left behind everything that was known to them, for this. She glanced at Jubal's drawn face reflected in the firelight and knew again that she could not have done anything else. She looked back at the quiet man, her lower lip caught firmly between her teeth to keep it from quivering. "I've never heard the name Farrway."

"I've never heard of it either, but that's what my grandpa said my name was. I'm called Farr."

"I guess you think I'm asking a lot of questions. It's just so dark out there, and the night is so long."

"I don't mind."

"What happened to your folks?" she asked in a small, weary voice.

"Bay fever cleaned out our village over on the Hudson. I was just a tyke and had gone off downriver with my grandpa on his durham boat. When we came back they were gone."

"You were lucky to have your grandpa. Poor little Mercy doesn't have anyone," she said sadly.

"After Grandpa died, I stayed with a couple of old mountain men." He chuckled. "Talk about odd names—guess they didn't pay any attention to mine because they were called True and Juicy. They taught me everything I know about staying alive in the woods." Farr suddenly realized that was the longest conversation he'd had with a woman since his last visit to Carrolltown and his talk with Cherish.

"Why did you decide to come out here?"

"I first came out here with True and Juicy when I was just a stripling. Later Sloan Carroll sent me, along with his son Colby, back east to school. While I was there, True passed on. When I came back, Juicy and I decided we wanted new country and came out here. We've seen a lot of change, people are moving in."

"I'd never been more than thirty miles from Middlecrossing when we came out here. I knew the journey would take several months, but I never imagined it would be so vast, so empty, so wild."

"It's getting too settled for some folk," he said. His eyes roamed the area before he spoke again. "You've got to move on in the morning, ma'am. Regardless of your man, you've got to move on."

"Because of Indians?"

"And the scum that prowl the river. You'd not stand a chance against them."

"Why are you walking? Don't you have a horse?"

"I have one. It was faster to pole downriver."

"Have you been to Vincennes?"

"A number of times."

"What's it like?"

"It's not big compared to Cincinnati or Louisville, but Fort Knox is nearby, and the governor has a fine home there. What do you plan to do, Mrs. Perry?"

"We have no choice but to go on to Vincennes to Hammond, my brother-in-law."

"Have you met him?"

"No." The thought flashed through Liberty's mind and she voiced it the same instant. "Do you know him?"

"I've met him. I don't think he's there. A few weeks ago a large group of men were sent north to Fort Harrison." Farr watched the look of disappointment cover her face.

Liberty closed her eyes briefly. A small groan escaped her. "Oh, my! Poor Jubal! All this way for . . . nothing."

"What had you planned to do, ma'am?" The look on her face was the saddest Farr had ever seen.

"What I still plan to do—farm. We were going to find a place by the river and Jubal was going to set up his potter's wheel and drying kiln. I wanted to plant fruit trees and farm. I have my seed, a fine plow blade and the oxen. For Amy's sake we need to be near other people."

"You could have stopped off at a number of places along the river."

"Jubal wanted to be near his brother. He was afraid—" She cut off her words and added, "It had been a long time since he'd seen him. Are Vincennes and Shawneetown the only settlements along the Wabash?"

"The settlement around my station is small. But almost a hundred people live within five miles. One family pulled up and moved on west to Saint Louis. The old man thought it was whistling that made the plow go . . ." Farr's voice trailed away. His narrowed eyes studied the girl.

Liberty sat immobile, expressionless, withdrawn. A faint pulse throbbed in her slender white throat. In the delicate shadow of her lashes her blue eyes shone with a strange intent light.

"Is any of the land already cleared?"

"The land beyond the Wabash is level prairie land except for patches of forest here and there. It stretches away like an ocean under a curving sky. From the Wabash to the Mississippi the land lies open to the sun."

"It's said that treeless land cannot produce crops," she said thoughtfully.

"Not so. I've seen corn grow as high as my head on that prairie land."

"Do you farm?"

"No."

Liberty could see his face in the dim light. His head was in constant motion, turning this way and that, but so slowly it seemed not to move at all. He was an extremely alert man, she decided, and beneath his calm manner lay something as inflexible as a stout axe handle.

In the silence that followed his last word, Liberty slowly leaned over to look into Jubal's face, knowing something was wrong, instinctively knowing something had happened that couldn't be changed.

"Jubal?" She placed her palm against his cheek. He had stopped struggling for breath and lay absolutely still. Life, for him, had ended. Somehow she had thought it would be different, that she would know and could hold his hand when the last breath left him. "Jubal. . . ."

She turned away and began to cry silently.

Chapter
Three

S ometime in the long hours before dawn, the wind came
roaring in from the southwest, tormenting the branches
of the giant oak trees, flinging a hail of broken twigs
down on the campsite, and sweeping leaves off the ground.

Liberty was jolted awake by the creaking of the wagon as
the wind pelted the canvas, covering it with huge rain drops.
She lay beneath the wagon with Amy and the child, Mercy,
her head pillowed on her arm. A fierce gust of wind
slammed the rain against the ground beside her, causing her
to rise in alarm. *Jubal was out there, alone, in the rain.*

"Jubal—"

"It's all right." Farr's voice came out of the darkness, and
a hand on her shoulder pressed her down.

"He'll . . . get wet."

"No."

"Where is he?"

"I rolled him in the canvas and put him in the wagon
alongside your pa."

Liberty sank back down, pulled the quilt up over her
shoulders and stared into the darkness. She recorded a
thought in her tormented mind to bring out and mull over at
a later date: how comforting it was to not be alone, to hear a
reassuring voice come out of the darkness. Her eyes became
glazed with tears as her mind swung back, remembering
Jubal alive, smiling.

"I'll be proud as a peacock to marry you, Liberty Carroll," he had said.

If she hadn't asked him to marry her he would be alive in

33

Middlecrossing, happily making his pots. There would have been no reason for him to sell out and go so far from home. Now he would never see home again or his brother, Hammond. He'd stay forever in this dark and lonely place. That was what she was thinking when the wooliness moved into her head and she went to sleep.

Liberty placed a bouquet of wild lupines, moss pinks and yellow wallflowers on the soft mound of earth. Farrway Quill had dug the grave before she awakened and had carried Jubal to it after she dressed him in his best shirt and smoothed his hair with her brush. He looked younger in death, and more peaceful than she'd ever seen him. Elija had read a verse from the Bible, and now he stood with Amy and Mercy, fidgeting, anxious to be away from this place.

"I want him to have a headboard. I want people who pass this way to know that he's here." Liberty spoke firmly and calmly, trying to deny with her tone how angry she was that Jubal had to die—Jubal, who was so kind, who never said a cross word to anyone. Jubal, who was a giver and not a taker. Jubal, who would have found beauty in this dark wood.

Farr stared into her blue eyes without speaking. She had folded the brim of her dark bonnet back, showing all of her face. The belligerent lift of her chin and the defiant glare in her eyes told him that she was holding in her grief, hiding it with anger.

"No, you don't." His brows came together in a scowl of impatience. He leaned the shovel against a tree, picked up a large rock and dumped it on the grave.

This angered Liberty beyond reason.

"He *will* have a headboard! I'll make it myself." She defied him with her eyes and dared him to contradict her.

"Not unless you want the Indians to dig him up and take his hair. They get paid by the scalp."

"They wouldn't do that!"

"Why not? A scalp's a scalp, and they'd only have to do a

little digging to get it." Farr continued to work. Finally Elija handed his Bible to Amy, and with a groan picked up a stone and carried it to the grave.

In the back of Liberty's fuzzy mind she knew he was right. Her heart gave a sickening lurch when she remembered what Hull Dexter had said about the wolves. She stood at the head of the grave silently watching the soft moist dirt being covered with stones, then continued to watch as Farr arranged deadfalls in such a way as to hide the grave.

"It's best we get moving." Farr stood back when he had finished and carefully surveyed the area.

"Come on, Libby." Elija turned to leave, and Liberty started to follow, then turned abruptly and walked back to the grave. Her father snorted impatiently. "Fer cryin' out loud! What ya doin' now? The man's dead, Libby. Grievin' ain't agoin' to bring 'em back."

"She knows that," Farr said curtly and took her arm to lead her away.

"How do you know how I feel?" Liberty jerked away from Farr's hand and tears filled her eyes for the first time since she awakened.

"I'm jist sayin' we ort a be agoin'. Stayin' ain't agoin' to bring 'em back. Jubal—"

"You didn't even like him!" Liberty threw the words at her father in a quiet but scathing tone. "You've never had one good word to say about him. He did the best he could for you and you did nothing but run him down." Her voice began to rise as the words tumbled from her mouth. "He was a good *man*, I tell you. He was a man and he had courage, which is more than you've got, Elija Carroll. He had courage and an adventurous spirit, even if he didn't weigh much more than eight stone. He knew he wasn't cut out for this kind of life, but he was willing to try. You think now that he's gone, I'll go back and marry Stith, and you can live nice and easy. You fool! Stith would have worked you to death," she shouted. "He'd have worked all of us to death. I'll never go back. Never!" She covered her face with her hands and cried.

"Ya jist gotta blame somebody. Cause I'm here it's me. Ya

jist ain't agoin' to own up that it's your own doin'. Makin' us come out here what's done it. I won't be surprised none if'n I ain't the next. I ain't cut out for this traipsin'—"

"Take the girls back to the wagon," Farr said impatiently. He made no attempt to hide the disgusted expression on his face. Dark brows were drawn together over eyes as cold as a green pond. They narrowed threateningly.

Elija threw up his hands and, pushing Amy and Mercy ahead of him, walked away.

Farr said nothing more, allowing Liberty's grief to work itself out. Finally she quieted and wiped her eyes.

"He was a good, kind man, and I'll never forget him."

"That's the important thing."

"No one cared a whit for him. He was just there. People walked around him like he was a porch post."

"There'd be no roof without a porch post."

"He could see beauty in a lot of things—"

"Men see what they want to see."

"He liked to read—"

"He was lucky someone took the time to teach him."

"I hate to leave him like this!" she wailed.

"There's nothing else you can do."

"He was scared—"

"All men are scared at one time or another."

"He depended on me!"

"Do you want to stay?"

She looked up at him with a glazed look in her eyes. Farr, wise in the ways of grief, recognized the signs of near hysteria. He shook her roughly until her eyes blazed at him angrily.

"Get your hands off me, you . . . heathen! You're just like Papa! You don't care that he's dead," she accused.

"I didn't know him."

"He was a human being!"

"So were my folks. Do you feel sad about the fever taking them?"

The anger went out of her as suddenly as it appeared.

"We should have stayed in Middlecrossing," she whispered. Her voice was so full of surrender that it angered him.

"Your life lies ahead of you, not behind you. You'll marry again and have a dozen younguns." He glared down at her. The words were half snarled and his mouth snapped shut, causing the scar beside it to whiten.

Liberty's eyes focused on the scar. Why was he angry? Why the scowl of disapproval on his face? She was sure that she thoroughly detested this man. He had been kind and helpful, but he was a take-over kind of man, just the type who would bring a woman under the yoke, force her to submit to his control, shake her self-reliance. He was the kind of man who would break a woman if she loved him, and long ago she vowed never to let any man do that to her.

Anger at Farr and at herself for wasting her thoughts on him propelled her feet, and she briskly left the grave without a backward glance, walked beneath the trees and out onto the sunlit track. The early morning wind had blown the rain clouds away and the sun shone brightly. "Damn you, sun," she muttered angrily. "Jubal wanted you to come out, shine on him, warm him. Now it's too late."

"I ain't agoin'! I tell ya, Libby, I ain't agoin'!" Elija banged his fist against the wagon.

"You don't have to go, Papa. I'll give you a third of the coins Jubal left me. You can take one of the horses and go back to Middlecrossing."

"It's a man's place to decide what's best for his family, not a lass not yet ten and ten! I say we all go back home where we belong."

"Go if you want, Mr. Quill has offered to take us as far as his station. Amy and I have decided. We're going to find a place up along the Wabash and farm." Liberty finished stowing the pots in the wagon, then grabbed the bedding from beneath it and rolled and tied it. "Nothing is changed, Papa. Nothing at all."

"Why are ya doin' this to me, Libby? Ya know I can't go off 'n leave you 'n Amy out here in the wilds." Elija spread his hands appealingly and looked at Farr who stood holding the child in one hand and his rifle in the other. "Libby's a drivin' woman, Mr. Quill. She's hard on a man. Just like her mama. Stubborn, hard 'n drivin'. Always amakin' a man do things he warn't suited fer. She needs a strong hand is what she needs. A man ta learn her a woman's place. It warn't in Jubal ta take charge. He warn't no man ta handle a woman like—"

"That's enough!" Liberty snapped angrily. "I'm not going to argue with you, and I'll not hear a bad word about Jubal. Understand? Do what you want to do. I don't care. If you're coming, let's get started. If you're going back, good-bye."

"See there? See there, Quill? I tole ya she was hard!"

"Set Mercy up there on the seat beside Amy, Mr. Quill." Liberty turned her back on her father and ignored him. "She'll not let her fall off. You're welcome to ride the horse. I prefer to walk myself." She waited until Farr settled the child beside Amy and threw his pack into the back of the wagon before she struck the oxen lightly with her switch. "Get humping, Sally. You, too, Molly. Pull, girls."

Liberty didn't look back, but she knew her father was following close behind the wagon on one of the horses. He continued to grumble until Farr moved a good twenty-five yards ahead of the wagon, his long rifle held negligently in his arms. Then he fell silent.

It was the middle of May and the Indian apple was in full flower, the maples were in red bud, and numerous wild flowers grew where they could lift their faces to the sun. The woods were filled with bird song. But still Liberty felt an inner chill, a quaking that even this beauty failed to dispel. She was alone now. Without Jubal, his brother Hammond might not feel any responsibility for her. She wasn't worried so much for herself as for Amy.

Amy giggled and Liberty looked up to see Mercy smiling at her and patting her cheeks. Amy, the little mother, she thought. As she watched, her sister put her arm around the younger child and hugged her close.

The seriousness of their situation pressed down on Liberty. She was determined to go on as she and Jubal had planned. She drew in a deep and hurtful breath, passion rising again in her silent protest: Going back would mean she would live a life of servitude with Stith Lenning, and she would not do it! But would giving in to the yearnings of her willful heart cost her something even more precious than her independence? Would she lose Amy too? she wondered. Her father blamed her for Jubal's death, and in a way she was responsible, but, Lordy, what else could they have done?

Liberty trudged alongside the oxen, her thoughts tumbling in mad confusion. In only five months winter would set in. Would she be able to find a place in time to plant a garden? What of the man walking ahead? He hadn't really told her much about himself. He hadn't encouraged her to go on or turn back. He'd said only that the settler who moved on to Saint Louis, the one who thought it was whistling that made the plow go, had left a good cabin, and that they would be welcome to it if someone hadn't already moved in. It would be a place to rest, Liberty thought tiredly. A place to rest while she decided if she should go on to Vincennes and try to locate Hammond Perry or find a piece of land near other folks and begin to build the farm she had always dreamed of.

By the middle of the afternoon Liberty was so tired she was hanging onto the patient ox and the strong beast was helping her along the uneven track. She wondered if the man walking ahead ever tired. He had come back to the wagon one time for a drink of water, then moved out ahead again. At times he disappeared in the woods only to reappear suddenly, running at an easy trot.

Amy had complained that she and Mercy were hungry. Liberty had told her to open the sack of dried apples hanging from the curved bow of the wagon, but to watch for worms, and had reminded her of the hoecake left over from the previous night's supper.

Liberty glanced back one time to see her father lifting his jug of Bald Face out of the back of the wagon. He was already unsteady in the saddle, she thought dispiritedly, and by evening he would be dead drunk and no help at all. She was embarrassed that Farr would see him so. Minutes before, the woodsman had disappeared into the thick forest. As she idly watched for him to reappear, it occurred to her that in all her life she had never had a strong man to depend on, one who would both provide for her and keep her safe . . . and love her. Liberty felt a flash of guilt at the thought. Jubal had loved her . . . in his own way.

She was startled when Farr came out of the woods and loped back down the track toward her. She knew something was wrong before he spoke.

"Stop! Stay here," he said curtly as he checked the priming of his rifle. He lifted his head and sniffed as an animal might have done.

"What is it? Indians?" Liberty pulled the team to a halt.

"Stay here," he said again, and disappeared into the thick growth beside the trail.

Farr had known immediately when the familiar sounds of the woods began to change. He had walked another fifty yards before the sweet sickening odor of the dead reached him. The sounds he'd heard were the cries of the scavengers: buzzards, crows, and other flesh-eating creatures. There was something else, too. A faint mewing wail. He made his way, running lightly, through the thick stand of oaks, cottonwoods and sycamores. The tallest were crowned by the foliage of huge grapevines, their trunks entwined with ropes the size of a man's leg. A whippoorwill swooped overhead, trailing his melodious repeated cry, unmindful of the buckskin-clad figure leaping the deadfalls and slipping through the tangle of berry bushes.

Five minutes after he left Liberty, he was peering through the bushes at a sight that, although he was hardened to sudden death on the frontier, made the bile rise in his throat and an almost uncontrollable rage shake his strong body. The squawking of the birds had ceased, the silence making the forest seem more ominous than the previous uproar. The eerie silence persisted and a vision of another time, another place, and another young woman sprawled in the dirt floated across Farr's mind and seared into his consciousness like a burning ember.

The camp had been attacked at night. The women who lay sprawled beside the wagons wore their nightdresses. The weak wailing sound he had heard came from a small child sitting on the ground beside his dead mother. He was looking at her face, twisted into a mask of agony, and pounding his small fist on her blood-encrusted breasts. Farr surveyed the area keenly, then strode quickly to the child and picked him up. The boy locked his arms around his neck, and rage like a red tide washed over Farr. He felt once again the almost overwhelming desire to hunt a man and kill him.

Four women and one young girl not much older than Amy had been fiendishly raped before they were killed. The five men had died in their pallets beneath the wagons. White men had done this. White men who were supposedly civilized. They had murdered and raped for oxen, horses, and what little money the pilgrims had with them.

Carrying the child in his arms, Farr went to each of the men and bent down to peer at their faces. He was not surprised to find that Hull Dexter was not among them. The wagons had been looted. Clothing and the personal belongings were strewn about. In one of the wagons Farr found the body of a young boy who lay where he had tried to crawl under the bed and hide. His throat had been cut. He made a silent vow to hunt down the men responsible and kill them.

After Farr made the rounds of each wagon he turned to see Liberty coming up the trail. The sun shone on tendrils of her startling hair and for just an instant he saw Fawnella. He shook his head. No, it couldn't be Fawnella. This woman was taller, her hair lighter. Liberty was well ahead of the wagon, but it was still coming.

"What is it?" she called. "What's happened?"

Farr was breathing hard when he reached her. "I told you

to stay back! What in the name of God is wrong with you? Get back there and turn that wagon around!"

Liberty's eyes swept over the destruction of the camp and the bodies sprawled on the ground. She gave a strangled cry, "Oh . . . oh, my God!"

"Take this child and go back! You don't want your sister to see this!" He jerked the rifle from her hands and thrust the boy into her arms.

"I'm going to throw up—"

"No, you're not. You're going to do what I tell you. Get back there and tell your pa to get up here. We've got to do something quick and get away from here."

"The savages! The damned heathens!"

"White savages! Keep that in mind! If your man hadn't come down sick you'd be here too. Get your pa."

Liberty hugged the small boy to her and pressed his face to her shoulder. "Pa's drunk," she managed to say.

"Good. What we've got to do won't be easy. We've got to put those bodies in a wagon and set fire to it."

"No, you can't! We traveled with them. We've got to bury them." In horrified fascination, Liberty's eyes swept the area again.

"We'll burn them," Farr argued.

"Burn them?" she echoed stupidly.

"Unless you want to leave them to be a meal for those scavengers." He flung his arm upward where the buzzards and the crows waited. "Unless you want to stay and dig ten graves and wait until Hull Dexter comes back to find out if your man had the flux. If not for that, you'd be here too."

"But . . . maybe some are alive."

"They're all dead! Now, take this rifle and go!"

"This one's alive," she persisted.

"I suspect his ma tossed him into the berry bushes. Look at him; he's scratched all over."

Liberty turned and stumbled blindly back down the trail. "Papa," she called. "Stop the wagon."

"What fer? Are ya agoin' back?" Elija reeled in the saddle. "Who's that?" He peered drunkenly at the child in her arms.

Anger and frustration washed over Liberty. "Act like a man for once in your life, Papa," she shouted. "Go help Mr. Quill." She dropped her rifle and slapped his mount so hard on the rump that her hand stung. The startled horse sprang forward. Elija grabbed the saddle horn.

"Why'd ya have to go 'n do that fer?" His complaining voice reached Liberty where she stood beside the wagon telling Amy to take Mercy and crawl into the back.

"Who's that, Libby? Why're you mad at Papa? Did we catch up with them other folks?"

"Yes, Amy, we did. I need your help, honey. Could you and Mercy take care of this poor little boy? He's gone to sleep, but I suspect he's hungry. Stay in the back of the wagon and hold him. Sing to him so he'll know he's not alone."

"That's the little Phelps boy, Libby. I threw a ball to him one day. His name's Daniel. Where's his mama?"

"She's dead. They're all dead. Now, don't think about it, just take care of Daniel and Mercy. I'm going back and help Mr. Quill."

"Did they get the lung sickness like Jubal?"

"No. I'll tell you about it later. Stay in the back with the little ones. Play like you're their mama, honey. If Daniel wakes up, give him some of the cold pap and put some syrup on it. Give Mercy some too. I'll not be gone long."

Liberty dreaded going back to the clearing more than she ever dreaded anything in her life. But knowing Elija's condition, she doubted that he'd be any help to Farr. She grasped her rifle and ran up the track to the massacre site. The first thing she saw was her father's horse, cropping the grass, dragging the reins. Elija was holding onto a young sapling and emptying his stomach on the ground.

Farr was carrying the stiffened body of one of the women toward a topless wagon. He had tied his handkerchief over the lower part of his face, and his voice when it came to her was muffled. "Go back."

"No. You need help and you'll not get it from him." Liberty tossed her head toward Elija who was moaning and retching at the same time.

"Then gather up all the dry timber you can find. Small twigs and grass to cover the bodies, big stuff to go on top. We'll burn them in the wagon."

"But won't they see the smoke?"

"We have to take the chance. We either burn them or let the wolves have them." He turned back to another dead body, knelt beside the woman and covered her privates with her nightdress before he lifted her.

Liberty worked fast and mindlessly. She carried armload after armload of dry branches and piled them beside the wagon where Farr was placing the bodies of the ill-fated group. She used the axe that had been embedded in a stump by one of the murdered men. No doubt he planned to chop wood for the breakfast fire. She hacked and carried wood until Farr took the axe from her hand. Together they tossed the grass and the wood onto the wagon until the bodies were covered. Farr took a flint from the pouch that hung from his belt and struck a spark, blew on it, then nourished it within his cupped hands until the grass caught. By that time Liberty had gathered several large handfuls to use as torches, handed them to Farr, and turned her back on the burning pyre. He took them from her hand without a glance and soon the wagon was aflame. Thick dark smoke filled the clearing and billowed above the trees.

"That's all we can do. Come on."

"But . . . a prayer—"

"We don't have time. We must get as far from here as we can. I figure they were here the night before last, but they couldn't travel fast with oxen unless they put them on a barge and floated them downriver. No doubt they had their sights set on someone who needed them and could pay the price," he said with a curl of his lips. He took her arm and urged her out of the clearing.

Elija stood with his head resting on the neck of his horse and his hand in the small of his back.

"Come on, Papa. We've got to go," Liberty said quietly, too shocked at what she had just witnessed to be ashamed of her father's weakness. She went to the tree where she'd left her rifle and then, with a quaking stomach and trying not to breathe too deeply of the smoke coming from the pyre, she walked on down the track beside Farr.

"We'll turn off into the woods and leave the wagon," Farr said when they reached it. "If we travel all night we'll be at my station by noon tomorrow."

Liberty, struggling to keep him from knowing how frightened she was, looked up at his still, grim face and felt a choking reluctance to begin asking questions, but it was not her nature to hold back. "Must we leave the wagon? It's all we have."

"You have your life, and your sister and father have theirs. What are these things compared to that?" His penetrating eyes searched her face; and had Liberty been less distraught, she would have seen admiration there.

She caught her lower lip firmly between her teeth and nodded. Her cornflower-blue eyes were full of torment, but her voice was steady when she said, "You're right, Mr. Quill. We'll do what you think best. Just tell us what to do."

"Good girl." A ghost of a smile played around his grim mouth. His hand cupped her shoulder and squeezed gently. "I'll come back for the wagon. I promise." Farr was a man who appreciated courage in others, and without a doubt this slight woman was blessed with an abundance of it.

Farr turned the wagon around, and they went back down the road a hundred yards. They were turning the oxen into the woods when Elija rode up. He didn't say anything, just followed along behind the wagon, his shoulders slumped, his chin on his chest. Farr led them at a fast pace until they were deep into the forest. He urged the oxen around deadfalls and beneath branches so low they scraped the top of the wagon. Liberty walked behind the wagon leading the extra horse. She was exhausted when Farr finally stopped.

"There's no way we can hide the tracks. Let's hope, if they come back, they'll look no farther than the road. The way we turned the wagon, they may think you've turned back. Fill a bag with your valuables and some food, Liberty, and hurry." Her name came so easily from his lips that he wasn't aware he had said it. He helped her climb into the back of the wagon. "Amy can ride with her pa. You take the boy up with you and I'll carry Mercy."

Liberty turned to look down at him. "No," she said quietly. "I'll hold the boy and Amy can ride behind me. Papa can hold Mercy in front of him. I think the sight back there sobered him."

Farr nodded. He opened his pack and took out powder and shot and another small pouch. He looked at Amy sitting on the floor of the wagon holding the small boy and winked. When she smiled, her whole face lit up. She would be a beauty someday, he thought. After he sat Mercy in front of Elija, he opened the pouch, took out a hard, brown flat cake, and held it up to the child. She looked at it, but made no move to reach for it. He put it to his mouth, then to hers. Her small red tongue came out, and then a smile appeared. He closed her small fingers around it and went back to hobble the oxen so they wouldn't stray far from the wagon.

When she was ready, Liberty led the horse to the wagon so she could climb up on the wheel to reach the stirrups. The bag she hung on the saddle horn contained her coins, some of her mother's letters, tea, dried apples and corn meal. In another bag she had put her packets of garden seeds. She hated to leave Jubal's pottery behind. Just the night before she had promised him she would keep it forever. She didn't have time to think about it because Farr was lifting Amy up behind her. He then placed the sleeping boy, wrapped in a shirt, in front of her.

"Hand me the shawls, Mr. Quill. It may be cold tonight. I've got one each for Amy and Mercy. I'll wrap the boy in mine."

He brought the shawls to her, and she looked deeply into his eyes. "Why do men do such shameful things, Mr. Quill?"

His eyes were almost tender as he looked at her. "I don't know, Liberty."

She noticed his use of her given name and was pleased. They looked at each other for a long time.

"Do you think Daniel will . . . remember?"

"You know his name?"

"Of course. Daniel Phelps."

"He'll remember. It will lie there somewhere in the back of his mind for as long as he lives. But he hasn't lost everything. He'll know who he is. It's more than Mercy will know."

"Thank you for staying with us."

"You're welcome, Liberty Bell." His eyes twinkled for just a moment. "I know you're tired, but we've got to travel fast. Here are some sweets I bought from a Frenchman just up from New Orleans. I gave one to Mercy. You and Amy have some. Sweetening will carry you a long way. When the boy wakes, he'll be hungry. Try to keep him quiet."

"I will. Amy fed him some pap and cleaned the poor little thing. He must not have moved from his mama all night long."

"Good girl, Amy." Farr's praise brought a wide grin from the child. He glanced around the site while tying his powder and shot bag around his waist; then he flung a water bag over his shoulder and picked up both rifles. "Let's get clear of this place. You may not be able to see me all the time, Liberty. Keep moving toward the sunset. I may backtrack, but I'll catch up. Be as quiet as you can; voices carry in these woods. Everyone within sight of that smoke will be curious about it."

"We'll do what you say, Mr. Quill."

He nodded and started off through the woods. Liberty followed, blessing fate for having thrown them in the path of Farr Quill.

Chapter
Four

Moonlight filtered through the trees in ghostly patches and the woods seemed ominously quiet. Liberty's arms ached from holding Daniel; her legs and buttocks ached from hours in the saddle. When darkness came, Farr had taken the reins from her hands to lead the horse along a path that wound through the silent forest of trees whose branches seemed to reach to the heavens. Amy was asleep, resting against Liberty's back. Farr had tied the ends of her shawl around Liberty's waist to make sure she didn't fall off the horse. The boy awakened several times during the night and cried for his mother. His whimpering, little cries were the saddest thing Liberty had ever heard. She cuddled him close, crooned to him, and after a while he fell into an exhausted slumber.

They came out of the woods and into a clearing where the grass was so high it stroked the belly of the horse. Farr led the party along the edge of the forest in the shadows of the giant trees that surrounded the clearing. The breeze from the south still carried the faint odor of wood smoke even at this distance. Dazed by fatigue and hunger, Liberty was scarcely aware the horse had stopped until Farr was at her side, his hand on her arm. She was thinking about roast turkey, plum pudding and a warm soft bed. She would eat, sleep and rest, rest . . . and sleep. . . .

"Liberty?" he whispered. "Liberty, are you awake?"

"Of course," she said testily, becoming fully alert. "What is it?"

"We'll rest here for an hour."

"I don't need to rest—"

"The horses do. We can water them here, and they can feed while we rest. Give me the boy. I'll lay him down and come back for Amy and Mercy."

Her arms felt magically light when the boy was taken from them. Now only Amy rested against her. She scarcely had had time to untie the shawl when Farr returned and lifted Amy into his arms. Liberty flexed her shoulders and moved her head in a circular motion in an effort to ease her tired muscles. Her father sat his horse directly behind her. Farr went to him and lifted Mercy down from in front of him.

Liberty knew she should get off the horse, but she was powerless to move. Pain, like a giant hand, was squeezing her legs and thighs. Her bottom was numb and her back ached from her tailbone to the base of her skull.

"Let me help you."

"I'll get off in a minute."

Ignoring her protest, he lifted her from the horse with strong hands at her waist. She didn't know when her feet touched the ground because they were numb, and her legs seemed boneless. She sagged against Farr, clinging to him to keep from falling. A whimper escaped her lips as the blood rushed to her numbed limbs. Her mind was mixed and unclear, but she knew that the arms that held her were strong, and there was no threat in that strength. Her face pressed against a smooth buckskin shirt that smelled of smoke, male body, and the peculiar, heavy, yet clean odor that was found only in tall timber.

He tilted his head downward, the better to see her face. "Are you all right?"

She laughed nervously and tried to step back, but her knees bent. "I'm not used to riding." Before she finished speaking he had swung her up in his arms. "Oh, no! I can walk." She hadn't been carried since she was a child. Afraid of being so high off the ground, she raised her arms to encircle his neck and cling.

Farr carried her to where he had placed the children, knelt, and gently set her on the ground beside them. They lay on one shawl and were covered with the other. When his arms left her she instantly felt the cool, damp air.

"Don't fall asleep." The words were breathed in her ear before he released her. "Sit for a bit, then move around, or you'll get stiff."

"I'll help with the horses."

"Your pa can help. You stay here," he said firmly and left her, moving swiftly and silently.

Liberty sat for a moment, then rolled over onto her knees and got slowly and carefully to her feet. Her buttocks and thighs ached, and every muscle in her body quaked with weakness. She stumbled to a tree, put her palms flat on the trunk and stood there until her light-headedness passed and the terrific pounding of her heart subsided a little.

Farr removed the saddle from her horse and after a few murmured words to Elija, he followed suit. They led the horses to where a ribbon of glimmering water snaked through the clearing. Liberty picked up the water bag he had left on the ground beside the children and stumbled after them.

"I ain't seein' no need a ridin' all night with them young-uns and jist awearin' ourselves out," Elija said when Liberty came up beside him and knelt down to fill the water bag. "We ain't agoin' to outrun nobody. We'll jist—"

"Please hush up, Papa," she said tiredly. "You could have turned back, but you chose to come with us. You'll do just as Mr. Quill tells you to do. Can't you see that he's doing his best to save our lives?"

"Life ain't hardly worth livin' out here'n this place God forgot about, nohow. Twarn't worth much back home, either, what with ya always naggin' do this, do that, and hold-in' so tight to the purse strings a man'd die a thirst afore ya squeezed out a shillin'. Work is all ya want to do. I ain't been fishin' fer so long I've plumb forgot how."

Farr led the horse back from the stream and staked him in the shadows of the huge trees so he could eat the tall grass. Grumbling, Elija followed.

Liberty stood beside the stream after her father left her,

her head bowed, her unseeing gaze on the rippling water. Tears of frustration filled her eyes. Her unruly hair had worked loose and its shining curls made a decorative frame for her strong, still, beautiful face. In her chest her heart pounded to the rhythm of the words that beat in her mind. It was not true! It was not true! She nagged because she had to, she cried silently, and she held the purse strings tight because otherwise it would all have been spent at the Bloody Red Ox.

An owl hooted nearby, and an answer came from some distant place. Like a doe who sensed danger, she tensed, poised, and tilted her head in a listening position. Stories of Indian atrocities flooded her mind.

"It *was* an owl." Farr's voice came out of the darkness and she turned to see him beside her.

"How do you know?"

"The crickets are still singing back in the woods. I'm reasonably sure we're all right here for a while, but put your shawl over your head. That hair of yours shines like a candle in the moonlight." He lay down on the rocks bordering the stream, removed his hat, and plunged his face into the water.

Liberty draped the shawl over her head, held it together beneath her chin, and watched him. He was the most confident man she had ever known. There was something plain and honest and earthy in his manner, not at all like the men in Middlecrossing. It amazed her that Farrway Quill, a stranger, had stepped in and assumed responsibility for them. Farrway Quill. She liked his name, his face, his gentleness with the children, his quick decisions. He was the type of man who would tame this vast wilderness.

She had yearned to be a part of the western movement, to build a home in a new land. She still wanted that despite all that had happened since they started the journey. She would have a house standing by itself in the center of her land, she mused. One that would withstand summer storms, give warmth in winter and protect her from wild things. Before the sun was up she would be hard at work growing vegetables, flax and corn, finding berries and greens and nuts in the woods. She would make hot breads and meat stews for her man when he came in from a hard day of labor. They would go to a bed spread with woolen sheets she had woven. . . .

All these thoughts flashed through Liberty's mind while she watched Farr wipe the water from his face with his two hands and slam his hat back on his head. She was grateful for the darkness that hid her flaming face when he looked at her and was ashamed that she could think of another man with her husband so newly laid to rest. But Jubal was not a *husband*, she reasoned, more like a dear friend. She had never lain in his arms, he had never lifted her and held her to his chest, or kissed her with passion. Jubal was not strong enough to take care of himself, much less a wife. He was not strong about anything. The main difference between him and her father was that Jubal didn't complain.

Farr stood looking down at her, his long body relaxed, a boneless grace that was neither anxious nor indifferent. While he waited for her to speak, time and space seemed to shrink to the small, rocky place where they stood beside the stream.

"Liberty?" He said her name slowly.

"You think it's a silly name."

"No. It suits you."

"My mother's people came from Philadelphia. When the Liberty Bell arrived from London in 1752, my great-grand-father helped to place it in Independence Hall. And twenty-four years later, my mother was allowed to tug on the rope when the bell rang on Independence Day. Because she was very proud of that, she named me Liberty."

She met his look with unsmiling calm while an almost frantic uneasiness leaped within her. Actually this man was a stranger. Could it be that only one night, a day and part of another night had passed since she first set eyes on him? So much had happened in such a short time. Why did she babble on and on when she was with him? Did he think she was bragging about her mother's connection with the famous bell?

"What are you thinking about when you stand so still, watching me with those big, sad eyes?" His voice was soft and intimate. She thought it had a teasing quality too, but he was not smiling.

She turned away, letting her glance move around the meadow to the trees that edged it. She knew she must speak, and speak casually. She looked back at him, then dropped her eyes. It was a strange feeling that washed over her, as if she lacked breath, as if she were sad to the point of tears, yet she was excited to be alone with him.

"I don't know that I should tell you."

"Why?"

"You'd think I've taken leave of my senses." She tilted her face, looked up at him, and smiled provocatively, unaware that she was doing so. Her mouth was wide and straight, its beauty was in the swift mobile movements of her lips as they parted over her even white teeth.

"I might. I don't know much about women."

"And I don't know much about men . . . like you."

"Like me? Why am I different? I'm a man like any other. I get tired, hungry, angry, scared. I get lonely, I dream—"

"About what?"

"About most things a man dreams about, I guess."

"Why did you stay with us?" she asked, wishing she were less conscious of his nearness.

"Maybe I wanted you to take Mercy off my hands."

"Is that the only reason?"

"No."

"Why, then? Hull Dexter went off and left us."

"I like to think I'm a cut above Hull Dexter," he said with a touch of sarcasm in his voice.

"Do you think he ran off and left those folks?"

"What else can I think? I saw no sign of a fight."

"It would be like him. He ran off and left us! He should be brought to justice!"

"By whom? There's very little white man's law out here, Liberty. It's every man for himself. Self-preservation is the first law of the frontier."

"But that's uncivilized. What about the Indians?"

"They have their own laws and punish their own people."

"I mean what about the Indians who raid and kill? Is there no one to punish them?"

"The militia does what it can to keep the peace. Don't forget that it's the Indians' land that's being taken away. Wouldn't you fight for your home?"

"You sound as if you're on *their* side," she said coolly.

"I have a certain sympathy for their predicament. They've lived here for hundreds of years. Now a steady stream of whites is invading their territory, killing off the game, clearing and plowing the land."

"Well, I don't have any sympathy for them. There's enough room for everyone. They've no right to kill . . . and take hair just because they don't want us here!"

"White men started the custom of paying for scalps. They offered the Indians a bonus for scalps. The Indians are not the only savages on the frontier. Yesterday you saw what white men are capable of doing to their own kind. They've done even worse to Indian women. I advise you to give a lot of thought about staying out here, especially without a man to protect you. An unmarried woman is fair game to such as Hull Dexter and others who want a woman. You'll be courted by every single man between sixteen and sixty within a hundred square miles."

"You, too?" The words popped out of her mouth before she could stop them. She felt the blood rush to her face as the embarrassing words left her parted lips; but she forced herself to hold up her head, and her steady blue eyes looked directly into his eyes.

"I'm not ready to settle down. I've got rivers to cross and mountains to climb. A woman would be like a millstone around my neck." His tone was light, but he did not smile. His words irritated her.

"I'm not looking for a man to protect me. More than likely I'd have to protect *him*. If ever I marry again it will be to a settled man, a providing man, one who wants to share *my* life, not one who goes off chasing rainbows. I'll walk beside him, not behind him, and I'll have my *say*!" Liberty held her head high with a kind of necessary dignity because he was looking at her with an air that said he was amused by her declaration. Her soft mouth was set stubbornly and her eyes dared him to deny her right.

"I bet you will!" A deep chuckle escaped Farr and his wide lips spread in a grin.

A wave of anger washed over Liberty. He was making fun of her! He was just like the rest of the conceited asses that thought women were good enough for drudges but were too stupid to voice an opinion. She wanted to kick him, to wipe that smirk off his face, to tell him that her brain was every bit as good as his. She wanted to make him admit she *was* a person of worth.

"Don't you dare laugh at me, you . . . you backwoods, mountain-climbing river-crosser!"

His deep chuckle escalated into soft but full-blown laughter.

"I wasn't laughing at you, Liberty. I was laughing at something my Indian friend told me. He said white woman's mouth open all the time. You beat—she shut it."

"So they beat their women too! I'm not surprised," she said with a look of indignation on her face. She thrust her chin out at a defiant angle. Her back was up, *good*. He would have known it even if she had not shot him the withering look.

"Only when they need it. Come on, let's get back. I want to sit for a while before we go on."

The night had passed slowly for Farr, and he welcomed the rising sun when it broke over the eastern hills and poured a radiance upon the trail. He led the party at a steady pace along a familiar path, one he had used many times. The land was more open here. They had made better time than he had anticipated. He figured they should be at the station by the middle of the morning.

He glanced back to see Liberty sitting erect in the saddle, the child in her arms and her sister sleeping against her back. She was a strong woman; strong and gutsy. Maybe too gutsy for her own good, he reflected uneasily. She had held herself together at a time when it was difficult even for him to do what had to be done, and he had seen violent death many times. Damned if he could think of another white woman who would have done half as well.

More likely than not she would see worse if she stayed in Indian country, he thought grimly. Without a doubt war would be breaking out soon. All along the frontier there had been acts of violence. British agents were providing the Indians with arms and ammunition. Tenskwatawa, the Shawnee chief known as the Prophet, was stirring up superstitions among all the tribes, and his brother, Tecumseh, was calling for a military alliance among the tribes, urging them to stop giving up their land and drive the white settlers out of the country.

Farr was eager to get home so he could start building a stockade at his station to protect the settlers in his area. It would take several months of hard work even with the help of a man from each family. Governor Harrison had confided to him that the settlers all along the Wabash were in danger from Tecumseh's warriors and from the British to the north. Harrison was careful to explain that no soldiers would be garrisoned at Quill's Station. It was up to the settlers to band together and prepare to protect themselves from an all out Indian attack. But for now he had to concentrate on getting Liberty and the children to the station.

It was painful to admit it, but when he held her soft body in his arms he had felt a surge of longing for a woman's love. Maybe he just needed a woman, he thought bitterly, a woman's body, not her love. It was purely a physical interest he felt for her and that was all. The night her husband died she had seemed small and defenseless with the firelight shining on her light hair, her eyes large and sad. Yet she couldn't have loved the man as he had loved Fawnella. Suddenly he saw the image of Fawnella's young, sweet face, and he ground his teeth against the pain that filled him. *Fawnella*. He couldn't seem to get used to being without her. With an effort he shifted his thoughts back to Liberty.

She would probably marry her brother-in-law, Hammond Perry, he mused. He was ambitious, and a woman as pretty and smart as Liberty would be an asset to one who so desperately wanted to be the governor's right hand man. The thought of Liberty and Hammond Perry together was not a pleasant one and brought a scowl to his face. Hammond was not only ambitious, he was domineering, and if Liberty wanted a man who would let her have her say, Hammond Perry was not the man. Farr shrugged. Liberty's choice of a husband was her affair.

His immediate problem was what to do about Mercy if Liberty wouldn't keep her. And there was the boy, Daniel. Farr doubted he would be able to find Daniel's kin, if he had any, so he had to find a home for him too. He tried to think of a family near his station (other than one of the Sufferites, a religious sect) who might take on an extra mouth to feed, and he couldn't think of any who would even consider it. If the children were old enough to work they would be welcomed into a number of homes. He himself had been lucky to have his grandfather when his folks were taken with the fever. Then he had had the Carrolls, and True and Juicy, who had treated him as if he were their own son.

The thought entered his mind that if no one had moved into the cabin old Shellenberger had left behind when he moved on west, Liberty might stay there with the children until he could make other arrangements for them. Of course, he would help feed them. He'd send down one of his two cows, and either he or young Rain Tallman would do their hunting so they'd have meat.

Liberty's father would be little use to her, other than to supply fish, he thought with a tinge of impatience. Elija had just given up. Suddenly remembering the man, he looked back to see him slouched in the saddle. It wasn't the first time Farr had seen men lose their spirit and whine their lives away. If the sight of the massacred settlers the day before hadn't shocked him out of his self-pity, nothing would.

Farr knew he would have to send word to Vincennes about the massacre with the first boat upriver, but he had little hope that the murderers would be brought to justice. In a week's time they would have taken the stock downriver and sold it to some unsuspecting traveler going into Missouri or Arkansas. Hull Dexter would have his own story to tell, but Farr would deal with that bastard if he ever got his hands on him.

As soon as he got Liberty and the children to the station, he'd go back for her wagon and the oxen if they were still there. She had hated leaving her possessions behind, but she hadn't complained about it. A gentle smile softened Farr's usually grim mouth, taking years from his face and leaving him looking as vulnerable as a callow lad.

By the time full daylight arrived, Liberty was desperately in need of going to the bushes. Daniel had slept so soundly that he had wet, soaking the front of her dress. Poor little tyke. He had been in such a state and had clung to her all night long. He was a big, sturdy child and at least a couple of years older than Mercy. Liberty remembered his running and playing and chattering happily. She wondered if the sight of his mother, her skirts around her waist, lying spread-eagled on the ground, would stay in his memory forever. She hoped and prayed he wasn't aware of the indignities she suffered before she died.

They stopped beside another stream, and Farr came to lift Amy down. He tried to take Daniel from Liberty's arms, but the child shrieked with terror and clung to Liberty, hiding his face against her.

"It's all right, Daniel. Mr. Quill won't hurt you. He's the man who found you. He just wants to hold you so I can get down." Liberty held him and pressed kisses to his wet cheeks. "Don't cry, lovey. It's going to be all right. Soon it'll not hurt so much."

"Mama. I want Ma . . . ma."

"Oh, sweet little boy. . ." Liberty felt hot tears behind her eyelids and closed them to trap them there, but they spilled over and ran down her cheeks. "You're tired and hungry. I bet Mr. Quill has some more sugarhards. Let him hold you so I can get down."

Farr lifted the boy from her arms, and Liberty quickly got off the horse, then reached for him. The small arms circled her neck, his legs her waist, and held onto her fiercely. Her wet dress no longer mattered. Her heart ached for a little boy whose world had been torn apart.

Amy tried to get his attention. "Daniel, remember me? Amy. I played a game with you and gave you a whistle. Oh, shoot, Libby, I shouldn't have said that. His pa wouldn't let him have it."

Farr set Mercy on her feet and Amy took her hand.

"Come on, Amy," Liberty said, keeping her face turned away from the tall, silent man who stood watching. "The children need to . . . we'll take them over there." She headed for a clump of tall weeds with a heavy purple flower topping the slender stems.

"Not there, Liberty," Farr called. "Those are nettle weeds."

"Well, for goodness sake! Why didn't you say so sooner?" She carefully backed away from the thorny branches that grabbed at her skirts. "Pick up Mercy, Amy. She'll get stickers in her feet." She walked quickly back along the narrow animal path, then turned into the woods where interlaced fallen timber offered endless opportunities for cover. "This is a good place for you and Mercy," she said, stopping beside a large tree that had been uprooted by a storm. "I'll take Daniel to the other side and you wait for us out in the path."

On the other side of the tree she pried the boy's arms from around her neck and lowered him to the ground. He wrapped his arms around her legs and hid his face in her skirt. She gently pushed the small body away so she could bend down.

"Are you hungry, Daniel? Make water and we'll go back and get something to eat." She put her fingers beneath his chin, and gently turned his face toward her. It was dirt-streaked and scratched; his large, brown eyes were swollen from crying, and the pleading look in them tore at Liberty's heart.

"Mama?" he said in a small frightened voice.

"Oh, Daniel. I wish I could tell you she's coming back, but I can't. Your mama and your papa have gone away. They're up in heaven—"

"They . . . hurt Mama." His lips quivered and he tried hard not to cry.

"I know they did, darling. But God took her to heaven so she wouldn't hurt any more."

"I want to go with Mama."

"You can't, darling. Not now. Someday . . ." A wave of pity shook Liberty, forcing a flood of tears to her eyes. She fought against weeping as she remembered her own fear of being alone when her mother died.

"I . . . want . . . Mama."

"You'll see her someday. My mama is up there too, Daniel. She left me a long time ago. I know how lost and lonely you feel. You're not alone. You've got me and Amy and Mr. Quill—"

"I'll kill the mean man." Tears rolled down his cheeks.

"Try not to think about it, honey. Think about how glad your mama would be to know that you didn't get hurt, and that Mr. Quill came to find you. She would want you to be brave and to grow up to be a big man she'd be proud of."

"But where'll I . . . sleep?" He leaned against her and she folded him in her arms.

"Don't worry about that, darling." She kissed his wet cheeks and smoothed his hair. "You'll be taken care of. Mercy doesn't have a mama either. Maybe you can help me and Amy take care of Mercy. You like Amy, don't you?"

"Uh huh . . ."

"She likes you too. Can you make water, so we can go back?"

"I . . . did." He cowered at her side, covering his face with his hands.

"Oh, that's all right, it happens sometimes. You were tired and sleeping soundly."

"Papa'd whup me."

"Then he'd have to whup me too. Look, I'm all wet." She stood and gently pushed him from her, hoping her pretense would ease his guilty feeling. "You go over there and I'll go here. Keep your back turned until I say you can look." He moved away, looking back to be sure she was still there. "I'll not leave. When you finish we'll go back to Amy and Mercy."

When they returned to the trail, Amy was holding a huge butterfly in her cupped hands for Mercy to see. Liberty suddenly noticed how tall Amy was. It seemed she had grown inches since they left Middlecrossing. The hem of her dress was above her shoe tops, and the bodice of her dress strained against her budding young breasts. Her sister was growing up. In just a year or two she would be marriageable age. Many girls were married and had babies by the time they were fourteen. The thought alarmed Liberty. What if her father got it into his head to marry Amy off to someone like Stith Lenning so he could live a life of ease? Again the fear that Stith would follow washed over her, and unconsciously she glanced back down the trail.

Dear God, she prayed, help her keep Amy safe until she was ready to choose her own man.

A few hours later they arrived at the bank of the Wabash River. The path to the river wound through the tall meadow grass. There were no cultivated fields or orchards, no roads filled with moving wagons or carriages to stir up dust to fill the eyes and clog the nose. Twice since the morning stop they had flushed deer from their beds, and while they were crossing a marshy section, a flock of teal took to the air with a loud beat of wings.

All along the riverbank the sycamores, walnut and cottonwood trees attained an enormous size. Beneath the trees and skirting the river, rushes and nettles and briers grew in matted profusion. Raucous clouds of waterfowl swarmed up as they approached the river. Liberty cherished the wildness. A woman, she thought, should have the right to decide on the kind of life she wanted, and this was what she had yearned for since she was a small child listening to stories about the frontier, new lands, and rugged living away from all the hypocrisy of towns. This was where she would spend the rest of her life, she vowed.

Farr led them along the river path to a place where the bank had been cut away and a log ramp had been laid. A thick rope running through a pulley lashed to a sycamore tree ran to the other side of the river. Farr emitted a shrill, intermittent whistle, shaded his eyes with his hand, and looked across the expanse of slowly moving water. A loud whoop came from the other side. A man came down to the river and jumped onto a raft that bobbled and bumped against a log mooring. Soon the rope began to move through the pulley and a wide log raft with pole handrails came toward them from the far side.

A gigantic young Negro, stripped to the waist, was turning a windlass on the raft. He was black as midnight. As the craft neared the shore, Liberty could see that he was tall, lean, straight and wide-shouldered. Thick muscles corded his shoulders and his bare chest glistened with sweat. His head was shaved except for a topknot. A large silver ring swung from each earlobe and from his nostrils. His mouth was wide, a deep, red chasm lined with large white teeth.

"How do, Mista Farr?"

"How do, Mr. Washington?"

"It purely is a fine day." The huge black threw a loop over a thick post to hold the raft and leaped to shore. He held out his hand and Farr shook it warmly.

"It purely is. Is the world treating you all right, Mr. Washington?"

"Jist fair to middlin', Mistah Farr. Jist fair to middlin'."

"This is Mrs. Perry, and her father Mr. Carroll."

"How do, ma'am?" The Negro made an elaborate bow.

"How do?" Liberty nodded.

"And you, suh? It's a mighty fine, showy day." Mr. Washington faced Elija squarely with his hands on his hips.

"Gawd!" Elija snorted, turned his back and began fiddling with a strap on his saddle.

With a tight, expressionless face, Mr. Washington looked long and hard at Elija's back while Liberty waited in an agony of suspense, hoping and praying that for once her father would keep his mouth shut. When the young giant swung around, his face was split by a huge smile.

"You 'n the folks wantin' to cross of my ferry, Mistah Farr?"

"We'd be obliged. What's the price today?"

The black put his fingers to his chin, looked up and down the river, walked around the horses, stood back and studied Elija, then turned his attention to Liberty and the children, all the time fingering his chin.

"You knows I like chillin's, Mistah Farr. I ain't never take no coin to take chillin's on my ferry, 'n they gots to have their mama come, so I don't take no coin for her. And I owes you a ride fer a sack a salt." He eyed Elija for a full minute, then threw out his hands as if he had come to a hard decision. "Fer the horses 'n the gent, I gots to have a bucket a clabber milk and a shillin'. You can take it or not, Mistah Farr."

"We'll take it, Mr. Washington. You'll have the clabber by sunset." Farr came to lift Amy from the horse, then reached for Daniel. The child went to him willingly.

"What was that all about?" Liberty asked when she was on the ground.

Farr grinned. "It's Mr. Washington's ferry. He likes ceremony and he likes to dicker."

"I ain't paying no black bastard a shilling to carry me fifty yards across a river. That's robbery!" Elija growled. "Who's he belong to, anyhow?"

"He belongs to himself. He's as free as you are." There was no mistaking the chill in Farr's voice. "If you couldn't pay, he'd take you for nothing. If you can pay and don't wish to, then swim across."

"We'll pay the shilling, but what about the clabber milk?" Liberty flung the sack containing her valuables over her shoulder and took Daniel's hand.

"That'll come from my place." Farr began hacking at the long grass with his knife and stacking it. "This will give the horses something to eat while they're on the raft and they'll be too busy to be scared."

"I ain't alikin' it," Elija grumbled and then snorted. "I ain't never called no nigger *mister*, and I ain't never heard of nobody else adoin' it, neither. It ain't decent, is what it ain't. I'll be dad-blamed if'n this ain't the gawdawfullest, hell-bent-to-Betsy land I ever heared of."

Farr carried an armful of grass to the raft and dumped it. On his way back he paused beside Elija.

"I advise you to watch your mouth, Mr. Carroll. *Mr.* Washington can be a valued friend or he can be a powerful enemy. He'll take your measure; and if he finds you lacking, you'll not cross on this ferry again. He don't take kindly to those who feel they're superior because their skin is white." He stalked away without giving Elija a chance to answer.

"Well, I'll be blamed if'n I can understand it," Elija muttered to his back. "It don't make no sense a'tall how things is done out here in this heathen land. They's things a man can stomach 'n things he cain't. This'n I cain't. I ain't makin' no talk or shakin' no hands with a nigger—"

"Libby, Papa's going to make a show of himself," Amy said anxiously. "What's Mr. Quill going to say? I wish Papa'd hush up just for once." She set Mercy on her hip to keep her small bare feet out of the sandburrs growing along the riverbank.

"He can't hush up. It isn't in him to hush up. And it's better that Mr. Quill knows how Papa is right off, because there's nothing we can do to change him. Papa brings trouble on himself, and it has nothing to do with us. Just hold your head up and be nice and polite to Mr. Washington." Liberty suppressed a giggle. "It is kind of funny."

Farr and Mr. Washington led the horses onto the raft and tied them. Farr came back for the children. He held one in each arm, jumped lightly to the bobbing craft, and handed them over to the huge black man. Liberty held her breath for fear they would scream. To her utter astonishment, they accepted him readily. He smiled broadly when Mercy's small hand reached up to touch the rings in his ears.

Leaving Elija to get aboard on his own, Farr assisted Amy and Liberty down the slanting ramp and led them to the pole handrail where they could hold on until they could sit down on the floor of the raft. He brought the children to them, sat them down, and went to throw off the rope that held the raft to the shore.

For Liberty it was a scary, but fascinating ride. Amy seemed to have no fear at all. Her eyes were bright with excitement, and to Liberty's surprise neither Daniel nor Mercy showed the slightest fear. They sat close together, and after Farr helped to push the raft out into deeper water with a stout pole, he came to stand protectively over them. Daniel looped an arm about Farr's leg and watched the moving water. Mercy clapped her hands happily. Her childish laughter floated out over the water like the song of a bird. Hearing it, Mr. Washington laughed. It was a soft, rolling chuckle as he strained to turn the windlass.

Elija stood with his back to the others, his hands gripping the rails. Liberty wanted to call to him, share the excitement with him, but from the set of his shoulders she knew he had little inclination to join them.

Farr's narrowed gaze sought Liberty's face time and again. The damp river air had turned all the loose hair floating around her face into tight curls. Her steady blue eyes watched everything with interest, and, as usual, she was hiding any apprehension she might be feeling from the children. Farr thought he had never seen a prettier, more lively woman in all his twenty-six years. There was a lot he liked about this slip of a girl; not the least being how she looked him straight in the eye, honestly, steadily. She even faced the unpleasant task they shared at the massacre site without a trace of feminine nonsense; not screaming, not fainting, retaining, even in that moment, the spirit to talk back, to tell him her views.

His association with white women had been limited to Cherish Carroll, who had been like a mother to him, and Orah Delle, the Carrolls' daughter, who lived in Virginia. He also knew the wives of the farmers who lived near his station and the Thompsons' spoiled brat of a daughter, Harriet. Their indentured girl, Willa, was so shy she ran at the sight of him. Of course, there had been a few loose women in New Orleans who had been accommodating. After he lost Fawnella he had died inside. He had vowed to never again expose himself to such gut-crushing pain. He still wanted a son to carry his name into the next generation, and he would need a wife for that. When the time came, he would choose her much as he would a horse. He would get a good, strong, serviceable woman of childbearing age, one who wouldn't nag him or interfere with his business or try to stop his wanderings. He'd get one who was willing to move on west when his work here was done. He wanted a quiet companion for the long winter evenings, one who would not question or—

Liberty looked up and his thoughts left him. He was so intent on looking at her that he scarcely realized, at first, that she was speaking to him.

"I had expected the raft to bob up and down like a cork and that we'd get all wet. It's much smaller than the one that brought us down the Ohio."

"This is a good time to cross. The snow melt has already run down and there hasn't been much rain lately. Mr. Washington has crossed hundreds of times and knows the current. He wouldn't take the children unless he thought it was perfectly safe."

"Is . . . is he a runaway?"

"No. He has his freedom papers. He's been out here almost as long as I have. He built this raft, patterned it after one in Virginia. Many men live the lives they want, but not many get to choose their own names." His eyes twinkled as they danced over her face, studying every contour. Liberty felt her body grow tense under his gaze. She lost herself in luminous green eyes and forgot to breathe until rebellious lungs jerked her back to reality.

"I wondered about that," she said breathlessly, then turned away from him and stroked the hair back from her temples with a quick, nervous motion.

The raft bumped against the log mooring as Mr. Washington brought it to the shore. He threw out the rope loop to secure it, raised his arms wide and announced, "Folks, you is now in the Illinois."

Chapter
Five

The air was fresh and invigorating, the sky a cloudless blue. A road ran parallel with, but back from the river. They had gone only a short distance when they came to four identical houses, set several rods apart, all fronting the road. Behind them was a carefully tended communal garden, a barn as large as the four houses combined, and a plowed field. While the place was clean and neat, there wasn't a bush, flower, fence, or anything at all to lend warmth or humanity to the settlement.

As they passed, a man with a dark beard along his lower jaws, wearing a loose white shirt and black hat, came from the barn and called a greeting to Farr. Women with small children clinging to their skirts came out and stood with their hands wrapped in the white aprons tied around their waists. Small white caps completely covered their heads. They stared at Liberty riding astride the horse with her sunbonnet hanging from the strings about her neck. Liberty waved, but only one of the women acknowledged her greeting with a slight lift of her hand.

Around a bend they saw another cluster of buildings. They were set about a hundred yards back in the timber above the river where it turned to form a deep bend. There in the cradle of the horseshoe bend was Quill's Station. The main building was hewn timber set upright in the ground and chinked with stone and mortar. Attached to the side was the long narrow room Farr had said was a storage shed for his salt and supplies not only for this station but for other settlers farther downriver. Both the building and the addition had steeply pitched roofs, starting at the gables and ending flat at the porch eaves. There was a barn with large double doors and an open shed. Beside the shed was a small cobblestone structure that looked to be a smokehouse. Liberty could see two cows, each staked on a long tether, several white geese and a few speckled chickens.

"I hope this is where Mr. Quill lives, Libby. My hindside is tired," Amy said.

"It must be his place."

"Is this all there is to his town?"

"He never said he had a *town*. He said there were nearly a hundred people that lived within five miles of his station."

"The ones back there looked like those Sufferites we saw in Louisville. If that's all that's here, let's go on. I didn't like them—they looked so sour."

"We have to wait for our wagon. I don't know what we'll do if it's gone when Farr goes back for it."

Farr strode on ahead, and when a man came out of the long, narrow building to stand on the porch, his hand shading his eyes, Farr shouted a greeting.

"Hello!"

The man let out a ringing whoop, came down off the porch and stood waiting. He was big, built like a barrel, and his gray hair hung to his shoulders. His white whiskers were braided in four strands, dangling in front of his buckskin shirt. When Farr approached, the man let loose a warlike yell, made two jumps and they were locked together, straining, their hands pounding each other's backs. They shouted, stomped and rocked back and forth as if they were in a death struggle. Finally, Farr broke free and stepped back.

"Well . . . I see you aren't dead yet, you old goat!" he said buoyantly.

"I reckon I ain't, ya blasted clabberhead!" The man's huge, gnarled hand gripped Farr's shoulder with affection and Farr lifted a hand to grip his. They stood at arm's length, smiling at each other. "Glad yo're back, boy." There was a huskiness in the old man's voice.

"I'm glad to be back, Juicy. Things all right here?"

"Fair to middlin' a late. Not much movin' on the river 'cept fer a Shawnee canoe ever' once in a while."

"I've brought some folks who've had a mite of trouble. This is Mrs. Perry and her sister, Amy Carroll."

"How do, ma'am? Little missy? Now then, ain't you all jist a sight to these old eyes!"

"This is their pa, Mr. Carroll."

"Carroll, ya say? Carroll? Any kin to Sloan Carroll up at Carrolltown?"

"I already asked them that, Juicy."

"Could be shirttail relation," Elija said, stepping out of the saddle. "My folks is a branch of the Virginia Carrolls."

Farr set Mercy on her feet and lifted Amy from the horse. He took Daniel, and Liberty slid to the ground trying to keep as much leg as possible from showing.

"There's a water bucket and a wash trough over there by the cabin, if you want to wash up," Farr said before he turned to the old man. "Where are Colby and Rain?"

"They be up at the salt lick. Had a mite of trouble thar. They be bringin' in the kettles 'n sich."

"What kind of trouble?"

"Injun women ain't makin' salt no more. Jist packed up 'n cleared out. Left the kettles 'n salt piled neat like, tho'. That Frenchie ya helped out last fall come by ta tell it, 'n Colby 'n Rain beat it up there."

"Do you think Tecumseh called them in?"

"Them womenfolk don't do nothin' on their own. Ya know that."

"When will Colby and Rain be back?"

"Ort a be back anytime."

Farr watched the group about the water bucket. Elija had drunk his fill, then leaned up against the cabin.

"You can water the horses down at the creek out back, Mr. Carroll," he called.

Elija wearily pushed himself away from the wall, picked up the reins, and with slow, dragging steps went around the house. Farr saw Liberty turn her back as if ashamed her father had to be told to take care of the animals.

Liberty and Amy, he noted, had taken care to see the children had water before they themselves drank, and now they were wiping the dust from their faces and hands with a wet cloth. He felt a swift, mysterious jab of apprehension that Liberty would move on to Vincennes to find Hammond Perry. With great suddenness he was struck by an ache of emptiness. At that instant she looked at him; and although thirty feet or more separated them, it was as if they were held together by an invisible thread.

"Is anyone on Shellenberger's place, Juicy?" He spoke with his eyes still on Liberty's face.

"No. Ain't been nobody through here alookin' fer somewheres to light."

"These folks are looking for a place. We had to leave their wagon and two oxen back near the Shawneetown road."

"Injuns?"

"River scum. Seen anything of Hull Dexter?"

"He in on it?"

"Either that or he ran out on a party of eleven and left them to be massacred."

"Gawddamned bastid! I always knowed he warn't no good."

"These folks might want to take over Shellenberger's place. It's hard for a woman to start from scratch even with a man to help. Her pa isn't much of a worker. She'd be better off to go on to Saint Louis."

"Shellenberger put up a stout cabin. Thar's flat land thar fer plantin'. Ain't she got no man?"

"Buried him a couple of days ago."

"Too bad. But I be thinkin' she ain't agoin' to have no trouble gettin' another one, sightly as she be. Ain't no woman—"

"I'm going back for her wagon," Farr said abruptly. "I'd take her pa, but if there's trouble, he'd be about as much good as a leaf in a whirlwind."

"Humpt!" Juicy snorted. "I knowed that afore he got off'n the horse. Take Colby or young Rain."

Liberty watched the two men walk over to the porch of

the long building. Farr was doing most of the talking, and she imagined he was telling his friend about the massacre. She stood still, looking around her. It was a wonderful, beautiful land. It was good to see an open stretch of sky after so many days in the dense forest. The grass in the meadow behind the station was a rich green, knee-high, and moved gently in the southern breeze. She had noticed that the earth was black when they passed a turned field. Here they would stay, she decided. It had been in the back of her mind since Farr told her about the land beyond the Wabash and the abandoned homestead.

Her only disappointment was that the people she had seen so far were a religious sect that was not friendly to outsiders. There would be no friendship there, but so be it. More people would come. She and Amy had been a long time without friends, they could wait a little longer. She would ask Farr how she could send word to Hammond Perry that she was here, and if he wanted to see her he would come.

Suddenly she noticed Mercy heading across the yard toward Farr on her stubby little legs. The single garment she wore hung on her small body like a rag. Amy had braided her hair and tied the ends with strips torn from the shirt. Her bare little feet were tough, and she seemed to not notice the wood chips she crossed to reach the hardpacked dirt in front of the porch. Suddenly she stopped, squatted down and picked up something from the ground with her chubby fingers.

"No, Mercy!" Liberty dashed to the child and grabbed her hand, but she was too late to keep her from popping her find into her mouth. She looked up at Liberty and smiled broadly, spit dribbling from her chin. Liberty shoved a forefinger into her mouth to extract a gooey mess. "Oh! Ugh, Mercy! Nasty! Nasty!" She slung the child on her hip and hurried to the waterbucket. "Get me a wet rag, Amy."

"What did she do?"

"She ate some . . . some—"

"Oh! Phew! It looks like chicken doo!"

"It *is* chicken doo! Oh, Lordy!" Liberty poked the rag in

the child's mouth until she gagged. "Don't put that old nasty stuff in your mouth, Mercy. It'll make you sick."

"Ma'am..." Daniel tugged on her dress and Liberty looked down into a worried little face. His large, round, brown eyes were pleading. "Don't whup her. Please! She don't know no better."

"For goodness sake! Of course I won't whup her! She's just a baby, Daniel. You'll have to help us watch to see that she doesn't put such stuff in her mouth. There. I've cleaned out as much as I can. Give her a drink of water, Amy."

"Mercy ate some chicken doo, Mr. Quill." Amy gave him a slanted look and waited for an answer.

Liberty looked around to see Farr standing nearby. She would have been surprised to know that while he watched her with Mercy, his thoughts rocked to and fro with the futile rhythm of a rocking horse. She was a spunky woman, he thought. But how would she manage out at Shellenberger's place? Would her father help her plant and tend a field? he wondered. If she decided to go to Vincennes, Farr knew he would take her. But he couldn't see how he could ask her to take Mercy and the boy with her. She had enough on her plate as it was with her sister and her father.

Farr decided his only alternative was to ask the Sufferites to care for Daniel and Mercy until he could get them upriver to Carrolltown or find homesteaders to take them. Hell! The last thing he wanted to do was to leave them at the mercy of righteous folk who thought it a sin to do anything but work. They had beat the fun and laughter out of their own children, and he hated to think of what they would do to two that were not their own.

Farr waited so long to speak that Liberty became uncomfortable and the color in her cheeks deepened. Feeling ridiculously self-conscious, she looked away.

"I'm going back to get your wagon."

Her eyes swung back to him quickly. "You can't. You've not had any sleep and you've walked all the way."

"I'll get a couple hours sleep and by that time my friend Colby Carroll and a young fellow that stays here with us may be back. One of them will go with me. You'll be all right here with Juicy." A sudden bright smile spread across his face. "Juicy likes nothing better than good cooking. Likes pretty girls, too," he said with his eyes on Amy. He laughed when she blushed miserably and avoided his eyes. He reached over and plucked Mercy from Liberty's arms. "What have you been up to, little wiggle wart? Have you been giving Liberty trouble?" His big hand spread over her stomach and his fingers tickled her. Squeals of happy laughter erupted from the child.

Liberty felt a small hand creep into hers. She looked down to see Daniel gazing with rapt attention at Farr and Mercy. Then she remembered seeing his father's stern face and hearing his harsh voice shouting at his son. It was no wonder the child was fascinated by the play between the man and the child. There was an unmistakable look of longing in Daniel's brown eyes. Liberty lifted her eyes to Farr's and saw that he was looking intently at the boy. He stood Mercy on her feet and squatted down on his heels.

"How old are you, Daniel?"

"Four." He held out four fingers.

"That old? Then I reckon you're old enough to look after my pet crow while I go back to get Mrs. Perry's wagon? He usually hangs out around the barn. Sometimes he flies down and sits on my shoulder. Let's go see if we can find him." Farr stood, removed his hat and hung it on a peg above the water bucket. He reached down, lifted Daniel and set him astride his neck. The boy's smile came quickly, then faded just as fast, as if it was something he shouldn't do. Farr's eyes caught and held Liberty's. He saw the tired lines in her face shift into a smile. "Make yourselves to home. I'll send him back in a while. I'll bed down in the barn for a few hours of sleep before I go."

Liberty felt hot tears behind her eyelids and closed them to trap them there. Farrway Quill, frontiersman, had seen the loneliness in the small boy's face and had responded. She swallowed the assortment of lumps in her throat, opened

her eyes, and stared hard at his back as he walked away with
the small boy perched on his shoulders.

The large square room attached to the long building was
gloomy, Liberty observed from the doorway. It smelled of
ashes, tobacco and hides. There was a table and stools for
sitting, beds in three of the corners, and a cobblestone fireplace in the fourth. The beds were pole beds, up off the floor
and covered with patchwork quilts. The nicest thing in the
room was a walnut cupboard, whittled and carved and put
together with pegs. It had double doors at the top and three
deep drawers at the bottom.

"Come right on in." The old man stood in the doorway
going into the long building. His gravelly voice boomed in
the silence. "Make yoreselves to home. If'n the younguns is
hungry, stir 'em up some vittles."

"Thank you. We have cornmeal—"

"Ain't no call to be a usin' it. I'll fetch ya in a bait a deer
meat from the smokehouse. There be milk 'n butter in the
root cellar. I got to fetch clabber milk anyways to send down
to Mr. Washington. Colby brung us in some wheat flour, but
ain't none of us no hand at makin' up bread." He tilted his
head to one side, his blue eyes twinkled, and the whiskers
around his mouth shifted so that Liberty knew he was smiling.

"I'll make bread, but it'll take some time."

"We can wait. Times me 'n Farr'd give a prime pelt fer a
hunk a good wheat bread."

"How far is the Shellenberger place from here, Mr.
Juicy?" Liberty reached to catch Mercy's hand before she
pulled a wooden trencher off the table.

"Ain't no need to be puttin' mister to my name, Mrs.
Perry. I be jist Juicy to one 'n all."

The old man's sharp eyes gleamed as he watched her, his
smile wide across his whiskered face.

"Then don't be putting a mistress to my name, Juicy. I'm

just Liberty, or Libby, if you prefer." There was a friendly sparkle in her eyes.

Juicy laughed, and turning, poked at the cookfire with a long iron poker before he spoke.

"The Shellenberger place ain't but down the road a piece. Good stout cabin is what it is. Hit was all Shellenberger knowed how to do, I reckon. Good builder, but he warn't no hand a'tall puttin' in a crop."

"Is the cabin on the road where people pass?"

"If'n they be on the river or the road they go by if'n they be aimin' fer Vincennes or Shawneetown."

"It's near the river then?"

"Right slap dab on, but on a rise. Ain't much risk of gettin' flooded out."

Liberty brushed a strand of hair back off her forehead, then slowly turned her face toward the open doorway and looked out into the bright sunlight. Her mind was busy sorting out the sudden flood of ideas that had flowed into it while talking to the old man.

"I reckon the younguns is hungry," Juicy said. "I'll fetch the milk 'n meat. Got taters, too, tho' they be sprouted some."

"Sprouted? Shouldn't they be planted by now?"

"I ain't much hand at puttin' in a patch. We get sich from them folks ya passed back yonder, or from folks that trade fer salt 'n sich," he said and was gone.

He returned with a large crock cradled in one arm and a small one in the other. He saw Liberty eyeing the fly floating on the top of the milk.

"I allus forget ta cover it. Now Farr, he be more persnickety," he said with a sheepish grin. "Him 'n that boy youngun is sleepin' in the barn. The little feller is curled up right by him like a pup to his ma." He hooked a stool from beneath the table and sat down. Mercy pulled her hand from Amy's and went toward him. "I allus did like purty little gal younguns." Juicy lifted her and sat her down on his knee. The child pulled on his whiskers and his roar of laughter filled the room. "Ya be a lively one, ya little scutter."

* * *

After the noon meal Liberty pushed the pot containing what was left of the deer meat and potatoes to the back of the hearth to keep warm for Farr and Daniel and made up a batch of wheat bread. Elija sat on a bench just outside the door, and she could hear him telling Juicy about Middle-crossing, the wonderful life they'd had there, and the hard-ships he'd endured on the long journey to the Wabash.

Liberty gritted her teeth and continued to work. The heat from the fireplace had brought a rosiness to her cheeks and dampness to the curls around her face. As her mind churned with plans, the excitement in her body grew, encompassing her heart and expanding into her soul. Somewhere in her heart she had known all along that she had done the right thing in coming to Quill's Station. Now she was sure of it.

Amy stuck her head in the door. "Mr. Quill's coming," she announced.

Liberty suddenly felt shy. She stood with her back to the doorway, her chest rising with the deep breath she permitted herself to draw. She heard Farr ask Juicy if Colby and Rain had returned, heard Juicy tell him no.

"Something smells mighty good." His voice was deep and rich and came from a few feet behind her.

Liberty turned. The picture of him standing there with the small boy's hand in his brought a lump to her throat. The silence went on for a long while before she spoke.

"Are you hungry?" she asked and knew immediately that it was a stupid thing to say. He hadn't had a meal in two days. "There are meat and potatoes in the pot."

"I'm hungry enough to eat a bear, but we'd better wash up first, huh, Daniel? I don't think women like men sitting at the table with dirty faces and hands." He looked down at the boy with a pretended frown, glanced at Liberty, and the two of them left the doorway.

Liberty had bowls of the steaming stew on the table when they returned. She set a cup of milk beside Daniel's bowl and tea beside Farr's. They ate in silence. Both were hungry. Liberty watched and refilled Farr's bowl without him having to ask.

Daniel's eyes seldom left Farr's face. Liberty eyed him sideways with amusement in her eyes. Daniel was completely captivated by the big frontiersman. More than likely it was the first time a man had shown him kindness, Liberty thought, remembering his gruff, bearded father who appeared to be as old or older than Elija. He had had no patience with his young son.

When they were almost finished Liberty filled a mug with tea and sat down at the table. She wanted to talk with Farr alone before he left, and she figured this would be her only chance.

"I want to pay you for going back for my wagon."

Farr looked up sharply. He was solemn as an owl. "Have I asked for pay?"

"No, but you've already done so much for us."

"Out here people do for each other, Liberty. It's the only way to survive. If you stay, you'll have to take help as well as give it when it's needed."

"Yes, I can understand that. Juicy said the Shellenberger place isn't far from here. I'm anxious to see it."

"A half mile or so. It's the first place north. There's some cleared ground—"

"Enough for a big garden and a corn patch?"

"Plenty for that."

"I want to plant fruit trees and berry bushes. Farr," she said breathlessly, "what do you think about an inn? Juicy said people going from Vincennes to Shawneetown, either by river or the road, pass by that place. He said sometimes he'd give a prime pelt for a hunk of good wheat bread. I think there may be others who feel the same."

"Seems to me Juicy's been saying quite a bit. The Shellenberger cabin isn't much bigger than this room, although it has a loft."

"I'll build an adjoining room for the travelers to sleep in.

Pa will have to help. He can plant a corn patch and cut grass for hay. Amy and I will cook.''

"There'll be a problem about supplies. The nearest mill is at Vincennes."

"Why don't you build a water wheel?"

"Why don't I what?"

"Build a water wheel. Why go all the way to Vincennes when you've got the perfect place for a mill?"

He studied her for a long moment and saw the excitement in her eyes. When he spoke again, it was to Daniel.

"Did you get enough?" he asked.

Daniel nodded, his eyes still on Farr's face.

"Then go keep an eye on Amy and Mercy while I talk to Liberty."

"Poor child. At times he seems so much older than four," Liberty said when they were alone.

"What do you know about him?"

"Only that his parents were with the group that hired Hull Dexter in Louisville. His mother was young, shy, and completely dominated by her husband. His father was an older man, harsh and very opinionated. Amy gave Daniel a whistle, but his father wouldn't allow him to have it. He said it was of the devil and told Amy to stay away from his son with her frivolous devil toys. Mr. Phelps didn't allow his wife to have anything to do with me. He thought I had bewitched my husband because he let me make some of the decisions."

"Then you wouldn't know if Daniel had kinfolk out here," Farr said as if to himself. "I may go back to the massacre site and see what I can find. There could be letters or something. But more than likely the wagons are gone by now. The people who passed would have taken what they needed. That's as it should be. Nothing should be wasted."

"Do you think our wagon will be gone?" Her calm tone belied the fact that her stomach was churning at the thought.

"No. I expect it's still there. That trail is known to only a few, other than the folks hereabout."

"I hope so. I try not to think about what I'll do if I lose it. Everything we own, except for the coins, is there."

"Don't worry about it. I'll have it back here by late tomorrow night."

He dismissed the subject by going to the kettle and pouring more hot tea in his mug.

When he was seated again, Liberty asked, "What do you plan to do with Daniel and Mercy?"

"Find them a home. It'll be no trouble at all." He lifted his shoulders in a careless shrug, but his eyes glinted mischievously as he observed the stiffening of her shoulders and the abrupt way she turned to stare at him. "The Sufferites down the road will take them. In a few years they'll be big enough to work in the fields. They'll get plenty to eat and be brought up to mind their manners. and work. Any foolishness, like book learning, singing and dancing will be knocked out of their heads at an early age."

"No!" Liberty drew her breath in quickly, her straight brows coming together with a frown, and she glared at him angrily. "You'll not give them to that bunch of sanctimonious hypocrites. We camped beside a group of them in Louisville. They wring all the joy out of a child's life. They're never permitted to laugh or play! I'll not have it, Farr," she said with a proud lift of her head, her furious eyes doing battle with his and failing to see the amusement in their green depths.

"What else can I do? I can't keep them."

"You should give them to someone who will make them feel wanted and loved."

"Who might that be?" he asked softly.

"Me."

"You?"

The questioning tone in his voice made her wide, generous mouth tighten. Her hands gripped the mug until her knuckles whitened.

"You say that as if you think I'm not capable of raising two children. I'll have you know, Mr. Quill, I've taken care of Amy since the day she was born. I taught her to read and cipher as well as to be kind and generous to those less fortunate than we are. Amy can bake bread, card wool, weave and sew. Don't you dare tell me I'm not capable of raising Mercy and Daniel."

"I never said you're not capable, Liberty. It's just that I feel responsible for them and want to be around to see how they're doing. If you should decide you'd rather be in a town and take off for Vincennes, I'd not know how they were faring."

"Who said I was going to Vincennes? There's nothing for me in Vincennes." Her voice rose in anger. "I'm staying here, that is, if we can have that vacant homestead. I'm going to open a place where a traveler can stay the night, have a clean bed to sleep in and a decent meal. I've made up my mind. I've seen travel inns all along the way from New York State. Tell me one good reason, Farr, why I can't run one as well as the next person."

"Well, for one thing you'll be expected to serve spirits—"

"I'll not have a grog shop in my home! Any drinking that is done will be done in the barn."

"These are unsettled times, Liberty. America is impatient. She covets all the Indian land east of the Mississippi, and Governor Harrison has orders to take it. The Shawnee will not give it up without a fight."

"Then we'll just have to take our chances along with everyone else."

"What will your father say to all this?" The grave expression on his face eased away as they looked at each other. His admiration for this slight, blond woman grew. He grinned as the humor of the situation took the upper hand, and Liberty's eyes began to shine and the corners of her lips lifted, causing a dimple to appear in her cheek. Farr stared at it and scarcely heard what she said.

"You know the answer to that question."

Before he could answer, Amy darted into the room.

"Someone's coming in a wagon," she said breathlessly.

In the distance there was a shout. "Juicy!" The voice carried into the cabin.

"Farr," Juicy yelled. "Colby 'n Rain acomin'."

Farr went to the door, glanced over his shoulder at the sisters standing beside the table, then went out.

A flatbed wagon pulled by two mules and loaded with black iron kettles, bags of salt, and the carcass of an elk pulled up and stopped a few yards from the porch. A hatless young man, his blond hair shining in the sun and a broad smile on his face, leaped from the wagon, made two jumps for Farr, and they began to pound on each other. It was the same ritual Farr and Juicy had gone through earlier in the day. The two men strained against each other, their breath whistling through their teeth. Being heavier, Farr looped a foot behind the other man's leg and threw him against the porch post. The impact shook the entire building. They fell to the ground, rolled, and lay still.

Watching in openmouthed amazement, Liberty was sure the two had lost their minds. It was a disgrace, she thought, for grown men to act so childishly. Daniel stood close to her, holding onto her skirt and occasionally turning his face into it. Mercy, on the other hand, loved the performance, clapped her hands and squealed with glee.

Farr rolled off his friend and got to his feet. He reached down and pulled the man up beside him. They shook hands and grinned at each other.

"You're ugly as ever, you old son of a gun." Colby was not as tall as Farr, and slightly heavier.

"You'd take no prizes, you young whelp."

"It took you long enough to get to Kaintuck and back. Did you get lost?"

"No. I smelled me a polecat and followed the scent on home."

They laughed and shoved at each other like two youngsters. Then Farr looked around. He spied the tall gangly youth who leaned against the wagon.

"Rain! I swear you've grown a foot." The youth's thin, dark face broke into a smile as he pumped Farr's hand vigorously.

"I ain't gettin' taller. You're gettin' shorter, Farr."

"I can still lick you, by granny."

"You still braggin' 'bout that?"

Rain tossed his hat onto the wagon bed and the two squared off. They circled each other, waiting for a chance to attack. Farr moved suddenly. The youth sprang back, feinted, spun around and kicked Farr on the thigh. It knocked the larger man off balance. The youth laughed. He was incredibly swift, incredibly agile. Farr moved, seemed to slip, and the youth sprang in. Farr turned and hooked him around the neck with a powerful arm. A booted foot struck behind Farr's knee. The two went down, rolling over and over. They finally separated and lay in the dirt, laughing.

Farr sprang to his feet and ran his fingers through hair that had come loose from the thong that held it. Rain stood and Farr clapped his shoulder. To Liberty watching from the doorway, there was no doubt that there was great affection between Farr and his friends. During the fracas Juicy shouted with laughter and Elija watched with amazement.

"In another year or two, Rain, you'll whip every bear that growls at you in the bushes."

Farr introduced Colby and Rain, and Liberty heard her father say once again he was a Virginia Carroll, but he doubted if he were kin to Sloan Carroll of Carrolltown.

Colby Carroll was as friendly as Rain Tallman was shy. The youth's dark eyes passed briefly over the women, he nodded politely, then disappeared around the corner of the cabin. Colby's eyes were plainly admiring as he was presented to Liberty. He bowed over her hand.

"Your servant, ma'am. Dang it all, old Farr has all the luck."

"We were the lucky ones, Mr. Carroll. If Mr. Quill hadn't found us, heaven only knows where we'd be by now." Liberty's eyes flicked to Farr and found him studying her from beneath half-shuttered lids. She pulled Amy up beside her. "This is my sister, Amy."

Colby made a sweeping bow. When he lifted his head he looked directly into Amy's eyes and winked. Instantly, the giggling young girl was in love.

"By jinks! I don't know if my heart can take all this beauty, Farr!"

"Never fear. It'll stand the strain," Farr said dryly. "Let's get the salt in the warehouse. I've a few things to tell you before I leave."

"Leave? You're leaving again?"

"Come on. I'll tell you about it while we work."

Rain had moved the wagon up close to the door of the long room. Each of the men shouldered a sack of salt and carried it inside.

"Do you think Tecumseh sent word for the women to leave?" Farr asked. "I had a deal with him. If he let the women work the salt lick, he could have a third of the salt. I've not heard of him going back on his word."

"They were scared off. There was a party of Sac and Fox on the river not many days ago. I heard, too, that Black Hawk, their chief, is getting ornery. The Sioux don't like it, and everyone seems to be gathering all their friendly relations around them. An Indian war is brewing, sure as shooting."

"We're pretty far south. It's the Shawnee we've got to worry about. Harrison said there was a need for a dozen forts between here and Fort Washington, but there's no appropriation to pay for them. It's up to the people, Colby."

"What do you plan to do?"

"Build a stockade right here. It's the logical site. The ground around it is cleared. The visibility is good. It's on a rise and we have the spring. In case of a siege, it's the only chance many of these folks would have."

Colby dropped the bag from his shoulder and looked at his friend. The warehouse was gloomy, but he could see the worried look on his face.

"That's going to be quite an undertaking. How much time do you think we've got to build it?"

"It's got to be done before fall."

"By jinks damn!" Colby exclaimed.

"My thoughts exactly."

Chapter
Six

In the middle of the afternoon, Liberty was rolling dough and forming it into loaves of bread. She had sent Amy to fetch a pail of water. At the sound of heavy steps, she turned to see her father with the pail.

"Where's Amy?"

"I tole her to watch the younguns 'n keep 'em out from under Quill's feet."

Liberty stopped working the dough. "Mr. Quill? Hasn't he left yet?"

"Ain't agoin'. He sent Colby 'n the boy."

She turned her back to the grumpy look on her father's face and braced herself for the argument she knew was coming.

"He must have changed his mind about going himself," she said over her shoulder.

"I heared what ya was atalkin' 'bout to 'em. What's this 'bout openin' a inn? If'n that ain't the most harebrained thin' ya've thought up yet. I ain't never heared the like. It plumb flummoxes me where ya get them foolish notions. Not even yore ma'd thought up that. She warn't no rattle-head even if'n she was headstrong."

"We've got to do something to make a living." Liberty pushed a lock of hair back from her brow with the back of her sticky hands.

"I reckon we do, now ya got us in this fix. I'm atellin' ya now, Libby, it ain't agoin' to turn out. We'd best get on up to Vincennes 'n try 'n set things right with Hammond Perry. Now Jubal's gone he might not claim us as kin."

Liberty set the bread close to the hearth and covered it with a cloth. She had known her father would be against the idea of a travel inn. As long as she could remember he had been against any new idea she had presented without even discussing it with her. She vowed she wouldn't let him discourage her. Her mind was made up. It would do no good to argue with him, to try to make him see things her way. It was best to go ahead, and eventually he would become reconciled to it and settle down. Not that he would cease his complaining, she thought wearily. He would never do that.

"I wonder why Farr sent Colby and Rain to fetch our wagon," she said, hoping to change the subject to something they could talk about without arguing.

"I know what yo're adoin'. Yo're thinkin' ta get my mind off'n the inn. Ya ain't agoin' to talk 'bout it. Yo're jist agoin' ahead n' doin' what ya want. Ya don't care a whit what me 'n Amy want to do."

"I talked it over with Amy. She's old enough to know what she wants to do. Forget it for now, Papa. We'll talk about it later. I wonder why Farr sent Colby and Rain," she said again.

"I don't know the *whys* or *whens* a anythin' no more. They took clabber milk to that uppity nigger on the way. It beats me all hollow hearin' a nigger called mister." Elija sat down on a stool. "Fetch me some tea, Libby. I'll swear if'n my back ain't 'bout to kill me."

Liberty washed her hands, then filled a mug with tea, sweetened it with molasses and set it on the table.

"I hope they find the wagon. Farr thinks it will still be there. He said not many people use that trail."

"I ain't acountin' on ever havin' more'n what's on my back right now. Them heathens'll have found the wagon 'n ruint ever'thin' in it. They've done et Molly 'n Sally by now." He stared at her accusingly.

"Maybe not. Oh, I hope not!"

"I'll be dogfetched if I know what'll become a us. That old Juicy says there's bound to be a Indian uprisin' afore long. Did ya know Quill's gettin' set to build up a stock-ade?"

"No, but it sounds to me like it's something that should be done if they're expecting Indian trouble. It'll be comforting to know we have a place to come to. Papa, there's a good cabin and some cleared land about a half mile from here. Would you like to go see it?"

"Libby! I swan to goodness. If ya ain't the beatin'est woman I ever did see. Why're ya so dead set on stayin' here fer? Ya ain't took a shine to Colby or Quill, have ya? Ya can't be thinkin' a bein' so foolish as to set yore cap fer one of them fellers. They ain't got nothin' but this place out here'n the middle of nowhere."

"I've not set my cap for anyone," she said testily. "Who would want me, Papa? He'd have to take in you and Amy too. I've decided that I'm going to stay right here because this place is going to grow into a town someday and I'll have been one of the first."

"A town? When? Ya'll be dead 'n gone afore a town's here. How're we goin' to live? Ya ain't meanin' to run a travel inn 'n grow crops too, are ya?"

"Yes, I'm aiming to do just that. Didn't you see the patch the Sufferites put in? This is good fertile land, Papa. We'll grow what we can and trade what we don't need for goods or cash money."

"Trade! Fer cryin' out loud! There ain't nobody to trade with!"

"There must be. The people here are trading with some-one. Maybe they're trading at Vincennes or sending their crops downriver."

"Lordy, mercy me. Ya want me to break my back agrow-in' corn, wheat 'n punkins on the chance we can send 'em downriver?"

"And a garden," she said matter-of-factly. "I've got the seed. Drink your tea, Papa. I'm going out to see about the children."

"That's another thin'. What's Quill agoin' to do with them younguns, anyways? If'n ya ain't careful, he'll shove 'em off on you, Libby. We didn't find 'em. It ain't up to us to look out fer 'em. We can't hardly feed our ownselves. If'n ya'd had your own younguns ya'd not been so set on pullin' up 'n comin' out to the wilds fer 'em to be took by the savages. Not that I'm thinkin' Jubal was man enough—"

Liberty slipped through the door and walked hastily from the cabin before she said something she would be sorry for later. There were times when she could take her father's complaining, cantankerous ways and other times, like now, when she wished he were a million miles away.

She heard Mercy's squeals of happy laughter coming from the barn and wished fervently for the carefree days of her own childhood. Then she thought of Daniel and his unhappy, fearful association with his father. No doubt his young mother had many times shielded him from the harsh discipline of the old man, taking the brunt of his anger herself. When she tossed him from the wagon into the berry bushes, she had probably cautioned him to stay quiet. He was used to obeying, and that training was what had saved his life.

Mercy's laughter rang out again. What a difference a couple of years made in the life of a child, Liberty thought. Mercy had been taken from the security of her family the same as Daniel had been. Yet in just a few days she had adjusted to a new family and could run and play and laugh. Daniel was old enough to remember and to realize what had happened to his mother who had made up his whole world. All of Liberty's womanly impulses urged her to lift the burden from his little heart and to make him feel he belonged to someone.

She headed for the barn, but when she saw Farr coming from the pen where he had enclosed the cows, she veered sharply and went toward him.

"Farr," she called. "Papa said you sent Colby and Rain to get our wagon. I—"

"I didn't *send* them. They insisted on going."

"What if they can't find it?"

Farr grinned. "Don't worry. Between the two of them they

could find a flea on the back of a buffalo. They'll not have any trouble finding a wagon and a couple of oxen."

"I hope so. I hate to think of wearing this dress much longer without washing it."

"I've got an extra pair of buckskins."

His twinkling green eyes teased her all the way down to her toes. The awakening of some emotion she didn't quite understand coursed through her as she looked into the clear green pools. She wanted to laugh. Instead, she eyed him with an odd smile and, as if being alerted by his close scrutiny, her heartbeat quickened. She felt light-headed and foolish, and her eyes clung to his. She didn't know why, but she had never been less articulate in her life, or more comfortable and relaxed, even if Farr did excite her. In fact she had never felt so acutely aware of a man before. It was as if she had been carrying a hollow spot inside of her that was suddenly filled. It didn't make sense. She didn't understand it or want to analyze it. She just wanted to enjoy it.

"Mercy!"

Amy's yell broke the spell that throbbed between them, and reluctantly, Liberty turned to see the child run from the barn. Daniel darted out after her. He caught her just before she slipped beneath the rails and into the pen where the cows had stopped chewing their cuds to watch her.

"No, no, Mercy. You'd get yourself hurt in there." He took her hand and gently but firmly led her back to Amy. Mercy protested briefly, then obediently trotted alongside him as he led her back to the barn.

"He's such a good little boy," Liberty said absently.

"You like little ones, don't you?"

"Of course, I do. Why wouldn't I?"

"You didn't have any."

Liberty felt the heat of the blood that rushed to her cheeks. She swallowed hard and, before thinking too much about it said, "I was married only a year."

They were quiet for a long while. Liberty could feel the warmth of his body, far too close to hers, and the warmth of the telltale blood that covered her face and neck. To hide it, she bent her head and looked down at her hands clasped in front of her and occupied herself with trying to think of something to say. When the words finally came the relief was enormous that they came out evenly.

"The children need clothes."

"There are bolts of cloth in the warehouse."

"They need shoes too."

"Rain and Juicy will make them some moccasins."

She turned to look up at him and was almost frightened by the quiet strength in his face, but not too frightened to say, "I'll accept the shoes, but not the cloth. I'll use Jubal's things to make clothes for Daniel, and Amy's outgrown things for Mercy. We'll not be dependent upon you, Mr. Quill." His face changed, not to anger, but to sheer amusement. He burst into hearty laughter. "What did I say that was so funny?" she asked quietly. When he didn't answer, she said, "You laugh at the most inappropriate times!"

"I'm sorry, Liberty," he said, still laughing. "But you get your back up over the strangest things." He tilted his head to look into her eyes.

"I'm happy to know that I amuse you," she said stiffly. His green eyes and sensuous mouth were far too close. She backed away, hoping he didn't know just how much she was bothered by his closeness.

His hand closed over her wrist. "Don't run away. I need to talk to you."

The touch of his hand on her arm caused her nerves to dance along the entire length of her spine. She felt again the warmth, but this time she also felt a sense of connection. It pulsed powerfully between them through the warm pressure of his flesh on hers. Oh, dear God, she thought. She must not get to liking him too much. A woman would be like a millstone around his neck, he had told her. He had rivers to cross and mountains to climb. Yet he was so gentle, so sweet, so . . . strong. A small light exploded in her heart. She wanted to reach out, lay her head on his shoulder, and say that she was tired; for him to please take care of her, love her. . . .

"Walk with me to the spring."

They walked alongside the rail fence toward a small stone building, sharing companionable silence. The sun fell warm and golden on Liberty's face. Suddenly she decided that whatever came later for her, she was going to enjoy herself. She felt light and young and was unable to deny herself the excitement of being with him. The future would have to take care of itself; today was hers.

One of the geese waddled up beside them, scampered ahead, and strolled majestically down the path ahead of them. Liberty looked up at Farr and laughed.

"I like geese. They're as good as a watchdog. They set up a terrible racket if they hear something in the night they don't understand."

"They're better than a watchdog," he said and smiled down at her. "And you can eat them too."

The springhouse was backed up to a low stone rise. Farr opened the door and Liberty looked inside. Water cascaded out of the rocks, ran into a trough that passed under the door, and spilled down to form a small stream that flowed toward the river. It was cool and damp inside the building. A shelf was built along one wall. Several covered crocks sat on the shelf. This must have been where Juicy had come to get the milk.

Farr lifted the end of the log that had been halved and scooped out to form a trough and moved it so that water could run from the spring into a stone-lined pond that extended inside the cow pen.

"What a lovely spring. Does it run all year?" Liberty asked.

"It has for the last five. Sometimes during January and February we have to chip the ice from around it. It gets pretty cold here."

"Couldn't be worse than upper New York. We had so much snow that at times we didn't get out of the house for weeks."

They leaned on the rail fence and watched the pond slowly fill.

"There are a few things I want you to know before you decide to stay here, Liberty."

She glanced up at him. His face had turned serious and his voice had deepened.

"Farr, I know what you're going to say. You're going to tell me again about the danger of the Indian uprising. Papa has already told me that you're going to build a stockade around this place."

"It's got to be done, Libby. There's bound to be a major uprising, if not this year, surely by next summer. Meanwhile there will be some overanxious young warriors who'll not wait for a word from Tecumseh or Prophet. They'll raid up and down the river. You and Amy will be much safer in Vincennes." His eyes held hers as her mind absorbed the meaning of his words.

Her retort was quick. "I don't want to go to Vincennes. I want to stay here." Instinctively she reached out to place her hand on his arm. "We'll be safe inside your stockade." She said the words simply, trustingly.

"You'd be a mile from the stockade, Libby. There may come a time when you can't get here. You'll have to be alert every minute. The warriors will come by river or through the woods behind the house. They'll kill your stock, burn your crops and kill you if they can. I want you to know that."

"What about the other settlers? Will they leave? Will they give up all they've worked for and let the land go back to the Indians?"

"That's what I intend to find out. Before Colby and Rain left to fetch your wagon, they started the word for the settlers to gather here—"

"Started the word?"

She had forgotten that her hand still gripped his arm. And Farr, without being completely aware of it, moved his hand to cover hers. Her gaze lifted to his. There was a mesmerizing fascination in the soft, sweet smile that curved her lips and was reflected in her eyes. His own eyes mirrored his admiration.

"Colby started it to the south, Rain to the north. They left word at the first farm. It will be passed from farm to farm and by night everyone within five or six miles will know that there's something they should know, or I'd not have called the meeting."

"Will some of them pull out?"

"I don't know. Most of them have put a lot of sweat and blood into their farms and won't want to leave. I must make them understand that we have to protect ourselves. We'll not have any help from the militia."

"How do you know that? The territorial governor wouldn't abandon us—would he?"

"Governor Harrison says that he doesn't have enough troops to protect the whole frontier. It's up to us to protect ourselves, or leave."

"Do you know him?"

"I know him, and I know Tecumseh. Both are stubborn, proud men. But the outcome is inevitable. The Indians can't hope to stand against the hordes of whites coming in. I can't blame them for fighting for what has always been theirs, yet I can't excuse the killing of innocent women and children."

"You sound as if that makes you sad, Farr."

"It does, in a way. I have good friends among the Indians —Tecumseh, John Spotted Elk, whom I've known all my life, and a chief named Blue Jacket who is a white man adopted by the Shawnee when he was a lad. His white name is Marmaduke Van Swearingen." He watched the smile light her eyes.

"That's a mouthful. It's no wonder they call him Blue Jacket." The smile dimpled her cheeks and Farr almost forgot what he was talking about.

"Rain was raised by my friend John Spotted Elk."

"Is he Indian?"

"No. He and his mother were captured up north and taken south to be sold as slaves. John Spotted Elk bought them, fell in love with Rain's mother and married her. John's mother was white. About four years ago, while Rain's mother lay dying, she pleaded with John to let Rain be raised among his own people. John sent for me, and I promised her I would take care of the lad until he was old enough to fend for himself. At that time he could choose. Rain is about as much Indian as he is white. It will be hard for him to fight his Indian brothers and hard for him to go against me and Colby and Juicy."

Liberty looked down at the hand that lay atop hers. Her gaze lifted involuntarily to his and saw that under slanting dark brows, Farr's green eyes were clear and searching. She made no attempt to loosen her hand from his or look away from him. The discovery that she enjoyed this sensual contact with him caused a shudder to ripple under her skin as she tried to retain her composure.

How strange, Farr thought, that he'd known her for such a short time, and yet they could be together like this. Aside from being pleasant to look upon, she was a listening woman as well as an independent, spunky one. It was as if she understood him and shared the feeling he had for the land. A huge feeling of protectiveness came over him, and then a sudden deep hunger for the soft warmth and tenderness, the sweetness of her. Crowding in on this emotion was an agonizing wave of guilt that he could feel this way about a woman after knowing the sweetness of Fawnella.

"I'd better be getting back—" She left the last word hanging, not really wanting this time with him to end.

"Are you going to stay after what I've told you?"

"You haven't said anything to change my mind. There isn't a place in all this vast territory that's absolutely safe. Amy and I will take our chances here. I can't speak for Papa, but knowing him, he'll not go without me and Amy. Don't worry about us. We'll not be a bother to you."

"Good Lord!" He gripped her hand tightly. "I've not said that—"

"I know you haven't. But I don't want you to feel responsible if something happens. Don't worry about Mercy and Daniel. Amy and I will take care of them. Papa will complain and grouch; that's just the way he is." A broad smile spread across her lips. "Papa loves all his ailments."

Farr smiled into her eyes. "I wasn't counting on his help,

but I was hoping for the use of the oxen in dragging timber up from the river."

"If Colby and Rain bring them back, you most certainly can use them."

"They'll bring them back." Holding her eyes with his, words he didn't dare utter floated through his mind. He liked the companionship, the just being with her. He hadn't realized how lonely his life had become. *Fawnella, sweet gentle Fawnella.* Farr knew the comfortable feeling he had with Liberty had nothing to do with the way he had loved Fawnella, yet there was still an uneasy feeling—guilt?—in the back of his mind.

"The pond is running over." Her softly spoken words reached into his consciousness.

She watched the surprised look appear on his face when he glanced down at the widening puddle of water. She was sure she had never seen such beautiful eyes on a man. His thick, dark lashes made a perfect frame for the intense summer green of his eyes.

"So it has."

He had been so completely engrossed in his thoughts that he had totally forgotten the pond. He didn't seem to be in the same world he'd been in a day ago, he thought impatiently. He moved the trough and they walked back toward the cabin.

He would have been surprised to know that Liberty was floating alongside him on a cloud of happiness, feeling a buoyancy which walked hand in hand with the singing in her heart.

The sound of an axe against wood woke Liberty. She went to the door, opened it a crack and looked out. To the east there was a grayness, the first promise of dawn, and outlined against that was the tall silhouette of Farrway Quill working with axe and hatchet. Beside him was a growing pile of pointed stakes. Closing the door, she went to where she had hung her dress after she had washed it the night before. It was dry. She felt Amy's and the children's clothes. All were dry. Before putting the children to bed, she had stripped and washed them. Then, after Amy had bathed and gotten into one of the bunks, she'd washed herself and all their clothes. She had cringed at the thought of meeting the people who would be her neighbors in the dirty dress she had worn since leaving the wagon.

At the fireplace Liberty knelt and carefully raked aside the ashes to find the glowing coals, blew on them and fed small slivers of kindling until they burst into flame. She added larger pieces of wood, and when the fire burned brightly she turned the iron crane holding the teakettle over the blaze.

She washed her face and hands and dressed. Then she groped in her knapsack for her hairbrush. Bending over so that the silver masses hung from the top of her head, she brushed, then twisted them into a rope, coiled and wound it before pinning it securely to her crown. Oh, the sweet freedom of not having to wear a blasted day cap, she thought, as she worked by the light of the fire.

As soon as the men finished their breakfast and left the cabin, she set the children up to the table and filled their bowls with sweetened cornmeal mush. While they were eating, she went out to have a word with Farr. She found him at the woodpile, swinging the axe with firm, sure strokes. She waited for him to look up and acknowledge her.

"What are these for?" she asked, indicating the pile of stakes.

"To mark off the walls of the stockade." He swung the axe and the chips flew.

She waited for him to finish before she spoke again. When he had cut through the piece he was working on, he straightened and leaned the axe against the stump.

"Will the people be here at mealtime?"

He wiped the dampness from his face with the sleeve of his shirt before he answered. "Some will be here most of the day. A few of the men will ride in alone, but each family that comes will bring something, and usually the women try to outdo each other. Any kind of a get-together calls for a meal. However, it's customary for whoever calls the meeting to furnish the meat. I spoke to Mr. Washington last night and he'll be bringing up a side of venison and some catfish."

"Already cooked?"

Farr grinned. "Sure."

"What do you want me to cook?"

"Pie." His eyes played with hers, glowing devilishly. "I get hungry for pie."

"What kind?" She almost choked on the happy giggle that bubbled up inside her.

"Whatever you can find. If I had time I'd pick some blackberries. I know where there's a fine patch."

"There's no time for that. How about bread pudding with nuts and raisins?"

His wide smile was her answer. "There's a nutmeg in a can on the shelf."

"I'll find it."

Liberty didn't want these magical moments to end, but she knew they must. She found the feeling of being with him exhilarating beyond her wildest fantasies. There was a tightness in her chest, a fullness in her throat, and she couldn't utter another word.

She went back to the cabin, her eyes shimmering with happiness.

Chapter
Seven

At mid-morning a handsome two-seated buggy pulled by two prancing, black horses pulled up in front of the cabin. Liberty quickly washed her hands, smoothed her hair, and went to the doorway. Farr was helping a large woman in a stiff black dress from the buggy. Her body was as round as a barrel, and her head sat on her shoulders without her seeming to have a neck. She wore a ruffled black bonnet, the strings disappearing somewhere beneath her numerous chins.

"Thank you, Mr. Quill." Her overly cultured voice and manner revealed that she clearly considered herself in the upper classes. "Harriet, dear, wait for Mr. Quill to help you."

Farr reached to lift a smaller version of the mother from the buggy. The girl's face was round and very white. She had large, round eyes and a pouting red mouth. Her blue silk dress was cut low at the neckline and edged with white lace. The full skirt failed to conceal the rolls of fat around her middle. The matching bonnet had even more ruffles than her mother's.

The girl put her hands on Farr's shoulders as he swung her down. "Oh . . . my goodness, Farr, you do that so easily."

"Harriet could hardly wait to get here, Mr. Quill," Mrs. Thompson trilled. "It's been a while since you've come to call."

"I've been away." Farr turned and extended his hand to the man who came from the other side of the buggy. He was shorter than his wife and not as round. His flushed face was clean-shaven, except for the whiskers that edged his jawline. He looked harried and wiped the perspiration from his brow with a white handkerchief. "Howdy, George. Is everything all right out at your place?"

"Fair to middlin'. Got the crops in a week early this year. If we don't flood out, we should make out all right."

Liberty saw a girl slide off the platform on the back of the buggy and lean over to pull a large basket from under the seat. She was small, yet it was impossible to tell if she was a child. Her loose fitting dress ended above her ankles and showed the heavy wooden clogs on her feet. Farr seemed to see her for the first time and went to help her.

"Here, miss. Let me help you." He took the basket from her arms.

"Oh, Willa can do it, Mr. Quill. Land sakes! We don't coddle our servants like some folks do. We only brought her along because we knew you'd need some help, what with no woman here and all. We come early so we could take charge . . ." She looked up, saw Liberty standing just outside the doorway, and her words trailed away.

"Come meet Mrs. Perry." Farr set the basket on the bench beside the door.

"*Mrs.* Perry?" The stout woman's face shifted from a frown into a broad smile. "I'm Florence Thompson, dear, and this is my daughter, Harriet."

"Hello. Can I help you with—"

"Don't bother with us. We've been here so many times we know exactly where things are and what's to be done. Harriet will take charge. Tell Willa what to do, dear, while I sit here and visit with Mrs. Perry." She had a smile on her face when she looked at Liberty, but her small dark eyes narrowed as if warning her not to interfere with her plans for Harriet to take over.

"Tell me how you want things done, Farr, and I'll see to it." Harriet was almost purring. She took off her bonnet, showing masses of thick, light brown hair, and smiled up at him demurely.

Liberty had never flirted with a man in her entire life. To

do so had never even occurred to her. Now she pressed her lips together to keep from smiling. Farr caught the amused glance she threw at him and looked away quickly.

"I'll leave that up to Mrs. Perry. Come on, George. We'll unhitch and water the horses." Farr walked away with the shorter man hurrying to keep up with him.

As soon as they were out of sight, Mrs. Thompson heaved herself up off the bench and began to issue orders.

"Take the basket inside, Willa. Be careful and don't upset the cream. Hang up your bonnet, Harriet. Sit out here where it's cool so you won't get all sweaty. Mr. Quill will want to visit with you." She shot a meaningful look at Liberty. "Mind what I say, Willa—"

Harriet disregarded her mother's orders and followed her inside. A pout pulled the bow of her lips out of shape. Willa struggled with the heavy basket until she got it up onto the table. Before she could step aside, the older woman elbowed her out of the way and reached to lift the cover.

"Oh!" Mrs. Thompson shrieked, jerked on her skirt and jumped back. "What in the world!"

Liberty looked under the table and her laugh rang out. Mercy and Daniel were squatting there, and Mercy had grabbed onto the shiny black material of Mrs. Thompson's skirt. Daniel's hand still held the tiny one he'd jerked loose.

"I didn't know you were in here, you little troublemakers. Come on out and go find Amy. I'll bet she's down at the barn with the little colt." Daniel crawled out, holding onto Mercy's hand and dragging her along with him. He looked as if he expected to be punished. Liberty knelt and placed a kiss on Mercy's cheek and then on his. "Don't look so worried," she whispered in his ear. "It's all right." She watched them scramble out the door, wishing she had had time to make them decent clothes. She saw Mrs. Thompson eyeing them with disgust, and her hackles rose sharply.

"They gave me a terrible fright," Mrs. Thompson said, fanning her perspiring face with the stiff brim of her bonnet.

"They didn't mean to frighten you. Mercy just wanted to feel your dress."

Florence looked down at her skirt. "They should be taught some manners, Mrs. Perry. They could have torn or soiled it. Children can be so . . . destructive."

Her words were like a wind against the flame of Liberty's temper. It flared instantly. "Mercy didn't hurt your dress. And *my* children are not destructive."

"I didn't say *your* children, Mrs. Perry." She lifted the cloth from the basket, peered inside and flung the cloth back down. She turned quickly and gave Willa a stinging slap on the cheek. "Oh, you good-for-nothing slut. I told you to be careful of that cream. Just look what a mess you've made."

Liberty was dumbfounded. The fat woman's action had caught her completely by surprise. When she recovered, her heart ached with pity for the small girl who stood with her hands clutching the edge of the table. Willa's face was drained of color, her eyes vacant pools that suddenly filled with tears. Almost instantly the red print of Mrs. Thompson's hand appeared on her cheek.

"I was careful—"

"Don't you dare sass me, girl!"

Willa sucked her lower lip in between her teeth, held it there and looked down at the floor. The skin of her face was stretched tightly over an oval frame. Her mouth was generous, her nose straight and small, her large eyes spaced wide apart and slightly tilted. Her dark hair was slicked tightly back from her face and braided in a queue that hung to her hips. She was small-boned and thin. It was impossible even to guess her age, but she would be pretty, Liberty thought, if she wasn't so cowed by this overbearing woman. Her humiliation was the saddest thing Liberty had ever witnessed.

"Don't stand there like a clumsy fool. Clean up this mess before Mr. Quill comes in." Mrs. Thompson's voice was shrill, her fat cheeks red and shaking.

Liberty was suddenly so angry she was tempted to strike the overbearing, fat cow of a woman! Being unable to strike out at Liberty, Mrs. Thompson was taking her spite out on Willa. Liberty had to remind herself that this was Farr's home, these people his guests. She tried to think of something that would ease the girl's plight.

"It was the jostling in the buggy that spilled it, Mrs. Thompson," she said icily and her blue eyes dared the older woman to say another word. *"I'll* help Willa clean out the basket." She made no attempt to keep the anger out of her voice. She brought a wet cloth, lifted a jar from the basket and wiped it off.

"Willa will do it, Mrs. Perry." Florence's voice rang with authority. "She made the mess and she will clean it up. Come, Harriet. It's too hot in here for you. We'll sit outside. Mind that you don't spill the greens on the honeycake, Willa. My land, I told George not to take that girl in, but he bought her indenture papers anyway, just like she was as smart as anyone else. Humph! He could of got another field hand and a nigger for us for what he paid for her. Men! Sometimes I think all they've got between their ears is air."

Liberty ignored Mrs. Thompson's orders and lifted the dishes and crocks out of the basket. Willa moved mechanically from one chore to the other. Liberty tried to talk to her, but her one word answers discouraged that. Finally she decided the miserable girl wanted to be left alone to enjoy a few peaceful moments away from the two who sat on the bench outside the door. When they finished, Willa pulled a stool out from under the table and wearily sank down on it.

Next to arrive was Donald Luscomb and his family. Farr explained that they lived a mile beyond the Shellenberger place and would be Liberty's nearest neighbors. He was a tall, slow-spoken Tennesseean. He wore his beard tucked into his shirt front and his hair queued up in the back. He brought along his wife, Dorrie, and three of their four children, one a newborn babe. The other one had stayed at home with Luscomb's mother and young brother.

Farr introduced Elija and Liberty. The children gathered around Mercy and Daniel, who stared at them in awed silence. When Mercy broke loose to play with them, Daniel followed hesitantly. Dorrie Luscomb was a heavy woman.

Childbearing and hard work had made her look older than her thirty-three years. With her babe in her arms, she sank down wearily on a chair as if she rarely had time for the luxury of doing nothing.

Two whiskered men dressed in duck pants and homespun shirts rode in on horseback, and a third came downriver in a canoe. The men gathered near the woodpile, the women under the porch roof. Elija was enjoying himself, Liberty noted. He was the focus of attention as he told of the trip down the Ohio, and how Hull Dexter and the others had deserted them, and how fate had dealt with them for their cowardly action.

Edward Brown and his wife came in a cart pulled by a donkey. Mr. Brown was heavy and middle-aged, she a spare woman, almost frail. They had six children and had brought along the youngest, a boy near Daniel's age. Mrs. Luscomb and Mrs. Brown were glad to see each other, and after a few friendly words with Liberty they began to relate family news to each other while giving Liberty curious glances.

The Thompson women spoke to them when they arrived, but had little else to say. It was plain to Liberty they considered themselves a cut higher than the other women. They had scarcely been civil to her since the scene with Willa, and even less after they discovered she was a widow and Elija was her father and not her husband, as they had at first believed. It was plain to Liberty that Harriet, with her mother's blessing, had set her cap for Farr. Liberty looked from the tall man beside the woodpile to the plump girl perched on the chair beside her mother and found her watching him like a cat eyeing a pan of cream. Liberty couldn't blame her. Farr was a fine looking man. Liberty also knew Harriet had about as much chance of landing him as a cow had of growing wings.

Just before noon Juicy and Mr. Washington arrived. Juicy drove the wagon under the large cottonwood tree near the front of the cabin. Mr. Washington stood in the back, threw a rope over a limb and hoisted up a side of venison that had been roasted to perfection. He jumped off the wagon bed and secured the end of the rope to the tree trunk. The delicious aroma of the meat drew the attention of all. Juicy drove to the barn and returned a little later with barrels and plank boards to make a long table. It took only a few minutes to set it up, and shortly after that Mr. Washington was filling pans with meat and smoked catfish and setting them on the table.

Liberty heard a grunt of displeasure from Mrs. Thompson as a wagon approached. The woman on the wagon seat wore a blue flowered dress and a neat bonnet void of frills.

"Always late so the men will be bunched to watch her arrive," Mrs. Thompson whispered cattily to Harriet, but loud enough for the women to hear. "She's looking for a man."

Maude Perkins was a widow with three grown sons. One of the boys was with her. He was a tall, strong boy in his late teens with large square teeth and a head of hair that looked like straw. Mrs. Perkins greeted the Thompsons coolly but politely, then turned her back on them and exclaimed warmly over Dorrie Luscomb's newborn babe.

Liberty knew instantly that there was no friendship between the Thompsons and Mrs. Perkins, which made her like the woman all the more.

By the time the baskets were unloaded and Liberty's wheat bread and bread pies were added, the table looked as if it were set for a Thanksgiving feast. The men, already fortified by brandy from the keg Farr had set out, filed by the table, heaped their plates and retired to the woodpile to sit on stumps and eat. They were hungry for news as well as for food. The women filled plates for the children and settled them down beneath the oak tree before they took care of their own needs.

Willa had brought out the food from the Thompson basket, placed it on the table and returned to the cabin. The Thompson women made no attempt to help her or call her out to eat. Mrs. Thompson bellowed one time for Willa to bring Harriet a cup of water. The girl brought it and then scurried back inside. This angered Liberty. She filled a plate, left Amy to see to Mercy and Daniel, and carried it into the cabin.

Willa sat on one of the bunks in the far corner of the room. Her head was bent so low her chin rested on her chest and her hands were clasped together in her lap.

"I brought you some food, Willa. But wouldn't you rather come out and eat with the rest of us?" The girl shook her head but didn't speak. Liberty set the plate on the table, went to the bunk, and looked down on the girl's bent head. "Are you sick?" There was no answer. "Willa?" She placed her hand on Willa's thin shoulder in a gesture of friendliness. Instantly the girl shrugged away from her hand, and she heard the gasp of pain that burst from her lips. "Oh, my goodness! You *are* sick."

Liberty knelt down so she could look into the girl's face. Huge tears were rolling down her flushed cheeks. She touched the palm of her hand to Willa's forehead.

"Why . . . you're burning up with fever! Does Mrs. Thompson know you're sick?"

"No, ma'am," she replied in a very small voice. Liberty sat down on the bunk and put her arm across the girl's shoulder. "Oh! Don't, ma'am—"

"You're not only sick, you're hurt," Liberty blurted. She tried to control her anger at the two who sat on the bench outside stuffing their faces.

"No. No, ma'am. Please don't." Willa raised her head and turned her face toward Liberty.

Liberty's heart sank as she saw her pallor. Willa's eyes were so large they dominated all her other features.

"Let me help you." Liberty took her limp hand and held it in her lap while she stared at the girl's pale, drawn face.

Willa shook her head slowly. "No one can help."

"Let me see your back." Liberty spoke quietly but firmly.

"Please, they'll know." She shook her head and began to shiver.

Liberty pulled her to her feet and lifted the loose garment up and over her head. She wore only a thin ragged shift beneath her dress. Liberty swallowed hard and swore under her breath when she saw her back. Shoulder blades and bones were clearly visible beneath the thin layer of skin that covered them. Her entire back was covered with dark, ugly bruises, and crisscrossed with bloody welts.

"Who did this?" Liberty demanded.

"Please . . . I got to sit down." Willa grabbed her dress from Liberty's hand and sank down on the bunk. She tried to put it on, but the effort was too much for her. She gave up and buried her face in her hands. "Oh, ma'am, don't tell. They'll be so mad."

Liberty helped her slip back into the garment and pulled it down over her back. "Can't you eat something?" she asked gently.

Willa shook her head.

Liberty went to the water bucket and poured a dipper of water over a cloth, wrung it out and went back to the bunk.

"Lie down, Willa. You've got a fever."

"I can't—"

"Yes, you can." Liberty eased her down so that she lay on her side and placed the damp cloth on her forehead.

"They'll want me," Willa protested, but closed her eyes wearily.

"They can wait on—"

Her words were interrupted by a bellow from Mrs. Thompson.

"Willa! Come here, girl."

Liberty's hand kept Willa from rising. "Stay here. I'll go."

"No, I got to—"

"Willa!"

Liberty pressed her down on the bunk and went quickly to the door.

"Get me some of that honey cake," Mrs. Thompson demanded without looking around.

Liberty stepped around so Mrs. Thompson could see her.

"Willa is sick. You'll have to get it yourself." She spoke loudly and firmly. An instant quiet fell on the group as heads swiveled toward her. The men at the woodpile had also heard and were looking at her.

"Sick? She ain't no such thing. I guess I know when she's sick. Lazy is what she is—"

"She is *sick*. She should be in bed," Liberty insisted firmly and loud enough for all to hear. "That's not all she's suffering from, Mrs. Thompson," she added in a low, meaningful voice as her eyes did battle with those of the older woman.

"Oh! Well." Mrs. Thompson heaved herself up off the bench with a show of indifference and went to the table to load her plate with the sweets.

Liberty stood in the doorway until Mrs. Thompson was seated again. She looked across to the woodpile where Farr sat with the men. He had turned to watch and continued to watch even when the others resumed talking. Liberty returned his look coolly. She intended her cold stare to carry the message that she was angry, and to show her contempt for the Thompsons.

Liberty hurriedly ate the plate of food she had brought for Willa, all the while keeping wet cloths on Willa's hot forehead. At times Willa shivered uncontrollably, at other times she seemed to be sleeping. When it came time to clear the table, Maude Perkins came in.

"How is the poor girl feeling?"

"I think she's sleeping."

"No, ma'am. I'm not sleepin'. I got to help—" Willa tried to sit up, but Liberty pressed her down.

"You stay right here. Amy and I will do your work."

"I'll sit with her and see that she stays put," Maude said. "You go ahead and do what you have to do, Mrs. Perry. I think Farr is about to call the meeting, not that the men will let us women have much of a say. That's why I brought my oldest. They'd listen to him before they'd listen to me."

"I don't know why we can't have our say," Liberty sputtered, her old resentment against male domination rising. "We live here too, or we're going to live on the Shellenberger place."

"I'm so glad, dear. I've missed having a genteel young woman to visit with. I've got boys, you know, and they're not much for woman talk." She laughed and sat down on a stool beside the bunk. "What seems to be ailin' her?"

Willa's eyes flew open. Liberty read the silent plea.

"She's probably got a touch of fever," she said over her shoulder and went out the door. Mrs. Thompson and Harriet were still on the bench, and the others were busy packing their baskets.

"I'll pack up your things, Mrs. Thompson, that is if you and Harriet can't do it." Liberty made no attempt to keep the sarcasm out of her voice.

Mrs. Thompson jumped to her feet, her sagging jowls red and quivering with anger. "We'll take care of our own things without any help from you."

"I'm glad to hear it." Liberty turned her back on the Thompsons and caught the admiring glances of Dorrie and Mrs. Brown before they bowed their heads to hide their grins. "Amy, wrap the bread in a cloth and bring in the pie pan."

"I'm going to hold Mrs. Luscomb's baby."

"That's nice. It'll give Mrs. Luscomb time to take care of her things. I'll take care of ours. Where's Mercy?"

"Under the table. Daniel's watching her."

"Humph!" Mrs. Thompson snorted and held her skirt back from the table as she passed.

Liberty grinned at her openly in a way she knew made Mrs. Thompson want to slap her. She had made an enemy, but that was nothing new. Middlecrossing matrons had been outraged more than once by her blunt speech and independent ways. She vowed silently that before the day was over Mrs. Thompson and her fat daughter would wish they had not come to Quill's Station that day.

* * *

Liberty was carrying the last of the milk crocks into the house to wash when she saw the four black-clad men walking up the road toward the station. The male members of the Sufferites were coming to the meeting. One of the women had already told her that they kept apart from the others, never allowing the women and children to come to any social gatherings. Dressed all in black, their faces clean-shaven except for the beards that edged their jawbones, and flat-crowned hats sitting square on their heads, they reminded Liberty of four black crows walking side by side. They nodded solemnly to the men, ignored the women and children, then stood in a row, legs spread and hands clasped behind their backs.

Farr stood and held up his hand for silence. The children's sharp shrieks of pleasure were cut off when mothers grabbed them and cautioned them to be quiet. Mrs. Luscomb's baby began to cry. She took it from Amy's arms, turned her back and opened her dress for it to nurse. The silence that followed was a pressure that made everyone turn their heads toward Farr.

Liberty stood in the doorway of the cabin, not wanting to leave lest Mrs. Thompson swoop in and harass Willa, who appeared to be sleeping. She had a good view of the side of Farr's face as he stood waiting to speak.

"For the benefit of our neighbors to the south," he nodded toward the four black-clad men, "I'll go over again what we've been discussing." He raised his voice slightly to give emphasis to what he was saying. "There's an Indian war brewing. The tribes all along the river are beginning to resist the takeover of their land. This past month I've met with Governor Harrison in Vincennes, and I've also visited the Shawnee villages to the south. The tribes are uniting. There's no doubt about it. Tecumseh and his brothers are preparing their people for war. Prophet stirs up superstition while Tecumseh rouses patriotism. Tenskwatawa, the really hostile brother, has been visiting the warlike and well-armed tribes of the Potawatomi, Ottawa, Chippewa, Delaware, and Miami. He has hinted strongly that the Shawnee have been solicited by the British to join them in war against us." Farr paused for his solemn words to sink into the minds of the listeners.

"Governor Harrison doesn't have enough troops to protect the entire frontier, so it's going to be up to us to protect ourselves."

Harriet Thompson let out a small cry of alarm. Liberty didn't take her eyes off Farr, but she heard Mrs. Thompson trying to console her and the grunts of disgust that came from the other women.

"The governor has suggested that we build a stockade and a shot house here." Farr waited for someone to say something, and when no one did, he continued. "We'll also have to build a barracks to temporarily house at least fifty soldiers and four officers."

"A fort here warn't do us no good, Farr. Hit'd take two hours fer us ta get here," one of the men who had come downriver in a canoe said.

"Two hours? But you could bring your family in by way of the river."

"I ain't leavin' my cows fer them blasted savages," the man said fervently.

"That will be up to you," Farr said and turned to look at the next man who spoke.

"Why're ya building a barracks if'n the soldiers ain't acomin'?"

"I volunteered to build a temporary shelter for patrols. In turn Harrison agreed to give us powder, iron, and lead to make shot if we provide an adequate supply base here. He also said that if you folk would furnish food supplies, payment would be made in trade goods or scrip."

"Thunderation! The gove'ment so poor they can't pay the sojers. Scrip ain't no good." Donald Luscomb shuffled his feet and spit on the ground.

"We'll take their scrip." The voice came from the back of the group and all heads turned to look at the Sufferites.

"I never said I warn't goin' ta take it," Luscomb retorted.

"We'll all have to pitch in and do what we can. We need to have it finished by fall—" Farr was talking again, but was interrupted by the Perkins boy.

"Why here?"

"Yeah. Why not my place or Brown's?" another man asked.

"Because there's an equal number of families to the north and to the south. It's the easiest place to defend and near enough to the river that the troops could get in here if we were pinned down. Any more questions about the site?" There was silence. "The sawyer camp will be down there in the timber by the river. We'll rig up a shelter for those who want to stay. I'm staking out the line for the stockade tomorrow, and we'll start digging the trench."

"We'll furnish two men and two oxen a day until our crops are going, then three men and three oxen." The elder of the four Sufferites spoke again.

Farr nodded, then said, "How about you, Brown?"

"I can send up one a my boys, but we ain't got no animal to spare."

"Palmer?"

"We ain't got no animal to spare either, but my boy can come."

"Thompson?"

"I'll send my nigger and a mule. Neither one's got the sense of a goose, but you're welcome to them."

Liberty darted a look at Mr. Washington to see if he took offense. He didn't seem to notice. He stood as tall and straight as an oak tree, his eyes on Farr.

"That nigger we're sending ain't worth a hoot. He's so slow and lazy the fleas crawl off him." Mrs. Thompson's voice reached beyond the group of women to her husband, who gave her a quelling look.

Farr went around the circle, calling on each man for his opinion. Each man pledged to send one or two men or boys from their families and what mules and oxen they could spare to drag the heavy timbers up from the river.

"'Pears to me ya'll need more teams," Palmer said. "Didn't ya say ya had oxen, Carroll?"

Surprised to be called on, Elija didn't know what to say. His mouth pursed, then pulled to first one side and then the other. He looked at Liberty and then away.

"I ain't . . . we ain't jest set on if'n we're stayin' or agoin' on to Vincennes yet."

"We're staying, Papa," Liberty said more sharply than she intended. Then, to take some of the bossy sting out of her words, she added, "We decided that this morning. Remember?" She stepped away from the doorway and walked a few paces out into the yard. "You can have the use of the oxen, Farr. But first I'll need them to plow a patch—"

"I was talkin' to yore pa." Palmer's gruff voice interrupted her. His beard was so thick and matted she couldn't see his mouth, but she knew it was there because his beard was stained with tobacco juice. "Are ya puttin' out like the rest a us, Carroll?"

"Well . . . I don't rightly know. Ya see, we ain't rightly come ta decidin'—"

"We'll do our share of the work the same as the rest of you. And I think the sooner the work is started the better," Liberty said.

"I was talkin' to yore pa," Palmer said again. He turned, eyed her with disgust, and spit a thick yellow stream of tobacco juice on the ground.

"Since the oxen are mine, you'd better talk to me," Liberty retorted sharply.

"Was you mine," Palmer retorted just as heatedly, "I'd learn ya to keep a civil tongue in yore head 'n yore nose outta men's business."

"I'm not yours, so you don't have to bother your head about it," Liberty replied sharply. She was vaguely aware that she was making a spectacle of herself, but her anger overrode her judgment.

The man spoke to Elija while his small, angry eyes were

still on the slim blond woman who stood glaring at him so defiantly.

"A woman's place is with women, not stickin' her nose in men's business. Tell yore girl to go gab with 'em, Carroll. She's paradin' herself like a cat on a back fence—"

"Palmer! Hush that talk!" Farr said sharply. His eyes were as cold as a frozen pond when he looked at the man. "The oxen belong to Mrs. Perry, and she has the right to speak her piece—"

"Well, blame it! If'n petticoats is goin' ta run things, count me outta it."

"Just because a woman expresses her opinion doesn't mean she's running things. I'm planning on the women and children making shot and loading rifles if it comes to a showdown. A lot will depend on them." He turned away from Palmer, making it clear that the subject was closed. "I know you're anxious to get started home. I've said all I need to say. If anyone has anything he wants to bring up, now's the time to do it." Farr waited, and when no one spoke, he said, "There's still brandy in the keg. Help yourselves."

Liberty looked around to see the Sufferites walking back down the road. Either the argument had made them uncomfortable or they had found out what they came to find out and it was time to leave.

The rest of the men talked among themselves for a few minutes and then, after helping themselves to the brandy, went to saddle their horses or hitch up the wagons for the trip home. Liberty waited anxiously until Farr was alone, then she went to him.

"I must talk to you. And I want to show you something." Her voice was urgent.

Farr looked down at her set, determined face and saw the anger smoldering in her eyes.

"What is it? Is something wrong?"

"There most certainly is something wrong. The most disgraceful thing I've ever seen, and I intend to do something about it."

"What's got you so riled up?"

"Riled up?" she echoed. "I'm damn mad! Get Mr. Thompson and come inside. I'll show you."

"George Thompson? What's he got to—"

Liberty glanced back over her shoulder and saw that Mrs. Thompson and Harriet were no longer on the bench beside the door. Abruptly she spun on her heels and hurried toward the cabin.

Farr watched her until she disappeared inside. With a worried frown on his face he went to the barn to find George Thompson.

Chapter
Eight

"Get up off that bed! You're not sick!"

Mrs. Thompson's shrill voice reached Liberty and stirred the anger already boiling inside her. She hurried past Maude, Mrs. Brown and Dorrie Luscomb who were busily packing their baskets but paused to look questioningly at her. Liberty was angry, so angry that she was oblivious to them or anything except what was taking place inside the cabin.

Liberty went through the doorway and straight to the bunk where Willa sat. The girl was hunched miserably on the edge, her hands covering her face, her hair loose from its braid and clinging to her cheeks. Mrs. Thompson and Harriet stood over her.

"You're nothin' but a lazy, worthless strumpet. I warned you about bringin' attention to yourself. You're a servant, is what you are, and nothin' else! We took you in, fed you, put up with your laziness and now you've shamed us. You've played on that woman's sympathy, but you'll regret it when I get you home. Get off that bed before I take a switch to you!"

Liberty took a long, slow breath to steady herself and spoke in a low, controlled voice. But every word came out and found its mark like a carefully aimed arrow.

"Mrs. Thompson! You are mean, and you are stupid if you think I'll stand by and let you beat Willa one more time. You brought that sick girl here so you could flaunt your servant before the other women. Willa is not going back with you. She's staying right here until she's well."

Both women spun around to face her. Mrs. Thompson's

face turned a mottled red, Harriet's deadly white. For an endless moment they stood staring dumbly at the silver-haired, cold-eyed woman, their senses shocked by the anger and determination on her face. Mrs. Thompson opened her mouth and then closed it as if she were strangling.

"You . . . you—"

"Don't you dare call *me* a slut, Mrs. Thompson! I'm not afraid of you. I'll pull every hair out of your head, even if you are old enough to be my grandmother!"

"Why . . . why you," Florence sputtered. "You've no right to interfere. We bought her. She belongs to me. She'll do what I tell her to do or I'll—"

"You'll not beat her and you'll not heap insults on her, either. She's not a mule or a dog; she's a person with feelings. You've treated her like dirt because you didn't think she had anyone to take up for her. But she has me now, and I intend to see that everyone in the territory knows what you've done to her." Liberty's aroused voice overrode that of Mrs. Thompson who was spitting and sputtering with rage.

"Why, you . . . Harriet, get George."

Liberty glanced over her shoulder. The doorway was filled with women and children, all watching and listening with rapt attention, shocked at the scene, but some had grins of admiration on their faces.

"Don't bother, Harriet. I've already sent for Mr. Thompson. He's coming now with Mr. Quill." As she spoke Mr. Thompson squeezed through the doorway, followed by Farr.

"George! I'm glad you're here." Mrs. Thompson took a handkerchief from her sleeve and let it flutter before lifting it to blot the sweat from her face. "I've never been so insulted in all my life. This woman said that she's going to take Willa away from us."

"What? What's going on here?" George Thompson's worried eyes went from one woman to the other. "What've you been up to, Florence?"

"There you go! You always blame me when things go

wrong. Ask her what she's been up to." She pointed a quivering finger at Liberty. "Ask this . . . this chippie—"

"I warned you before about calling me names. And I'll do what I said if you don't stop it." Liberty's sharp voice brought Mr. Thompson's head around. She met his stare head-on with a determined stare of her own, glanced up at Farr, then back at George Thompson before she spoke. "I'll tell you what your wife and your daughter have been up to. They have cruelly mistreated an indentured servant, which is against the law." Liberty was surprised at her own tenacity. She didn't know of any such law, but she spoke as confidently as if she did.

"What are you talking about?" Mr. Thompson demanded angrily. A dark red stained his weathered face and his small dark eyes went from Liberty to his wife and then to the quivering girl on the bunk.

"In New York State an indentured female servant can be released from servitude if it's proven she has suffered bodily harm to the extent that her life is in danger. That is a well-known fact, Mr. Thompson."

"Bodily harm? Hellfire!" George snorted. "First, I'll remind you, young woman, this is Illinois and not New York State. Then I will also remind you to tend to your own business as Mr. Palmer suggested a while ago. We will take Willa home. If she's sick, she'll be taken care of."

"She's not just sick! And you're not taking her back to be whipped and beaten like an animal by your wife and your fat, lazy daughter!"

"What are you talking about, Liberty?" This came from Farr. He watched as if he couldn't believe what he was seeing and hearing.

"I mean what I say, Farr. I'll go to Vincennes to see the governor if I have to. These two women have beaten Willa until she's so cowed and so weak she can hardly stand. I think she may even have broken ribs. If you men stand by and let a woman be so abused, you're not worth much in my estimation." Liberty folded her arms across her breast and stood glaring up at him.

"She's lying!" Mrs. Thompson shouted, then turned her bulk so she could look at Farr. Harriet moved around behind her mother, held her palms to her pink cheeks and watched, her eyes round with fear. "Mr. Quill! Where did this terrible woman come from?"

"Beat Willa? Broken ribs? That's ridiculous." George Thompson looked outraged at the suggestion. "We've treated her well, Quill. No one's laid a hand on her."

"Does she have folk around here, George?"

"Not that I know of. We got her from some traveling people coming down from Vincennes. They were going on down to Cairo and needed traveling money. They said she was a docile girl and a good worker. She has two years to go before she's paid her debt. I don't know where this young woman got the idea we mistreated her."

"If Willa said we did, she lied," Florence stated confidently, a triumphant expression settling on her fat face.

"She didn't *tell* me. She was afraid to. I could see for myself. You were very careful to strike her where the bruises wouldn't show, weren't you, Mrs. Thompson?" Liberty took a blanket from the end of the bunk and knelt down beside Willa who sat with her hands covering her face. Her back was erect as if it were too painful to bend over. "Willa, we'll have to show them."

"No, ma'am. Please don't."

"I'll hold up the blanket while you pull up your dress," Liberty whispered. "I want Mr. Quill and Mr. Thompson to see what they've done to you."

"I can't. It'll just make it worse when I go back."

"We've got to show them, Willa. It can't be worse than it already is." Liberty turned a determined face to Farr. "You'll have to hold up the blanket so I can help her."

Behind the blanket Farr held in his outstretched arms, Liberty helped Willa out of her dress. When she pulled on the shift, the thin, worn material tore and fell down around her ankles. The bruises and lacerations on the girl's naked body were even worse than Liberty had at first believed. Across her breasts and buttocks were the crisscross cuts of a willow switch, and bruises, old and new, covered most of her torso.

Anger made Liberty's hands shake as she took the blanket from the bed and draped it about the thin, trembling girl.

"Come around here, Mr. Thompson, or do you want Farr to drop the blanket and let all those folk standing in the doorway be witness to what your wife and daughter have done? You look too, Farr. Look, and tell me that they've not mistreated her." Mr. Thompson walked around and stood beside the bunk. Willa's head rested on Liberty's shoulder and Liberty dropped the blanket down to expose her back.

"God in heaven!" Mr. Thompson exclaimed. "What happened to you, girl?"

Willa rolled her head back and forth.

Liberty's angry eyes met Farr's and saw anger and pity there. "This isn't all. She's got cuts from a switch on her stomach and breasts, her legs and her buttocks. Some of them are open cuts with pus in them. She can hardly catch her breath. One of her ribs may be cracked or broken. What did they hit her with, Mr. Thompson? A piece of firewood?"

George Thompson could feel the contempt from this lovely young woman wash over him in a chilling tide. No man, unless he were wholly lacking in pride or personal integrity, would fail to notice her determination, her strength of right and purpose.

"I didn't do that, George," Florence whined. "The girl fell down the cellar steps. You know how clumsy she is. And she was out picking berries. That's what made the marks, thorns on the berry bushes—"

"Shut up, Florence."

"I won't shut up. This is not *her* business. It's like Mr. Palmer said—"

"Shut up, Florence!" Mr. Thompson thundered.

Liberty eased Willa down on the bunk, took the blanket from Farr and covered her. She looked at him when she spoke.

"She's not going with them. I want her indenture papers."

"What?" Florence squeaked.

"I want her indenture papers," Liberty said again firmly.

"How much do you want for them, George?" Farr's eyes met Liberty's before he turned to the man. "I want to believe that you didn't know about this."

"I don't understand what the fuss is about," Florence fumed. "Everybody beats their niggers if they want to get any work out of them. She's white, but she's trash. A lazy slut is what she is." The fat woman's jaws were quivering and her face was a plum red. The words burst from the tight mouth, reverberating in the small room.

"Florence, I'm warning you not to say another word or you'll be sorry when I get you home." Her husband spoke quietly, but there was no doubt about the anger in his voice. "Quill, I certainly didn't know about this. The girl never said anything. Florence kept tellin' me she wasn't bright, and I figured that was the reason she didn't talk much. I bought her papers thinking she'd be company and help to the women. I don't beat my nigger, my animals or my women." He glared at his wife and added, "Even if they need it. I'll have the boy bring the girl's papers when he comes down to help with the fort."

"Papa!" Harriet moved from behind her mother. Only Liberty saw the hand that pulled her around to plead with her father. "Make her go home with us! Who'll slop the hogs? Who'll milk, Papa? And hoe? And wash? Mamma and I can't do everything."

"Yes, you can," he said, coldly eyeing his daughter. "You're getting as fat as your mother, Harriet. It'll do you good to work from sunup till dark like this girl's been doing."

"How much do you want for Willa's papers, Mr. Thompson?" Liberty asked.

"Libby, for Gawd's sake! Ya cain't be meanin' ta pay this girl's debt." Elija pushed through the crowd around the door and came into the room. "We ain't got money ta be throwin' good after bad."

"Don't interfere, Papa. It's my money. Jubal left it to me."

"All we got is the clothes on our backs. Lordy. We ain't even got our wagon back, or—"

"We'll discuss it later," Liberty said firmly.

"Dang fool girl ain't got a jugful a common sense. She'll be the ruination a me," Elija muttered.

"I'll buy her papers, George." Farr spoke quietly. His eyes flicked from Liberty's set face to George's harried one.

"I ain't sellin' 'em, Quill, but I'll give 'em to you and take the money out of the purse I set aside to buy a iron stove the women want." His look dared Florence to protest. "There'll be no dress goods or bonnets when I go to Vincennes," he told her. "You'll spin and weave the cloth or go without. You'll tend the garden, cut the kindling, and work in the field when the boy comes here to help Quill."

"Papa! You're bein' mean!" Harriet wailed.

"Don't give me any sass, girl. Get out to the buggy."

"But—"

"You too, Florence, and don't give me any buts," Mr. Thompson shouted. "Go, or so help me Gawd I'll give you the back of my hand!"

The two women gaped in surprise for a moment, then hurried to the door. On the way they gave Liberty a look loaded with pure hatred. Farr followed them out the door. When Liberty moved to follow, her father put his hand on her arm.

"Now, hold on fer jist a dang blasted minute. What fool thin' are ya gettin' us in? Ya ain't meanin' ta take in another mouth to feed, are ya?"

"Later, Papa. The ladies are leaving and I want to tell them good-bye. Amy," she said to her sister who was hovering near the door, "stay with Willa."

The Thompsons made a hurried departure, leaving without a nod or a wave of the hand. Liberty felt sorry for Mr. Thompson. He had been terribly embarrassed. But making a scene in front of the others was the only way she could get Willa out of the clutches of his wife and daughter, she reasoned. Nothing riled her more than seeing a woman or a girl treated as if they had no worth because they were female and had no man to stand up for them. She didn't dwell on the consequences of her action as she spoke to each of the women as they prepared to leave.

"We'll be right down the road, Dorrie. Mr. Quill said I can almost see your place from where we'll be. Come anytime."

"If there's anythin' I can do to help you get settled, just give a holler. Anything a'tall. It's goin' to be grand havin' close neighbors."

"I'll let you know. Bye, Mrs. Brown. You know where we'll be. Come anytime."

"I'll do that, Mrs. Perry. It's right nice knowin' ya." Her mouth twitched in a grin and her eyes twinkled as she jerked her head at the departing buggy.

Maude Perkins was the last to leave. She stood beside the door talking to Elija while she waited for her son to bring up the wagon.

"Your girl's right spunky, Mr. Carroll."

"She ain't had a woman to show her a woman's ways in a right smart spell. She's pert nigh got outta pocket." He allowed his shoulders to slump dejectedly.

"Don't be discouraged, Mr. Carroll. Young women who've not had a strong man to lean on, as I have, get some bossy notions. It takes time for them to learn their place. I had my husband to take care of me, and now that he's gone, I depend on my boys. If I can ever be of any help . . ." Her words trailed away and she smiled shyly at him.

"Ain't that good a ya. I knowed ya was a lady right off."

"Thank you, Mr. Carroll. Your daughter must have married young."

"The younguns ain't hers, ma'am. She's jest lookin' after 'em fer Quill."

"What happened to her man? Mrs. Brown said he died on the way out here."

"Lung fever. He left her well fixed with cash money, two good horses and oxen. I was well set back in Middlecrossin', but I had ta pull up 'n come with 'em ta look after her 'n Amy when they sold out ta come here. Her man warn't much a'tall. He warn't no hand at handlin' a headstrong woman or we'd a not sold out all we had. She's awantin' to settle here, 'n I jist may do it ta give her a taste a hard life."

Maude smiled into Elija's eyes. "I can see you're the kind of man who takes charge. I wish you folks had looked at land adjoining our place, Mr. Carroll."

"There ain't nothin' fer sure 'bout us takin' the Shellenberger place, Mrs. Perkins. Libby's got her sights set on it, but I ain't decided yet. She ort a go on to our kin in Vincennes is what she ort a do."

"Then you'd be leaving." Maude gave a deep sigh. "Just when we were getting to know each . . . getting acquainted."

"It ain't sure, now. More'n likely I'll decide to stay right here. Amy, that's my other girl, is a fine youngun. Ain't no sassiness in Amy."

"I can see that she's a well-mannered child. I hope you stay, Mr. Carroll. We need some quality folk along the river. I'd like you to come out to the farm and meet the other boys. They've carried on since John died. I'm not one for bragging, but we have as fine a farm as you'll find along the Wabash."

"Why, thanky for the invite. I'd be right proud to come."

Elija saw the admiring look in her eyes before she dropped them and timidly murmured, "You're welcome anytime."

He straightened his shoulders and smoothed his mustache with his thumb and forefinger to hide his pleased smile. She was a comely woman, he thought, and not so all-fired set and bossy. She would look up to a man instead of belittling him all the time. The invitation was plain. She liked him and wanted to know him better. And she had a fine farm and sons to work it.

In the late afternoon, Juicy came in with a pail of fresh milk. "Is there somethin' I kin do fer the lass?"

"I don't think so. She's sleeping. The poor thing's worn

out. I washed her cuts with vinegar and she hardly let out a peep."

"It's a shame, is what it is. I ain't never seen her but onct. Me'n Farr was at the Thompsons' afore Farr taked off on his jaunt. The little one was flighty as a bird 'n stayed clear outta sight. I reckon that Thompson gal was feared she'd latch onto Farr. If'n ya want to strain this here milk, I'll take it to the spring."

"All right. I'll hold the cloth over the crock."

They worked together without speaking for several minutes. Juicy lifted the heavy bucket and poured the fresh warm milk into the cloth Liberty held over the empty crock.

"Ya stirred things up right good, missy." He set the pail on the workbench and reached for a hunk of bread. "But ya make a fine mess a bread." His grizzled face broke into a grin.

"I'm sorry if the scene I made embarrassed anyone. I was so mad I didn't even think about what Farr would say. I just knew I couldn't let Willa go back with the Thompsons after I saw what they'd done to her."

"Don't bother yore head none 'bout Farr. Warn't no way fer him ta know the little missy was in bad shape. If'n he'd a knowed it, he'd a taken Thompson ta task. He's soft 'bout younguns, women 'n critters. He took a whip ta a feller onct fer hittin' a mule in the head with a fence post 'n knockin' him senseless. Farr can cut a real sockdolager when he's riled up. Farr does what he's got ta do."

"He offered to buy Willa's papers, but Mr. Thompson said he'd give them to him. She'll be a big help with the cooking and washing." Liberty spread a clean cloth over the top of the milk crock.

"Why, missy, I ain't areckonin' that's what he buyed her fer."

Liberty's head came up and she looked at him in shocked surprise. "Oh!"

Juicy's eyes teased her and his laughter was little more like a hen's cackle. "Farr ain't wantin' to bed the gal, if'n that's what ya mean by 'Oh!'"

Liberty felt the crimson blush that covered her face. "I didn't mean that!" she snapped.

"What're ya gettin' yore hackles up fer?" Juicy regarded her carefully and his eyes contained a suppressed amusement.

"I'm not!"

"'Pears like ya are."

"Well, for goodness sake!"

"Farr ain't agoin' to take no poor little ole whip-thin gal fer his woman. Now, if'n ya ask me, I'd tell that ya'd be more to his likin'. I'm athinkin'—"

"I'm not asking you, Mr. Juicy. The kind of woman Mr. Quill wants is no concern of mine." Liberty's voice was calm and disguised her embarrassment beautifully. It was a small triumph, and she clung to it long enough to get out the door. She paused just outside, and with an impatient nervous gesture drew her shawl tighter around her shoulders when she heard Juicy's teasing laughter.

Evening shadows were growing deeper. A fresh wind was coming up and overhead, dark blue rain clouds were rolling toward them from the southwest. Amy and the children were trying to entice Farr's pet crow to come down from his perch in the oak tree by holding up bits of meat scraps. Knowing they were occupied for the time being and feeling the need for a few minutes alone, Liberty walked down the path toward the river passing from shadow to lightness to shadow again.

She stood on the bank of the Wabash and watched the water flow past her on its journey to the Ohio. From there it would go into the great Mississippi and on to the sea. Rivers had always fascinated her. That fascination had led her mother to teach her to swim at an early age. She thought of that now, and felt a sudden longing for the gentle stream of her childhood, yet this place was wild, and more beautiful than any she'd ever seen.

In the evening light the vista as far as she could see was an Arcadia of peace and beauty. The pale green of the budding cottonwoods, the brighter green of willows, and the dark green of cedars were a background for the glowing redbud and the snow white blooms of the wild pear and plum trees. The smell of the dank water mingled with mint weed along the bank. Liberty drew in a long, satisfied breath, consciously permitting herself to enjoy the view.

It was a lonesome river, she thought. It was lonesome, as she was lonesome for someone of her very own. The thought shocked her, and brought Farr forward in her mind. Since she had met him, no matter what her concentration on more pressing matters was, he remained in her recollection as a somewhat disturbing presence. Now, to her surprise, she could see him clearly as he had looked at Willa. His face had softened, his eyes had examined every line of Willa's face, but when he had offered to buy her papers his expression was hard, uncompromising. A swarm of challenging thoughts floated through her mind. What would he have done if Mr. Thompson had insisted on taking Willa? Was he attracted to the clinging, submissive type of woman? And how did he feel about herself? Had she embarrassed him in front of his friends today at the meeting? If so, why had he defended her right to speak?

Liberty took a deep breath to steady the tremor that ran through her and walked slowly along a path that followed the river. It climbed steadily until it reached a small clearing almost ten feet above the water. She stopped to look once again at the rolling, restless river. The evening was serene and beautiful. In the near twilight the woods were alive with pleasant cheeps and chirps. A whippoorwill swooped overhead, trailing his melodious repeated cry, and distant colonies of ducks quacked companionably. She was not afraid to be alone there. Farr had told her to listen to the familiar sounds of the forest creatures. If something unknown to them moved among them their cadence would be interrupted.

With a deep sigh Liberty turned to retrace her steps. It was then she saw the headboard marking a grave. Behind it were wild rose bushes, their long stems laden with blooms. Along each side were forest ferns and in front of these, yellow buttercups. In a large half circle surrounding the glade were white blooming dogwood trees and red blooming judas. The small garden had been carefully planned and laid out. It was well-tended and lovely beyond words.

Feeling as if she were an intruder, Liberty moved closer to the marker at the head of the grave and knelt down. She had never seen a lovelier headboard to mark a final resting place. It was made from a slab of oak about six inches thick, and perched on the rounded top was the carved image of a dove. The headboard had weathered, but amid the carved vines and flowers, the letters, outlined with dabs of stain, were as easy to read as the day they were put there.

FAWNELLA QUILL
beloved of
Farrway Quill
1787–Oct. 22, 1803
My love for you through life will last.

Liberty felt a tightness in her throat. Farr's wife had been only sixteen years old when she died. He would have been only a little older than the boy, Rain. He must have loved her very much to tend this place all these years. Liberty's eyes blurred with tears. *My love for you through life will last.* A shudder of longing worked its way down her body. Fawnella Quill had had a wealth of love in her short lifetime, more than Liberty hoped to have if she lived a million years.

She was stroking the head of the dove with her fingertips when she saw Farr. She looked up and he was there.

"Colby and Rain are coming with your wagon."

Liberty stood quickly, her heart beating a mad tattoo against her ribs. In her haste to get to her feet she lost her balance and a foot went dangerously close to stepping on the grave. She stepped back hastily.

"I'm sorry," she said in a breathless whisper. She expected him to say something, but instead he simply stood as still as stone and looked at her steadily. "It's a beautiful place," she murmured.

When he still didn't speak, she turned her face away from him and looked around. There was something like panic running just below the controlled surface she presented. She closed her eyes tightly for an instant. Even with her eyes closed she could still picture his face. It was not the smooth beauty of youth as Fawnella had known it; the age lines around his mouth and eyes showed evidence of his grief. She turned to look at him again and through her tears could barely discern his profile.

"I'm glad they found the wagon," she said when she found her voice. "I'd better go."

"It'll be a while before they get here. They're crossing over on the ferry now."

"How do you know that?"

"We've worked out a system with Mr. Washington. Three blasts on the horn says he's going over to bring someone across. A short, a long and another short says things are all right."

When Liberty moved away from the grave she passed close to where Farr was standing. She could feel every nerve in her body respond to his lean hardness. She wanted to press close to his broad chest, and have his powerful arms hold her. She wanted to comfort him, tell him that if Fawnella loved him as he had loved her she would want him to be happy. But she only glanced at his face as she passed.

"I'd better go," she said again and walked quickly down the path.

Farr watched her leave. This was the first time he'd seen her when she was unsure of herself. In every other encounter he'd had with her she had faced things squarely, standing up to them, sober, truthful, and earnest. Now she seemed apprehensive. What astonished him was that her disquiet about being found here troubled him.

Farr didn't understand himself at all. And then the truth hit him like a blow between the shoulders. Here he was in the place he had made for Fawnella and he was lusting for another woman.

What he'd had with Fawnella had been rare and beautiful. A man couldn't ask for a greater love than the one she had given to him, he told himself sternly. Yet as much as he had loved her, he still wanted Liberty. It wasn't a question of love, it was purely physical attraction, he reasoned. He wanted to bed with her! He wanted to bury himself in her softness, watch her face when she went wild beneath him, wanted her to cry out his name while in the throes of passion as the whore had done in New Orleans. But no, not like that! He wanted her to mean it!

Chapter
Nine

Farr squatted down and pulled the grass from around the marker that had taken him an entire winter to make. He gazed at the likeness of the dove, saw the crudeness of the sculpture, and wished that he'd had the skill then that he had now. But in that first winter of his grief he had not tried his hand at carving; he had simply known what he wanted and had set about carving it. Later, he was to think the labor had saved his sanity.

Memories flooded his mind, taking him back to his youth, to the summer of 1803. . . .

Eighteen-year-old Farrway Quill, in black oiled buckskins and moccasins, inched his way along the shelf above the Wabash River and peered over the edge. Coming from the salt spring he and Juicy had discovered, he had been drawn by the sound of jubilant laughter to this place. Two boats were beached below on the sandy bar that jutted out into the swiftly moving water. One, a light Indian canoe, had the body of a dead Indian in it. Another Indian floated facedown in the shallows, his legs caught in a sawyer at the end of the bar.

The other boat, flat-bottomed and laden with bales of fur, was drawn up onto the shore. Farr knew at a glance that the boatmen had overtaken the canoe, killed the Indians and taken their captive.

The guttural laughter came from two bearded, fur-clad trappers. They were stalking a nearly naked, fair-skinned girl. She made no sound but shook her head, waved her arms and frantically darted back and forth. Although small, not much larger than a child, she was not a child. Her light brown hair hung in a tangle over her shoulders and small, rounded, naked breasts. A dirty rag that had once been a woman's dress hung in tatters from her waist to her knees. The trappers frolicked like two cub bears in the spring. They danced in a semi-circle on widespread, bent legs, their arms outstretched, keeping the terrified girl pinned between them and the river.

"Whoopsy! Whappsy!" The gleeful shouts echoed through the thick forest that lined the river.

"White! White! Ain't no nigger, ain't no squaw. White, white woman." The grizzly bear of a man sang the words and waved his arms up and down in a frenzied, berserk manner.

"Hi-bye, diddly di-do." The voice of the other man was a shrill imitation of a woman's. "Thar's bells a tollin', 'n chains a clinkin', mad howlin' 'n screamin'. I is dippin' my pecker, says I, say I. I is dippin' my pecker, says I—"

It was the strangest sight Farr had ever seen. His mind ground to a halt for a mere instant. The men were mad! They had been too long in the wilds and were more beasts than men. *What* to do was the question. It never entered his mind that he would not try to help the girl. Farr checked the load in his rifle, touched the shaft of the knife in his belt. Wait, he told himself. Wait, plan, and act—in that order, Juicy had told him time and again.

What occurred next was so obscene, the thought to wait and plan left his mind, and a red rage filled it, rage at the indignity the young girl was suffering.

The trappers, worked into a lustful frenzy, dropped their britches down around their knees and were flaunting their swollen shafts. They continued their grotesque dance, their male organs bobbing up and down, stopping every other step to jerk their pelvises so that the young girl had no doubt of their intentions. They laughed uproariously at the horrified look on her face. Her mouth opened and closed, opened and closed, but not a sound came from her throat. In desperation she dashed toward the river. A rough hand caught the loose hair flying out behind her and jerked her back. She fell hard, and one of the men fell on top of her.

Farr stood, aimed at the center of the back of the man standing over the couple on the ground, and fired. The blast resounded down the river and a flock of birds rose and fanned out against the sky. Before the man on top of the girl could shove his dead companion off him, Farr had leaped to the beach, raced across the bar, and plunged his knife in his back time and again. Never before had he killed a man who was not trying to kill him. Now, in the space of ten seconds he had killed two, and he thought no more about it than if he had killed a rattlesnake and a copperhead.

In a frenzy to see if the girl had been injured, he pulled the dead men off her. She lay there unmoving, pressed into the sand by the heavy bodies. Blood from the man he had shot covered her upper torso, and a splotch of wet, red blood smeared her chin. She was as still as death, her eyes wide and staring at the sky above her.

"You'll be all right now, ma'am. You'll be all right. I killed them." The girl continued to stare straight up, and Farr shook her gently. "Ma'am, are you hurt?"

There was no answer. His young mind groped for a reason and found one. She was in a stupor. The poor little thing had been scared almost to death. Farr picked her up in his arms and carried her to the water's edge. He stripped her of the tattered dress and used it to wash the blood from her face and body. He had never seen a fully naked woman before, but that fact never occurred to him. This pitiful little creature needed his help. When he was finished, he wrapped her in a blanket he found in the Indian canoe. That done, he reloaded his rifle, something he had never failed to do immediately after firing, pulled his knife from the back of the mad trapper, and shoved the bodies out into the river until the current caught them and they were swept downstream.

By the time he was ready to leave for the camp he and Juicy had set up, the girl was thrashing her arms and trying to rid herself of the blanket. Not a sound came from her throat when Farr went to kneel down beside her, but her eyes, focused now, were wild with fright.

"They're gone. I'll not hurt you. You'll be all right now, little girl." Farr spoke softly and brushed the tangles of hair back from her face. "You don't have to be afraid. I'll take care of you—"

Something in his sincere young face must have reached into the depths of her understanding. She quieted, her face crumbled and she began to cry. Her mouth worked, but no sound came from it. The tears that filled her eyes ran down her cheeks. Her eyes clung to his face in mute appeal.

"Ah . . . don't cry, little girl." Farr lifted her onto his lap and cradled her to him, rocking her as if she were a baby. She curled her arm up about his neck, turned her face to his shoulder and silent sobs shook her thin body. "Don't cry, little pet," he crooned. "You've had a hard time, but it's over now."

Gradually she quieted, and when Farr tilted her head back to rest in the crook of his arm, he saw that she was asleep. Brown, gold-tipped lashes, the same color as her hair, fanned down onto her cheeks. She had a sprinkling of freckles on her nose, but otherwise the skin on her face was clear and smooth as velvet. Her mouth was wide, her lower lip somewhat fuller than the upper one. She was young, he thought, so very young to have had to endure what she had just been through.

A yearning to protect this small, helpless creature came over him with such a rush that his arms held her to him with fierce determination. As he held her, he studied her still features and gently brushed the hair back over her ear. In all his young life he'd never held a girl in his arms, never felt a soft arm about his neck, never had anyone turn so trustingly to him and depend so completely on him. In the space of that instant, young Farr lost his heart to the helpless young girl.

He carried her back to the camp he and Juicy were using while they built their cabin. And in the weeks and months that followed he devoted himself to her. She couldn't speak, but she could purse her lips and whistle. When he asked her if she had ever spoken she shook her head. Farr asked her name and told her his. She shook her head again, sadly. He never knew where she had come from or how she happened to be on the river with the Indians.

Farr named her Fawn because she reminded him of one, and then added Ella, his mother's name, to it. She accepted the name with a broad smile. At first she was afraid of Juicy and clung to Farr when he was near. Then gradually she began to trust the old mountain man. As the days went by, she became stronger, took over the cooking chores, laughed at Juicy's antics, and hugged him when he presented her with a pair of moccasins. She had been wearing Farr's shirts and the britches he had cut off for her, but his moccasins were so large she couldn't keep them on her feet.

Fawnella and Farr spent every waking hour together. He talked and she listened. He told her about Carrolltown, his schooling in Virginia, about Cherish and Sloan Carroll. When he told her of the death of his parents, she buried her face against his shoulder and clung to him, showing her regret. Their love and devotion for each other grew until it was all-consuming, and the only world they wanted was in that clearing beside the Wabash.

By summer's end the cabin was up and they moved in. Juicy began to prepare for his annual fall trip downriver to Cairo. He would trade the prime furs from the trappers' boat and bags of salt from their salt spring for supplies to last the winter.

Juicy asked Farr to go, take Fawnella, and try to find out something about her people. Farr spoke of this to Fawnella. She shook her head vigorously, took his hand and pulled him toward the cabin.

"It's all right, honey. We won't go if you don't want to. We'll stay here. Juicy just thought you might want to find your folks."

She shook her head again, put her fingers on his chest, and then on her own. He knew she was telling him that *he* was her folks. He was all she wanted, and his love for her swelled in his young heart.

They waved good-bye to Juicy one morning in late September and watched the boat take him down the Wabash. The journey would take him almost a month. They walked back to the cabin. It seemed strange to be alone, and at first they were shy with one another. Juicy had always been with them or was close by.

The first two nights Farr tossed and turned in his bunk. Sleep seemed to evade him. He couldn't get his mind off the girl who slept in the bunk across the room. His healthy young body responded to his thoughts, and he would turn over on his belly and grind his teeth in frustration.

On the third night he was wakened out of a deep sleep. Fawnella lifted his blanket, crept into bed beside him and curled up in his arms. The sweet softness of her body pressed against his, and the trusting way she nuzzled her head to his shoulder and curled an arm about his neck brought a groan from his throat. He wrapped her in his arms, pulling her so close he couldn't tell if the loud thumping between them was his heart or hers.

An instinct born from a woman's desire to comfort man caused the child-woman in his arms to move sweetly against him. She held him in her arms, caressed him with her hands and lips, showed him in every way she wanted to mate with him as a woman mated with the man she loved.

"You want to, little sweetling?" he asked hoarsely. "Are you wanting me to take you for my . . . wife? Are you sure?" Her answer was to place little kisses on his face. "Oh, little darlin', I've not done it. I don't know—I might hurt you." More kisses stopped his words. "Ah . . . sweetheart. You're my woman . . . you are, you are! Sweet, sweet girl . . . I want to touch you everywhere, I want you to touch me."

She responded to him eagerly. Lightly his mouth touched hers, moving tenderly over her parted, breathless lips. Her warm taste filled him. Like two children in paradise, they fondled each other's bodies, discovered hidden pleasures, became bolder as their passion grew. Instinct guided them.

Farr waited until he was sure she was ready to receive him, but he held back for so long that it was Fawnella who pulled him on top of her and they were finally united. Their release was immediate, instantaneous and glorious. It left them pantingly breathless and holding on to each other.

Farr knew the sweet bliss of holding her all through the night, of feeling her damp cheek on his chest, knowing she was where she wanted to be. He scattered soft kisses over the top of her head and his hand gently ran up and down her spine as if to reassure himself that she was really in his arms.

It was the beginning of the most wonderful time in his life. He called her wife, told her that her name was now Fawnella Quill, that she belonged to him and only to him, forever and ever. She blossomed under his loving devotion. Their days were filled with work and play. At almost any time she would come to where he was working, put her arms around him and pull him down on to the soft grass, her face filled with silent laughter at the pleasure she found in his. In the evenings, when the work was done, they ran to the river together, played, bathed each other, and during the long nights they lay entwined in the bunk built into the side of the cabin wall.

Farr talked to her as he had never talked to anyone. He told her his innermost thoughts and dreams. They communicated with touch and eyes. He knew what she was thinking by the expression on her face; there was little need for words between them. He gave her all the love his boyish heart possessed, and she gave him a bottomless, unending love, its gentle flow like a sunbeam bathing him. There was no way he could count its worth. His world had suddenly become bright, new and beautiful.

From the notches they made each day on the stick, they knew that soon Juicy would be back, and so the morning they heard the shout from the river, they ran hand in hand across the clearing and through the trees to the bank. The canoe that was beached there was not Juicy's, but that of a Frenchman who had came down from the north. He was a big man with a thick black beard and bright dancing eyes. He wore a knitted red-tasseled cap tilted at a jaunty angle on his head.

"Ho, mon ami, it is good to see someone without a feather in his hair. I smelled the smoke from your fire."

"You're welcome to a meal. I'm Farrway Quill, and this is my wife, Fawnella."

The Frenchman jerked the cap from his head and bowed low. "It is indeed a pleasure, Mademoiselle."

Farr held tightly to Fawnella's hand and smiled down at her proudly. She pressed close to him, nodded to the Frenchman, but didn't smile.

"Not mademoiselle, Monsieur. She is Madame Quill," Farr corrected, knowing it meant little to Fawnella, but wanting to make sure the Frenchman knew she was his wife.

"Oui, you are indeed a lucky man, my friend."

"Come on up to the cabin," Farr invited, "and tell us the news from Vincennes."

The Frenchman spent most of the day. He talked to Farr, but his eyes followed Fawnella. Farr decided he didn't like the man and let the conversation lag, hoping he would leave.

"Your woman . . . she don't talk much, no?"

"Not much."

"Mademoiselle—ah, madame, forgive my poor eyes, but your beauty makes such a feast for them."

Fawnella glanced quickly at Farr, and then moved around to sit behind him.

When it came time for the Frenchman to leave, Farr was not sorry. He walked with him to the river's edge. When the canoe turned the bend in the river and was out of sight, he hurried back to the cabin and the girl who waited for him.

The next morning, while Fawnella peeled and sliced the pumpkins to dry, Farr took his rifle and walked out into the woods behind the cabin. For two days he'd seen a large stag come almost to within rifle shot distance of the cabin. Their meat supply was getting low, and it was a good opportunity to replenish it without having to go far. Time went by faster than he expected, and soon he was an hour's walk from the cabin before he realized it and turned back without sighting the stag.

He shouted when he came out of the woods, and looked expectantly at the door of the cabin for Fawnella to appear and race down the path to meet him. After the second, and then the third shout, a dark, deep, frightening fear that something was terribly wrong possessed him. He began to run.

Farr found her lying in the dirt beside the cabin. Her britches were off and her lower limbs were covered with blood. Her head was thrown back and she was gasping for air. When she saw him, her arms reached for him and her eyes pleaded for him to hold her.

"Darling . . . Oh, my darling girl." He fell on his knees beside her, gathered her in his arms and kissed her face. "Oh, sweet girl. Who did this? Who did this?" he demanded. She opened her fingers and the tassel from the Frenchman's cap fell from her hand. "Oh, God! I'm sorry . . . I'll kill him, I'll kill him," he whispered fiercely.

He carried her into the cabin and placed her on their bed. One of her eyes was almost swollen shut, her jaw was bruised and her lower lip cut and bleeding. Farr washed her the best he could and placed a blanket between her legs to try and stop the flow of blood that continued to come. He pushed all thoughts of the Frenchman from his mind as he worked. Finally, when he had done all he could, he sat beside the bunk and held her hand.

"Darling girl, forgive me for leaving you here alone." The agonized words tore from his throat and tears rolled unashamed from his eyes.

Her eyes remained on his face, her fingers tightened on his, and her swollen lips formed words. "No, no," she was trying to say.

"I love you more than I ever thought I could love anything. You're everything that's beautiful; you're my love, my life." He knelt down, gathered her in his arms, and kissed every part of her face that he could without giving her pain, kissed her desperately, lovingly. The pain in his heart cried out don't die! Please don't die!

Farr held her all through the afternoon while the blood slowly drained from her. He talked to her, told her how much she meant to him, how happy she had made him the last few weeks. He begged her not to fall asleep. But gradually her eyes drifted shut, and her fingers could no longer grip his. He had to face what he had known all along: he was losing her.

"Don't leave me, Fawnella," he pleaded. "Don't leave me, my love! Wake up and look at me."

At the end, a small bubble of breath came from her parted lips. It was the last breath to leave her frail body. Still he held her, his eyes on her face. She seemed even smaller now that life had left her. The crushing grief that pressed down on Farr in the hours that followed seemed to drain all reason from his mind. He wondered if he were going mad. He couldn't imagine how he was going to live without her. He placed his head on the pillow beside hers, and agonizing sobs shook him.

Slowly the tears were drained from him. He sat beside the bed and watched the bright October sunlight come in through the open door, making a path across the floor to where Fawnella lay as if she were sleeping. Evening came and light faded. He sat unmoving. All through the long, lonely night he sat beside her, not leaving his chair for as much as a drink of water. Morning came and he set about doing what his logical mind told him had to be done.

Farr washed Fawnella and dressed her in his best shirt and britches. He combed her hair and tied it the way she liked to wear it. When he was finished, he went to the shed for the spade and took it to their favorite place, a small grassy clearing on a high bank beside the river. They had gone there often, frolicked in the grass, played, made love.

Farr buried his Fawnella deep in the earth. He carried stones from the river to partially fill the grave and then finished filling it with soft earth. He carefully replaced the sod and the wild flowers on the top, and when it was done, he collapsed on the grave, weeping uncontrollably.

It took Farr three days walking cross-country to reach the Ohio. At Shawneetown he learned the Frenchman was headed for Cairo. He followed the river south and one day out of Cairo overtook him where he had camped for the night. Farr walked into the camp. When the startled Frenchman stood, Farr tilted his rifle and fired point blank without even raising the weapon to his shoulder.

The force of the double load flung the Frenchman ten feet back. He was dead before he hit the ground, but Farr followed. He drew his knife and slit the man's buckskins. With a single stroke of the sharp blade he cut the sex organ from the dead body and tossed it into the fire. Then he spit in the face of the man he had killed and headed back to the cabin on the Wabash, the place where he had known his greatest happiness and deepest sorrow. . . .

The memories were less painful now as they floated through Farr's mind. It all seemed so long ago. He didn't come here as often as he used to do. He carried the memory of Fawnella in his heart. She would always be there, though he be a million miles from this place. Today when he had looked at the young girl, Willa, and had seen the marks of cruelty on her back, memories of what Fawnella had endured had come rushing back to haunt him. He had wanted to sink his fist in George Thompson's fat face. Even though he was not the one who had mistreated the girl, he had permitted it to happen.

Farr left the clearing and followed the path Liberty had taken minutes before. He came out of the woods and saw the train of three wagons approaching. The lead wagon was a heavy freight wagon pulled by four oxen, Liberty's wagon was next, and behind that was another large freight wagon followed by a span of mules.

Colby and Rain spurred their mounts and came on ahead.

"Yeehaw, ole hoss!" Colby shouted. "We found it, just where you said it was." He pulled his mount to a stop beside Farr. "We hit luck this time, Farr. We ran into Mrs. Perry's kin from New York State and brought him on."

Chapter
Ten

"It's Molly and Sally!" Amy called out happily. "Oh, Libby, I was so afraid we'd never see them again. Pa said they'd be ate up by now."

Liberty sat on the doorstone with Mercy on her lap. Her wagon was second in line and a big man sat on the wagon seat. An uneasy feeling began to work its way into her stomach. Slowly she stood and set the child on her feet. Daniel, sensitive to her moods, knew she was disturbed and took Mercy's hand.

"Oh, Pa! They're coming, they're coming!"

Amy's excitement brought Elija up from where he was sitting on a stump beneath the oak tree. "By jinks damn!"

"Molly and Sally didn't get eat up by the savages, Papa."

"I'll be dogfetched if they ain't bringin' it. Ne'er thought to see it again a'tall."

Colby and Rain had come on ahead and were talking with Farr. Farr waved to the lead wagon to turn up the lane to the station.

The wagons came on. Liberty's eyes were on the man driving hers. As they neared, realization of who he was hit Liberty like a dash of icy water. Then a blazing hot, consuming anger washed over her, blotting her vision for an instant, making her heart pound so hard she could scarcely breathe. The lead wagon reached the cabin and passed her. By the time her wagon stopped, she was trembling so violently her legs threatened to collapse beneath her.

Instinctively, she grabbed Mercy to keep her from getting

too close to the oxen, and then relinquished her hold as she realized Daniel was pulling her back.

Amy was suddenly quiet.

"Get off my wagon!" Liberty's strident shout overrode the creaking of the wagons, the commands of the drivers, and the snorts from the tired mules.

"Hello, Libby."

"Get off my wagon . . . damn you!"

The man who sat quietly looking down at her was big, even taller than Farr. He wore a felt hat with a wide ribbon wound around it for a band. Into this was thrust a long-stemmed pipe. His light hair was braided into a queue, the end tied with a colored ribbon. He was a man in his middle thirties with a broad, handsome, completely shaven face and large, wide-set eyes so light a gray they were almost colorless. Taking his time, he slowly wound the reins around the brake handle.

"That's no way to greet a friend, Libby."

"Friend? You belly-crawling snake! You're no friend of mine! You're nothing but a damned, dirty bastard! You're a cheating, lying, smooth-talking son of a bitch!"

"Libby!" Elija shouted. "Watch yore mouth!"

Liberty jerked the whip from the holder on the side of the wagon. "Get off my wagon!" she shrieked. "Or I'll strip the hide off your rotten carcass!"

"Libby, fer Gawd's sake! Yo're shamin' us all 'n making' a show of yoreself is what yo're doin'." Elija grabbed the whip from her hand and threw his arm across her chest to hold her back. "Ya got here soon'er I figured ya would, Stith. Step on down. Pay no mind to Libby. She's jist a mite upset 'n don't mean nothin'—"

"Papa! Shut up! For once in your life let me do my own talking!" She turned on the man climbing down over the wheel of the wagon. "I mean exactly what I'm saying, Stith Lenning. I don't want anything to do with you. Stay away from me and Amy. Hear?" She turned to Elija. "How could you do this, Papa? You know how I feel about him, yet you told him we were coming here and made plans to meet him.

You did this in spite of all Jubal did for you." Liberty never felt more like crying in her life, but anger kept the tears of betrayal at bay.

"Don't get yoreself in a snit. It's best Stith has come now that Jubal's gone 'n ya don't have no man ta look after ya."

"Jubal didn't last long, did he? Carroll said you buried him back on the trace." A half-smile changed the shape of Stith's thin mouth. "I told you what you needed was a real man, but you wouldn't listen."

Liberty saw the satisfied smirk settle on Stith's face. Her hand lashed out and she struck him with a resounding blow on his cheek.

"You're not fit to mention his name!"

As fast as a striking snake, Stith's big hand clamped down on her wrist. He held it up between them and nudged her chin with her own fist while stepping back to avoid her feet that were aiming for his shins.

"I've warned you about striking me, Libby."

"Get your hands off the lady." Farr spoke quietly from behind Liberty.

Stith looked up from Liberty's furious blue eyes into green ones as cold as a well. The two men stared at each other over Libby's blond head.

"Who are you?" Stith asked.

"The man who's going to tear you up if you don't move your hand . . . now."

Stith dropped Liberty's wrist, but he didn't back up. His big head jutted forward, and he eyed Farr like gentry eyeing a peasant.

"The *lady* is a hot-tempered little shrew who needs a wallop daily. She was promised to me and I intend to wed her before the week is out."

"That's for the lady to decide."

"That's for me and her pa to decide. He promised her to me before she up and wed Jubal Perry. She's soiled now, but that don't matter. She's mine." Stith ignored Liberty's gasp of anger as she moved back beside Farr, and his voice rose to a near shout as he continued, "I keep what's mine if I have to travel a thousand miles to fetch it. My advice to you, mister, is keep your nose out of my business, or you might find it smashed all over your face."

Farr knew he was going to hit him, not only for what he had said about Libby, but because he didn't like his looks or his attitude. He just wanted to hit him, and he did. He put all his strength behind the blow that caught Stith square on the chin. It propelled him backward a half a dozen steps before he hit the ground like a fallen timber.

There was a murmured grumble from one of Stith's men, a saddle creaked, and then an instant quiet. It was as if no one present even breathed.

Stith lay where he had fallen, then slowly raised a hand and wiped the blood from his mouth. There was stunned disbelief on his face.

Farr followed to stand over him.

"My advice to you, *mister*, is stay away from Mrs. Perry unless she invites your attention. Now get up from there, get your wagons, and get off my land."

"Oh, Lordy! Oh, dang bustit!" Elija hopped around Farr to help Stith to his feet, but Stith angrily shrugged off his hands. "Ya ain't ort a done that, Quill. Stith here's a friend a mine."

"You have some mighty ill-mannered friends."

"He didn't mean nothin'. Ain't that right, Stith?"

"Papa! Stay out of this." Liberty placed her hand on Elija's arm, but he shrugged it off. "Haven't you done enough?" she asked angrily. "I'll never forgive you for telling him we were coming here!"

Stith got up off the ground and stood swaying like a wind-rocked tree. Elija picked up his hat, stuck the pipe down in the band and handed it to him.

"What's your name, mister?" Stith spoke out of the side of his mouth.

"Farrway Quill."

"This isn't the end of this."

"I didn't think it was."

"I'm going to be the most man in these parts. The time will come when you'll come to me if you want something."

"I doubt that. You won't live that long." Farr looked steadily at him. "Popinjays like you come through here all the time. They don't last long."

Stith slammed his hat down on his head, his colorless eyes turned to Liberty and then swept the area and focused on Amy. "I'm not giving up on you, Libby. Get yourself ready to leave. We're going to Vincennes to be wed, all legal and proper."

"You . . . popinjay," it was the only word that came to her mind, "I wouldn't marry you if my life depended on it!"

"No? How about someone else's life? Huh? You thought to escape me by marrying that milksop Jubal Perry. He was nothing. He up and died on you before you got here."

"Jubal was ten times the man you are. You don't scare me with your threats." But she was afraid. She knew he was capable of doing anything to get what he wanted. Her anger goaded her to say, "You're nothing but a big mouth! You run roughshod over everyone. The people in Middlecrossing hated you, but you always arranged it so they had to trade with you and you got the best of every—"

"Hush up! You'll not run off at the mouth when you're wed to me." Stith cut her off. His body was stiff with resentment when he turned to speak to Farr. "I'm here to get my woman. I'm a man who stands by his word. Ask Elija. He's known me twenty years."

"I know all I want to know about you," Farr said. "I saw it all in one look."

"Come on, Stith. Let's go off somere's 'n cool off." Elija fidgeted from one foot to the other and refused to look at his daughter's resentful face.

"All right. Turn them wagons round, men. We'll camp down there in that clearing by the river."

"No, you won't. That's my land. Go on down the road, or back the way you came from." Farr stood with his feet spread, his arms folded across his chest.

Stith turned to face him, anger a flat shine in his eyes. "You'd better stop pushing me, mister."

"Come on, Stith," Elija said hurriedly. "Come on. I'll show ya a place to camp."

Stith climbed up onto the wagon and Elija took a seat beside him. Liberty watched them leave and tried hard not to let the last bit of love she had for her father leave with them.

Farr stood motionless; Colby and Rain still sat their horses. Juicy lounged in the doorway of the cabin. Even the children were quiet. Liberty noticed Colby's hand was on his rifle, and the boy, Rain, sat with his rifle across the neck of his horse. Juicy's old musket was tucked in his belt. It was then she realized how dangerous they considered the situation to be. They were ready to back Farr.

"Why did he have to come, Libby? I hate him!" Amy cried. "Papa don't have no sense at all or he'd see he's just a rotten old scalawag!"

"Papa only sees what he wants to see," Liberty said tiredly. She was so ashamed she couldn't look at Farr when she murmured, "Thank you, Farr. I'm sorry we've brought this trouble down on you."

"Don't give it a worry."

Liberty rejected that with a slow shake of her head. "He won't forget it. He's a mean enemy. He has no rules of fair play." There was a tremor in her voice as she issued the warning.

"Neither do I. If a snake needs killing, I kill it. I've locked horns with some of the meanest."

There was no brag in his voice. Liberty's eyes searched his face. She found herself suddenly in awe of this big, quiet, self-assured man. The look of complete sincerity in his green eyes rendered Liberty less and less sure of herself. When Amy's excited voice drew his attention, she was relieved.

"Oh, I'm so glad to see Molly and Sally." Amy rubbed the spaces between the eyes of the patient oxen. "Thank you for bringing them, Mr. Carroll. You, too, Rain."

"Yes. I thank you, too." Liberty walked around to the end of the wagon and looked in. "Everything seems to be here."

Rain slid from his horse. "I'll unhitch, ma'am. We pushed hard and the beasts are plumb wore out. Where do you want the wagon?"

"Pull it up alongside the cabin, Rain," Farr said.

"I'll help you, Rain." Amy took hold of the yoke and tugged. "Come on, girls. Just a little more and you can go rest."

"I don't need help," Rain said and swatted Molly on the rump.

"I can help."

"I don't need no help," he repeated stubbornly.

"Yes, you do too," Amy retorted sassily. "They know me. They don't know you."

"They don't have to *know* me—"

"Why are you so mean? They're our oxen and I'll help if I want to."

Amy was so childishly direct, Liberty thought. She would be thirteen in a few days. At that age many girls were preparing for marriage and were mothers by age fourteen. Her sister was physically mature; rounded, lovely, graceful, but she showed no other signs of growing up.

She heard Farr chuckle and turned to look at him. In the last light of evening she could see that he was watching Rain and Amy.

"What's funny?" she asked.

He looked at her then. "I was just thinking that in another year that young lady will be a handful. You Carroll girls have more spunk than you know what to do with."

"Oh, fiddle! I know how to handle oxen." Amy's sputtering voice came out of the darkness. "Didn't I come all the way from New York State with them? Didn't I? Rain? Listen to me, Rain—"

Colby walked over to Liberty and nervously cleared his throat. "I'm plumb sorry about bringing that fellow here, Mrs Perry. We found your wagon and went on down the trace to the massacre site like Farr told us." Colby turned to

Farr as if suddenly remembering something he hadn't told him. "There wasn't anything there, Farr. Somebody come through and carried off every board, almost. All that was left was the burned-out wagon and a few rags."

"I thought that might be the case," Farr said. "It was worth a try for Daniel's sake. I wish now I'd brought something along that was his. At the time I was thinking only of getting the women away from there."

"It's what I'd a done." Colby looked anxiously at Liberty. "When we run on to Lenning, he asked if you had come through. He said he was your kin, and you were to meet up at Vincennes."

"He's a distant cousin of my mother's, I'm sorry to say. It doesn't matter, Colby. He'd have found us sooner or later."

"Your pa seems to set store by him. Why is that?"

Liberty looked up at Colby and then away to where Daniel and Mercy sat on the doorstone. Mercy was asleep, her head in the patient little boy's lap.

"He has a way of getting around Papa," she said finally. "Papa thinks he's grand because he's rich. He can't see what he's *really* like. Sometimes . . . I'm not proud of Papa."

Liberty went to the end of her wagon, now pulled up close to the side of the cabin. More than anything in the world she wanted to climb in the wagon, lower the end flap, and let all the misery flow out of her. She reminded herself that she had known that this day might come. The shock of seeing Stith again in this place was even more horrendous than she had imagined.

Nothing would be gained by sulking in the dark. The thought came to her out of the chaos in her mind. She had long been trained to face whatever had to be faced and do the best she could. She took a long, deep breath and tossed her braid back over her shoulder. Daniel's little head was bobbing, and she couldn't afford the luxury of feeling sorry for herself right now. She turned on her heels and went to the children. Farr was by her side when she reached them.

"Let me help you." When he picked Mercy up in his arms, Daniel roused. "It's time for bed, Daniel."

Liberty lit a candle from the glowing coals in the fireplace and saw Willa sitting on the edge of the bunk, a blanket around her shoulders.

"How do you feel?" Liberty went to her and laid the palm of her hand on her forehead.

"Better. Much better. Is it true? I don't have to go back to the Thompsons?"

"It's really true. Mr. Thompson promised to send your papers to Mr. Quill. He'll be kind to you, Willa. No one will strike you again."

"Thank you, ma'am." She grabbed Liberty's hand and held it to her cheek. When she looked at Farr, tears streaked her face. "I'll be a help. I'll work hard, sir."

Farr placed Mercy on the bunk and Daniel crawled up beside her. He covered them with a blanket before he spoke.

"What I had in mind was for you to help Mrs. Perry, Willa. She'll need help if she keeps Daniel and Mercy. Are you still of a mind to go on to the Shellenberger place, Liberty?"

Liberty looked at Willa's expectant face and then up at Farr. Tiredly she brushed the hair back from her face with the back of her hand. She had been able to keep from crying only by keeping her anger alive. Now that her anger was dead, depression held her in its tight grip.

"I've got to think about it. Things have changed now. Willa, you'd better eat something. You've not eaten all day," she said absently and walked out the door.

Liberty climbed into the back of her wagon and sat in the dark. She reached out to touch the trunk and ran her fingers over the two drawer chest. It had been a futile journey, one that had cost Jubal his life. Would she ever get over her guilt for asking him to come into this wilderness for which he was so unsuited?

She heard Amy and Rain come from the barn. Amy was talking and the boy was scarcely answering her.

"Why in the world don't you talk to me?" Amy demanded. "My goodness! I might as well talk to a stump!"

Liberty heard Farr's voice and then Juicy's and Colby's as

they walked away from the cabin. When all was quiet, she sat alone with her thoughts. Amy wouldn't have to suffer, she prayed, because of her rejection of Stith. What had he meant when he said, "someone else's life?" Had he meant her father? Or Amy? Would he try to kill Farr? Stith was foolish, but not that foolish, she decided. That he was capable of murder, she had no doubt. It had been rumored for years that he'd smothered his old uncle with a pillow so he could have the store in Middlecrossing.

Liberty allowed the tears to roll down her cheeks unchecked. What to do now? Her father was going to insist that she marry Stith. Back home he could force her and the law would back him. It was his right to give a daughter in marriage. Did the law still apply here in the wilderness?

Each person created the life he lived, Jubal had told her. Some did it through their failures, some through their dreams. Some did it by a single mistake or a single success. She wondered which applied to her. She had made a lot of mistakes, had a lot of dreams, and the only success she could take credit for was getting Willa away from the Thompsons . . . and, of course, she had met Farrway Quill who had brought them safely to this place.

A tear trickled down her wet cheek—a tear for a foolish dream. Because of Fawnella Quill, who lay in the lonely grave down by the river, there was no room in Farr's heart for her.

After a while Liberty lay down on the pallet and pillowed her head on her arm. Her eyes remained wide open. With so much on her mind, she was sure she would never sleep, but she fell into a deep, dreamless slumber that lasted until morning.

Willa knew morning was near when she heard the birds chirping in the branches that hung over the cabin. She had been awake for hours thinking about her good fortune, about the wonderful way things had worked out. She vowed that she would show her appreciation by working hard. She went over in her mind what she was going to do when there was enough light to see by. She would build up the fire, then wash and rebraid her hair so she would look presentable. She'd be sure the water bucket was full, and then she'd take the pails and go to the lot and milk the cows. She wondered if she could get all this done and have meat frying in the skillet by the time Mrs. Perry came in. Oh, she would work hard! That blessed woman with the light hair and eyes the color of a cloudless sky had stood by her against Mrs. Thompson and her fat daughter when she had been so sure she would stay with them until she died. She could not remember anyone doing that since her mother died, but that had been so long ago that now she had trouble recalling her face.

She heard the low murmur of men's voices coming from the next room and jumped out of bed. She groped for her dress, found it on the end of the bunk and slipped it over her head just as the door opened and Farr came in. He knelt at the fireplace, raked ashes from the banked coals, sprinkled them with wood chips and worked on them with the bellows until they burst into flame.

When the fire was going strong, he turned. In the flickering light he saw Willa standing beside the bunk as if she were poised for flight.

"Morning." He lit the small wick floating in its dish of oil and set it on the table before he spoke again. "Do you feel well enough to be up?"

"Yes, sir. I'm much better. Do you want that I go milk now?"

"Juicy has already gone, but I'm sure it would please him if you took over the chore while you're here. He hates cows," he said, a smile in his voice. He poured some water from the bucket into the washbasin, and then the rest of it in the black iron coffeepot and swung it over the flame. "If you're sure you're up to it, you can lay out the meat and bread left from yesterday's meal and make coffee. It's in the tin on the shelf above the bunk," he said and went out.

Willa hurriedly washed and combed back her hair with her fingers. While she tied it with a strip of cloth she took from her pocket, her mind went over and over what Farr had said. While she was there. What did he mean? Was Mrs. Perry leaving right away?

The coffeepot was boiling and she was warming the meat in a skillet when Farr returned with the water bucket. He was followed by a tall, dark, still-faced boy, and a blond-haired man who stood with his hands on his hips smiling at her.

"Another pretty lady. I'll declare, Farr, this place is getting plumb civilized. Howdy, ma'am. I'm Colby Carroll, this here skinny kid with me is Rain Tallman."

"Howdy." Willa felt the heat rise and flood her face. She hid her hot cheeks by bending to take the meat from the skillet with a long fork. She was grateful when Juicy came in with the milk and began to tell about the snake he had found in the barn.

"If there's anythin' I hate worser'n cows, it's snakes," he declared venomously.

The men were sitting down to breakfast hen Liberty hurried through the door. She had pinned her shining braids in a coil on the top of her head and was wearing a dark linsey dress and had a white apron tied about her waist.

"I overslept," she exclaimed and took the heavy coffeepot from Willa's hand. "You're not well enough to be out of bed," she scolded.

"I'm better. I can help—"

"Sit down here by Juicy and eat your breakfast. You can help later."

"But, Mrs. Perry, I—"

"Liberty, or Libby," Liberty corrected. "Sit down, Willa. I'll get you some milk."

"I can't . . . sit," Willa protested weakly.

"Why not?"

"Cause it ain't right."

"You might as well sit down and eat, Willa. You won't win an argument with Liberty," Farr said matter-of-factly.

"Is the butter all gone?" he asked and helped himself to the bread.

Liberty looked across the table and met Farr's eyes. She saw a teasing sparkle there that released from deep within her a short-lived burst of pleasure.

"It seems there's more butter left than bread," she said lightly, and set the crock on the table. "I don't know where it all went. I thought there was plenty."

"It was Rain, ma'am. He sneaked in here in the night and stuffed his gullet." Colby looked so serious that at first Liberty couldn't tell if he were teasing. "I didn't get hardly a taste. It's why I'm so weak and hungry this morning." He reached over and quickly lifted a thick slice of bread from Rain's plate.

"You're lucky I don't have my knife on me, or you'd be drawin' back a stub," Rain said quietly.

"You two quit your jawin' and get out of here before you wake up the younguns and Liberty takes a stick to you. Eat up, I need two strong backs today." Farr unfolded his long legs and got up from the table.

Colby groaned. "You know my back ain't strong, Farr."

"Mine ain't either." Juicy held his cup out for more coffee. "I be too ole ta be heftin' 'n tuggin' 'n pullin'. I'll look out fer the ladies today. They might be needin' a bucket a water or somethin'."

"Too old? Hellfire!" Farr snorted. "You're as strong as a mule and twice as ornery."

"It may be yo're right 'bout the strong part. I could whop yore hind if'n I took the notion. But somebody's got ta keep a eye on the womenfolk 'n see that Colby 'n Rain don't slip back in here 'n pester 'em."

Colby let out a snort of disgust. "Why can't I do that, Farr?"

"Cause they'd be safer with me, ya young scutter!"

Rain continued to eat with the appetite of youth. Liberty passed him the last slice of bread and smiled into his dark eyes as he reached for it. It was hard for her to smile. So much had changed with the coming of Stith Lenning.

"Farr? May I talk to you before you get started for the day?" She looked straight into his eyes, her determination clearly visible. The words were out. She had dreaded saying them, but once a decision was made, there was no holding back.

Farr looked steadily back at her, then nodded. "Come on out when you're ready." He went out the door and Liberty went over to press Willa back down on the stool with a gentle hand on her shoulder.

"Don't get up, Willa. Sit and rest a spell. We'll tidy up when I come back in." She lifted her shawl off the end of the bunk and followed Farr out the door.

Willa sat with her head bent. She never felt more uncomfortable in her life. She couldn't remember ever sitting at a table and having someone wait on her. She, Willa Carrathers, was sitting at the table with three men! She couldn't eat . . . she didn't know what to do with her hands. She jumped when a log in the fireplace burned through and popped. When she looked up, Colby Carroll, the man with the blond hair and violet blue eyes, was looking directly at her.

"I just never had nobody treat me so . . . good," she said, and to her horror she burst into tears. She got up quickly and went to the end of the room. Overcome with embarrassment, she wished herself anywhere but where she was. She stood with her back to the table while she wiped her eyes with her palms. She heard the scrape of the chair legs on the rough plank floor and knew the men had risen from the table. With relief she heard the closing of the door when they left the cabin.

Thinking she was alone, she turned. Colby Carroll was still at the table. Willa glanced at him and then away. She felt trapped. He was looking at her and she was conscious of nothing except the serious look on his face, the concern in his eyes. An uneasy silence seemed to go on and on. Willa's glance darted to the coffeepot.

"Can I get you some coffee, Mr. Carroll?"

"No, I don't need anything."

"I'm sorry for bawlin'. I don't usually—"

"You don't have to apologize, Willa. You've every right to cry if you want to."

"But . . . I don't want to. I just couldn't help it." Willa squeezed her eyes tightly shut as tears welled again. Her throat clogged and she had to struggle to keep the sobs from breaking loose.

"Ah . . . don't cry," he said anxiously and came to where she stood. "Farr told me what happened. You'll be all right with Mrs. Perry. We'll not let the Thompsons take you back." His voice came softly through the roar in her ears.

"I know it . . . now. It's why I keep cryin', I guess."

"Where did you come from, Willa?"

"Pittsburgh."

"I mean before that."

"Me and my mum come from London, but I was little bitty."

Her eyes were still closed. Colby lifted her chin, then wiped the tears from her cheeks with his fingertips.

"How did you end up with the Thompsons?" he asked softly.

She opened her eyes and looked up at him through lashes spiked with tears. He was so close, his voice was a mere whisper.

"When Mum died, her bond was passed on to me. The folks were real good to me. They died and my bond was passed on to their kin. They took me to Detroit, then Louisville, and then brought me out to Vincennes, but they wanted to go on to Saint Louis. They sold my papers to the Thompsons so they'd have money to go to Cairo, then to Saint Louis." It was so easy to talk to him, her words rushed out and were barely above a whisper.

"How long were you with the Thompsons?"

"Since last summer."

Colby swore softly. "You're not to worry, hear?"

"Yes," she said simply.

"Rain and I got something we got to do," he said as if he were suddenly uncomfortable. "Take it slow, like Mrs. Perry said." He went to the door, turned and looked back at her for a brief instant before he went out.

Willa stood with her hands clasped tightly in front of her. She had never before had such an intimate conversation with a man; and now that he was gone, she could scarcely believe that it had happened.

Chapter
Eleven

The sun was making its presence known, and streaks of light lit up the eastern sky when Liberty stepped out the door. She sniffed the fresh cool air, took a few steps out into the yard, turned and looked back. Breakfast smoke came from the chimney of the cabin. The solid log structure looked sturdy and permanent compared to her frail wagon that sat beside it. Within the walls of Farr's cabin there was safety, she thought wistfully. A place like this was what she had been searching for. Nothing real big or fancy, just a spot on this earth that was hers.

The day before she had felt secure knowing she had the Shellenberger place to go to. She had belonged to the community—her oxen would help build the stockade that would protect them from the Indian raids. She and Amy would bake bread and cook meat pies for the men who would come to help Farr. Now she had none of that to look forward to. She was scared, not only for herself, but for Amy.

"I'm here, Liberty." Farr's voice broke into her thoughts. He came from around the side of the house. He had a piece of straight-grained hickory in his hand. "Come over and talk while I work on this axe handle." He headed for the wood-pile and the tree stumps that would serve as places to sit down.

Liberty sat down and watched as he took his knife from his belt and began to whittle on the wood. She stared bleakly at his strong brown hands as they worked. Words were not coming easily to her, and yet she knew that she must find words to make him understand her situation. She thought of many ways to begin, but they seemed empty and meaningless. It was not easy to speak when feelings were deep and strong. Knowing the longer she waited, the harder it would be, she rushed into speech.

"I want to tell you again how much I appreciate what you've done for us. If not for you, we wouldn't be here at all. I'm fully aware of how foolish Jubal and I were to strike out for Vincennes just on the chance Hammond Perry would be there and would help us to get a start here in this new country. I didn't realize the danger and how ill-equipped we were to cope. Papa was right in that respect, although I hate to admit it. I want you to know, too, that I'm sorry you were drawn into the fuss between me and Stith."

"Don't mention it. I wasn't *drawn* in. I stepped in because I wanted to."

"Stith is the reason Jubal and I left Middlecrossing. He was the one Jubal was talking about the night he died."

"I figured that."

"Stith's pride couldn't stand it when I turned him down. He was humiliated because he was one of the richest men in town and we were some of the poorest. It was his pride that goaded him to follow us here, not any love for me. He won't rest until he has me completely in control and shames me as he believes I shamed him."

"He must be a mule-headed bastard to want a woman who doesn't want him."

"He's that and more. I thought I had things worked out so that Amy and I could stay here, but that's all changed now. I've been thinking about what to do—"

"Why do anything? Tell him how you feel and let that be the end of it. If he tries to force himself on you, fill his hide with buckshot. You carry that gun like you know how to use it."

"I've been telling him for years that I don't want to marry him. I'm not afraid he'll hurt *me*. It would be his way to hurt Papa or Amy or . . . Mercy and Daniel, if he thought they meant something to me."

"He must be a real, low-down son of a bitch!" Farr's

voice was as hard as iron. His knife bit deeper into the wood than he intended and he bit out a curse.

"As I see it I have only two choices. One is to go on out to the Shellenberger place with Amy and the children. I can't depend on any help from Papa, but I don't think Stith will put up with him for long when he finally realizes that I'm not going to marry him."

She watched him move the knife steadily down the long shaft of hickory, slicing paper thin sheets from the wood.

"That's one. What's your other choice?"

"My other choice is to take Amy and go on to Vincennes like Jubal and I planned." She drew a deep, hurtful breath. What she was going to say wouldn't be easy to put into words. "I won't be able to take Mercy and Daniel with me. Not right now. But you'll have Willa here to take care of them."

"Seems like you're giving up on Mercy and Daniel mighty quick."

"I don't want to give up on them. I just won't be able to take care of them for a while. When I get settled, I'll send for them. Willa has had such a hard time herself that she'll be good to them. They need to be with someone who loves them. And I do—"

"Seems like you're giving up on Willa too. You're the one who wanted her papers."

"Of course I did. When I saw how they were treating her I wanted to pull all the hair out of Mrs. Thompson's head," Liberty said spiritedly. "But because I'm a woman, Mr. Thompson gave the papers to you."

She thought she saw the shadow of a smile twitch Farr's lips and impatience flared in her eyes. He cut off her retort with his logical question.

"If Lenning is as determined to have you as you say, won't he follow you to Vincennes?" Farr moved his palms up and down the wooden shaft, feeling for the places he wanted to work on.

"Surely Hammond Perry can . . . discourage him."

"Hammond Perry?" He looked at her then. "I'd not count on Hammond helping you."

"But he's my brother-in-law."

"What difference does that make?"

"Well, we're kin, sort of."

Farr held the piece of wood up to his eyes and sighted down the length of it.

"You can forget going to the Shellenberger place. Lenning has moved in there, lock, stock and barrel."

His calm words shocked her speechless for a moment.

"No!" She ground out the word from between clenched teeth. Then, "Did Papa take him there?"

"Straight as a string. I went up there last night and again early this morning to see what was going on. He's moved in, taken over; his men are putting up a pole pen by the shed."

"Can't you make them leave?"

"No. It's not my land. It's there for the taking and he got there first. Your pa must have told him it was an abandoned homestead."

Liberty was silent for a long while before she spoke. She didn't want to go on to Vincennes, but now she had no choice.

"I guess that settles it. I hate to ask, Farr, knowing how much you're trying to get done this summer, but could you spare Colby or Rain to take me and Amy to Vincennes?"

"No."

Liberty gasped at his blunt answer. She was embarrassed now that she had asked. Paralysis gripped her throat, preventing her from saying anything. There was a sudden wall of silence between them. She pulled her shawl tightly about her shoulders and got slowly to her feet.

"Sit down, Libby. You have another choice."

The words were spoken kindly and broke down the wall between them. Without even thinking about it, she sat down, and words of anguish poured out of her.

"You don't understand, Farr. If Stith Lenning stays, I've got to go, or one way or another he'll force me to marry him. I saw him eyeing Amy. If Papa can't make me marry him, he'll ask for Amy. He knows I'll marry him before I let him have my sister." She ground her teeth in frustration.

"Amy? Hell!" Farr's head came up with a jerk. His eyes were cold, his brows drew together in a frown, and the white scar at the edge of his mouth deepened. "Amy's just a little girl yet."

"She'll be thirteen soon. Some girls marry at thirteen and die in childbirth at fourteen! I'll . . . kill him before I let him have Amy." Just saying the words aloud sent a shiver of dread down her spine.

The scowl lines changed like magic, and Farr grinned. His green eyes held hers like a magnet. "I bet you'd do it too."

Not even the note of admiration in his voice could keep Liberty's shoulders from slumping. Some of the desperation she was feeling made itself known by lips that quivered of their own volition.

"Papa will be back soon. He never stays away for long. I've got to decide what to do. You said I had another choice."

Farr lifted the axe handle again and sighted down the length. He made a notch at one end with the tip of his knife before he spoke.

"You can marry me."

Liberty's shoulders jerked up and her eyes sought his face. He was drawing the knife blade down the wood and appeared to be concentrating on what he was doing. She looked at him for so long that her eyes compelled his to meet them. She wondered if he knew that her stomach was churning and that her heart might leap from her breast. His eyes were curiously devoid of expression.

Her mouth was parted in surprise and she managed to say, "Marry you? Why?" There was a kind of desperation in the jerky way she spoke.

"For the same reason you married Jubal Perry."

She searched his face with puzzled eyes, but there was no crack in his invulnerable self-assurance, no expression to tell her what he was thinking.

"But I don't—you don't—"

"You don't what? Love me? It didn't appear to me that you loved Perry either. Leastways not like a wife should love her man. That didn't stop you from marrying him."

"Why would you do it?"

He shrugged and didn't answer.

"You . . . don't love *me*," Liberty insisted.

"And Jubal Perry did."

"Yes, he did, and I loved him . . . sort of." She shook her head in disbelief. "I don't understand you. You said a woman would be like a millstone about your neck. You said you had mountains to climb, rivers to cross—"

"Maybe I've changed my mind about the millstone. Women have their uses. Without them none of us would be here." His hands stilled and he looked at her steadily. "I can still cross rivers and climb mountains. Maybe it's time I took a wife—that's what Juicy is always telling me. If I am going to do it, I might as well have one that won't fold up on me the first time she hears a musket fired."

"And you think I wouldn't? Is that the only reason you asked me?" A hectic flush stained her cheeks when she realized the implication of her question, but her eyes narrowed dangerously and gave him back stare for stare.

"No. I have the desire to mate like any other man, to have a son of my own flesh and blood. I'd like to know there would be another generation of Quills after I'm gone." He spoke simply as if this were an everyday topic of conversation, but the measured words left no doubt as to their rock-hard meaning.

Liberty felt a new wave of crimson wash up from her neck and flood her face. He was telling her that he meant to avail himself of all the privileges he was entitled to have if she became his wife. As she looked at him, shock receded, and in its place came logic.

"Stith will ask for Amy and Papa will give her to him if he thinks it will make life easier for him," she said bluntly, forgetting a lifelong habit of whitewashing over her father's faults.

"Then it'd be my job to kill Lenning, and not yours."

"You'd do that?"

"It's best that you know about me right now, Liberty." He looked her straight in the eyes, his green ones taking on a shine that contrasted strongly with his dark face. "I do what has to be done to keep my hair on my head and my hide on my back. And I do it in whatever manner suits the place and the time. This is a hard land where only the strongest survive. I'm like Lenning in one respect. I keep what's mine and do my best to see that no harm comes to it. If that means killing, I kill."

"Me and Amy being the 'it'?"

"If we marry, you, Amy and the children will be my family, along with Juicy, Colby and Rain."

A blanket of silence covered them after his words. He looked at her as if he knew every line and hair on her body. Consciously she willed herself to remember that this man was all that was standing between her and a life of pure hell with Stith Lenning.

"It's a lot for you to take on," she said with a deep sigh. "Are you sure you want to?"

"I don't say things I don't mean, especially something that will change my life."

"Marriage is . . . forever." Her voice was flat and strained.

"No. It's just until one of us dies."

"But what about Juicy?"

"He stays with me for as long as he lives."

"I didn't mean that. I meant what will he think?"

"What difference does it make to you what he thinks?"

"Well. . . ."

"Well what? Get it all out, Liberty."

"I like him. I don't want him to think we're pushing him out of his cabin. That's five extra people, Farr. Six, counting Papa."

"I've thought of that. It'll only take a couple days' work to make over the front part of the storage shed into a snug room for Juicy, Colby and Rain. We're not using it now that the Indian trade isn't what it was. We can fix up the loft. It'll make a snug room for Willa, Amy and the kids."

"What if . . . what if Papa comes back?"

"He's welcome to sleep in the barn," Farr said without looking up. "But he'll pull his own weight. I want you to understand that."

"There's one more thing—the most important. Stith will try to kill you."

He dismissed her statement with a shrug. "Let him try."

"But it isn't fair that you have the most to lose and I have the most to gain. You'll be giving me and my sister a home, protecting us. What do we give you in return?"

"I've told you one thing. And you'll do the things women do, cook, wash, milk, plant a garden, make a home out of this place." He looked up and she saw a glimmer of laughter in his eyes. "Juicy will wallow in all the attention. He doesn't admit it, but he's getting old and enjoys his comforts."

"How long were you and Fawnella married?"

Liberty saw his hands still for just an instant, and when she looked at his face she saw a muscle was jumping in his tightly clenched jaw. She wished with all her heart that she could recall the words.

"Not long. That time in my life has nothing to do with you."

Liberty was stunned by the cold tone in his voice. A wave of sickness rose into her throat, and she fought it down. The silence lengthened. She felt as if the breath had been knocked out of her, but she refused to let him see how his words had affected her.

It seemed to Liberty that they had been by the woodpile for only a few minutes, but the sun was up and bathing everything with its bright light. She could feel the heat on her back through the shawl. She didn't understand why the thought of Farr with Fawnella depressed her so. If she married him, would the ghost of the love he and Fawnella shared stand between them? The panic in her stomach began to build.

"Well, what are you going to do?" Farr was watching the knife slice into the hickory wood.

"I don't seem to have a choice."

"No, you don't," he agreed matter-of-factly. "You've got yourself into a peck of trouble."

"When did you think . . . When do you want to . . . do it?"

"Now. It's as good a time as any."

"Now?"

He wiped the blade of his knife on his buckskin pants and shoved it into the band that circled his waist.

"Now. Come on. I've got to get back and finish this axe handle. Today we're going to mark the trees to be felled. I sure hate to use green wood, but there's no helping it." He started off down the path that led to the road and she hurried to catch up with him. "I wish I'd known last year what I know now. We could have cut the poles and they would have been cured out. As it is they'll be so damn green they'll warp out of shape if we don't lash them tight."

"Farr! Wait. Don't walk so fast. Where are we going?"

"To be wed." He stopped and looked at her with a frown. "Have you changed your mind?"

"No, but where are we going? Who'll . . . do it?"

"The preacher man down at the Sufferites' homestead. Vernon Ellefson. It'll be legal. He'll give us a paper. If you have doubts about it, I can send it up to Vincennes for Harrison to sign."

"No. If you say it's legal I believe you. I'm just surprised that we're . . . doing it so fast. When I put this dress on this morning I never dreamed it would be my wedding dress."

"It looks fine to me. Come on. Ellefson may already be out in the field. He doesn't waste much time." Farr started off, then stopped. "Wait. He'll not even talk to you unless your head is covered. He thinks a woman's hair lures men into their clutches."

"Well, for goodness sake! If that isn't the most ridiculous thing I ever heard. I thought I'd left all that nonsense back in Middlecrossing."

"He's got some tough ideas where women are concerned.

He rules his women with an iron hand. Don't be surprised if he's pretty harsh with you. Take off your apron." Farr reached behind her and pulled the sash to untie it. He whipped it off, looked at it, and then draped the waistband across the top of her head and tied the sash under her chin. "That'll do it. They'll think it's the style back East." Before she could comment, he took her arm and propelled her down the road.

Liberty was conscious of the warmth of his hand through the sleeve of her dress. It was a pleasant feeling. Suddenly she was jolted by the realization that she was on her way to be married to this man! She was losing her mind was her next thought. She knew nothing about him. At least she'd known Jubal all her life. Then, overwhelmed by a feeling of warmth and completeness that was new to her, the stiffness went out of her body and she was conscious of nothing except firm warm fingers on her arm leading her into the future as the wife of Farrway Quill.

Farr passed three houses and stopped in front of the fourth. He called a greeting from the road and a man came out onto the porch. He was one of the black-clad men who had come to the meeting.

"Good morning, Mr. Quill."

"Good morning, Preacher Ellefson."

"What brings you to my door?"

"I came to ask you to marry me to this woman."

Sharp blue eyes swung to Liberty, and he looked her up and down. A deep frown settled on his broad, seamed face.

"Have you given this considerable thought, Mr. Quill? Isn't this the woman who made a spectacle of herself at the meeting yesterday?"

"Yes. But in time I will teach her respect, and she will know that a woman's place is behind her man, not beside him."

"Farr!" Liberty almost strangled.

"Hush!" he hissed, and she did.

"Spare the rod and you'll spoil her, Mr. Quill. Remember that. A switching every day or so will keep her docile. God gave man a woman to do for him. If I wed you to her, do you swear you'll set her feet on the right path?"

"I'll do my best, Preacher Ellefson. I've already got a hickory switch cut and laid aside."

"Good. Good. Come up to the edge of the porch and I'll get my Bible." He turned back into the house and Liberty could hear him issuing orders. "Prudence, go slop the hogs. Hope, you've et enough, get to the field. Mary Magdalen, get that youngun out from under my feet," he said with an unmistakable sneer in his voice.

"I don't like him! I don't like him at all," Liberty protested as Farr's hand on her elbow pushed her toward the porch. "What did he mean about a hickory switch? That old fool is nothing but a bigoted windbag! There are a few things I'd like to say to that puffed-up peacock! He's a mule-brained son of a jackass, is what he——"

"Hush up!" He gripped her elbow tightly and held her close to his side. "He's the only person this side of Vincennes that can marry us."

Preacher Ellefson came back out onto the porch. He wore his black coat, black hat and carried a large Bible. Beneath dark shaggy brows, his piercing eyes focused on Liberty's face.

"Woman, are you pure in thought and act?" he demanded.

"What do you mean?"

"Are you unsullied?"

"Unsullied?" she echoed in disbelief.

"Mrs. Perry is a widow," Farr said. "Her husband died a few days back."

"Are you sure of this? Women are deceitful creatures."

"I helped to bury him."

The preacher nodded, then resumed his questioning.

"Have you ever lusted for a man's body?"

"No! I——"

"Sold yourself for profit?"

Liberty almost strangled as she shouted her answer.

"Has any man other than your husband seen you naked?"

"No! Not——"

"You do realize that you came from man, and to man you do belong?"

"I know that the Bible says God took a rib from man and made woman. I don't take that to mean—"

"She understands it, Preacher Ellefson—or she soon will," Farr added threateningly.

"Mr. Quill, can you assure me this woman is decent, modest and free from all taint of what is lewd or salacious?"

"I'd stake my life on it, Preacher Ellefson." Farr's fingers were bruisingly tight on her elbow.

"Be it on your head, Mr. Quill, should she not be." He opened his Bible, spread his legs, and squared his shoulders. "What's your name, woman?"

"Liberty Carroll Perry."

Liberty was angry. What should be one of the most sacred moments in her life was being ruined by this jackass of a preacher. His clear eyes were honed in on her as if she were some defiled creature not fit to be standing beside a man. He was preaching to *her* about sin, chastity, purity and obedience. He spoke in a booming voice about the end of the world, hellfire and brimstone, purity of conduct and even abstention from sexual intercourse when she had her woman's time. Liberty could feel the blood swelling in her veins. This fanatical old man was disgusting and she wanted nothing more than to tell him so and would have except for the warning fingers on her arm.

Finally he got around to the marriage ceremony.

"Liberty Carroll Perry, do you take this man to be your husband, your master? Will you obey him in all things, love him above all others, including any children you may have? Will you care for him in sickness and in health? It is your duty to see to his needs, to open your body to him so that he may take comfort when he so desires. Do you understand this?"

The breath went from Liberty's lungs with a swish. Farr poked her with his elbow. When she spoke it was a croaked whisper, "I do."

"Farrway Quill, do you promise to chastise this woman for her wicked ways, guide and direct her wayward feet into the path of righteousness, provide food and clothing, beget her with child and provide for her get?"

"I do."

"You are man and wife." He closed the Bible. "I'll get the marriage paper." He turned and went back into the house.

"Well! I never! I've never been so insulted in all my life. Are you sure that awful man married us?"

To add to her anger, Farr chuckled. "We're married. The old man has all the papers to prove he's a preacher. He just puts his own touch to the ceremony."

"If I had known it would be like this I wouldn't have come." Liberty turned her head deliberately, giving him a view of her profile.

"That's not true and you know it. We could have jumped the broomstick and gotten under the sheets. But this and a marriage paper will make more of an impression on your pa and Lenning."

"But the things I promised—"

"Don't worry about it."

Preacher Ellefson came back out to the porch. "Make your mark, woman."

"I can write," she snapped.

"Then sign the paper." One of the children brought an ink horn and a quill. Liberty signed her name and handed the quill to Farr. He dipped it into the horn and signed. Preacher Ellefson waved the child back into the cabin with a flick of his hand and blew on the signatures to dry the ink before he handed the paper to Farr. "That will be five shillings."

Farr lifted his tunic and unhooked his moneybag. He counted the money and dropped it into the preacher's hand.

"I wed you to this man, woman. You mind him, hear? And don't be shaming him by making talk of yourself." The preacher's harsh voice rasped across Liberty's mind like sand.

"And if I do?" she snarled.

"I have Mr. Quill's promise to lay the switch on your back."

"Oh! Why—" Anger made her incapable of replying.

"And I will, Preacher Ellefson. I'll have her dancing to the hickory switch." Farr stuck the marriage paper into his belt, grabbed Liberty's arm and pushed her out into the road. "We'll take our leave. I've got work for her to do," he said over his shoulder. "She's got to clean out the barn, cut kindling, clean fish, stake out the cows and dress out an elk before she starts the noon meal. Then she's got the washing and the garden——"

"Busy hands will keep her from doing the devil's work, Mr. Quill," the preacher called gleefully.

When they reached the road, Liberty jerked her arm free from Farr's grasp, reached up and pulled on the sash that held the apron over her head. She yanked it off in an act of pure defiance. His hand in the center of her back propelled her on down the road.

"There! Let the old reprobate see my hair. I'll not cover it again for a man! Never! Do you hear me, Farrway Quill?"

"I hear you."

"That's a nasty minded old man! He's mean as a rutting moose! All he's got on his mind is fornicating. By jinks damn! I just bet he takes his pleasure from those *evil, lowly* women he browbeats. Master, be damned! Oh!" She turned and would have stopped, but Farr's greater strength kept her feet in motion. "Stop pushing me, you . . . you bully!"

"Cool off, Libby——"

"Cool off? Cool off! Let me tell you one thing, Farrway Quill. If you ever lay a switch on me you'd better never sleep again, because the minute you do, I'll lay your head open. Damned if I won't!"

"Stop swearing."

"I'll swear if I want to. Don't you dare tell me not to swear! And I'll not walk behind you, either. I'll not walk behind any man, I don't care if it's President Madison. All a man wants is some dumb heifer to breed." She was shouting at him now. She was so angry that tears were running down her face, but she didn't know it. "Are you wanting to trample on my pride, Farrway Quill? Is that what you want?"

"Libby, you're going to make talk of yourself." She was

too angry to hear the laughter in his voice. He pushed her off the road and into the shadows of the giant cottonwoods.

"What do you think you're doing?"

He released her arm, folded his hands across his chest and stood looking down at her. She spun around like a spitting cat and looked up at him. Stunned by the look on his face, she gaped at him. She had never seen his face so creased with smiles. There were smile lines at the corners of his eyes, at the sides of his wide mouth, and his eyes were shining with amusement.

Liberty was suddenly aware that she was behaving like a witless fool. Anger flowed out of her and the irony of the situation caused laughter to bubble up from deep within her. She threw back her head and giggles of pure delight escaped her.

"Oh! Farr! Wasn't he funny?" She continued to laugh.

Farr watched her with fascination, and to his surprise heard himself laughing too.

"He was dead serious."

"About keeping me busy so I'd not do the devil's work? And keeping my feet on the path of righteousness?"

"And about me being your master and using the switch if need be." Farr's green eyes smiled into hers.

"You wouldn't!" she exclaimed, smiling broadly.

"I might, if you make me angry enough," he said, still smiling broadly.

"I wonder what the preacher would have said if I'd said yes to some of his questions. I should have, just to shock him."

"He was probably hoping you would, then he could have found out about your sordid past. He's not used to women like you."

"Am I so different?"

"Hell, yes. His women don't dare open their mouths unless he tells them to."

"Why do they stay?"

"They have children, and it's the only life they've ever known."

"They have a lot of children."

"The old man works at it." Farr's grin widened when he saw realization dawn in Liberty's eyes.

"You mean . . . all of them are his?"

"I think so. The other men are forbidden any contact with women."

"Forever?"

"As far as I know."

"I can't believe they'd be so stupid. Why, that old goat has set himself up in a harem."

They looked into each other's eyes and laughed. Liberty's soft giggles mingled with Farr's deeper, hearty laughter.

"Come on. We've got to be getting back."

"I know. I've got to clean the barn, dress out an elk—" Another peal of laughter broke from her. "I've never dressed out anything bigger than a rabbit."

"You'll learn, or you'll get the hickory switch."

She tossed her head saucily and stepped out into the sunlight. The last few minutes had shown her a different side of the man she had just married. Farr had a sense of humor. She had not heard him laugh so heartily before. Perhaps, just perhaps, they could build a pleasant life together. She could never hope to have his love, but there was a chance they could be companionable.

Chapter
Twelve

"I saw you walk off with Farr. Where did you go?" Amy spoke as soon as Liberty entered the cabin. She lifted Mercy down from the chair and wiped her mouth on the end of her apron.

Liberty hesitated for a moment, then said, "Oh, just down the road a way. Amy, why don't you go through our trunks this morning and see what we have that we can make over for Mercy and Daniel? I have a dress Willa can have, and later we can make her another one."

"I thought we were going to the Shellenberger place today. You said we were going to live there."

"Stith has taken over the Shellenberger place. We're going to stay here."

"That old fart!"

"Amy! Watch your mouth. You shouldn't say such things in front of the children."

"Poot, then!"

"Not that either."

"Is fart bad?" Daniel asked and slid down off the stool. He looked up at Liberty with serious brown eyes, and his hand worked its way into hers.

"It's something we don't say." A giggle entered Liberty's voice as she added, "Even if Stith is one."

"Why is it a word if we don't say it?"

"There are a lot of words that are not quite nice. That's one of them."

"Fart . . . fart . . . fart . . ." Mercy sang and raced for the

174

door. Amy grabbed for her, caught the end of her shirt and the cloth ripped.

"Oh, shoot! Mercy! Look what we've done."

"Libby." Daniel jerked on her hand to get her attention. "Are we stayin' here too? Me and Mercy?"

Liberty saw the worry on the child's face. Poor little tyke, she thought. Everything he had known had been suddenly taken from him. He must be feeling so lost, so at loose ends. She sat down in a chair, pulled him up onto her lap, pressed his head to her shoulder and hugged him tightly to her.

"You and Mercy are going to stay with me, Daniel," she crooned softly and smoothed his thick dark hair back from his face so she could place light kisses on his forehead. His small arms went around her and clung tightly. "You're my little boy now. Farr and I will take care of you. We love you and want you to stay right here so we can watch you grow up to be a man your mama would be proud of."

"Mercy, too?"

"Mercy, too. You're not to worry about it, sweetheart."

"Is Willa stayin' with us?" Amy was watching with a puzzled look on her face.

Liberty looked across the room and saw another worried face. Willa's hands clutched the edge of the table as if the world were tilting and she was afraid she would fall off. She looked directly into Willa's eyes as she spoke to her sister.

"Willa is welcome to stay with us for as long as she wants to. She is to be considered a member of our family. We will *all* share the work, the good times and the bad. That's the way it's going to be."

Willa's mouth worked and she drew her lips between her teeth to stop their trembling.

Liberty let Daniel slip off her lap. "You and Mercy stay in here with Willa while Amy and I go through the trunks in the wagon."

"I'm handy with a needle," Willa said hesitantly.

"Good. I'm not," Liberty confessed. "Amy's stitches are much better than mine. We'll see what we've got in the trunks. Farr did say there was cloth in the storeroom, but we'll not use it now if we don't have to."

Amy followed Liberty to the wagon. She didn't speak until they were inside.

"What's happened, Libby? Why are you talking like we're staying here forever?"

Liberty sat down on a stool beside her trunk and reached for her sister's hand.

"Because we are. Farr and I were married this morning."

"What?" Amy's voice squeaked. "You *married* him?"

"Yes. Just a little while ago."

"Well, dog my cats!" Amy let loose a chortle of laughter. "You married him?" she repeated. "You married that big, handsome woodsman! By jinks damn! That'll take the starch out of Papa and that old pissant Stith. Oh, Libby! I'm so glad!" She threw her arms about Liberty and hugged her so hard they both almost fell off the stool.

"Calm down, Amy. We've got to talk. Papa will be madder than a stepped-on snake. He's got his heart set on Stith as a son-in-law. I don't know what he'll do. He might even try to take you away. You've got to stay close, hear?"

"He won't do that. He'd have to find a place for us to stay. That would mean work, and you know what Papa thinks about that..." Her words trailed off and her eyes widened as the meaning of Liberty's words became clear. "Do you think he'd take me to Stith's place?"

"I don't want to frighten you, Amy, but I'm not sure what he'll do. He might... might tell Stith he can marry you. I'm almost certain he'll ask for you." Liberty held tightly to her sister's hand.

"Ask to *marry* me!" Amy's face turned a deep crimson red. "But I'm not grown up yet. I'm not ready to marry. Flitter, Libby. I'm not a... woman!"

"You got your woman's time last winter, and I'm sure Papa knows it. If Stith puts enough pressure on him he might consent to a wedding."

"No! Papa wouldn't!"

"I hope not. Oh, I hope not."

"I hate Stith! He's a fart, a turd, a . . . pissant! Papa loves me. He wouldn't just give me away. Would he, Libby?"

"Who knows what Papa will do. But if he does, there will be trouble. Farr won't let him marry you to Stith if you're against it." She hugged her sister. "Don't worry about what *might* happen. Just don't go wandering away from the homestead by yourself until we find out what Papa is going to do and if Stith is staying on here."

"Did Farr say he'd not let Papa do that?"

"He said that if we married, it would be his job to keep his family safe. He said you would be a part of our family."

"I'm glad you married him, Libby. I like him better than Jubal. Jubal wasn't . . . able to do much."

"He wasn't a strong, forceful man like Farr, but he did the best he could. If not for Jubal we'd be back in Middlecrossing and I'd be married to Stith. Remember that, Amy. Jubal was a brave man to go up against Stith and take something Stith wanted. For that reason I'll cherish his memory always."

"I didn't mean he was like Papa is always saying he was. Papa talks like Jubal didn't have any sense at all. I just mean nobody listened when Jubal said something. Farr is . . . well, I'm not afraid at all when Farr is with us."

"Neither am I. And I'm grateful to him. We'll have a home here and he'll stand between us and Stith."

"I'm glad Farr hit old Stith. I hope Farr kills him!" Amy sat down hard on her trunk. Her usually smiling lips were turned down at the corners and her eyes were filled with the awful hurt of her father's betrayal. "I've always tried to . . . love Papa."

"And we will continue to love him. He's our father, but that doesn't mean we have to *like* him!"

"Old Stith's a poot-head and a mule's ass," Amy blurted. "All the kids in Middlecrossing hated him. They were afraid to stick their tongue out at him, but I did once."

"Stith is everything you say he is, but there's no use talking about it." Liberty lifted the lid on the trunk. "This is what I thought we could do. I have a couple of dresses that you can have. Yours are getting too small for you. Do you think you can make them over for Mercy?"

"I suppose so." Amy's face softened and she grinned impishly. "She's a lot of trouble, but not so much with Daniel helping to watch her."

"We can make some of Jubal's clothes over for Daniel. Now what about Willa?" She lifted a blue sprigged dress out of the trunk and held it up. "I was saving this for you to grow into. It should be just right for Willa. Did you know that she doesn't have a stitch of underclothes? Isn't that a shame? She can use some of mine and a nightgown too. We'll make her some as soon as we can."

"Do you know what, Libby?" Amy hadn't moved from the trunk. She had a dreamy look on her face. "I bet Rain will grow up to be just like Farr." She looked out the end of the wagon and then back at her sister. "I think I'll marry him when I grow up. By then he might not be so damn stubborn!"

"Don't swear, Amy love."

"I won't in front of the kids, but sometimes I just like to. Libby?" She sat up as if a thought had pulled her erect. "When you married Farr, did that make Rain my brother?"

Liberty laughed. "No, silly. Get the sewing box. We've got a lot to do. Amy," she said before she climbed down out of the wagon, "don't say anything about the wedding. I think it's best that Farr tells Juicy and the others."

"Uncle Juicy will be tickled. He said you were the kind of woman Farr should take."

"Uncle Juicy?"

"He told me and Mercy and Daniel to call him that. I was getting tired of saying Mr. Juicy."

"Are you going to like it here, Amy? We've always made our decisions together. I had to make this one alone; there wasn't time to talk with you about it."

"Oh, yes! I want to stay here for ever and ever. I was even dreading going to the Shellenberger place."

"Amy Carroll, you've set your sights on Rain," Liberty teased.

"I've not done any such thing!" Amy's face reddened, then she giggled helplessly. "Yes, I have, but don't you dare tell, Libby. Don't tell Farr or anyone. Rain's so quiet and stubborn and stingy with words you'd think every one cost him a shilling! How can I get him to talk to me?"

"I was never much for trying to win someone over," Liberty said seriously. "But I remember my mother saying that if you say a nice thing about something dear to a person, you have a better chance of his liking you."

"I tried that. I told him his horse was the prettiest horse I'd ever seen. I even told him how smart I thought *he* was. I bragged on his moccasins because he said he made them. I told him I bet he could take on a whole band of Indians and kill them all. He just growled at me when I said that and looked at me like I was just a silly kid with no sense at all. He makes me so mad I want to kick him!"

Liberty tried hard to keep the smile off her face as they climbed down out of the wagon. This was terribly important to Amy. She remembered how close to the surface her own feelings were at that age.

"Well, in that case you'll just have to wait until he wakes up and sees how sweet and pretty you are."

"Will I be as pretty as you are, Libby?"

"Oh, honey! You'll outshine me a hundred times or my name isn't Liberty Carroll—Quill."

The shock of hearing her new name slowed Liberty's steps. The enormity of what she had done was just now sinking in. How well she understood the kind of rosy dreams a young girl like Amy had concerning the man she would some day marry, how many babies she would have, and what she would name them. When she was younger, the thought of being a bride was a beautiful thing, but she had married Jubal and had stored those dreams away. Today she was another man's bride—today she had committed herself to live the rest of her life with a man who was tormented by the memory of his lost love.

The deep sigh that slumped Liberty's shoulders made a small sound as it left her parted lips.

*   *   *

The sun was directly overhead when the men came from the thick stand of timber where they were marking the trees to be felled to make the fifteen-foot pickets for the stockade and the logs for the shot buildings.

Mercy and Daniel were sitting on the doorstone. Liberty heard Mercy squeal, looked out, and saw her running toward the four men walking up the path. The child stopped, let out a cry, and hopped on one foot. Another burr, Liberty thought, as she watched Farr swing the child up with one arm and set her on his hip without breaking stride. His other hand gripped his rifle.

Liberty stepped outside, her knees unsteady. She was nervous about this meeting. Had Farr told Juicy, Colby and Rain about the wedding? What would they think? For men who were used to being alone, how were they going to feel about suddenly having three women and two children thrust upon them?

After Liberty had confided the news to Willa, the three women had gone to work. The cabin was spotlessly clean, the table set, and the meal ready to be served up. They had brought in a few things from the wagon. Libby's quilts covered the bunks and her rocking chair was placed beside the hearth. When the work was done they had set about making themselves presentable.

Liberty still wore the brown linsey with the clean side of her white apron turned out. Willa wore the blue sprigged dress; and with her hair brushed and pinned to the back of her head, she didn't look like the same waif who had arrived with the Thompsons the day before. Knowing this was an occasion, Amy had brushed her hair back and tied it with a ribbon. In one of Liberty's dresses she looked like a pretty young woman, and Liberty felt a dread of what her father would do when he discovered she had once again evaded Stith.

"This youngun's got a burr in her foot," Farr said as soon as he reached the cabin. He turned so that Liberty could take

Mercy's foot in her hand. "We'll have to see about making her and Daniel some moccasins."

It was such a normal, everyday thing to say that some of the anxiety Liberty had been feeling left her. She found the burr, pulled it out, lifted the child from Farr's arm and set her on her feet.

"The meal is ready," she said without looking at him. "Soap and towels are on the wash shelf."

"Now ain't that plumb handy," Juicy said, his sharp blue eyes going from Liberty's suddenly red face to Farr. "I swear but somethin' do smell larrupin'." He headed for the side of the house and Rain followed. Farr and Colby stepped inside to place their rifles on the pegs just inside the door, then went out.

Liberty had lengthened the table by moving a smaller one up close to it. It wasn't as high as the regular table, but she planned to sit at the end with one of the children on each side of her. She assumed it was customary, even here in the wilderness, for the men to eat first and the women and children later. She had always detested the custom and decided she would start off the way she planned to continue. They would all sit down and eat together.

"Waugh!" Juicy came in, followed by Rain. He looked around and shook his head in wonderment. "I jist never knowed this place could look so homelike. I'm figgerin' ta get plumb spoiled. What's that thar in the pot? It be ticklin' my insides clear down to my toes."

"Meat stew and potatoes," Liberty said, taking a loaf of fresh bread from the side oven.

"Taters? Lordy! Them those old rotten taters we had?"

"They weren't rotten. They just needed to be eyed. Amy eyed them this morning, and we're eating what's left. Find a place to sit, Juicy. You, too, Rain."

Willa filled bowls from the big iron pot and Amy carried them to the table. Liberty set a sliced loaf of bread at each end and the large crock of butter in the middle. She was acutely aware when Farr and Colby came into the cabin. She saw Farr turn and take a long, deep look around the room. She saw him note the neat quilts covering the bunks, the orderly shelves, the extension to the table. When his eyes came to her, she could see the smile in them although it didn't reach his mouth. She knew instinctively that he was pleased she was making this cabin into a home.

Colby stood with his hands on his hips, his head tilted toward the iron kettle, sniffing appreciatively. "I don't hardly know how to act, things so ready and waiting, pretty women to eat with and all." His smiling eyes lingered on Willa even after she had turned her back to hide her blushing face.

"Might as well get used to it," Farr said casually as he went to the head of the table and sat down.

Liberty picked Mercy up off the floor where she was playing with a spool and sat her on the chair. After the sound of chair legs being scraped on the rough plank floor, and they were all seated, an unusual quiet settled. It was as if each one of them were waiting for something. Liberty had put a small amount of stew from her bowl in Mercy's, mashed the potatoes with a fork, and now she placed the spoon in the child's hand.

"It's cool, honey. Go ahead and eat," she murmured.

Mercy looked up at her with wide, twinkling blue eyes and banged the spoon against the side of the bowl.

"Fart, fart, fart," she said proudly. The words came out loud and clear and so shocked Liberty that her lower jaw dropped and her mouth hung open while crimson rushed up and covered her neck and face.

"Shh . . . eat your stew."

"Fart, fart," Mercy said happily.

"Shh," Liberty said again, dipping the spoon in the bowl and putting it to the child's mouth.

Amy's giggle was followed by a chuckle from Colby and then even Willa, with her face so low her chin rested on her chest, let out a gurgle of laughter. Juicy's loud guffaws followed.

"Someone's going to have to watch what they say in front of this child from now on. I wonder where she heard that?" Farr said matter-of-factly and helped himself to bread.

"I forgot to pour coffee." Amy jumped up and turned her

back to hide her red face from Rain's piercing dark gaze that had lifted to it on hearing Farr's words.

"She didn't know it wasn't nice," Daniel said with a worried frown. He sat with his spoon in his hand and looked at each of the grownups with his serious brown eyes before they rested on Farr.

"I know that, Daniel."

"Now, I ain't athinkin' it's all that bad. The little scutter's a smart 'un, is what she is." Juicy sat hunched over his bowl with a happy smile on his face. Now and then his eyes went from Liberty to Farr and back again.

The meal progressed. Liberty was happy to note the men ate heartily. They talked about the size and number of trees they had found suitable for the pickets that would surround the homestead, how long it would take to fell and trim them, and the possibility of the work being completed before the summer was over. After they had discussed building a sled to drag the logs up to the building site, Farr looked down the table and spoke directly to Liberty.

"Is there anything we can bring in out of your wagon before we go back to work?"

"Amy and I can move everything except the trunks and the chest. We brought in some of the cooking things and . . . the rocking chair," she finished lamely.

"Liberty and I were wed this morning." Farr spoke in a tone he might use for discussing the weather and continued on in the same tone. "Obviously the cabin will have to be enlarged. I don't see why we can't extend it into the storage shed, do you, Juicy?"

Liberty's face had turned red again, and she didn't know why. It irritated her to be embarrassed. Farr spoke as casually about being wed that morning as if it were of no importance. She looked quickly at Juicy and then at Colby. Both were looking at her and had huge grins on their faces.

"Wal, dog my cats! I knowed somethin' had took place, cause you was so dang quiet, boy. Dang bust if'n that ain't the best news I heared in a coon's age. A sudden like, I got me a daughter 'n grandkids!"

Liberty's eyes circled the table and then returned to rest on the old man. She smiled at him fondly. She had no doubt that he loved Farr like a son. He was probably very fond of Colby and Rain, but Farr was special to him. That he accepted her as Farr's wife meant a lot to her. A soft, loving light shone from her eyes.

"Sly old dog!" Colby reached over and swatted Farr on the back, causing coffee to slosh from his mug. "All it took was a pretty blond woman to knock those dreams of climbing mountains and crossing rivers out of your ugly head." Colby turned to Liberty. "I've known him all my life. He's a good man in a fight, he'll take on a pack a wildcats, can outrun a bear or an Indian squaw . . . Farr Quill's pure hickory! But there's something about him you should know, Mrs. Quill. His feet stink!"

It was strange to hear herself called Mrs. Quill. Almost guiltily, Liberty's gaze lifted involuntarily to Farr. His head was tilted slightly and he was laughing at Colby. Then his gaze turned to her, and it never wavered beneath her direct stare. A deep inner restlessness flickered to life in the pit of her stomach. Why had she never noticed his beautiful white teeth? she wondered. Now that the news was out, she felt better. She felt a lot better, almost happy. She could speak, now, without fearing there would be a quiver in her voice.

"There are sawed boards in the bottom of the wagon if you want to use them, Farr. We set the trunks and things right on top of them."

He nodded. "They'll be handy for making chairs. We'll make a longer table too. What do you think, Juicy, about running a partition across the front of the storage room and later putting down a board floor, building in bunks, and a fireplace at the end?"

"Don't know why it wouldn' work out jist right."

"We can make a room in the loft too. It'll be nice and warm in the winter."

"That won't be no chore at all with the good stout ceiling we put in."

Liberty watched closely for the men's reaction to the work

Farr was laying out. Colby looked at Juicy and winked when Farr mentioned the room in the loft. Rain's face was unreadable as usual. Liberty looked at him closely. He was a handsome boy. She wished he would smile more often.

"Dang it, Farr. It seems like you got the summer crammed full of work," Colby said. "That's going to shoot our trip to Saint Louis all to hell, Rain."

"We wasn't going to Saint Louis till he could go with us."

There was silence after Rain's softly spoken words. Liberty quailed inwardly as Farr's words came back to haunt her. *I can still climb mountains and cross rivers.* A quick glance at Farr's face told her nothing.

"There'll be times when you men will wish you didn't have us women underfoot." Liberty said the first thing that came to mind in order to change the subject. "You've been here alone for a long time."

"Too long," Juicy snorted.

"We . . . ah, Amy, Willa and I will take over milking and watering the stock from now on, Juicy. I'll set some hens and plant a garden as soon as we can get a spot plowed. I brought the seeds—" She stopped speaking and her eyes sought Farr's at the other end of the table. Did she see a tender regard for her there? Her heart thudded painfully at the thought. "We'll do our best not to make you sorry you took us in."

A strained silence was broken when Juicy said, "Hellfire! This place's been needin' a woman doin' fer it. God musta knowed we be purty nice fellers. He jist opened up a hole in heaven 'n dropped us three of 'em. It'll be plumb comfortin' ta have a purty woman takin' care a me when I get old."

"When you *get* old? Just this morning you were saying you were too old to work," Colby said teasingly.

"Yo're always ashootin' off yore mouth, Colby Carroll. Ya didn't get yore manners from yore ma, or yore pa, for that matter. Ya ort a show more respect fer gray hair, is what ya ort a do."

Farr stood and moved his stool under the table with his foot.

"Let's help Libby unload the wagon so we can get back to work. I want to start digging the trench for the poles this afternoon. I figure to hitch the oxen to the plow and dig as deep a furrow as we can before we start digging by hand."

Farr guided the plow being pulled by the oxen. It was work that required very little thought and his mind was free to wander. Something strange had happened to him. Liberty's face, framed with its crown of hair the color of eggshells, had nudged itself past the hard crust he had built around himself as a protection against ever loving, wanting, or needing a woman again. From the first he had liked having her in his house. And today it had been pleasant to come up for nooning, to have the meal ready, and to see her at the end of the table with a child on each side of her.

He had given considerable thought about asking Liberty to stay on as his wife even before the arrival of Stith Lenning. Of late he had yearned for a home spot, not just a cabin with a place to eat and sleep, but a place where someone waited just for him. At times he was desperately in need of a woman's body, and unlike many of the white men in the territory he refused to take an Indian woman to satisfy his lust. He thought about that now without the small, bitter flame of guilt he always felt when he thought of being closely entwined with another woman as he had been with Fawnella.

Time had dulled the pain of losing his first love. Fawnella was a part of his youth, a sweet and cherished memory. They had come together in mutual love for each other, and together had discovered the joy of consummating their love.

It would be different mating with Liberty. She did not love him and was too honest to pretend that she did. She had taken him as a protector to stand between her and a man she detested. He had no doubt that she would do her *duty* by him. After all she was not a stranger to a man's desires. They had made a fair bargain, he told himself. She would make a home, give him children, take care of Juicy, and he would protect her with his life if necessary. What more could she ask for?

By the middle of the afternoon Farr had made three trips around the compound and the furrow was becoming too deep for the plow. He stopped to adjust the iron blade and saw Liberty coming toward him carrying a pail. He continued to work and didn't look up until she was standing beside him.

"I thought you might like a drink of water." Her glance wavered beneath his direct stare.

"I'm dry as a bone." He took the pail from her hand, tilted it and drank deeply. When he finished he handed her the pail, and wiped his mouth with the back of his hand. "Thank you."

"How many more times do you have to go around?"

"About three more times. Then we start digging by hand." Farr studied her face but she avoided a direct glance.

"I thought I'd plow a garden tomorrow, that is, if you don't need Molly and Sally," Liberty said.

"I'll start a spot for you tonight after supper and add a little to it each night. You can't rake it and plant all at once anyway."

Liberty looked into his green, somber eyes, then down to his large brown hand on the handle of the plow. She looked away from him, pondering her unease. He was an intelligent man; his eyes absorbed everything they pierced, his mind was quick and alert. She had a feeling he knew her every thought. He was starkly handsome. She couldn't deny that her heart fluttered more quickly in his presence. That was a natural reaction, she reasoned. Then, thinking about what the night would bring, her heart beat wildly and a shudder rippled under her skin as she tried to retain her composure.

"I've got to be getting back."

Farr watched her go off toward the cabin, then turned back to the plow.

Chapter
Thirteen

The sun had made its daily trip across the sky and was sinking low in the west when Amy came in to announce that their father was riding up the lane on one of Stith's horses.

"Papa's coming," she said breathlessly. "He'll be madder than a flitter about you marryin', Libby! Do you want me to go get Farr?"

"Farr probably saw Papa before you did. No, I want to leave him out of it if I can. This is a family matter and I'll handle it."

"What if he wants me to go back to Stith's with him?" Fear was in her voice and confusion on her young face.

"I'll not let him do that. Take the children and go out to the barn."

"No! I'll stay and talk to Papa too. I'm . . . almost grown up."

"I'd rather he think of you as a little girl, Amy. Now go before he sees you in that dress and realizes that you really are almost grown up. I'll be all right. He'll be angry and shout, but that's all he'll do. Go with her, Willa, and keep them away until Papa quiets down."

Liberty watched them go to the side of the cabin where the children were playing in the dirt. Mercy squealed in protest, but Amy dragged her along determinedly. When they disappeared inside the barn, Liberty went out to stand in front of the cabin and wait for her father.

Elija reined in a dozen feet from where Liberty stood.

"What's Quill diggin' round this place fer?"

"He's digging a trench for the stockade."

"Is that all the bigger it's goin' ta be? Why, that ain't big enough ta skin a cat in."

"I'm sure he knows what he's doing. The barracks wall will be part of it."

"Ya give him the loan of the oxen. Is that why ya ain't come on up ta the place? Stith'd sent his men ta get the wagon if he'd knowed Quill was usin' the team."

"You led Stith straight to the Shellenberger place, didn't you, Papa? You let him get there first and claim it, although you knew I wanted that homestead." Anger and resentment were in her voice.

"You couldn't a run a inn by yoreself, Libby," Elija said with exaggerated patience. "Stith'll build ya one, just like ya wanted. He'll have a tavern with it, 'n a tradin' station, 'n brin' in a wench or two ta help ya out." He paused when Liberty lifted her eyebrows, pursed her lips, and nodded her head.

"That's mighty kind of him," she said scornfully.

"I done tole ya that ya had Stith all wrong. He ain't a bad sort. He's awantin' nothin' but ta treat ya right, Libby. Ya coulda had ever'thin' ya wanted back in Middlecrossin', but ya up 'n wed Jubal. Stith come on cause he knowed Jubal couldn't a took care of ya." Elija got down from the horse and looked around. "Where's Amy?"

"In the barn."

"Get her. Quill's unhitchin' 'n I'll put the oxen ta the wagon so we can be gone."

"Where do you plan to take us?" she asked with a calm composure she was far from feeling.

Elija's head turned and he looked at her cautiously. It was the smooth, indifferent tone of her voice more than her words that made him watch her uneasily.

"Down ta Stith's place. He's got it fixed up fer ya, and he be waitin'."

"You haven't heard a thing I've said for the last five years, have you, Papa?" Heartbreak made her voice shrill. "I despise Stith Lenning. He is a cruel, hateful man who wants

me because I don't want him. How can you, my father, want
me to marry such a man, bed him, live with him for the rest
of my life, take his abuse?" Liberty drew in a deep breath,
but never allowed her eyes to waver from her father's.

"I know what's best fer ya!" Elija cursed under his breath.

Liberty could feel her knees weakening, but not from terror. Anger started down in her stomach and surged up.

"Don't you mean what's best for *you?*"

"All of us—me 'n Amy too. I be head a this family, what
I say goes. It ain't fer a woman ta be makin' the choice!
Beddin' goes with marryin'. It's a woman's duty ta her
man." His voice rose angrily.

"What about your duty to me and Amy?"

"A man does what he can fer girls he's got. He gets 'em a
man ta look out fer 'em. Ya got them notions 'bout a woman
havin' her say from yore ma." He snorted angrily.

"Yes, I did, and I thank God she had the sense to teach me
that I have the same amount of brains in my head as any man
alive!"

"A woman ain't got no more sense than a hen chicken.
She's there ta give eggs, have a rooster ta ride her 'n pay no
mind ta her squawkin'.''

"That sounds like something Stith would say. Don't you
have any thoughts of your own, Papa?"

"Yo're jist deaf, dumb and blind ta a woman's ways, is
what ya are."

"Don't you dare talk to me like I had no more sense than a
hen waiting for a rooster to ride me!" Liberty's temper flared
out of control and she almost choked getting the words out.

"Don't ya raise yore voice ta me!" he said with more
determination than she had heard in a long time. "Stith's still
willin' ta take ya, jist as if'n ya ain't been had by Jubal.
Jubal had the say of ya fer a while, but he's gone. Yo're
back under my say, 'n I say you'll marry up with Stith like
ya ort a done, 'n we'd not be in this gawdforsaken place."

"I suppose Stith reminded you that I'm back under your
control?" Liberty's anger faded and she was able to speak in
an unnaturally quiet voice. Her father reminded her of

Preacher Ellefson and would be just like him, she thought, if he had a strong enough character.

"Stith ain't no fool. He knows the law."

Liberty watched Farr working with the oxen. He was out of earshot, but within calling distance.

"You can tell Stith that he might as well pack up and go back to Middlecrossing. I'm not coming with you, now or ever. This is the parting for us, Papa. Go back home with Stith. You've said repeatedly that you don't like the wilderness." She watched the anxiety fill Elija's eyes and anger goaded her to say, "You don't care a whit for me and Amy anyway except to use us to make an easy life for yourself."

"That's a mean thin' ta say. Ya've always been headstrong 'n mouthy, ain't ya? Ya always stick your bill in when I'm tryin' ta do right by ya. Ya ain't got no gratitude in ya a'tall fer me workin' 'n raisin' ya up like I done. I'd like ta take a stick to your backside is what I'd like ta do."

"I don't think I'd try that if I were you." Liberty looked over her father's shoulder and saw Farr walk up behind him. He came around and took her hand. It was trembling and he held it tightly.

"Is your pa staying for supper?" he asked casually.

"None a us is stayin'." Elija cleared his throat. "If yo're done with the oxen, I'll hitch up. We got ta be agoin'. Get Amy, Libby."

"You're not taking my *wife* anywhere. She stays here with me. I understand the oxen and the wagon are hers. They stay too." Farr's voice was moderate, reasonable as he dropped his quiet words into the silence.

Elija looked at Farr stupidly. Farr looked back at him steadily until finally Elija glanced down at Liberty's hand clasped in his big brown one.

"Ya ain't wed. There ain't no place—" he stammered as if his throat were raw and he was having trouble speaking.

"Yes, there is. We are wed and have a paper to prove it. It's legal and binding in the Illinois Territory. My wife brought to our marriage the oxen, the wagon, and the two horses. They stay here too."

"He can have one of the horses," Liberty said.

"All right. Take one of the horses. I want you to understand this, Carroll. Liberty and her sister are under my protection now. You tell that blowed-up bastard who's taken over the Shellenberger place that if he as much as touches a hair on the head of either one of them, I'll draw and quarter him and hang him out to dry." Farr's cold green eyes slashed across Elija's face like the sharp edge of a knife.

"Ya can't be wed," Elija protested and scrubbed his hand over the stubble around his mouth.

"We are wed, Papa," Liberty said almost kindly. "Face it. Go back and tell Stith to forget about me. Maybe he'll go back home and you can go with him."

"It ain't right, ya up 'n weddin' without yore own pa knowin'. It's like ya done when ya wed Jubal." His shoulders began to slump and a whine came into his voice. "Nothin's gone right."

"You're welcome to come see Liberty and Amy, but if you stay, you work for your keep," Farr said bluntly.

Elija stood silently for a moment, fingering the reins in his hand, and Liberty thought he was going to mount and ride away. When he looked at them, there was a defiant gleam in his eye.

"Ya ain't wed to Amy. I'm her pa 'n I got the say over her. She's acomin' to Stith's with me." He led his horse to the rail and tied the reins.

Farr dropped Liberty's hand and with a few quick steps was in front of him, blocking his way.

"You're not taking Amy down to stay with a bunch of rough men. Get that through your head and we'll avoid trouble. Her place is here with her sister." Farr spoke calmly but firmly, and Liberty was grateful that she had him beside her.

"You ain't got no right ta be tellin' me what ta do 'bout Amy. I'm her pa."

"I have the right because it's the decent thing to do."

"Papa! Amy's been with me all her life." Liberty's heart had given a sickening leap and was still pounding so hard she could scarcely speak.

"Stith'll get the soldiers. Stith said—"

"He said if you couldn't make me come to bring Amy," Liberty finished bitterly. "Isn't that right?"

"Carroll, I don't want any trouble with you because you're my wife's father. But you're going to get plenty if you insist on taking Amy away from her sister."

"Libby—" Elija turned to Liberty, but she turned abruptly away and closed him out as sure as if she had slammed a stout door in his face. "It ain't right, losin' both my girls."

"You're free now to do as you please, Papa," Liberty said without looking at him. "Take one of the horses and go. I'm making my home here, with Farr. Someday Amy will marry and make her own home. Until that time comes she'll stay with us."

It seemed to Liberty she had come out of a long, dark, frightening tunnel and into the light. She had always had to stand alone against her father and Stith. This time Farr had stood beside her. Her emotions in check, Liberty looked at her father, and soon her anger gave way to pity for the man whose heart was so lacking in love for her and her sister. He was not an evil man. As far as she knew, he had never harmed anyone. He was just willing to trade his daughters for what he sincerely believed to be a life of ease. He cared for no one and nothing but himself.

"Good-bye, Papa."

Her eyes met his briefly, then she turned away and walked swiftly to the barn and didn't look back.

Evening had turned into night by the time the evening meal was over. Amy washed the children, and almost as soon as she put them to bed they were asleep. Willa and Liberty cleaned up by the faint light from the floating oil lamp. Supper had been quieter than the noon meal. Juicy and Colby joshed each other as was their habit. Rain and Farr ate in silence. When the meal was over, the men went out into the storeroom with a stub of candle Liberty had placed on the mantle, and she could hear them talking about the partition they were going to build to make the extra room.

"I like light in the evening." Liberty rushed into conversation to break the silence. "I'm glad I brought the tin molds. We'll melt down some beeswax before winter—"

"There's not much soap, and what we've got isn't much good," Willa said hesitantly. "Mr. Juicy said they got this from the Sufferites."

"We'll make our own soap from now on. I'll ask Juicy to build us a lye box and we'll start soaking down the ashes. There's a crock of lard in the springhouse. I don't think they've kept it covered, so it'll not be good for anything but making soap. We'll make a batch and put some honey in it. Have you tried that? It's nice to wash your face with. I've used beeswax, too, but I like honey better." Liberty talked on about making soap and adding rose oil to make it scented. She told of the garden seed she had brought with her. "I've got marigold seed too," she admitted.

Willa asked her about the carded wool in her trunk. They talked about knitting warm stockings, gloves and caps after it was spun into yarn.

Liberty's nerves were like a jumping jack by the time the work was finished and it was time to retire for the night. Amy seemed to be blissfully unaware of her sister's anxiety and chattered endlessly about how happy she was that they were staying with Farr and Juicy, Colby and Rain. That they had made a permanent break with their father didn't seem to affect her at all.

Willa came to the wash shelf where Liberty was washing her face and hands with a wet cloth and a small bar of scented soap Jubal had given her before they left New York.

"Don't be so worried," she said quietly. "Mr. Quill is a kind man." Soft brown eyes looked anxiously into Liberty's and Willa's work-roughened hands clasped her arm.

"How did you know I was worried?" She answered her own question before Willa could open her mouth. "I have been running off at the mouth, haven't I?" She sighed deeply. "I always dreamed it would be . . . different. Since I was a little girl, I've dreamed I'd be with a man who loved me. Mr. Quill doesn't love me—"

"Oh, he must! How could he not? You're so nice and so pretty."

"Have you ever been with a man, Willa?" Liberty's face reddened as she whispered the words.

Even in the dim shadows Liberty could see the fear and tension that flitted across Willa's face, and wished she could withdraw the question.

"Once . . . but it wasn't like it's supposed to be. I didn't want to do it. Catherine, Mrs. Coulter, the lady who had my bond, told me being with a man wasn't anything to be scared of. She said it was real nice to . . . do it, when she and Mr. Coulter were young."

"Did he—"

"Oh, no. Not Mr. Coulter. He died first, then when Mrs. Coulter died, her kin got my papers. He . . . he came to my room one time. His wife found out and made him sell my bond to Mr. Thompson."

"He forced you?"

"Yes." Willa shuddered. "He was so hairy. . ." She clasped Liberty's arm. "But Mr. Quill won't be like that," she said quickly.

"He wants children."

"But . . . you were married. You know what they do."

"My husband treated me like a younger sister. He never made any attempt to take me to bed. I don't think he even thought about it."

"Oh . . ." Willa's eyes filled with pity. She watched Liberty through dark, thick lashes. In all her young life, Willa had known little love, and much loneliness, longing and hardship. There had been years of impossible struggle. And from that struggle, she had learned to judge men. "Mr. Quill isn't the *taking* kind of man," she said firmly, and searched Liberty's face, trying to decide if the dampness on her cheeks was caused by tears or the wet cloth.

Liberty avoided her eyes. "He isn't the *asking* kind of

man either." She felt faintly giddy and her face, framed by the blond hair, paled. "I'm going on out to the wagon. He'll . . . know where I am."

Amy was sitting quietly in the rocking chair, and Liberty dropped a kiss on her forehead as she passed her.

"Night, Libby." There was a pitying quality to her voice that brought home to Liberty the fact that Amy was aware her sister was now the wife of a man who would expect her to be a wife in every sense of the word. While married to Jubal she had slept most of the time with Amy. It occurred to her that sometime in the future, after she had experienced what happened between a man and a woman, she should talk to her sister and tell her things that had never been told to her.

Forcing a lightness in her voice, Liberty said, "Night, honey. In the morning we've got to plant the potato eyes and make something decent for Mercy and Daniel to wear."

A full moon rode high in a sky full of floating, drifting clouds that allowed its light to shine through one moment and concealed it the next. The cottonwood leaves were whispering and the peeper frogs down by the river seemed unusually loud in the quiet night. With no other noise, the smallest sounds were obvious, such as the loud creaking of the wagon as Liberty climbed inside.

She sat down on her straw pallet and took the pins from her hair. She looked out the end of the wagon, staring into the shadows, transfixed, literally shaking inside. She swallowed hard, fighting back the tears. A poignant longing for her mother surged through her. For a moment all the years rolled away and Liberty could hear her talking. *Someday you will meet a man and a miracle will happen. You will love each other very much. He will be the center of your universe. It will be as if you are not whole without him.*

It was years after her mother died that a distant cousin told Liberty about her mother's younger days. The love of her life had been killed by a Tory bullet, and in the midst of her grief and depression she had married Elija Carroll, a man who was the complete opposite of the man she had loved so desperately.

Thinking about her mother's life, and how she had bedded with a man she didn't love and who didn't love her, Liberty slipped out of her dress and underclothes and into her nightdress. Filled with tension, she sat on the pallet and raked her fingers through her hair. Finally she lay down and pulled a cover over her. She was sure that her brain was too tired and too confused to think about what she would do when Farr came to her. But her mind refused to be turned off. Knowing she was merely *paying* for his protection, she wondered how she was going to share the most intimate act a woman could share with a man—especially a man who stirred longings in her. She would never have his love. Fawnella, sleeping on the hill above the river, would always have his heart. Liberty meant no more to him than a woman who would give him children, keep his house, and work beside him in return for his protection.

Tears trickled from her eyes. Soon the tiredness in her body overcame her restless mind and she slept.

She awakened suddenly. A fierce gust of wind had rocked the wagon and she could hear a tin bucket rolling across the yard.

"It's only a windstorm." Farr's voice came out of the darkness. "Go back to sleep. The clouds are thin, and it will pass."

Liberty sank back down and pulled the quilt up over her shoulders. It was the same as the night Jubal died. His voice had come out of the darkness to reassure her. She had not even awakened when he had come to the wagon and lain down beside her. Would he turn to her now and demand his right? No. He had said for her to go back to sleep. She lay still, almost afraid to breathe lest she draw attention to herself. Her eyes became accustomed to the darkness and she could see the shape of his shoulders as he lay with his back to her.

Her last thought before she drifted off to sleep was that Farrway Quill was a strange man—kind, but strange. And she wondered about the little spark of disappointment that flickered through her mind.

Morning came and Liberty awakened to find herself alone. Light rain was falling and a mist hugged the ground. She dressed quickly, and with an old leather jacket over her head dashed for the door of the cabin.

"Mornin'."

Willa spoke from where she was bending over a pan of frying meat. The smell of coffee boiling permeated the room. A faint light from the storage room shone through the open doorway and Liberty could hear Juicy's gravelly voice and Colby's light teasing one.

"Oh, flitter! I overslept again. I don't know what's the matter with me."

"You didn't oversleep. I got up extra early. 'Sides, Mr. Quill came in early and stoked up the fire. He said you were still sleeping."

Liberty felt the warmth of the blush that covered her face and was grateful that Willa didn't look at her. She washed, dried on a towel that was damp from previous dryings and wondered if it was Farr who had run the cloth over his face to rid it of wash water. There were so many things about him she didn't understand; his explosive temper when he struck Stith, his tenderness with the children, his kindness to Willa. She knew nothing about his personal habits except that he was clean, very clean.

She turned from the wash bench to see him coming through the doorway.

"Morning," he said. "It'll be too wet for you to work the garden today. But the rain will soften the clods and make raking easier when you do work it."

"Will the rain slow you down much?" She was surprised she could carry on a normal conversation.

"We'll fell trees today. Colby and Rain are like two water rats," he said and smiled. "Juicy will work on the extra room. Coffee smells good."

"Sit and I'll get you some."

The men filed in and took their places at the table. There were no sly glances, no indication of the teasing that usually followed a wedding night. Voices were kept low so as not to waken the children. Liberty saw Rain cast his eyes toward Amy's bunk. She lay with her back to the room, her loose hair spread over the quilt that covered her.

When the meal was over, Farr lit a candle and asked her to come into the storage room. He told her their plans for building bunks and a cobblestone fireplace before winter. He took her to the back and showed her bolts of material stacked on a shelf. Alongside were needles, threads, garters, leggings, white goods and blankets.

"Use what you want of this to fix up the house," he said casually. "Women like curtains . . . and things."

"I don't have to have curtains. . . ."

He shrugged. "Then make the children some clothes. Rain and Juicy will make them moccasins." He led the way farther back into the storeroom. "Back here we have kegs, sacks of salt, lead, powder, guns, gun screws, knife blades, and the like. Keep the little ones away from here or they're liable to get hurt."

"I will. Farr? Do you mind if I put my clock and some of Jubal's best pots on the mantle?"

"Put out what you like. It's your home."

"It's yours and Juicy's and Colby's and Rain's too."

"It was mine and Juicy's. Now it's yours and Amy's and Willa's. Colby and Rain come and go as the mood strikes them. Rain is beginning to be uneasy about the Indian war. He'll not want to stay and fight against his Indian brothers. He won't fight against us, either. I suspect he and Colby will go west before fall."

"Had you planned to go with them?" The question was out before she could stop it.

"No. I committed to Harrison that I'd stay here until

things settle down along the Wabash. Besides, I'd not stay away from Juicy for long. He's slowed down a lot. He won't admit it, but he has."

Liberty followed Farr back to the front of the darkened storeroom. Juicy and Rain were there, and Rain was helping the old man shift bags of salt and bales of furs away from the front wall. Through the open doorway she could see Colby sitting at the table with Willa. His head was bent toward her and he was talking. Liberty backed away from the doorway, instinctively knowing it was no time to intrude.

As soon as the others left the room and it was evident Colby was going to stay, Willa jumped up from the table on the pretense of fetching the coffeepot. She filled Colby's cup and would have moved away, but his words stopped her.

"Sit down and talk to me."

"What do you want to talk about?"

She was breathless and felt stupid and weak. Events were happening so fast her head was spinning. She wanted him to go and she wanted him to stay. What she really wanted was for her crazy heart to stop galloping like a runaway horse so she could gather her scattered thoughts into some kind of order before she made a complete fool of herself.

"How are you feeling?" he asked when she was seated.

"All right." Her tongue was stuck on the roof of her mouth and she kept her eyes on the plate in front of her.

"Do you like it here?"

"Oh, yes. Mrs. Perry—ah, Mrs. Quill's real nice."

"That was something, wasn't it? Old Farr jumping the broomstick. I never thought it would happen."

"Why not? He's not old."

"He's older than I am by six years or so. How old are you, Willa?"

"Sixteen." She kept her head bent and refused to look at him.

"Let me see your pretty eyes." He placed his forefinger

beneath her chin and tilted her face. Startled, she backed away from his finger and her frightened eyes looked into his. "They're just as pretty as I remembered. Are you afraid of me, Willa?" His brows had drawn together in surprise and there was honest regret in his voice.

Willa shook her head vigorously. "I'm not scared . . . I'm just jumpy."

"I can understand that after what you've been through. Don't ever be afraid of me. I'll never hurt you. You believe that, don't you?"

"Yes."

"I thought about you all day yesterday. It made the day go so fast it was over before I knew it." His eyes were warm and bright, his mouth was slightly parted and his lips tilted at the corners.

"Why did you do that?"

"I don't know. I'd be on the other end of the saw with Rain, and suddenly a little heart-shaped face with big, sad brown eyes would just be there right in front of my eyes. I wanted to hurry back and be sure you were still here, that I hadn't dreamed you."

Willa stared straight ahead of her, her face red, her hands dug deep in her lap. She couldn't have gotten a word out if her life had depended on it.

"You're not all talked out, are you?" Colby's voice held a trace of amusement and her eyes darted to him. From the laughter in his eyes she knew he was teasing, and her pounding heart released a flood of happiness that reflected in her shy smile.

"I think you're full of clabber, Mr. Carroll." She couldn't believe she had said that. Her face flamed and she drew in a deep breath. She heard his low chuckling laugh. It warmed her, and she stared at his bright blue eyes and handsome, laughing face before turning away in confusion.

"I want to know about you, Willa. I want to know all about you." He said it so kindly, so sincerely. His blue eyes watched every expression that flicked across her face.

A long silence followed his words. Willa's mind searched

for something to say, and then from behind her she heard Mercy's little voice.

"Pee, pee."

Willa jumped up from the table and went to her. The child was sitting up in the bed rubbing her eyes. She held up her arms for Willa to take her.

"Are you sure, love?" Willa whispered.

"Pee, pee," Mercy said again, loud and clear.

Willa gritted her teeth and kept her red face turned away from Colby. She lifted the child in her arms and with relief heard the scrape of Colby's chair on the floor as he got to his feet.

"I have the feeling that this is no place for me right now." A small chuckle followed his words. He went into the store-room and closed the door.

Willa's embarrassment was so acute she wanted to cry. Instead she pulled the china pot out from under the bunk and sat the child down on it. She let water go immediately and when she was finished, Willa replaced the lid and slid the pot back under the bunk. She lifted Mercy in her arms and the child wound her arms about her neck.

Willa carried her to the rocking chair beside the hearth and sat down. "Go back to sleep, baby," she crooned and kissed the little smooth cheek that snuggled against her. It was comforting to hold the small warm body, and Willa's thoughts roamed.

Did Colby Carroll consider her fair game because she was an indentured servant? She was trying desperately to believe he was a nice, decent man and wasn't just trying to get her under the blanket as others had done when they had been nice to her.

She couldn't get to liking him, she cautioned herself. If she had learned one thing it was that men like Colby Carroll never considered a woman like her when they chose a wife.

Chapter
Fourteen

Liberty's wagon was still parked beside the cabin. Four days had passed since she and Farr had married. Each night they had slept beneath its canvas top. He came to bed long after she retired and was up before she awakened. The first few nights she had expected him to reach for her and take the right that was due him, but he had not as much as touched her or spoken to her since the first night during the windstorm.

The early summer heat was growing strong. Inside the wagon, Liberty stripped off her dress, then two petticoats, and put her dress back on, using only her pantalets and waist shift for a foundation. The sudden airiness made her smile, and she wished she had a mirror so she could see herself without the bulky padding. When the weather turned hot a man could take off his shirt, she thought, but a woman had to work and swelter beneath a long, heavy skirt and at least two petticoats. She would not do it, she decided. She would wear the long skirt, and what she had under it was her business.

Breaking up the rich Illinois dirt was back-wrenching labor. Liberty had chosen to work the garden and leave the cooking, cleaning and sewing to Willa and Amy. Each night Farr had plowed an addition to her garden, and when she was satisfied it was big enough, he had dragged a knobby log across the ground to break up the clods.

All day Liberty worked in the soil. It was a labor of love. Her face and arms were turning brown from the sun, and small freckles had popped out on her nose. While she worked she could hear the ring of axes, the rip of saws, the slough of adzes and the crackling crash of falling timber. The work was progressing well, according to the conversation among the men when they came to the house to eat the hearty noon meal. A member of the Sufferite community had come to help Farr, but he never stayed for a meal, so Liberty had not seen him except from a distance. In a few days other men would arrive, and she, Willa and Amy would be really busy with meals.

When the last seed was planted, Liberty slowly straightened. Her back was too stiff for flexibility. She placed her sore hands in the small of her back and stretched carefully. That morning at breakfast Farr had taken her hands in his and spread them palm up, exposing raw and blistered flesh.

"Are you about finished with the planting?" he had asked.

"Today should do it."

"I'll get some salve. Put it on your hands, then wrap them with a cloth."

Liberty thought of it now. He hadn't scolded or made too much of the fact that she had worked from daylight to dark. He had not asked if her hands hurt, and if he had, she wouldn't have told him that at times they hurt her so badly she bit her lips to keep from crying. He had merely handed her the salve and walked away.

She stood back and let her eyes wander over the rich black soil and the neat rows she had planted with sticks to mark each end. Later she would tie some string to the sticks and attach small scraps of cloth to flutter in the breeze to scare away the birds that would feast on the bounty. It wasn't a big garden. She had brought with her only one small bag of seeds, but it gave her an enormous amount of satisfaction to know it was all her doing. Farr had promised to drag up some brush from the sawyer camp and make a brush fence around the small plot to discourage deer and other animals from trampling the tender shoots.

Liberty knew Farr was pleased with the changes she had made to his home although he never voiced the fact. She had seen him pause in the doorway, his eyes going to the hand-carved clock with the glass face and short pendulum. She had wound it, set it by guess, and placed it on the mantel. The soft ticking had caught his attention. A glass lamp with a shiny chimney and filled with what was left of her precious lamp oil was there beside the clock. Pots were hung, trenchers lined up on the shelves, ashes from the fireplace had been removed and dumped into the lye box. Clean towels were on the rack beside the wash bench.

He had surveyed his home with an expressionless face. Her own eyes had held a sparkle of deep pleasure as she watched him. He had nodded his approval and passed on through to the storeroom.

That morning Willa and Amy had washed clothes at the creek and now they were spread on the bushes to dry. Juicy sat in front of the cabin smoking his pipe and watching the children play on the sack swing Rain and Colby had made for them. A log had dropped on his foot the day before. Luckily no bones were broken, but Farr insisted he stay off it for a few days.

It was all so peaceful, Liberty thought as she headed back to the house. Four days had passed without a word from her father or Stith Lenning, but she didn't allow that to lull her into believing that she had heard the last of them. During the noon meal today, Colby had mentioned that if the men at the Shellenberger place expected to seek protection at the fort, they damn well better do some of the work. Farr had merely grunted a reply, but Liberty suspected that was because he didn't want to talk about it in front of her and Amy.

Her sister came running to meet her.

"Libby! Are you through with the plantin'?"

"Yes, thank goodness. I don't think my hands would have lasted another day."

"Let's go down to the sawyer camp. Just for a little while?" Her eyes were bright and she barely suppressed a giggle, when Liberty eyed her knowingly and smiled.

"Are you sure it's the *sawyer camp* you want to see?"

The giggle came floating out on the breeze, and Amy

flipped her loose hair back behind her ears. "Well . . ." she admitted.

"Amy Carroll. What would the matrons in Middlecrossing think about you if they could see you with your hair loose and your skirt above your ankles?"

"They'd think I was a . . . fallen woman."

"Fallen woman! What do you know of such as that?"

Amy tossed her head. "I know a lot more than you think I do, Libby." She grabbed her sister's wrist and pulled her toward the path leading to the thick stand of trees where the men were working. "Come on. Willa will watch Daniel and Mercy. I asked Uncle Juicy if we could go down there and he said we could if we didn't get in the way. He said be careful if we went to the river, 'cause it was high."

Liberty admitted silently that she was curious to see what was going on in the timber beside the river. She allowed Amy to guide her to the camp and they sat down on a stump to watch the operation. Colby and Rain were doing the felling, limbing and cutting the trees into sixteen-foot lengths. A team harnessed three-abreast was being handled by a black-bearded man from the Sufferite community. He skidded the logs in pairs to the pit, where they were worked onto a large A-frame and ripped. A pit had been dug and over it a stout scaffolding erected. Liberty was amazed at the amount of work that had been done in such a short time.

Farr and Mr. Washington were in the pit handling the huge two-man saw. The pit was a hot and dirty place. Both men, stripped to the waist, were covered with sweat and sawdust. Sweat ran in streaks down Farr's sides, and his hair was stuck to the back of his neck. They sawed for thirty minutes before pausing, and that was only to walk to the other end to start another cut. Each log was squared off, then ripped into planks four inches thick. Already a stack was growing on the flat area beside the pit. The boards they were ripping were for the barracks Farr had told her would be built first. Then the stockade would fan out from each end of it. The work was slow and brutal, and after seeing it, Liberty understood why Colby had said all who would benefit should share in the work.

If Farr was aware of her presence he never let on. Liberty suspected that nothing went on that he *wasn't* aware of. Amy was craning her neck so she could watch Rain. The young boy never as much as glanced their way as far as Liberty knew, but Colby shouted and waved.

Liberty began to feel uncomfortable sitting there watching the men work. She wanted to yell out and ask if there was something she could do, but she didn't because she feared her offer would embarrass Farr.

"Let's go, Amy."

"Let's see the river first. Uncle Juicy said there have been floods up north and the river is full. I bet that's why Mr. Washington's here. He didn't want to take his ferry across."

"All right, but just for a few minutes. I've got work to do."

They took the path to the river that Liberty had used the day she had discovered Fawnella's grave. She thought of it now, and wondered if the marigolds she had planted around the headboard were up. When she thought of the girl on the hill who filled every corner of Farr's heart she wanted to cry. She felt an aching torment knowing she would never have her husband's love. He had promised her nothing but his protection, she told herself sternly. Her heart skipped a few beats and then settled into a dull ache. More and more often now she found herself yearning that someday he would turn to her with love in his eyes. She tried to crowd that hope out of her heart with other thoughts, but it remained secure in a small corner to flare up at the most unexpected times.

Amy had boundless energy. She danced up and down the path plucking flowers from among the dense growth on each side of the narrow lane.

"Look at these!" she laughed, waving a fistful of light blue flowers in Liberty's face.

"Watch out for snakes," Liberty cautioned.

"They're just the color of your eyes, Libby," Amy said, ignoring her warning.

"And yours are the color of cattails.''

"Your hair is like...dirty snow!" Amy laughed and danced away.

"It is not! Yours is like that old shaggy dog we had back home.''

"It is not! It's like ermine fur! You told me that yourself." Amy's laugh rang out and she raced down the path. "Your nose is like a pig's snout!" she shouted. It was a game they had played since she was a little girl not much older than Mercy.

They reached the river bank and Liberty steered Amy to the south, along an animal path away from Fawnella's grave. When they came to an opening in the dense growth of young willows that lined the river, they passed through and came out onto a lip. The lazy river of a few days before was now a raging, muddy torrent that came up to within a foot of where they stood. It rolled and thundered as it swept past them carrying decayed vegetation and small uprooted trees.

"For goodness sake! They must have had a terrible flood up north of here. No wonder Juicy told you to be careful. Stand back, Amy. This bank could give way any minute.''

"Look, Libby! Oh, looky there," Amy yelled over the roar of the water as she pointed upriver.

A canoe, riding the swiftly moving water, came careening down the river. It spun against a boulder, struck the bank, turned and came on sideways. An Indian woman knelt on the bottom, her hands fastened to the sides, her long, black hair wet and sticking to the sides of her face. As the canoe turned, Liberty could see a small child strapped in a carrier on her back.

"Oh, my God! She'll drown!"

The words had no more than left Liberty's mouth when a huge wall of water came rushing down to lift the canoe as if it were a toy. The woman was swept up and thrown to the top of the crest. Her terrified screams ceased suddenly as she sank beneath the roiling water. The thick brown river poured over her head, and when she reappeared, Liberty could see her groping and grabbing before she sank out of sight again.

Whimpering sounds of horror came from Amy as they witnessed what was sure death for the woman and her child. Then to their amazement, the woman's body surfaced, was swept up and thrown again, crashing her cruelly into a tree trunk that had been wedged between two boulders. In a wild panic she flung her arms around the trunk and clung to the only solid thing in the plunging flood.

"Hang on! Hang on!" Liberty shouted. She grabbed the hem of her dress, pulled it off over her head, and ran to a place along the bank where she could get into the water. "Hang on! I'm coming!"

"Libby! You can't go in—"

"I must. Stay here and help me pull her out!" She took a deep breath and plunged into the cold, swiftly moving water.

Liberty was a strong swimmer. Against all the prejudices of her day about a woman learning how to swim, her mother had insisted that her uncle teach her. She opened her eyes as soon as she surfaced and stared over the water to where the woman still clung to the branch. The water beat at her with its cold, mighty force as she swam against the strong current, grateful she was upriver from the stuck tree trunk because the current was pulling her down. She took great gulps of air when she could and prayed she could reach the middle of the stream before she was swept past the boulders and the tree trunk where the woman clung. Lifting her head high out of the water she saw the red band of cloth that was wrapped about the woman's head, and increased her effort.

By the time she reached the boulder and inched her way around, choking, and clawing at the slick rock, she was tired. The woman's terrified eyes clung to her, and when she reached out a hand to her, the woman shook her head vigorously. Clinging to the trunk with one arm she reached to unfasten the harness that held her child to her back. Liberty understood and turned, slipped her arms into the straps and settled the child high on her back between her shoulder blades.

"I'll be back," she croaked and pushed herself away just as she felt the tree trunk break loose from the rocks. Muddy water washed over her. She gasped at the air when she came up, looked wildly around for the child's mother, and when she didn't see her, began to swim with the current, the weight of the child on her back holding her low in the water. She heard Amy calling and used all her strength to keep her arms and legs moving. When she reached the bank, Amy was there. She pulled and tugged until Liberty could get her foot anchored in a tree root so she could heave herself up out of the water. She choked and gulped cold air into her burning lungs.

"The woman," she gasped and pulled her arms free from the harness. The baby's little face was puckered as if it were crying loudly, but only soft mewing sounds came from its little mouth.

Amy was crying too. Liberty shoved the child into her arms and turned to search the river for the child's mother.

"Amy!" she cried desperately. "Where did she go?"

"There! Down there . . ." Amy pointed downstream.

Liberty ran along the bank, her eyes searching. She saw the green of a tree top, and then the red headband. The woman had both arms wrapped around the tree trunk. The current had washed the tree closer to the bank and it appeared the end was stuck in the mud. Without hesitation, Liberty jumped into the water again. The current was not as strong there, and when she reached the tree her feet could almost touch the slimy bottom. The woman was so terrified that Liberty had to pry her hands from the trunk. Her throat was too raw to talk to her, so she placed the woman's hands on her shoulders and pushed the two of them away from the tree before the woman realized what she was doing.

Liberty could feel her strength leaving her as she flailed the water with her arms and legs. Each of her limbs felt as if it were tied to a heavy weight. Using every ounce of power she possessed, she inched them toward the bank. As they neared, her feet felt the bottom and she sagged. She was beyond tired. She couldn't lift herself up out of the water.

Amy, with the child in her arms, shouted encouragement

and tried to reach her with an outstretched arm. The Indian woman seemed to come to life, and with a surge of strength pushed Liberty up onto the bank, and then, slipping and sliding in the mud, managed to crawl up herself. When she reached for her child, Amy placed it in her arms and then tried to help Liberty stand.

"Get Farr—" Liberty gasped. She slipped out of Amy's arms and fell facedown on the grass, battered, bruised, her clothes torn and muddy.

Farr knew the moment Liberty and Amy came in sight of the sawyer camp and the instant they got up to follow the path to the river. He had glanced up and seen them. The first thing he noticed was the sun shining on her hair. It was braided and wound around her head like a crown, held in place by three long, silver hairpins. He knew this because he had seen them lying on the box in the wagon where she placed them every night. There were many crinkly little waves struggling to escape the braid. The skin on her face and arms was now an ivory tan after hours in the sun. Without even looking at her he could visualize the arch of her brows, the molding of her nose and mouth, the chiseling of cheekbones and chin. Every angle of her was just right. It amazed him, and yet he felt an undercurrent of anger, as though a trick had been played on him, when he found himself thinking those thoughts about her.

He had meant to consummate the marriage that first night, for she had agreed to the terms. He had made sure she fully understood his reasons for taking a wife. He had gone to the creek to bathe, and when he returned, she was in the wagon asleep. Every night since, for some reason that he himself didn't understand, he had waited until he was sure she was sleeping before he crawled in beside her. The last four nights had been agony. He had lain in torment for hours, wanting to reach for her, knowing that she would come to him, yet also knowing that inwardly she would cringe away. He had endured the terrible ache in his loins, aware that relief was a mere foot away if only he reached for it. The hours were long until the tiredness of his body released him from that torture and he went to sleep.

Thinking about it now, he pushed and pulled on the saw handle with vigorous strokes. The young black giant on the other end of the saw glanced at him questioningly. He had seen Farr's head turn more than once and his eyes flick over his young wife while she was sitting on the stump.

"Lawdy!" he murmured, his thick lips barely moving. "Mr. Quill's done gone 'n lost his heart as sure as the sun is comin' up in the mornin'. It didn't take him long, not long a'tall."

"Farr! Farr!" The sound of the nearly hysterical female voice overrode the buzz of the saw, the jingle of harnesses and the sound made by the dragging logs. Farr lifted his head in alarm. Then his heart leaped into his throat when he saw Amy running toward the camp. He jumped out of the pit, snatched up his rifle and ran to meet her.

"Farr! Farr! Come . . . quick."

"What is it? Where's Libby?"

"In . . . the river . . . She . . . Indian . . ." Amy was so breathless she could say no more.

Farr ran toward the river as if he were being chased by a pack of mad dogs. Libby! Libby! Sweet, sweet girl! He wasn't even aware of the thoughts that pounded in his head or the ugly, blasphemous words that poured from his mouth when he reached the river and paused to read the tracks. He saw the imprint of Liberty's shoes going south and turned and ran along the animal path. He came out onto the lip where Amy and Liberty had first seen the canoe. He found Liberty's discarded dress, picked it up, but then dropped it when he heard a faint mewing sound over the roar of the river.

He forced his way through a tangle of underbrush and saw Liberty lying on the grass. Her hair was wet and muddy and her sodden underclothes, covered with river slime, clung to her body. An Indian woman as wet and bedraggled as Liberty knelt beside her. The mewing sound had come from a baby who lay in a wet and muddied blanket beside the woman.

The scene of Fawnella lying in the dirt beside the cabin flashed through Farr's mind and the feeling of déjà vu caused a lump of fear to knot in his throat.

"*Machemenetoo sepe tschi, machemenetoo sepe tschi.*" The Indian woman was rocking back and forth on her knees, her hands clasped in front of her.

Devil river kill. The Shawnee words almost knocked the breath out of Farr. He fell on his knees, grasped Liberty's shoulders and turned her over. She was as limp as a rag. Wet and covered with mud, she was almost unrecognizable. He wiped the mud from her face with the palm of his hand and tried to feel for a pulse in her throat with his fingertips, but his own pulse was hammering so hard he couldn't feel anything. He bent his head and placed his ear on her breast. When he heard the strong beat of her heart he wanted to shout his relief. She was all right! His guess was that she had worn herself out and had either swooned or was in an exhausted sleep. He gathered her slim body up in his arms and held her tightly to his breast while waves of thankfulness flowed over him.

"*No nepwa!* Not dead, not dead," he repeated until he was sure the Indian woman understood.

Colby and Rain, with Mr. Washington and Amy behind him, broke through the tangle of bushes. Amy fell on her knees beside her sister.

"Is she all right? Farr! Farr! Libby's got to be all right!" she wailed.

"I think she is. I think she swooned."

"Amy said Libby jumped in the river and saved an Indian woman and baby," Colby said with disbelief. "My God! I've never known a woman who could swim."

Farr held Liberty against him, cradling her head with one hand, hiding her nakedness, because every line of her breast and belly were clearly visible through the thin material of her wet underclothes.

"Libby can," Amy said stoutly. "Libby can swim better than any man I ever saw." She looked pointedly at Rain. "Libby just jumped right in! Oh! I was so scared for her!"

Amy told about seeing the canoe come careening down the river, about the woman clinging to the tree and Liberty swimming out to take first the baby, and then going back for the mother. Liberty slept on during the telling. Farr held her and the men kept their eyes averted.

"Amy, get her dress and we'll get her up to the house. Rain, see if you can find out where this woman came from and tell her to come with us and get dried out."

Rain knelt down beside the Indian woman and placed his hand on her shoulder.

"Mother," he said in the language of the Shawnee. "Why were you on the river with your child?"

Surprised to hear the white boy speak her language so fluently, she gazed at him for a moment and then placed her hand over her heart before she spoke.

"My heart cries for my people." She picked up the baby and held it in her arms. "Four seasons ago I was taken by the white man to the country in the south. When he go in great canoe down big river, I hide myself for many days from white man who would make me slave. I walk until the moon change and come to little river where I found the canoe. Big rain come and swell the little river. I could not paddle against the great water. White-haired woman come like a fish and take my son. I think I die, but rejoice that my son would be in the land of the Shawnee. White-haired woman come back and I am here."

Rain briefly repeated her story to Farr who had understood snatches of it. Then he asked, "Why did you not walk, mother?"

She moved aside her sodden skirt to show him her foot. Her ankle was swollen to an enormous size and there was a deep, open gash on her heel.

"Lawdy!" Mr. Washington squatted on his heels to look at the foot. "It's fair swelled to bust!"

The Indian woman drew back slightly when the huge

black man with the silver rings in his ears and one in his nostrils came close to her.

"No wonder she took her chance on the river," Colby said. "She sure as hell couldn't walk on that foot. Were you headed for Prophetstown, mother?" he asked kindly. She understood, although Colby's skill at speaking her language was not nearly as good as Rain's.

"I am called Tecumapese. My brother is Tecumseh, the great chief of all the Shawnee," she said proudly. "I go to him and to my other brothers, the three who were born at one time."

"Thunderation! Did you get that, Farr?" Colby said in English. "She's a sister to Tecumseh and that other bast—"

"I got it." Farr cut in quickly not knowing how much English the woman understood. "This could make the difference whether or not we get burned out. But something's got to be done about her foot. Mr. Washington, Sugar Tree would know more about how to take care of it than anyone. Would you want to bring your wife here, or take the woman to your place?"

"Sugar Tree know." Mr. Washington nodded in agreement and stood. He fingered the silver ring in his nose as he studied the woman. "The Shawnee woman'll not want to come. She's scared of a black man."

"If she's been south she's seen one before. Rain, explain to her that Mr. Washington's wife is Shawnee and that she's his wife by choice. It will save time if you and Mr. Washington took her to Sugar Tree. If something isn't done soon, that foot might have to come off to save her life."

Rain began to explain to the woman that the black man would take her to his wife who would doctor her foot. At first she looked up at Mr. Washington with frightened eyes, but then gradually her face relaxed.

"Sugar Tree, his woman, is Shawnee. Sometimes she longs to visit with her people. She will make you welcome and use her skill to treat your foot. Sugar Tree's husband will carry you to their lodge, and I will carry your child."

Tecumapese nodded and trustingly handed Rain her son.

"That baby will be sick if it stays in those wet blankets!" Amy exclaimed. She had returned with Liberty's dress and Farr was slipping it over her sister's head. "You wait right here, Rain Tallman. Don't you move an inch with that baby until I can get you something dry to wrap it in." She darted back into the willows and returned a minute later with her white petticoat. Not the least embarrassed, she waved it at the red-faced Rain. "Give him to me and I'll wrap him in this. Men!" she snorted. "They don't know the first thing about babies."

She lifted the baby out of the wet blanket and placed him on the petticoat she had spread on the grass. Suddenly free of the blanket, he waved his tiny arms and legs. Amy cooed to him softly and carefully wrapped the naked little body in the dry petticoat.

"See. He's all right." She held the baby toward its mother so she could see his contented little face. "You be careful with him, hear?" she said sternly to Rain, and placed the child in his arms.

"What did you think I was going to do? Drag him by the heels?" he snarled. Rain waited while Mr. Washington picked the woman up in his arms as effortlessly as if she were a babe. Then, knowing she would be anxious about her child, he shot Amy an angry glance and led the way to the path.

"You two kids sure strike sparks off each other," Colby said with a chuckle.

"He thinks he knows everything!" Amy tossed her head and glared defiantly at Colby. "I know a lot more about babies than he does."

"I don't doubt that one bit."

"Then why did he act so smarty?"

"I didn't notice Rain bein' smarty. Did you, Farr?" Colby asked innocently.

"Well I did!" Amy said heatedly.

"Don't get all prickly, love. I'm on your side. I think you're much prettier than Rain. If you say he's smarty, I agree. As a matter of fact, I just might loosen a few of his teeth for being so smarty." Colby couldn't keep the grin off his face when he saw Amy's astonishment. When she realized he was teasing, her eyes began to dance, her lips tilted, and through a huge smile she stuck her tongue out at him.

"Oh, you!"

Farr got to his feet with Liberty in his arms. "Get my rifle, Colby. We've got to get Libby back to the house and out of these wet clothes."

Chapter
Fifteen

L iberty opened her eyes. She was being carried, cradled against a warm, naked chest. She wasn't dreaming because she could hear Amy chattering excitedly and Farr's deep voice close to her ear. She tilted her head and when her eyes began to focus properly, she saw his stern profile outlined against the blue sky. His cheek was covered with a day's growth of beard, all except for the white scar beside his mouth. Feeling the movement of her head on his shoulder, he looked down. Their faces were so close she could see the amber circles around the irises in his green eyes and a tiny mole amid the thick lashes on his lower lid.

"How did you get that scar?" When he didn't answer she realized the words had not come out, that she had merely croaked. She tried again. "Why are you carrying me?" Her throat was raw and her voice was strangely ragged.

"You swooned."

"I've never swooned."

"You did this time. Hush trying to talk. We'll be home soon."

Home. Events had happened so fast that she hadn't had time to settle in and think about Farr's home being her home. *Home.* A spot on the earth that was hers. Where she belonged. Where she had roots. It was a blessed, comforting word. Her mouth began to tremble, her eyes flooded, and she couldn't see.

"Why are you crying? You'll be all right. The woman and babe are safe too." His voice was strained. "Do you hurt? I was sure you didn't have any injuries other than being worn out." He had stopped walking. "Libby? Am I hurting you?" His question was anxious, caring.

"I'm all right."

"Then why are you crying?"

"I . . . I don't know."

"We'll be home soon," he repeated and started walking again. "You'll feel better when you get out of these wet clothes and get the river water out of your throat."

"I can walk."

"You've ruined your shoes. I'll have to make you some moccasins."

"But I'm so heavy."

"You're not heavy at all. Besides, I like carrying you . . ." The admission had come honestly, the last two words trailing as he looked away from her.

Amy danced alongside them, and Liberty didn't have time to ponder the meaning of Farr's words.

"Is she awake?"

"She's awake. Run ahead and tell Willa to heat some water and get a bed ready for her. Amy," he called, because she had taken off in a run toward the cabin, "tell Willa to make a hot rum toddy."

"I will. Oh, I will. Farr? I'm so glad Libby married up with you." Amy's voice rang with joy.

"So am I."

The words came out on a breath, and Liberty wasn't sure if she heard them or just wished them. She buried her face in the warm flesh of his neck and her hand inched up until her fingers slid into the soft hair at his nape. She savored his nearness, the strength of his arms, the warmth of his breath on her cheek, the strong beat of his heart against hers. Not for anything would she tell him that every bone in her body throbbed with pain and that her back felt as if it was being pierced by a thousand needles.

The instant Liberty's arm crept around his neck, Farr felt a wondrous spurt of happiness. There was far more to this woman he had taken for a wife than he had at first believed. He knew she was spunky, but to jump into a swollen river was something only one man out of a hundred would have done. All the odds were against her, but she hadn't stopped to think about that. She could easily have been sucked under and not come up until she was miles downriver or swept away by the tangle of trees washed down by the flood. He had no doubt the big wave the Indian woman and Amy spoke of was caused by the collapsing of a clay bank into the river.

His arms tightened around her as he thought of her narrow escape from death. She had brought such warmth and pride to his home with her loving, womanly ways. He liked her independent spirit and the way she refused to be put aside because she was a woman. Her coming had given the world a new brightness. His heart cried out to God that he didn't want to love this woman, that he couldn't endure the gut-crushing agony of losing her.

Amy and Colby had blurted out the story of what had happened at the river by the time Farr and Liberty reached the cabin. The place was abuzz with activity. Liberty, too weary to open her eyes, was almost asleep again when Farr lowered her to the bunk and knelt to take off her sodden, muddy shoes.

"She's worn out," he said huskily. "Wash her, Willa. And Amy, fetch a clean gown."

Suddenly Daniel launched himself at Farr, his small fists flailing, tears streaming down his cheeks. The surprise attack almost knocked Farr off his heels.

"Daniel! What—"

"You made her go to heaven!" he sobbed and continued to strike out at Farr until he caught the boy and held his small sobbing body in a tight grip.

"She's all right. Daniel? Do you hear me? Libby is all right. She's just tired."

Liberty roused. "What's the matter with Daniel?"

"He thinks you're dead," Amy said bluntly from where she stood at the end of the bunk.

"Oh, poor baby! Come here, love." Liberty held out her arms and when Farr released him, Daniel flung himself at her and clutched her tightly, burying his face against her. "Danny, darling. Don't cry. I'm all right. See? I'm all wet, but I'm all right." She stroked his hair and kissed his forehead.

"I don't want you to go to heaven," he sobbed.

"Don't worry, sweetheart. You'll not be left alone. You've got me and Farr and Amy and Willa. Don't cry, love." Liberty lifted her eyes, and found herself staring into Farr's serious, green ones. He knelt down beside the bunk.

"Daniel, we men have got to get out of here so Libby can get out of those wet clothes. How about coming with me down to the sawyer camp?" Farr gently pulled the little boy out of Liberty's arms. "Colby and I could use some help."

Liberty's eyes clung to Farr. The compassionate tone in his voice as he stood with his hand on the child's head almost moved her to tears again. Daniel looked up at Farr and nodded solemnly.

Later, when the three women were alone, Liberty stripped and washed the river mud from her body and hair. She was sore, but some of it was from the work in the garden, she reasoned. Amy had brought in a nightdress from the chest in the wagon where she was keeping her clothes, but Liberty sent her back for a dress and clean pantalets. She didn't intend to spend the rest of the day in bed being waited on. Willa had washed the mud from her shoes and set them beside the hearth to dry, so she put on a pair of Jubal's heavy stockings.

"Farr wanted you to stay in bed. He likes you a lot, Libby." Amy dropped Liberty's muddy clothes down in the bucket they had used to wash her hair. "Phew! That slimy old river mud stinks."

"He was concerned." Liberty fervently wished that what her sister said was true.

"It was more than that. You're his *wife*, for goodness sake! When I told him, he took off like a . . . scalded cat."

Willa giggled. "When did you ever see a scalded cat?"

"She's never seen one." Liberty talked without knowing what she was saying. The thought that perhaps Farr was fond of her sent her pulse skittering. "She was probably looking to see where Rain was and didn't even see Farr leave." She was toweling her hair and pushed it back out of her face so she could see her sister's.

"I wasn't any such thing," Amy protested heatedly, but she grinned saucily at Liberty and tossed the hair back over her shoulder. She had been primping more of late, Liberty observed, leaving her hair loose and trying to act more grown up.

"I suppose you didn't even know he was there," Willa teased.

"Of course I knew he was there, just like you know every time Colby comes near." Amy stood with her hands on her hips, smiling at Willa's red face. "I got you that time, Willa."

Amy, more than anyone, had been able to break through Willa's shyness, and the two girls had a real affection for each other. When the women were alone Willa was as open and talkative as any young girl her age, but when the men came in she found it difficult to enter the conversation. Not so Amy. She did enough talking for all of them.

Liberty sat in the rocking chair, her hair spread in a shining mass over her shoulders. For the first time in many years she felt as if she were home and among people who cared for her. Her eyes rested on the pine cupboard, the neatly made bunks, the table with the cloth spread over the necessaries in the center. One of Farr's buckskin shirts hung from a peg on the wall, and Juicy's pipe and tobacco were on the mantle next to the clock. This was where she wanted to spend the rest of her life, and maybe someday she and Farr—

She tried not to think that Farr's concern for her was any greater than he would have had for anyone. Although when he was carrying her, she had the feeling that it was lovingly and that he had held her closer to him than necessary. But no, she reasoned. She was tired and weepy and imagining it.

Evening came. The men didn't come up from the sawyer camp until almost dark, and supper was eaten by candlelight. As soon as Farr came in he asked Liberty how she was feeling, then sat quietly and listened while Colby teased her about being a silver fish.

"I've never known a woman who could swim."

"Why shouldn't a woman swim?" Liberty countered in a hoarse voice. "I think everyone should know how. You never know when you'll be thrown out of a boat or have to cross a river. My mother learned when she was a little girl, and she could outswim her brothers."

"Did she teach you?"

"No. My uncle did when I was very young. I grew up not being afraid of the water."

"It was lucky for Tecumapese that you did."

"You should have sent Amy for me," Farr said. "The river is treacherous when it's high."

"There was no time," Liberty said simply.

"Is the baby all right?" Amy looked directly across the table at Rain.

There was silence. Everyone waited for Rain to speak, but he continued to eat and ignored the question.

"Well, are you going to tell us or are you going to wait till you fill your hollow legs?" Colby asked and forked a piece of meat from the platter onto his plate.

"Tell you what?"

"If the baby is all right, and what did Sugar Tree say about Tecumseh's sister?"

"I guess the baby's all right, and she told Mr. Washington to go kill a chicken." Rain continued to eat, his eyes on his plate.

"Why did she tell him to kill a chicken?" Amy asked.

"To put on Tecumapese's foot." Rain glared across the table with a disgusted look on his face.

"What for?"

"To draw out the poison." Rain spoke as if he couldn't believe she didn't know why a dead chicken was put on a sore foot.

"How was I to know? Smarty."

"Humpt!" Juicy cleared his throat loudly. "If'n the

squaw's Tecumapese, she be Tecumseh's favorite sister. How are ya agoin' to get her up to Prophetstown, Farr?"

"I'm taking her," Rain said before Farr could speak. "I told her we'd go as soon as she can ride."

"I think you should take her, Rain. John Spotted Elk is there by now. You've been wanting to see him." Farr looked at young Rain and thought that with the training John had given him, he was as capable as any man he knew.

"Who's John Spotted Elk?" Amy was not to be put off by a shake of Liberty's head.

"He's a Shawnee who raised Rain." Farr spoke when he saw that Rain wasn't going to.

Rain lifted his dark eyes to Amy's. They were as cold as ice. "An *Indian*. A greasy, dirty, good-for-nothing redskin who has the gall to want to keep his own land." He spoke bitterly, and afterward there was a sudden quiet.

"Humpt! Now, take me," Juicy said matter-of-factly, "I ain't got me no use a'tall fer them triplet brothers of Tecumseh's. They ain't worth the powder to blow 'em up, but I'd stake my life on Tecumseh's word, if 'n he give it."

"I'm not askin' for any favors." Rain spoke in the same bitter tone and looked from one man to the other.

"We don't expect you to." Farr sat back and eyed his young friend, then stood. "Tecumseh will do what he thinks will help his cause despite any friendship with us, and we'll do the same. He'll expect us to. When you're finished, Rain, come into the storeroom. There are a few things I'd like to send to John."

The other men soon followed Farr into the storeroom, and the women began their nightly routine. Amy washed the children and got them ready for bed while Willa and Liberty cleaned up after the meal. Willa had taken over the milking and churned in the evening while Liberty set a pan of bread to rise. Between the three of them the work went fast.

As the time to retire drew nearer Liberty began to feel a little fluttering sensation in her stomach. Today a closer bond had been forged between her and Farr and she wanted to be alone so she could think about it.

The far-off twinkling stars were the only light in the sky when Liberty stepped out of the cabin and went to the wagon. These last days of May were warm, but the night breeze was cool. She shivered, crawled into the wagon, took her nightdress from the chest and fumbled with the buttons on her dress. She undressed hurriedly, then removed the pins from her hair and ran her fingers through the heavy masses. She usually brushed it before she went to bed, but tonight she had left her hairbrush in the cabin.

She snuggled down into the thick straw pallet and pulled the blanket up over her. She turned on her side and stared into a darkness no more confusing than her own thoughts. *Farr*. Farr saying that he liked carrying her. Farr telling her they would be home soon. Farr taking off her shoes. It was strange, she thought painfully, that she hadn't realized how lonely she had been until she met Farr. But how could she have missed what she didn't know? A few short weeks ago she had not known such a man as Farr existed. Now he was woven into the fabric of her life, making her aware of his every move, making her love him. Her mind stumbled over the word. *Love*. What did she know of loving a man? Did thinking of him during every waking moment mean she loved him? *Farr. Farr. Farr*. Tears of frustrtion and confusion trickled down from between her closed eyelids.

She awakened suddenly.

"Libby? Are you all right?"

"Farr..." Drowsy with sleep, his name came softly from her lips even as her hands reached for him.

"You called out. Were you dreaming?"

She remembered now. The dream had been lovely. Farr was kissing her. His lips were warm as they explored her mouth, her eyes, her throat. He was holding her, whispering loving words. The dream was so deeply real she didn't hesitate to reach for him now. Her hand came to rest at the back of his neck and then his arms, gentle but firm, closed around her.

"Libby?" Her arm tightened about his neck and he buried his face in her hair. "Oh, God, every night has been torture!

I've wanted to reach for you, hold you and kiss you for days." His voice was choked with the harsh sound of desire.

"Hold me. Kiss me, Farr..." A flood of sweet tenderness washed over her and she turned her face up to him, longing to kiss his lips with a sweet, lingering softness.

His lips covered hers and he murmured between kisses, "I want to hold you... I need your softness, your woman smell, your... warm hands on me. Libby, Libby, it's been so long, so lonely."

His mouth was sweet, his breath as cool as mint, his cheeks pleasantly rough against her face. His warm lips, at first tentative, became more demanding, and his long fingers entwined in her tousled hair to hold her to him. His mouth parted her lips, desperate in a search for fulfillment, and she clung to him, bonelessly melting into his hard body. Her skin tingled. Something deep within her stirred, bringing an ache to the nether regions between her legs. The kiss lasted endlessly as if they each found it impossible to end it. She moved restlessly closer to him, a hunger gnawing at her relentlessly.

So this was what it was like to kiss the man she loved! It was wonderful, she thought. The taste of him, the smell of him, the feel of him. She wanted to pull him inside her and keep him there forever.

His lips trailed down the side of her face to her throat. His heart was pounding violently against her soft breasts. He hadn't meant for this to happen tonight. She was tired and sore after her ordeal in the river, but when she turned to him and touched him he hadn't been able to help himself. Even as he was kissing her, a small voice in his head had told him to stop... that he would hurt her.

"Libby... I've got to know. I want you, but not unless you want me too. Do you... want me to leave you?" he whispered against her ear.

"Oh, please! Don't leave me, now!" Whatever came, this night was hers. The thought that followed her words was so tangible in her mind that she didn't know or care if she had voiced it. "Hold me, Farr. Hold me as if . . . you love me, just for tonight."

His kisses came upon her mouth, warm, devouring, fierce with passion. Liberty closed her eyes as the bliss of his kisses swept her every nerve with intense pleasure. She heard his harsh breathing in her ear, the hoarsely whispered words of how he had longed to reach for her. She murmured that she had wanted him, had waited for him. He trembled violently and groaned a muted, strangled, incoherent sound. Yes, she wanted this! She wanted to give herself completely. This was more wonderful, more frightening than anything she had ever imagined mating with a lover would be.

She felt briefly alone and lonely when he left her to slip out of his buckskins, but soon he was back under the blanket with her, bare and warm and pulling her into every curve of his body. Her arms went up to hold him closer as he leaned over her, her body strained against his. He covered her face with quick kisses, releasing his pent-up desire with each touch of his lips. He drew back as if trying to see her face.

"Am I hurting you?"

"No! No, sweet man. It's what I want." Liberty placed her palms on each side of his face and gazed at him with the soft light of love in her eyes. "Tell me," she whispered softly, "tell me what you want."

"Take off the gown," he breathed against her lips. "Come to me, all warm and soft and naked as the day you were born."

"Yes, love. Anything . . . for you. . . ."

His hands gently but insistently tugged the gown up and over her head. When she was free of it, he sank down against her, the hard nipples on her firm breasts snuggling into the hair on his chest, her soft flat belly against the hardness of his, the down between her legs pressed firmly to his aching, throbbing, elongated sex.

"Ah . . . you feel so good, so smooth, so soft."

Her lips moved along his cheek to find the corner of his mouth. He wanted to talk to her, but his lips could not seem to leave hers. He wanted to tell her how glad he was that she had come to his station, how pleased he was to have her for his wife. He wanted her to know that each night he had lain awake wanting her but was afraid she would receive him coldly, as if it were a duty. He wanted to say she was setting him on fire with desire for her, and he wanted to sleep with her in his arms every night for the rest of his life. But there was such a frenzied singing in his blood that grew so rapidly that the words beat against his brain and he never uttered them.

He rolled her on her back and pinned her with the length of his long body. Her head was caught in the crook of his arm and she couldn't move—not that she wanted to be anywhere but where she was. The part of him that throbbed so aggressively against her soft down was large and strong like the rest of him. It was all so sweet, so right, so natural. Her inexperienced hands stroked his furry chest, slid along muscles that quivered at her touch and down to his taut buttocks. Involuntarily his pelvis flexed as her hands moved over his hipbones, and she felt his sharp intake of breath. He moved his head down to kiss her breast and to worry her nipples with his lips; his breathing came fast and irregularly; his heart thudded above her.

"Little sweet woman . . ." It was as if he couldn't bear to linger another instant. He spread her thighs and lifted himself above her. She felt him large, hot and hard, pushing to slide into the warm cavern of her body. She became aware of a slow, gradual filling of that aching emptiness. He paused at the barrier that guarded her virginity, breathing raggedly. Then Liberty, afraid he would go no farther, pushed upward, seeking more of that glorious feeling. A sudden movement of his hips brought a pain-pleasure so intense that she cried out. "I had to . . . sweet little thing," he whispered raggedly. "I didn't know—"

She couldn't speak, but she kissed his face with wet passionate kisses and clutched at his buttocks to keep his throbbing warmth inside her. Lying beneath him, with his arms around her, a part of his body inside her, she wanted to cry out that a miracle had happened. Without him there she would never be whole again.

His mouth searched the sweetness of her lips, and his tongue searched for entry. Her hands moved impatiently over him, wanting to know and feel every inch of his body. Her legs, knees bent, rested on his and rubbed gently against his hair-roughened thighs. Her body and mouth were offered to him to do with as he wanted. His hands and his lips moved over every part of her he could reach. The deeply buried heat in her body flared out of control and stinging waves of pleasure traveled like quicksilver up and down her spine.

"I love you," she screamed inside and her body twisted as he took her to the edge of the world. They fell off together, locked tightly in each other's arms. Vaguely she heard his muffled cry and felt his body shudder as the hardness inside her jerked with release, sending a flow of warm soothing fluid where a moment ago there had been a pulsing, aching emptiness.

Wave after wave of pure pleasure washed over Farr. He felt as if he were one being with the woman joined with him. He had been lonely, a man burning for contentment, and here it was, all the joy he had thought would never be his. He poured himself into the sweet woman beneath him, groaning, shuddering, striving to reach her very soul with his possession. His heaving body was bound to hers in total consummation with both physical and emotional ties.

Afterward, still joined to her, he turned on his side, bringing her with him. They lay face to face, foreheads touching, breathing the same air. His arms and legs were wrapped around her, her arms about him. He moved his face so that his nose lay alongside hers, and his lips could reach her mouth. She hardly had strength to return his kisses. She was weak and lifeless in body, but her heart was so flooded with happiness and her spirit soaring so high that she wanted him to know how it was with her.

"I've not been with a man before. My husband never

touched me. You were the first, and you were... wonderful."

"I'm glad I was first. Although it would have made no difference." Tenderly, he pushed the damp hair from her face. He was filled with an indescribable joy and contentment even though, to his surprise, he was still fully extended inside of her. He placed his palm on her bottom and pressed her tightly against him. Reverently he kissed her forehead, and then her lips. "It will be a while before I get my fill of you," he whispered against her cheek. He flexed his hips, his palm on her bottom holding her to him, and she could feel the tip of him touching her womb. "Does that hurt?"

"No. It feels... good."

"It does to me too." His lips closed over hers. "You're a lot of woman for such a little thing," he breathed after his had almost taken her breath away. He moved her up until his mouth could reach her breast and he could suck her taut nipple. She stirred and he laughed softly as he pulled her down so he was buried deeply within her once again, and his mouth was once more on her lips. "Do you like mating with me? Do you enjoy this thing a husband does to his wife?"

"I'm not supposed to like it, but I do." She arched her back so she could see his face. "Farr? Do you mind that I like it?"

His laugh was soft and joyous. "Oh, Libby, Libby, you are a wonder. I could almost like Lenning for chasing you out of New York. Dear woman, you are what every man dreams of."

She set her teeth on the softness of his upper lip and bit gently. This freedom with him was making her giddy. Her lips pressed gently, then fiercely to the scar beside his mouth, and then slowly, steadily, he began to move within her, probing, writhing. Her arms locked around his neck and he moved both hands down to grasp her buttocks, moving her with him, pressing up while he pushed her down, until she thought the tip of him was touching her very soul. The pleasure went on and on, building until they were riding high on the soaring, swelling tide of rapture.

At the end Farr sucked gently at the flesh of her slender neck, and she smoothed the tumbled hair back from his face with gentle fingers. He fell away from her, then gathered her tenderly into his arms and held her to his strong, relaxed body, stroking his hand over her breast.

The clock inside the cabin struck two o'clock. The lassitude of plenty, the sense of a hunger fed caused a sigh of contentment to come from Farr.

"I want to tell you about Fawnella." He held Liberty cradled in his arms and whispered the quiet words against her hair.

"Are you sure you want to? She was part of your life a long time ago."

"Yes, I want to tell you."

"Then tell me," she whispered, kissing his ear.

"It was the first year that Juicy and I came to stay. We had been here before, but I had to go back to Carrolltown so I could go to school with Colby. Juicy waited until I got back from Virginia and we came on together. We had found the salt spring and decided to build our cabin in this bend on the Wabash. We had friends among the Shawnee. John Spotted Elk, the man who raised Rain, is a good friend of Sloan Carroll. Juicy and I had known him for years. One day I heard shouts down by the river. I found a young girl—"

Farr paused, as if almost wishing he hadn't started the story. Liberty waited, rubbing her palm soothingly over his cheek, trying to let him know that she understood how difficult it was for him.

He started talking again, telling her how he had killed the trappers and taken the terrified girl. He told her that he named the mute girl Fawnella because she reminded him of a shy, silent little fawn. He left nothing out in the telling. They had loved each other with all the passionate love of their young hearts, and when she died, the pain was so deep that he had vowed never to love another woman, never to expose himself to the agony of losing her.

"I realize now that my time with Fawnella was a special time, but that I can have other times in my life equally as special. Tonight, when you came to me openly and honestly, wanting me as I wanted you, was a special time. I had not met another woman I wanted to marry until I met you. Be patient with me, Libby. At times I have such a guilty feeling for wanting you. I feel that . . . somehow I'm betraying Fawnella, for if I'd not left her alone that morning, the Frenchman wouldn't have come back."

"You can't blame yourself. If Fawnella loved you, she wouldn't blame you. She'd want you to be happy."

"She loved me," he whispered.

"You're an easy man to love."

"I'll be good to you, take care of you—"

"I know that. Farr," she ignored her jumping heart and steadied her voice, "are you saying you can never . . . love me like you loved Fawnella?" Her breath caught, but she had to voice the question.

"No! I'm not saying that." His arms tightened. "I'm saying what I feel for you is . . . different. I'm different. I've been over the mountain, as Juicy says. I've been to New Orleans, seen the sights—"

"I understand. Really I do."

"I didn't fall desperately in love with you the moment I saw you as I did with Fawnella. My feeling for you grows as I learn more about you. I thought my heart would burst today when I saw you lying on the grass. And I thought, Oh God, how can I bear to lose her? Let's take each day as it comes, Libby. This is all so new."

"For me too."

Her kissing lips traced his brow, and she pulled his face into her breast, felt his lips take up the kissing, felt his hands on her hips, her belly, her thighs.

"Do you think you could . . . learn to love me?" He asked the question hesitantly, like a small boy.

Liberty's arms tightened and she wanted to say she didn't

have to learn. But it was too soon to lay all her feelings out in the open. Her fear of rejection was too great.

"You're an easy man to love, Farrway Quill."

Her answer seemed to satisfy him. His caressing hands lifted her to him. This time she took all of him in one long, gentle, sweet thrust, giving him comfort . . . and love.

Chapter
Sixteen

L iberty wakened when Farr removed his arm from beneath her head.

"You don't have to get up yet. Wait until I build up the fire," he whispered.

The first gray of dawn could be seen through the open end of the wagon. She watched him dress, his body silhouetted against the pale light. His body was more intimately known to her now than her own had ever been before. She lay there reveling in the new, wondrous feeling of belonging to him and watched him slip silently out into the new morning.

Later, he returned just as silently and placed a pan of warm water on the tailgate of the wagon. The damp cloth felt good against her aching femininity, and she marveled at the thoughtfulness of this woodsman she had married.

She washed and dressed. In the dim light of morning she looked down at her body. It had taken one night with Farr to make her aware of the gift God had given when he created man and woman and gave them the urge to procreate. She was a woman now, in every sense of the word. Her body had known the sharp thrust of her man's body; he had possessed every inch of it and she had given it freely. Nothing in her life up to now could compare with that experience. Even now her heart hammered with anticipation of what the coming nights with Farr could bring.

She smoothed, coiled and pinned her hair on the top of her head, wishing all the while for the hairbrush she had left in the cabin. Before she climbed out of the wagon, she checked to be sure her dress was buttoned properly and that her apron was reasonably clean.

She paused in the doorway of the lighted cabin. Willa was moving silently between the workbench and hearth. Farr turned when she entered. Their eyes caught and held. His green ones were warm and shining and looked long and deliberately into hers. Liberty thought she would stop breathing.

"Morning." Amused smile lines fanned out from the corners of his eyes and deepened the creases on each side of his mouth.

"Morning," she murmured, then spoke to Willa. "I'll make corn cakes if we have any sorghum left."

Willa lifted the crock jug with the cork stopper. "It's enough."

Liberty's hands were shaking as she poured water into the cornmeal. She could feel Farr's eyes and couldn't prevent her own from seeking them. When he smiled at her with amused tenderness, the thrill reached all the way to her toes, and her heart leaped joyfully.

It was the same all through the day. When he was near, their eyes caught and clung as if they shared a glorious secret. That night he came to the wagon shortly after she did, gathered her in his arms and whispered that he was a greedy man. He laughed and told her that the night before had only whetted his hunger for her. Slowly and sensuously they caressed each other's bodies without the shyness of the night before. He took his time with her quite deliberately, making the pleasure last until she was filled with a driving physical need which drummed through her veins like thunder, and she was conscious only of a need to please him, please herself.

Afterward, he pulled her snugly into the curve of his body, curled around her like a contented kitten, and slept.

Several weeks passed without any word from Elija or Stith Lenning. Liberty seldom thought of either of them. She had never been so happy. It seemed as if a heavy weight had been lifted from her heart. Farr filled every corner of it now. She no longer carried the heavy responsibility for Amy alone. She and Farr would take care of Amy. Liberty's world was suddenly bright and shining. She felt laughter bubbling up inside her at the most unusual times, and smiles of pure delight made her face radiant. She even pushed to the back of her mind the thought that her father and Stith were planning something evil. There was no room for anything inside her now but the wish to make a home for Farr and to anticipate her time alone with him.

George Thompson sent his black man and a mule to help with the stockade. Edward Brown sent his eldest son, a sturdy lad of fifteen who Amy said looked like a possum. He cast his shy glances at her, but she only had eyes for Rain, who ignored her as completely as she would allow. A day later the Palmer boy arrived and another man from the Sufferite community. The Sufferites refused to eat with them, and so Willa and Liberty cooked a hearty noon meal for eight men with enough left over for supper.

It was the middle of the morning. A thick stew was bubbling in the pot, fresh bread was cooling on the workbench, and the suet pudding was ready to dish up. Liberty was ripping the skirt from one of Amy's dresses so that Willa could cut a dress for Mercy. The little girl was playing happily with a rag doll Amy had made from a stocking. Amy and Daniel had gone down to the sawyer camp.

Willa came from the spring with a fresh bucket of water.

"Libby," she said breathlessly as she set the bucket on the shelf. "Militiamen coming."

"Militiamen?" Liberty got up and went to the door.

A group of horsemen were on the road. The two in front were officers. She could tell by the plumes on their tricorn leather hats, the bright blue coats and light trousers. The eight that followed in sets of twos were regular militiamen. There was no mistaking the two riders that followed. Her father rode the mare she had given him and Stith Lenning was mounted on a big gray. Apprehension knotted her stomach. She watched, expecting the group to turn up the lane to the house, but they continued on by.

"They're going to the sawyer camp." Willa's hand reached out and clasped Liberty's arm. "Amy's down there."

An icy hand squeezed Liberty's heart. "That's right! Oh, Willa! I've got to get down there."

"Go around the side of the house and through the trees. They'll not see you until you're almost there. Hurry!"

Liberty ran. She lifted her skirts to her knees and ran as if the devil were after her. Fear of what her father and Stith had in mind for Amy drove her recklessly on and caused her to disregard the stones and sticks that bruised her feet through the soles of the thin slippers.

The work in the pit had stopped. Farr and Colby had climbed out and were wiping the sweat and sawdust from their faces. Amy was coming back through the trees with Mr. Washington, Daniel riding on his shoulder. Her sister was laughing up at the huge black man, and Daniel was giggling and holding onto his topknot. Liberty saw all of this before she reached the camp.

She reached it slightly ahead of the party that came around by way of the road. Her face was red from exertion, and her hair had come loose from her braids, causing it to kink and curl down over her forehead. She went directly to Farr; her eyes met his and clung. His smile of cheerful reassurance was gentle, easygoing, half amused. He reached out his hand and she put hers in it.

"I thought a bear was after you. You can run fast when you have to, Liberty Bell." He had taken to calling her that. The light banter eased her anxiety. Just being with him made her feel confident.

"I had to get to you. Oh, Farr. What'll we do if Papa has come for Amy?"

"If he has we'll take care of it when the time comes. Don't worry."

They waited together for the horsemen to approach and together walked out to meet them.

Farr had known the militiamen were at Lenning's since

Donald Luscomb's brother had arrived that morning. The thin, wiry youth, called Peewee for so long he had almost forgotten that his real name was Melvin, had told Farr the patrol had spent the night at the Luscomb homestead. He had come as far as Lenning's with them. Farr had expected them to arrive earlier.

He had met Captain Nathan Heald when he first arrived from Fort Wayne to take command of Fort Dearborn, and he was curious to know why he was leading a patrol this far south. And he knew Lieutenant Hammond Perry.

The column stopped and a sergeant barked orders in a drill voice. Two men came to hold the horses while Captain Heald and the lieutenant dismounted. The captain's blue coat was faced with red, his leather hat trimmed with a roach of bearskin, cockade and a feather. An epaulet graced his right shoulder, establishing his rank as captain.

He came toward Farr and Liberty, clutching his sword to keep it from thrashing at his leg. He extended his gloved hand long before he was close enough to shake. His dark eyes made eye contact with Farr's and remained there.

"Howdy, Quill."

"Hello, Captain."

The captain's eyes brightened when he turned to Liberty. He hurriedly whipped off his hat and made a sweeping bow.

"Your servant, ma'am."

Farr introduced Liberty as his wife, and Captain Heald voiced his hearty good wishes. He scarcely acknowledged his lieutenant who came up beside him.

"Hello, Quill." There was disinterest in the voice of the lieutenant who was no taller than Liberty.

"Hello, Perry." Farr's greeting was barely civil.

Perry? Liberty's eyes went first to Farr and then to the face of the lieutenant. It was a thin face, dominated by piercing eyes set close together under brows that met over his nose. His lips were shaped like a woman's, full and red. The thin, reddish brown whiskers on his chin were an effort to disguise the fact that it receded sharply, giving his face the shape of an upside down bowl. He was small of stature, but stood with his shoulders held rigid and his head tilted far back as if he were looking down his nose. Could this be Jubal's brother?

"This is Hammond Perry, Libby. Your late husband's brother."

Liberty saw a look of irritation flit across Hammond's face. She held out her hand and he touched it briefly.

"Hello, Hammond. I've heard so much about you from Jubal and read the letters you sent to him. That's why—"

"Spare me the details. I've heard all about it from your father," he said in a tone that clearly relegated her to an inferior position.

Liberty was taken aback by his hostility, but made another effort to be friendly to the brother of the man who had been so kind to her.

"Then you know about Jubal's death. I'm sorry—" His only response was to wave his hand as if it were unimportant, but Liberty continued determinedly. "Jubal was a good man. We were married for almost a year."

"Carroll told me all that. You married *Jubal*? Name of a cow! Why? All he knew to do was whine and make pots, and who cares if jugs have two stripes or one? He had no business coming out here. You had no business insisting that he come. I'm not surprised he died on the way."

The unfeeling attack on Jubal fanned the anger that had been building in Liberty since Hammond's first words. It blossomed until she forgot the captain, forgot to be polite for Farr's sake, forgot everything but the need to defend Jubal. She placed her hands on her hips and faced his brother.

"Jubal was the best potter in New York State, and if you weren't so square-headed and full of yourself, you would know it. He made beautiful things and he didn't *whine*. He had dreams too. He had as much right to do what he wanted to do as you do."

"Don't you mean what *you* wanted, *Mrs*. Quill? My brother was weak as water. I knew it, my father knew it, and *if* you married him, you knew it. I imagine he was like clay in your hands. He didn't have an ounce of manhood," he finished scathingly.

"Don't you dare say that about Jubal, you cocky, little, strutting popinjay! He was a man—a good man—and he died trying to get to you. How disappointed he would have been if he had lived to see you." Liberty could use her voice to cut as deep as her words. She did that now.

"If you cared so much for him, *Mrs.* Quill, why did you remarry before he was cold in the ground?" His voice was fringed with sarcasm.

"Why you arrogant son of a bitch! That is none of your business!"

"Now, now." Captain Heald lifted his gloved hands. He glanced to see if Quill was going to interfere. He saw that he was watching his pretty wife, his eyes warm with admiration. Beneath the softness of this young woman, the captain decided, there was steel and determination. He liked her immediately. She reminded him of his Rebekah.

"Name of a name! Hush up, Libby. Ain't ya got no manners no more? Since ya come here, ya talk like a tavern wench." Elija, unsure of his reception with the men working on the stockade, had stood with the troops that had gathered to hear and gawk at Liberty, who was the prettiest woman most of them had ever seen. He confronted Hammond Perry. "She jist ain't been herself since we up 'n left civilization. She don't mean nothin'—"

"Shut up, Papa!" Liberty said sharply. "I do mean something. Don't you dare apologize for anything I say."

"Now, Libby—"

"And don't be 'now Libbying' me, either. I don't have to account to you for what I say and do. I'm accountable to my *husband* and that is all! Jubal loved this little pip-squeak and he isn't fit to lick Jubal's boots. I say Hammond Perry is a weasel; a mouthy little rooster who talks big and does nothing! Compared to Jubal he is lice and cabbage."

"Quill! Ain't ya agoin' ta do somethin'?" Elija's squeal was like that of a stuck pig. He groaned and sagged against his horse when he saw Farr smile proudly down at Liberty.

"What do you want me to do?" he asked when he looked back at Elija's worried face. "Liberty has the right to say what she wants to say. Besides, I agree with her. I always thought Perry was a strutting little something-or-other. Rooster fits. Weasel fits. And compared to almost anyone I know, he *is* lice and cabbage."

Hammond's face turned brick red; he clenched his fists and swallowed convulsively. There was a titter, followed by a low murmur of laughter. Hammond swung around, his hand on his sword, and the laughter ceased.

"It looks as if we're getting off on the wrong foot here, Quill. We need this fort. What we don't need is to fight among ourselves. There was a stiff Indian fight up near Rock Island last month. That's Black Hawk's country and he means to keep the whites out of it. The Sac and Fox will be pushed south before spring. When that happens the whole territory will be a battleground," Captain Heald said.

"It seems to me that talking peace would be easier than fighting."

"I agree. There are men in Kaskaskia who are working on getting Illinois admitted to statehood. When that time comes we'll have plenty of backing and the government can work at a permanent peace." His eyes roamed the camp. "You're making good time here. Any Indian trouble?"

"No. Don't expect any."

"Lenning said three canoes of warriors came downriver yesterday. Lenning fired on the canoes, but failed to hit anyone. I told him to come to you if he sees any more war parties."

"For God's sake! I wondered who was doing the shooting. The 'war party' Lenning fired on was a hunting party of Ottawa, as peaceful a tribe as any in this territory. It's damn fools like him that will start a war."

"Major Taylor has put Lieutenant Perry in charge of the lower Illinois Territory, Quill." Nathan Heald dropped the news into the conversation smoothly.

"Oh, my God! Has Zack Taylor lost his mind?"

"It isn't my place or yours to question Taylor's or the governor's decisions."

"I'll question it if it's my life and that of my family he endangers by making a foolish judgment." Farr spoke with hard conviction.

Captain Heald studied him for a moment before he spoke again. "I would appreciate it if you would cooperate with Lieutenant Perry—for the good of the territory."

"It is impossible to cooperate with Lieutenant Perry. He can be in charge of whatever he wants as long as he keeps his nose out of my business. I'm in charge here, and he'd better not forget it." Farr spoke quietly. He didn't need to shout to make his point.

"Now look here, Quill. Are you putting yourself above Major Taylor?" Hammond stood with his back straight and his hand on his sword. He had regained his composure, and feeling he had the backing of Captain Heald, he spoke sternly. "He's depending on me to see that this work is done here."

"Look here, Perry. The governor is a busy man and so is Zack Taylor. Usually I respect their judgment. But not this time. I'd not put you in charge of building a privy. I don't like you. I have never liked you since I heard that you shot two innocent Indians to teach the rest of the tribe a *lesson*. As a matter of fact, I hate your guts." Farr pointed his finger in Hammond's face. "You listen and listen good, because I'll say it only one time. Do your soldiering someplace else. You come nosing around here and I'll roast your butt over hot coals and send you downriver on a pike. Do you understand?"

"Damn you . . . Why, who the hell do you think you are to threaten me?" Hammond sputtered.

"Lieutenant, take the men and set up a noon camp." The captain issued the order crisply.

Hammond gave Farr a murderous look and yelled out orders to the sergeant for the troops to mount up. Farr saw the glance that passed between Hammond and Stith Lenning as the troops wheeled their horses and moved back toward the road.

"Would you be so kind as to excuse us, ma'am? I must have a private word with your husband." Captain Heald smiled charmingly and tilted his head toward Liberty.

She returned the smile. "Certainly. And captain, we would be pleased if *you* dined with us." She pointedly refused to invite Hammond.

"Thank you, Mrs. Quill. I'll be delighted to accept your hospitality."

Without even looking at her father, Liberty went to where Amy stood with Mr. Washington. Farr watched, as did the captain: Farr to see that Elija and Lenning didn't corner her before she reached the others, and the captain because he was impressed with her beauty, her bearing, and her independent spirit.

"You've got yourself some woman, Quill. It seems she takes to pioneer life, just as my Rebekah did. She's a spirited woman too."

Captain Heald put his hat back on his head and walked a few paces back from where Stith and Elija lounged. After the troops left, the other men had gone back to work with the exception of Mr. Washington, Juicy and Colby. They stood ready, as if Amy and Liberty would need protection.

"You've got yourself some trouble, Quill. Perry will go back to Vincennes and tell the major and Harrison what you said."

"I hope he does. I intend to send them a message myself. That little ass will start a war as sure as shooting."

"I'm inclined to agree, but that's off the record. You've got other troubles too. Carroll says you're holding his young girl. He says you've threatened him if he goes near her. He seems to think you want her for yourself along with her sister."

Farr laughed. "Do you believe that, Captain?"

"No, but Perry does. He can command his men to take the girl and turn her over to her father."

"There'll be a fight if he does. The girl is twelve years

old, for God's sake! She's lived with her sister all her life. Carroll wanted Liberty to marry Lenning; she refused and married me. Lenning wants to get back at Liberty by taking Amy. Carroll will let him marry the child thinking he'll have a soft spot for the rest of his life. I'm telling you now, Heald, Lenning isn't going to get his hands on that girl."

"Hell, Quill, you can't stand off ten men."

"You, too, Heald?"

"No, goddamnit! Nine men."

"Would you want your twelve-year-old sister taken to bed by a man like Lenning? Why, the bastard's as big as an ox. He'd split her in half!"

"You know I wouldn't. I'd kill the son of a bitch first!" Heald put emphasis to his words by slapping his gloves against his palm. "But she's not my sister, and the law is the law. The old man can give her to wife. It's the custom back East, and as wrong as it is it's the custom here."

"I'm not going to let him have Amy," Farr said firmly.

"I don't want to go against you, Quill, but what the hell am I to do?"

"You can give me a day to work things out. You can tell those two bastards over there to get the hell off my land and not to come back unless they've got guns in their hands. Give me this time to do what I can, or I'll take my family, which includes Amy, and pull out. Mr. Washington will go with me. Without us, who'll build your fort? Do you want to go back and tell Harrison that there'll be no fort on the Wabash?"

"You know where to grab a man where the hair's short, don't you, Quill? Well, I can't say that I blame you. What do you plan to do? Kill Lenning? Or Carroll?"

"It wouldn't cause me to lose a wink of sleep if it comes to that. I'll do it if I have to. But I've something else in mind. I'm not wanting to kill my wife's father, even if he is a low-down, lazy bastard."

"All right. I'll take the patrol on downriver. We'll be back tomorrow. Is that time enough?" Heald asked.

"Plenty. But there's something else you can do—for the good of the territory."

"What's that?"

"You can talk to Will Harrison and tell him he's made a mistake giving Perry so much authority. If he really wants peace with the tribes, he'd better keep Perry in Vincennes."

"I've already thought of that. I'll throw your name into the argument if it's all right with you. Will has great respect for your judgment."

"Tell him just what I said I'd do if Perry comes nosing around here. If he wants this fort built, he'd better keep him away."

"I'll do that. Now, about this fort. Harrison plans to send two boatloads of ore to feed the furnace in the shot tower along with two boatloads of supplies."

"I'll be ready for them in two months' time. We'll build the barracks and shot tower first. It will give us some protection while we're building the stockade. In two weeks' time I hope to have a crew of twenty men working full time."

"It's more than I thought you could do. Be careful with Lenning. From what I've observed of him in this short time I'd say he's a vindictive man."

"He may not stay. I've seen his kind come and go."

"I'd bet my last button he'll stay. He's all keyed up to open a trading post and build a town around that place he's got up there. He's forting it up too. It appears he's got the money to do it. Be careful of him."

"I mean to be. You'd better warn him about firing on everything that's got a red skin or he'll be burned out and scalped before the summer's over. What's more, he'll cause a lot of innocent people to be killed."

"I'll have a talk with him."

"Have you seen or heard anything about a fellow by the name of Hull Dexter?"

The captain thought for a moment, then shook his head. "No, I've not heard the name. Is he wanted for something?"

"I want him. He ran out on a train of four wagons and left the pilgrims to be slaughtered by river pirates. As far as I could tell there wasn't a shot fired. That young boy there with Mr. Washington is the only one who lived, and that was because his mother threw him into the berry bushes. Four women raped and murdered, four men and two children killed."

"He might not have run out. He may have escaped to save his own skin."

"I think he set them up."

"God in heaven! I'm constantly amazed at the uncivilized behavior of these people. How could he have done that to white people?"

"Any people, Captain Heald," Farr corrected. "Indians are people too."

"If I hear anything about him I'll send word."

"I mean to kill him."

Nathan Heald nodded. "Just be sure he did what you think he did."

He went over to speak with Elija and Stith, and Farr took that opportunity to ask Juicy and Mr. Washington if they would escort Liberty and Amy back to the cabin.

Lenning was angry. Elija was talking excitedly, waving his arms and casting hurried glances at his daughters as they went up through the woods with their escort. Farr and Colby watched until Elija and Stith mounted up and rode away.

"Old Elija is fit to be tied and that other fellow's real mad. The captain was reading them the book!" Colby grinned happily. "What are you going to do about that other cocky little bastard, Farr? I've never liked him. I don't think the captain likes him much either."

"Just what I said I'd do." Farr smiled at his friend. "Only maybe not in that order. He'll throw his weight around, but he'll get someone else to do his dirty work. I'm thinking that someone is Lenning."

"What can he do?"

"He could burn us out, try to kill me, or send his hench-man to do the job."

"Goddamn!"

"I hear he's forting up his place. I guess he plans to stay there if the war comes this way."

"Ha! He'd play hell protecting any place with a handful of men once Tecumseh goes on the warpath."

"He'll have to find that out for himself—if he lives that long. Come on, let's cut a few more boards before nooning."

With the help of Mr. Washington and Juicy, tables were set up in the yard for the men, and at Willa's insistence she and Amy waited on them so that Liberty could dine with Farr and the captain. As soon as she reached the cabin with the news they would have a guest for dinner, Liberty brought out a white linen cloth and reset the table. When she was satisfied the cabin was as neat and homey as she could make it, she went to the wagon and changed her dress. She brushed her hair and coiled it on top of her head, added a brooch to the neck of her dress, and then went back to the cabin. She wanted to make a good impression for Farr's sake.

The captain was suitably impressed. Smiling quietly, she served him and Farr and then took her place at the table. She was a gracious hostess but did not enter into the conversation unless asked a question or spoken to directly. When they had finished eating Captain Heald turned to her.

"My wife and I were married just a year at Fort Wayne, Mrs. Quill. We married in May, and our wedding journey was a brisk horseback trip over the spring prairies to Chicago. We traveled by compass over the grasslands and made good time, six days. Rebekah is a sturdy, spirited woman, who, like her uncle, Captain William Wells, took naturally to the wilderness. She likes the wild and lonely post of Fort Dearborn."

"I would like to meet her. Perhaps when peace comes to the territory you can make another journey, south this time, to visit us."

The captain laughed. "I don't know, Quill. With the two

of them, there might be more fireworks than we could handle."

Farr looked into Liberty's shining eyes, and what she saw in his quickened her pulses and set her heart to singing. There was a proud fondness in the depth of his green eyes. His lids narrowed slightly, yet he continued to look at her. His eyes possessed a mysterious magnetic force, and she couldn't look away. He smiled, and she felt immersed in a sumptuously delicious joy. She felt as if she were floating several inches above her chair.

The captain laughed again, and the spell was broken. "You two may have married in haste, but I'm certain your union is blessed with love since you have eyes only for each other. Excuse me, ma'am. I wish to speak with Colby Carroll. I know his father, Sloan Carroll, of Carrolltown. It will give your husband time to reassure you about . . . things that, er, trouble you."

Farr and Liberty stood, and Farr went to the door with the captain. Liberty took the silver candlestick she had set on the table for a decoration to the mantle. Farr came up behind her, wrapped his arms about her waist, and rested his chin on the top of her head. Liberty felt her insides warm with pleasure as she looked at their reflection in the glass door of the clock. . She had never before experienced this melting, letting go sensation that invaded her innermost being when she was with him.

"You were beautiful, and I was proud." He bent his head and pressed his face into the curve of her neck.

She turned in his arms and slipped hers about him. Her warm, moist lips traced the line of his jaw and moved upward to settle very gently on his mouth where they moved with sweet provocation. Love and tenderness welled within her. They stood quietly as if to absorb the feel of each other. When Farr pulled back, he tilted her chin with his finger so that he could see her face.

"I must go, but I'll be back in a little while. We've got a lot to talk about."

"Papa and Stith want to take Amy, and they're going to get Hammond to help them."

"Are you a witch, my pretty? How did you know?"

"It's what they would do. What can we do?" Fear made her eyes cloud and her mouth tremble.

"You're not to worry. You've got me now. That's my job."

"Oh, Farr! I'm so glad I didn't go to Vincennes to find Hammond. He's horrid. A real mule's ass!"

Farr chuckled. "I wasn't going to let you go. I was even glad when Lenning took over the Shellenberger place so you couldn't go there."

"Hold me for just a minute. You are the most wonderful man!" Her voice was weakened by the depth of her emotion.

When she looked up into his face again, there was a mischievous sparkle in his eyes.

"I hope you'll always think so. Remember what Colby said on the day we married?"

"What? Oh . . . about your feet?"

"It's true."

"Oh, you! Farr? Don't make me laugh. I don't feel like laughing, I want to cry. Poor little Amy."

Amy seemed to be blissfully unaware of what was going to happen. She flirted with the Luscomb boy, thinking to make Rain jealous, but he ignored both of them. Peewee got so flustered he forgot to eat and went back to the sawyer camp still hungry.

"Amy, stay in the house with Libby, or close to the house." Farr was on his way back to the sawyer camp and passed Amy swinging Mercy on the sack swing. "Those soldiers haven't seen a girl as pretty as you for a long time."

"It isn't the soldiers, is it, Farr? It's Papa. He's trying to take me to Stith's?"

"Yes, he's trying. But you don't have to go if you don't want to."

"I don't want to ever leave you and Libby. I hate Papa!"

"You should feel sorry for him. He's lost the love of two beautiful daughters." Farr put his hand on her head, and Amy leaned her forehead against him.

"I'll do what you say, Farr."

"Good girl."

Farr walked away and Rain ran a short way to catch up with him. "What's that all about?"

Farr's surprise at his young friend's question was not reflected in his face. Rain was troubled. He never asked questions or pried into other people's affairs.

"I thought you didn't like Amy."

"She'd be all right if she didn't talk so much."

"She's just trying to get your attention."

"Why me?"

"I don't know. Why any girl would choose you over Pee-wee is beyond me."

"Stop joshin', Farr. Old man Carroll and Lenning are up to something. Is it about Amy?"

"Yes, it's about Amy. It's something we've all got to talk about."

Chapter
Seventeen

Time passed slowly after the men went back to work. Amy came in and sat in the rocking chair with Mercy while Willa and Liberty washed the dishes. Soon Mercy was asleep. Amy placed her on the bunk and went back to the chair.

"Papa doesn't love me," she said quietly. "Why doesn't he love me, Libby? I tried to be good. You told me I was a good girl when I was little."

"Oh, honey, you were good. You are good and sweet and helpful now. I couldn't ask for a better sister. It isn't anything you've done or not done. And Papa loves you in his own way. He feels that life has cheated him. That's why he talks big, builds himself up, and takes credit for things he's had nothing to do with. It's the way he *wants* to be, but it isn't in him to do those things."

"He could if he'd try. He thinks everyone owes him something. Farr doesn't think that, or Uncle Juicy. I just never thought Papa would give away his own little girl so he'd not have to work."

"I don't know what to say, Amy. I don't want you to hate Papa, but there's no way I can defend him." Liberty wanted to cry for her little sister. Amy was hurt and scared. Her hands clutched the arms of the rocker as if she were hanging onto a raft in a swirling tide. "Farr will know what to do. We have him and Colby and Uncle Juicy and even Rain to help us."

"Does Papa know what Stith will do to me? How he'll hurt me?" Amy's eyes filled with huge tears.

"Yes, he knows. But a lot of men think that's just something a woman has to endure to pay for her keep." Liberty glanced at Willa and saw that she was keeping her face turned away because she was crying.

"Does Farr think that?"

"No. Farr would never force a woman." Liberty pulled up a chair and sat down in front of her sister. "Farr didn't touch me until he asked me if I wanted to . . . be with him that way. I wanted to because I love him. He was gentle with me, and it was wonderful. It was nothing to be ashamed of, as I've heard women say. It will be that way for you and the man you love."

"He didn't hurt you?"

"No, darling. He didn't hurt me at all. It was comforting to have him hold me."

"Farr loves you."

"He's never told me so."

"Libby? I saw Stith do something bad once. I've never told because I was afraid. Mary Clary and I were in Stith's barn hiding from prissy Hope Swenson. Mrs. Swenson's bond girl, Lucy, came in with a basket looking for eggs." Amy began to talk fast, scarcely taking a breath. "Stith came in right behind her and shut the doors. He threw her down on the hay. She got up and tried to run, but he caught her and . . . pulled her dress up over her head. She cried and begged him to leave her alone, but he laughed. Then . . . he got between her legs and took out his . . . thing. When he rammed it in her she screamed!" Tears were rolling down Amy's cheeks. "Lucy cried for a long time and tried to wipe away the blood—" Amy came up out of the chair, sat on Liberty's lap and put her arms around her neck as she had done when she was Mercy's age, and sobbed uncontrollably.

"Oh, darling! Don't cry and don't think about it. That won't happen to you. I swear it!"

"I can't help it. I'm so scared."

"I know, and so am I. Farr will think of something. He said for us not to worry."

* * *

Liberty and Amy were sitting on the bench beneath the oak tree when Farr, Colby, Rain and Juicy came walking up the lane from the road. Liberty was darning the holes in Farr's socks; Amy was aimlessly staring off into space. Willa and Daniel had gone to the barn to find the pet crow.

Farr picked up a bench as he passed the house and carried it out to the tree. He and Juicy sat down and Colby and Rain squatted on their heels.

"We've decided what we think is the best thing to do," Farr said as if he were adding to an ongoing conversation. He had noted Amy's swollen, tear-drenched eyes and Liberty's shaking hands and thought it best to get to the point.

"The captain tells me that Lieutenant Perry, backed by his men, has the authority to take Amy and turn her over to her father. I don't intend to let that happen," he added quickly when Amy clutched Liberty's arm fearfully. "Someone would be killed, preferably Perry, but when the bullets fly you can't be sure who will get hit."

"What can we do?" Liberty asked, strangely calm now that Farr had taken over the problem. "Hammond will be determined because he hates me and . . . you."

"We have an idea, but Amy will have to be the one to decide whether she's willing. The four of us have discussed it and come up with a solution. She can do what you did, Libby. She can marry. Then her husband would be responsible for her and not her father."

"Marry? Who?" Liberty gasped. "Good heavens, Farr, she's only twelve years old!"

"There's no age limit to when a woman can marry. Some do it at ten."

"I don't want to marry yet," Amy wailed and looked at Rain through teary eyes.

"We're not suggesting a *real* marriage. It would be to give your husband the right to take care of you and manage your affairs," Farr explained patiently. "Colby plans to ask someone to share his life, so that leaves—"

"Let me tell it to the youngun." Juicy's watery old eyes were filled with compassion for the young girl. "Listen ta ole Uncle Juicy, little purty. I know ya've been asettin' yore cap fer the boy here 'n it's a good choice ya made. He's as fine a lad as there is."

Amy blushed hearing his blunt words, and her eyes darted to Rain again. He was whirling a blade of grass between his fingers and looking off toward the barn.

"I'm not so sure about that," Colby murmured teasingly with an affectionate slap on Rain's back.

Juicy refused to be distracted by the horseplay.

"Rain's got him some growin' ta do 'n ya ain't full growed yoreself. Rain here's awantin' ta pull foot fer a spell till thin's quiet down some. It won't help none a'tall if 'n ya married up with him 'n him gone. Now I be eighty-two years, the best I can recollect. I got me two, three more years to live, maybe four on the outside. By the time I be gone, you'll be all growed up 'n free ta choose a man ya'd want."

Amy gaped at the old man.

"It's a solution, Amy." Farr's voice came to Amy through the pounding of blood in her ears. She turned slowly to look into his face. His eyes were full of concern—for her.

"I be far past the age ta bed a woman, child. Do ya fear me? Is that what troubles ya?"

Amy shook her head slowly from side to side. Her face changed in an instant and she burst out laughing.

"It's perfect! Oh, Uncle Juicy. I'll be ever so pleased to marry you." She jumped up and threw her arms around the old man's neck. "Won't Papa be fit to be tied?"

Juicy chortled happily. "I can't wait ta see his face when I call him Papa."

Farr got to his feet, took Liberty's hand and pulled her up beside him. "Libby? What do *you* think?"

"I'm trying to think of how I'm ever going to thank you and Juicy."

"Then Colby can go for Preacher Ellefson?"

Liberty grimaced. "That old mule's ass!" she whispered just to Farr.

He laughed. "He's the only preacher around and he'll do most anything for five shillings."

"Amy is just a child. Will he wonder why she's willing to marry Juicy?"

"He won't care if she's willing or not. In his lecherous old heart he considers a girl is old enough to marry if she can cook mush and boil coffee and that it's her duty to do so. You'd better prepare Amy, sweetheart. I know how shocked you were when you met him."

Sweetheart. The word echoed in Liberty's mind as she watched Farr go to the corral where Rain and Colby were each saddling a horse. She said a silent prayer that he would one day love her.

The mood was almost joyous as they waited for Colby to return with the preacher. Rain saddled his horse and Colby rode out, leading the sorrel for the preacher to return on. Rain stayed on in the barn.

Amy had listened patiently to what Liberty had told her about Preacher Ellefson and had promised to be docile and keep her head bowed. As soon as she could get away she took off to seek Rain. She found him rubbing bear grease on strips of leather hanging on the wall.

"Rain? Why're you staying out here? Are you coming to see me be married to Uncle Juicy?"

"No."

"Why? It's the only thing that'll keep Papa from making me marry Stith. You didn't want to marry me," she said accusingly.

"I'm not ready to get married."

"I'm not either, but I have to. I was going to marry you . . . if you're like Farr when you grow up." She put emphasis on the last words.

He dipped into the bucket and threw a handful of grease onto a soft doeskin rag. He worked on the leather strips as if she weren't there.

"Sometimes you make me so mad, Rain Tallman!" Even her sputtering, sarcastic voice failed to get a rise out of him. Amy wormed her way around so that she was almost between him and the wall, but he merely stepped back and pulled the strip with him. "Why are you so anxious to leave here? Where are you going to go after you take the Indian woman back to her people?"

"They're my people too. They raised me. And she's got a name. It's Tecumapese. Her son's name is Chiksika."

"What does that mean?"

"Gunshot."

"For goodness sake! Why did she name him that?"

"How do I know? It's her brother's name too." He shouted so loud she put her hands over her ears.

"Well! You don't have to be so mad, I was only asking. When are you leaving?"

"Two days, four days."

"I want to see Tecumapese and the baby again. Will you bring them by here?"

"I plan on it."

"How long will you be gone?"

"Don't you do anything but ask questions?"

"You are so stingy with your words, you make me sick! Some day I'll be grown up and so pretty that you'll want to talk to me and I won't say a word. I'll just stand there while you ask questions that I won't answer."

"When that time comes, the world will tremble and the rivers will flow backward."

"Oh! I don't know why I bother with you." Amy felt like she wanted to cry again. This time for a different reason. Rain acted like he hated her . . . and he was leaving. It could be months or years before she was alone with him again. "Rain? Please don't be mad at me," she pleaded. "I just want you to like me a little bit."

"I do. Now are you satisfied?"

"I want to kiss you before you go." Before he could move, she threw her arms about his neck and kissed him square on the mouth. "Bye, Rain. I know I'll see you again, but not like this."

Startled to feel soft lips on his for the first time, Rain's arms went around her and this time he touched his lips to hers, and held them there for a long moment. When he released her, Amy ran from the barn.

"Phew! What's that I smell?" Liberty was helping Amy out of her short everyday dress and into one that she had given to her. Preacher Ellefson would be arriving soon, and she wanted her sister to look as grownup as possible.

"Bear grease. I was in the barn with Rain. I kissed him right on the mouth, and he kissed me back."

"Well!" Liberty turned quickly to hide her smile. "That doesn't tell me how you got in the bear grease."

"Rain had it on his hands. He hugged me. He hugged me tight, Libby. I know he likes me, but he's too blasted stubborn to admit it."

"I don't know how anyone could help but to like you," Liberty said staunchly. "But then I'm your sister," she added teasingly. "Hurry now and fasten your dress. I'm going to pin your hair up on your head."

"Rain said he isn't coming to see me be married."

"He might change his mind."

"Rain doesn't change his mind. Oh, they're here." Amy darted back from the door.

"Cover your head with this shawl, Amy. It'll not matter if your hair is up or not. I forgot that the preacher thinks a woman's hair was put there to lure men into sinful ways."

"He thinks that?"

"He has a lot of foolish notions. Don't pay any attention to him. Cover your head. And Willa, cover yours too," Liberty said hurriedly.

The preacher got off the horse with his huge Bible in his hand. Juicy got up from the bench under the tree, knocked the ashes from his pipe and put it in his pocket. He and Farr shook hands with the preacher. Liberty could hear the man's booming voice asking the same questions of Juicy he had asked Farr the morning they were married.

"Will you properly chastise this woman? Make her docile and obedient? Set her feet on the path of righteousness?"

Juicy must have given the right answers, because Farr beckoned for them to come out into the yard.

It was no easier for Liberty to hear the insulting questions asked of Amy than it had been when they were asked of her. The only thing that kept her from lambasting the preacher with all the scathing remarks that came to mind was the fact that he was providing a means for Amy to escape Stith, and Amy didn't seem to mind.

When the ceremony was over, the preacher drew the paper from his pocket, and Farr sent Willa to the house to get the ink horn and the quill. Amy painstakingly signed her name to the paper and Juicy scratched his name also. Then he sat back down and took out his pipe as if being married was an everyday occurrence. Amy began to play with the kitten Daniel had brought from the barn. Farr dug into his moneybag for the shillings.

"I'm glad to see you've taken a firm hand with your woman, Mr. Quill. I had my doubts about your success. No doubt you've worn out a dozen willow switches, for I could see she had a rebellious spirit."

"Yes, she did, and she still does, Preacher Ellefson. I've made her dance to the swish of the willow switch more than once. Show him your legs, Libby." Only Liberty saw the mischief that danced in Farr's eyes.

"I'll do no such thing, and you can't make me." She tossed her head sassily, stuck her tongue out, and jerked the covering from her head.

She heard the preacher gasp with indignation.

"Get to the house, woman, before I lay my hand on your backside right out here in the yard. I mean to teach you that I'm your master."

Farr's shout was convincing. Liberty could hear the sympathetic words from the preacher as she ran giggling to the house.

She entered to see Colby and Willa standing beside the wash shelf. Colby had the dipper in his hand, but his eyes were on Willa's turned-up face and she was looking at him as if—as if he had just hung out the stars, she thought. This was not the first time Liberty had caught them alone. She backed out the door. They didn't even know she had been in the room.

There was much to mark the next morning different from the other mornings when Liberty and Willa had cooked breakfast for the men. Everyone was quieter than usual; the men ate more hurriedly. When Liberty went to wake Amy as she slept with Mercy, she jumped up at once and didn't plead for just a few more minutes of sleep. And finally, the children fed, the cabin tidied and the noon meal started, there was nothing to do but wait for Captain Heald and the troops to return.

Farr went to the sawyer camp to see that the work was started and to speak to Mr. Washington about what was to be done. Juicy, Colby and Rain stayed at the cabin. When Farr returned, they busied themselves at the woodpile making stakes. It was a place where they could see both the sawyer camp and the road.

Two hours after sunup the patrol came up the road from the south. The captain and Hammond Perry were in the lead; the others followed in an orderly fashion, Elija and Stith Lenning bringing up the rear. They rode up to within a dozen yards of the house. The captain held up his hand and the sergeant barked an order. The troops stopped, the captain and Hammond came on. Elija and Stith rode around the troops and followed the officers into the yard. They alighted and Captain Heald walked forward to meet Farr and shake his hand.

"Morning."

"Morning, Captain." Farr pointédly ignored Hammond.

"You know why we're here, Quill. Lieutenant Perry has business with you."

Farr turned frosty eyes on Hammond. A wave of anger stormed through him. Hammond arrogantly returned his stare. He stood with feet apart, balancing on the heels of his boots. Farr desperately wanted to wipe the satisfied smirk off his face.

"Say your piece, Perry, and then get off my land before I plant my fist in your face."

"Now, Quill, let's be civilized about this." Heald's words made the smirk on Hammond's face widen.

"Yes, Quill. Be civilized for *once* in your life."

"What do you want here?"

"I've been told by Mr. Elija Carroll that you have his daughter, Amy Louise Carroll, and that you refuse to allow him to see her or take her to the home he has provided for her." Hammond moved so he could look beyond Farr's tall frame that obstructed his view of the cabin. "You are to turn the girl over to him immediately. Where is she?"

"In the cabin."

"Call her out. Her father is here to fetch her."

"No."

Captain Heald had the feeling Farrway Quill was enjoying the encounter. He folded his arms and waited to see what card he would pull from his sleeve to avoid giving up the girl. He hoped to hell Quill had one.

"Must I remind you that I can take the girl by force?"

"You don't have to remind me. You're just stupid enough to try it."

Hammond's face turned a dull red, and his lips worked before he shouted, "Damn you! My patience is running out. Fetch the girl or—"

"Or what?" Farr taunted.

The captain decided he'd have to step in before things got out of hand.

"Quill, you know as well as I do that a female is under the jurisdiction of her father until she marries, and that he has the right to give her in marriage to a man he feels will make a suitable husband for her. If you have any proof that Mr. Carroll is not Miss Amy's father, please say so, and let's get this over with."

"Now see here, I ain't agoin' ta be talked of like I warn't even here. Ain't nobody can say Amy ain't mine. Ask Libby. She were there when Amy was born. Stith knowed her ma too, ain't that right Stith?"

Farr turned his frosty gaze on Elija.

"You're just about as rotten a father as I've come across. I've no proof that you didn't sire Amy or Liberty. God only knows how two fine women could have come from the likes of you."

Stith shouldered Elija aside. "I'm getting tired of this pussyfootin'. We come to get the girl, and by Gawd—"

"Shut your mouth and step aside," Nathan Heald said sternly. "This is none of your affair."

Stith's light eyes looked down on the shorter man as if he'd like to run him through with a saber. He seethed with the desire to lash out at the captain, but he didn't dare.

"Are you the law here or not? I'm athinkin' yo're scared a this backwoods clod!"

"Open your mouth again, Mr. Lenning, and I'll order the troops to seize you and give you ten lashes." Nathan Heald's eyes were dark with anger, his voice more deadly because he spoke softly. He deliberately turned his back and spoke to Farr. "Let's get on with this."

"Amy," Farr called without taking his eyes off Hammond. "Come out and say hello to your pa."

Elija started forward when Amy and Liberty came from the cabin, but Farr stepped in front of him. Amy went to where Colby, Rain and Juicy stood beneath the oak tree. She caught hold of Juicy's arm, and they moved forward a few paces.

"Hello, Papa."

"Amy, I'm wantin' ya to come—"

"Say hello to my husband, Papa." She hugged Juicy's arm and smiled up into his face.

There was flat silence while the statement and its ramifications were absorbed. Elija looked as if he had been struck in the stomach. Stith let out a bellow of rage and took a threatening step forward. The captain flung his hand out in warning and Stith moved back. Amy pressed close to Juicy and he put his arm around her.

Liberty watched Amy. She couldn't believe the show she was putting on. She fingered Juicy's beard and pressed her head to his shoulder. She had told her to act as if she were happy, but now she was afraid Amy would overdo it. Elija watched too. He sagged in defeat as Liberty had seen him do so many times before, but there was no pity in her heart for him this time.

Juicy held out his hand to Elija. "Howdy . . . Pa."

There were loud guffaws from the troops, who had inched up to hear what was going on. Hammond whirled to glare at them and they fell silent.

"Ya didn't—ya didn't wed this ole man?" Elija wailed.

"I married him. I am Mrs. Deverell, Papa. Isn't it grand? You wanted me to have a husband, and I loved Juicy right from the first."

"But . . . but he be old. He ain't—cain't—"

"Hold on, Papa!" Juicy pointed his gnarled finger at Elija. His white beard flopped on his chest as he shook his head angrily. "'Cause ya cain't, don't mean I cain't. I ain't havin' no sich talk made ta my wife. Not from her pa, not from nobody."

"This seems to settle it," Captain Heald said. He made no attempt to disguise the fact that he was pleased.

"I beg to differ, Captain." Hammond cleared his throat noisily. "Bedding this, ah, woman, doesn't make for a legal union." He eyed Amy rudely.

"Why, ya young whippersnipe! It be legal," Juicy roared. He dug beneath his tunic, pulled the marriage paper from his belt and waved it under Hammond's nose. When Hammond would have taken it, Juicy snatched it back and handed it to the captain. "Preacher Ellefson read the words 'n put his name ta the paper. Wedded and bedded. Ain't a damn thin' ya can do."

Stith let out a roar of rage. Before anyone realized his intentions, he lowered his head and charged at Farr, striking him in the chest with his head. The attack caught Farr unaware. The momentum carried both men six feet before they fell, Stith sprawled on top of Farr.

Rain sprang. As quick as a flash of lightning he was on Stith's back, his hand in his hair pulling his head back. The blade of his hunting knife was pressed to Stith's throat.

"Hold it, Rain. Don't kill him yet." Colby stood over them and touched Rain on the shoulder, then said to Stith, "Get off him, you piece of horseshit."

Stith was afraid to move. The blade bit into the skin of his neck.

"Let him up, Rain." Farr gasped. "Let me get my breath. I'm going to stomp his ass into the ground."

Rain removed the knife and stepped back. Stith got up and moved back until the tip of Rain's knife poked him in the spine. He stopped.

"I'm not fightin' a gawddamned kid!"

"No, but you wanted to take one to bed and ruin her." Rain spoke so softly that no one heard but Stith. "If you ever touch her I'll kill you." He pushed the tip of the knife blade into Stith's back to give emphasis to his words.

Farr got to his feet. Liberty grabbed his forearm with both hands.

"Are you all right? That was a cowardly thing for him to do!" She glared at Stith. "You've never done a *fair* thing in your life! Coward!" she flung at him.

"Stay back out of the way, Libby. I've wanted a piece of his hide since I first heard his name."

"Don't fight him. He—"

"Do as I say, Liberty Bell. Look to the kids. Colby, Rain, keep them out of the way." He gave Liberty a gentle shove toward Colby. "The man wants a fight, Captain, and I'm going to oblige him."

"I haven't seen a good fight in a long while. Got your wind back, Quill?"

"Just about." He breathed deeply, removed his buckskin shirt, his knife and a plunder bag that hung from the waist of his trousers. He handed these things to Rain while keeping his eyes on Stith. Lenning had removed his shirt and was talking to Elija. Farr nodded to the captain.

"Have at it," the captain said and stepped back.

"I'm agoin' to bust you up. I'm agoin' to stomp your guts loose," Stith bragged as he came toward Farr.

"You'll not do it jawing." Farr leaped and hit him. He threw the punch unexpectedly, a blow that would have stunned a normal man. Stith caught the fist flush in the mouth and reeled back, a tooth sheared completely off. When he spit it out his lips were covered with blood. For an instant he stared, unable to believe a man inches shorter and pounds lighter could do that. "That was for ramming me when I wasn't looking."

Stith charged with a bellow of rage, his boots pounding the grass. Farr threw up an arm to weather the windmilling attack, but a fist broke through, landing a blow to his jaw. Stith butted Farr's chest with his head. With a grunt of pain, Farr went backward, his feet stamping for purchase. He gained his balance and struck Stith a glancing blow over the left eye, opening a deep gash, but the huge man gave no indication that he had even been hit.

Stith was a grappling type of fighter. He tried to hug Farr, but Farr kept batting his arms away. Stith lowered his head for another charge and Farr let him come on, but before Stith could hit him, Farr's fist came up with such force that Stith's head snapped up and his body arched backward. He staggered, but didn't fall. The big man had the weight and the strength to plant his feet wide apart and become as rooted as an oak tree.

Stith stood panting, bleeding from the nose and mouth. He watched Farr move around him and he growled like an animal, deep in his chest.

Farr moved in swinging. Stith grabbed him around the

waist and applied pressure. Farr arched his back as he stiffened to resist this tremendous force, but Stith's arms had the strength of a bull as he squeezed. His heavy boots thrashed about, trying to stamp down on Farr's moccasined feet. Failing in this, Stith began to bring his head forward in short, sharp raps, striking Farr in the face. He bloodied Farr's nose and raised livid cuts over Farr's eyes. Then Farr cupped both hands, drew his arms apart and slapped Stith smartly over both ears.

Stith screamed, dropped his arms to clasp his hands over his ears, and doubled over. The sudden concussion rendered him momentarily helpless and Farr sank down on one knee, painfully drawing gulps of air into his tortured lungs. Slowly he pulled himself up and moved toward Stith. He struck him on the base of the skull with his fist, but lacked the power to knock him to the ground. Stith grabbed Farr by the ankle and threw him backward, then jumped on him. Farr turned and took the huge man's weight on his hip.

They were at the edge of the woodpile. Stith reached for a stake and swung it. Throwing up an arm, Farr deflected the blow with his upper arm. Pain shot through his arm and shoulder. For an instant he thought it was broken. A grunt escaped him and he heard a woman cry out.

Liberty felt as though her own body had been struck. She pressed both hands over her mouth. And then to her horror she saw Stith's hand grope and find the axe. In blind urgency she ran forward. Farr was gripping Stith's wrist, trying to keep him from raising the axe. The pile of stakes beside the woodpile were stout and over two feet long. Liberty grabbed one and swung, catching Stith on the shoulder. He yelped and dropped the axe to grab the stake. Liberty clung to it like a dog at the end of a rope.

"Goddamnit, Libby!" Colby shouted. He and Rain jerked her back, leaving the end of the stake in Stith's hand.

Stith, standing over Farr, raised the stake and brought it down. Farr, rolling to avoid the blow, saw the axe. He gripped it just above the blade and swung with all his strength. The handle caught Stith on the side of the head and stunned him. Farr got to his feet and swung again. The blow caught Stith on the collarbone and he yelled like a wounded bear. Stith tried to swing a backhanded blow, but he was disoriented and staggered blindly.

"Had . . . enough?" Farr gasped, dropped the axe and drew back his fist.

Stith looked at him stupidly. With the last of his strength Farr hit him. Stith's knees buckled slowly. He shook his head like a bull and mumbled something through his smashed mouth, then sank to the ground.

A cheer went up from the troops who had been shouting encouragement to Farr from the beginning. It was enough for them to favor Farr if the lieutenant was against him.

Farr turned, his eyes seeking Liberty. They found her, and he reeled toward her on not-quite-steady legs. She met him with tears streaming down her face. His was bruised and swollen. Blood oozed from a dozen cuts. He shrugged off her hands when she reached out to touch him.

"If you ever . . . step into my fight again, I'll . . . beat your butt!" he gasped. He wanted to say more, but it hurt too much.

Chapter
Eighteen

Hammond Perry stood ramrod stiff, his hands clasped behind his back, and watched the fight. He fervently hoped Lenning would gouge the bastard's eyes out. In all his thirty years, Hammond had never hated a man as he hated Farrway Quill. Quill had been a thorn in his side since the first day they had met over a year before. And to further increase Hammond's dislike, Governor Harrison held Quill up as an example of the type of person needed to settle and hold the territory until it could be brought into statehood.

On Hammond's first mission to the area, the governor had sent a message to Quill. He and his troops had camped at Quill's Station. Hammond had had a run-in with Quill that night over the disciplining of his men. Although the man he had ordered to be flogged had deserved the punishment for insubordination, Quill had interfered, and Hammond lost face with his men. After that Quill had bucked him each and every time they met. Quill had completely ignored Hammond when the governor entertained him and the officers at a dinner at the mansion a few months back, and Hammond still smarted from the snub.

This time Quill had gone too far, Hammond thought. He and the chit would pay for putting him down in front of Captain Heald and his troops. If Lenning didn't kill Quill, he would, or better yet, he would find a way to get to Quill through the chit. He had seen Quill looking at her as if she were a gold nugget. Hammond was convinced Quill was as obsessed with his brother's widow as Lenning was. Lenning hadn't been able to talk about anything except how he was going to make her rue the day she refused him.

The troops behind Hammond were cheering. He turned to give them a quelling look, but they were so wrapped up in the fight they didn't even look at him, and Hammond didn't dare shout an order. Captain Heald was cheering too.

Not everyone in the territory was wrapped up in Farrway Quill, Hammond thought smugly. Mrs. Thompson and her daughter had had nothing good to say about him or the Widow Perry the night he and the captain had supper with them. The mother had pushed the fat girl, Harriet, his way, and Hammond had walked out with her. It hadn't taken Hammond any time at all to learn everything that had taken place at Quill's Station during the last few months. At Lenning's homestead, Elija Carroll told him of Jubal's death and of his daughter's marriage to Quill.

Hammond's eyes swept the compound and settled on the indentured girl the Thompsons had told him about. He had seen her before. Willa Carrathers had been in Vincennes with Norman Cooley and his wife. Cooley had spent a great deal of his time in the tavern swilling ale, and when in his cups, he talked. Several times Cooley had hinted about the girl's mysterious past and her connection with someone high up in government circles.

According to the Thompson girl, Quill had demanded the indentured woman be turned over to him, and her father, afraid of Quill, complied. Having the girl in Quill's household could be something he could use now against Quill, Hammond thought with a satisfied smile.

The fight was over. Goddamn Quill. If not for the chit, Lenning might have split his head with the axe. He barked an order to the sergeant, and two men went to help Lenning get on his horse. An idea was beginning to form in Hammond's mind, an idea that would totally discredit Farrway Quill with the governor. He ran his eyes slowly over the girl, Willa. He would talk again to the Thompson woman, using the fact that she was angry with Quill and the chit for taking her servant. He would talk to Stith Lenning and use his hatred of Quill. He was sure he could find out all the tavern owner knew, and he would locate Norman Cooley.

Hammond rode away from the homestead with his mind full of plans.

Farr's rebuff cut Liberty to the core. She stood back against the cabin wall and watched the troops prepare to ride out. Elija didn't say a word to her or Amy or even look their way. He accepted the reins to Stith's horse, after a couple of the troopers heaved Stith, groggy but able to stand, into the saddle. The captain, with Hammond beside him, lifted his hand in a salute to the women and led the procession down the lane to the road. Elija followed and didn't look back.

Farr stood with legs spread, head up and blood running down the side of his face, until the men left his homestead. Then, without a glance at Liberty, he went toward the spring. Colby and Rain followed him.

Mercy's sniffles were the only sound that was heard after distance swallowed the hoofbeats of the departing patrol. Willa held her and tried to soothe her fears. The child had been frightened by the violence. All she understood was that someone was hurting Farr. During the fight Daniel had wrapped his arms about Juicy's leg and had watched with his usual quiet. Now he ran after Farr and slipped his hand into Colby's.

Juicy had seen the look of devastation that came over Liberty's face when Farr pushed her hands away and turned his back on her. Juicy watched her eyes follow Farr as he walked unsteadily away.

"He don't stay mad fer long, Libby. He's hurtin' now, but he'll see ya meant no harm."

Liberty turned tear-filled eyes to the old man. "I thought Stith was going to kill him. I had to try to help him."

"A man ain't wantin' nobody abuttin' in on his fight, 'specially a woman. It shames him somethin' fierce."

"I never meant to shame him. But I'd rather shame him

than stand by and see him killed!" Her blue eyes shone defiantly through the tears. "A woman should be able to fight for her loved ones. Oh, men and their damn pride make me sick!"

"It's the way a thin's here, Libby. Out here there's times all a man's got is pride. It keeps him goin'. Don't worry none 'bout it. Farr'll say his piece 'n set ya straight, but he ain't one to carry on."

"What'll I do? I love him!" Liberty blurted.

"I knowed it, little purty, 'n I be plumb tickled. Farr be needin' a sweet little thin' like ya be fer a long time."

"He told me about Fawnella. I'll never take her . . . place with . . ." Her voice lowered to a whisper and trailed away.

"Ya'll make yer own place. Fawnella be more child than woman. Ya be a woman fittin' ta stand by a man. Farr'll see it, if 'n he ain't a'ready."

"I hope so. Oh, Juicy, I should be happy because he beat Stith, and we don't have to worry about Papa taking Amy, but . . . I'm so miserable!"

"Farr'll have ta fight him again. He won't feel he beat him fair 'n square cause of yore buttin' in. Lenning won't forget it none, either."

"Oh, no! What'll I do, Juicy? I can't bear to have him angry at me."

"Leave him be." Juicy's voice was stern, and then he added gently, "He'll come to ya when he cleans hisself up."

Liberty slumped against the wall. "I've ruined things, haven't I?"

"No, ya ain't ruint nothin'. Perk up 'n hold that purty head a yores high. It's yore perky 'n pride he likes. I know my boy. He be havin' ta get it outta his craw. He'll chaw on ya, but that's all."

"I've got a lot to learn about him."

Juicy dug his pipe from the depths of one of the cavernous pockets of his tunic and busied himself packing it with tobacco.

"What're ya fixin' up ta eat?" He sniffed the air. "I can

smell it. This gettin' wedded up, meetin' my new pa 'n all this fightin' 'n carryin' on makes me powerful hungry."

Liberty couldn't suppress a small smile. "If you don't be careful, Juicy, I'm going to love you a powerful lot." She reached over and placed a kiss on his cheek.

Liberty was grateful when the men walked up from the sawyer camp for the noon meal. The work kept her busy. She and Willa carried the heavy pots to the tables in the yard and dished out the meat and dumplings. Colby and Rain came from the barn and ate with the men. Liberty was in the cabin cutting fresh loaves of bread when Farr came in and stood just inside the door. Willa, sensing the strain between them, quickly placed the bread on a cloth, wrapped it, and took it out to the tables.

Farr's head was wet. He had combed his hair and tied it back. One of his eyes was almost swollen shut. Salve was spread over the gash on his cheekbone. His nose was puffy, as was his upper lip. Silence bore down on Liberty as they looked across the room at each other.

"I'm sorry," she whispered from where she stood beside the table. "I never meant to shame you. Juicy said I did."

"Don't do it again. If I need your help I'll ask."

"I was afraid for you."

"It was an open fight. He fought fair."

"I'm ... so sorry. I just don't know what I'd do without you." A sob caught in her throat.

"You'll never be without me," he said quietly. He looked at her for a long moment, saw tears in her eyes, misery on her beautiful face. He opened his arms. "Come here," he whispered.

Liberty hurried to him, put her arms loosely about him and placed her head on his shoulder.

"I was never so scared in my life. Farr, if I'd had my gun I'd have shot Stith. It scares me to think that I could kill someone."

"Don't be scared. Someday you may have to. Juicy came out and chewed on me for making you cry. He likes you, likes you a lot."

"And you?" Liberty raised her head so she could see his face. He was smiling down at her. His hand came up to cradle her head, and he gently touched his swollen lips to hers.

"What do you think? I didn't whip your butt."

Liberty kissed his lips, his chin, the place on his throat that pulsed. He put his face in her hair and they stood quietly. She could feel him all through her and wanted to hold him forever. The world fell away, and for a moment there was just the two of them. But it had to end. She tilted her head to see his face. It was battered, rugged, almost primitive. She touched it with her fingertips.

"Oh, Farr, I—" She stopped herself before she told him of her love. "Your poor mouth. Can you eat? Does your jaw hurt?"

He looked down in her beautiful face, full of concern for him. His eyes held hers while his fingers worried the curls over her ears and then gently stroked her cheek. When he spoke, it was to say something totally disconnected from his thoughts.

"What hurts the most is my hands. I need some warm salt water to soak them in. I'm afraid I'll not be able to handle the saw for a day or two."

Four evenings later, at the supper table, Farr announced that Rain was leaving the following morning. Rain didn't raise his head when all eyes turned in his direction.

"Is Tecumapese's foot healed? I was hoping to see her before she goes. I'm anxious to meet Sugar Tree too." Liberty looked down the table at Farr and moved Mercy over onto her lap. The child was so sleepy she had no interest in eating.

"According to Sugar Tree it's well enough for her to walk on it."

"She's not going to walk and carry the baby, is she?" Amy asked. She'd had time to get used to the idea that Rain was going to leave. He looked up now, straight into her eyes.

"She'll ride my horse."

"What'll you ride?"

"I'll walk."

"Libby!" Amy turned stricken eyes to her sister. "Can't he use our horse?"

"He certainly can. I was going to suggest it. Is that all right with you, Farr?"

Farr gazed fondly at his wife. "It's your horse."

"I don't want to use your horse. I'm not coming back," Rain looked from Liberty to Farr to Amy.

"I know that," Farr said. "If Liberty wants you to take the horse, take it."

"No."

"What's the matter with you, Rain Tallman?" Amy sputtered. "You're the most mule-headed boy I've ever met. You'd walk all that way before you'd take a favor."

"Taking a horse isn't a favor. Men kill for a horse." Rain's dark eyes glinted angrily.

"I'll pay Libby for the horse. You and Colby have money coming from the salt in the storeroom. I'll use your pay and part of Colby's pay—"

"Now wait just a doggone minute! I'll not give up any of my pay to keep this skinny kid from walking to Prophetstown." Colby's bright gaze flashed around the table. "Let him walk. It'll do him good."

"Colby's pay?" Rain's dark eyes took on a shine. He tilted his head and looked at Farr.

"Colby's pay. It was his fault you lost half that load crossing the creek. You have your share coming, but not Colby." Farr's face was serious. "I'd planned to take it out of his pay."

"You're not going to let me forget that, are you?" Colby looked at Willa and winked.

"That's right." Rain gave Colby a half grin. "You were being smarty and the back wheels of the wagon sank in the bog." He looked back at Farr. "I'll take Colby's pay. Will that cover the cost of the horse?"

"He's not paying me for that horse, Farr," Liberty protested.

Farr nodded his answer to Rain, then said, "Hush, Libby. It's settled."

"Damn you, Farr. I'm going to need all of my pay." Colby dug his elbow in Rain's ribs. "I'm not forgetting this, *kid!*"

Liberty saw one of the rare smiles on Rain's face. He had beautiful white teeth, and when he smiled his lips spread and turned up in the corners. A deep, long crease appeared in each cheek. She glanced at Amy and saw her staring at the young boy with misty eyes. Farr was gazing at him fondly, and her love for this man who had worked out a way to give the boy a horse without wounding his pride grew another measure.

That night, as they lay side by side, Farr told her that her father was no longer at Stith Lenning's. According to the Luscomb boy, he had ridden north and hadn't returned.

"Do you think he went to Vincennes?"

"If he did he got a cold reception from Perry. Perry is a user himself. I've not heard of him doing much for anyone if it didn't benefit him in some way."

"I should feel sorry for Papa, but I don't. He leaned on my mother until she died. Then I had to take over. Amy's mother was a young girl of fifteen, fourteen when Papa married her. He thought her folks would keep us, but after their daughter died they'd not have anything to do with us."

"Don't talk about him. This is my time with you. Take off that nightdress. I want to feel your breasts against my chest, your heart beating against mine." He moved away from her for an instant. Then they were back together, naked and straining to feel every inch of each other.

His lips, sweet and firm and knowing, moved over hers. She felt the rough drag of his cheeks, the caressing touch of his wild hair against her forehead. His hand roamed over her back to her buttocks, caressing. She gave herself up to his kiss with an abandon that made hunger leap deep inside of him. His hands and mouth moved down over her body with a velvet touch. His lips captured her nipple, and the rough drag of his tongue was so painfully exquisite that she drew a gasping breath.

"Sweet woman, I need you like I need air, food, sleep." His words came in an agonized whisper against her breast.

She wrapped her arms around him, spread her legs so his thighs could sink between hers, and pulled his weight down on her. Cradled together, they rocked from side to side, but it wasn't enough. Only by blending together could they even begin to appease the hunger they had for each other. He lifted his hips as her hand urgently moved between them to guide him into her.

"Farr..." She arched against him in sensual pleasure.

"Am I too heavy on you, sweet?"

"No! No, darling!" His concern brought a mistiness to her eyes that turned to tears and rolled down her cheeks. She wanted to tell him that he was the moon and the stars, everything wonderful that life offered, but she held back the words. He turned his head and caught the tears with the tip of his tongue, then found her mouth and kissed her with lips wet with her tears.

"Why do you cry when we're like this?"

"Because I'm happiest when I'm with you like this." She tightened her arms around him, holding him inside her warmth, and hungrily turned her mouth to his.

The spasms of pleasure that followed were like a dance throughout her body. At times it was like an enormous wave crashing over her. At other times it was like a gentle wind caressing her wet, naked body. Her whole world was the man joined to her. His mouth and hers were one. He was at home in her, moving gently, caressing, loving. She arched her hips hungrily and he wildly took what she offered.

* * *

The next morning Farr, Colby, Juicy and Rain spent an hour together before Rain went to Mr. Washington's to get Tecumapese. When Rain returned with the Indian woman, Liberty wiped her hands on her apron and went out into the yard to greet them. Liberty walked up to the horse and held out her hand. The woman put hers into it and looked solemnly into Liberty's eyes.

She was the prettiest Indian woman Liberty had ever seen. Her hair was as black and shiny as a crow's wing, her skin smooth and golden brown. Large, soft, dark eyes dominated her small featured face. She was slim and carried herself proudly. Her baby rode in a cradle board on one side of the horse and a basket of provisions provided by Sugar Tree was on the other.

"I thank you for my life and for that of my son."

Liberty turned to Rain and he translated.

"I'm glad I was there to help you."

"I shall tell my brothers, Tecumseh and Prophet, that the White Dove on the Wabash is the bravest of all women."

Rain translated, then added, "She's named you White Dove because of your hair, and to honor you for what you did."

"Tell her I am honored, and that she and her people are welcome at Quill's Station. Tell her that if she's ever in need to come to me."

Rain spoke quietly and solemnly to Tecumapese. When he finished, she turned her dark eyes to Liberty and spoke in English.

"Good woman you."

Liberty smiled into her eyes and repeated, "Good woman you. Rain, ask her if I can hold the baby."

Rain repeated the words, and Tecumapese, lifting the child from the cradle board, put him in Liberty's arms.

"The Shawnee are very fond of their children," Rain said. "They seldom allow a white to touch them. This is another way she is expressing her thanks."

"He is beautiful," Liberty said softly, smiling down at the child she cradled in her arms. She pushed the dark hair back from his face with gentle fingers and smiled up at the watching mother. "You must be very proud of him."

Amy, who until now had eyes only for Rain, gazed at the baby with shiny eyes. "I didn't remember that he was so little. Oh, Libby, he could have drowned so easily."

"Yes. God must have a greater plan for him." She handed him up to his mother.

Rain had dismounted. He stood holding the reins of the horse that had come from New York with them. Amy rubbed the nose of the brown mare.

"Take care of Rain," she whispered, not knowing that her voice carried to the young boy and that her words touched him deeply.

"We'll miss you, Rain. Farr explained why you feel you must go and I understand. Take care of yourself and know that we're here thinking of you." Liberty wanted to put her arms around him, but she was sure he'd not appreciate a show of affection in front of Tecumapese, so she held out her hand. Rain gripped it tightly.

"I'll make out," he said gruffly and turned to swing into the saddle. Amy was there. "Bye, Amy."

"Bye."

Amy waited, and when he didn't look at her, she ran to the cabin.

Liberty stood in the yard and watched until the horses were in the trees and out of sight. Rain had not stopped at the sawyer camp on the way to the cabin, and now he avoided the road that would take him past the homesteaders. It suddenly occurred to her that it could be months or years before she saw the quiet young boy again.

Willa had never been happier in her young life. She had not been part of a family since her first mistress died six years before. At times she feared she was dreaming, the feel of Mrs. Thompson's switch would wake her and she would once again be under the control of that cruel woman. She and Liberty worked from dawn until dusk. Their hands and their mouths were never idle.

Amy and Liberty became the sisters she never had, Juicy the grandfather. She was still in awe of Farr. The big, quiet man moved so silently, spoke so little, and all the while his great knowing eyes were seeing everything. She had three dresses now and soft comfortable moccasins. Juicy, and Rain before he left, had spent evenings making moccasins. It surprised her how fast they made the footwear. The women and the children each had a pair.

Willa talked freely to Liberty about her life with Mrs. Coulter, but said little about Norman Cooley and his wife Bella, Mrs. Coulter's relatives who sold her indenture to the Thompsons. There were two things she kept carefully to herself. One was the fact that she was in love with Colby Carroll. The other was a secret told to her by Mrs. Coulter before she died, a secret that caused her to burn with shame when she thought about it now; but, at the time, it had been of little significance to an eleven-year-old girl. That dear lady had not realized she was dying until it was too late for her to make arrangements to free Willa from her debt. The Cooleys had been pleased to inherit a servant, quite put out when they discovered she was so young but delighted when they realized how capable she was.

Evening was the time of day Willa liked the best. Liberty had told her that she liked the morning because it was the beginning of the day and evening was the ending. Willa had argued that evening was quiet and golden. Liberty had laughed and said that morning was new and fresh.

Willa sat on the bench outside the door, worked the dasher up and down in the oak churn, and enjoyed the last moments of the day. Stars twinkled in the still-light sky. Before the milk yielded the butter there would be total darkness. The children had gone to bed, and Amy was reading to Juicy by the light of the candle. Each night she read a chapter to him from one of Daniel Defoe's novels. Farr had read them to him once before, but the old man was enjoying them just as much this second time. It seemed to Willa that Amy had reverted to being a little girl again after Rain left.

"Boo!"

Willa made a pretence of being scared. She couldn't disappoint Colby. She had known he was coming up behind her. In fact, she knew where he was every minute he was at the homestead.

"Colby! Stop that. One of these days I'm going to jump right out of my skin." She worked the dasher up and down in the churn vigorously because being close to him made her nervous.

"Don't do that. It's such pretty skin. Haven't you finished with that yet?"

"It's beginning to feel like it."

"How can you tell?"

"By the way the dasher feels as it goes up and down. It feels . . . heavier."

"Take a peek. If it's done, I'll carry it down to the spring. Then I'll have you all to myself. Tomorrow night it'll be my turn to be on guard down at the sawyer camp."

"I should dip out the butter first."

"Can't that wait until morning?"

"I suppose. We have enough butter for tomorrow."

She wondered if she sounded breathless. Being alone with Colby was the most exciting thing that had ever happened to her, and somehow she was always short of air for the first few minutes. She stood and smoothed down her skirt. Colby lifted the churn and cradled it in his arms.

"Be careful. You'll slop it down the front of your shirt."

"And you'd have to wash it again."

"Nothing smells worse than sour milk. Phew! It's a blimey smell."

Colby laughed. "Every once in a while you come out with one of those English expressions. When Farr and I were in school we knew a fellow from Dover, England. It was *bloody* this and *bloody* that. I've never heard you say it. Didn't they say bloody in London?"

"Of course they did. But I was taught not to say bad words."

"Bloody is a bad word?"

"Said only by men, and not in front of ladies."

"Well, what do you know!" he exclaimed.

Willa waited while Colby set the churn in the cool springhouse. When he came out, he took her hand and they walked along the little creek made by the flow of water from the spring. It was dark now, and it was as if the two of them were the only people in the world. The peeper frogs were singing and overhead an owl swished by on a nocturnal journey of its own.

"Tell me again about how your father found your mother down on the Kentucky River, saved her from the men who were tracking her and carried her to his cabin on the Ohio."

"You've heard that story," he teased. "I told you and I heard Juicy telling you and Libby. Juicy was the one who went out into the blizzard and led Pa to the house. Pa told me that Juicy taught him how to stay alive in the wilderness when he first came out from Virginia."

"And Juicy taught you and Farr."

"Yes. He brought Farr out first. Then he and Farr taught me. There's still a lot I don't know. Someday I hope to be the man Farr is."

"You are now!" Willa said emphatically.

Colby's laugh rang out and he squeezed her hand tightly. "I've only shown you my good side. It could be that you're prejudiced. I hope you are." They walked on in silence. They came to the edge of the woods and stopped. "You would like my mother, Willa. She's small like you. When she was young she had red hair. It's got some gray in it now. Juicy said she was the prettiest thing he'd ever seen. Pa loves her to distraction."

Willa sighed. "It's wonderful."

"What is?"

"That they love each other still."

"Is that so strange?" He pulled her around to face him.

"I don't know of any men who love their wives to

distraction after they've been married a long time. They usually want someone . . . younger."

"You haven't met my father. Farr will be that way too. He's tail over teakettle in love with Libby. He can't take his eyes off her when she's near. Haven't you noticed how he's always touching her and listening to every word she says?"

"You've noticed all of that?"

"And more. My eyes can't leave *you*. I'm tail over teakettle in love with *you* and listen to every word *you* say." His other hand clasped hers and drew her to him. "You like me, I know. But . . . do you love me, Willa?" His words and the softness of his voice turned her to butter.

Willa thought her heart would leap up through her throat. She couldn't answer. She didn't dare tell him that she loved him with all her heart and soul and that as long as she lived she'd cherish these moments alone with him. She couldn't tell him that she loved him too much to try to share his life with him, that someday he would despise her, and she couldn't endure that.

"Willa?" he urged.

"I like you," she whispered. "I'm not sure what love is."

"I'm going to kiss you."

"No! Please don't."

"You always pull away when I try to get close to you. Are you afraid of me? I'll not force you."

"I know you won't."

"Then let me kiss you. You can move away anytime you want to." He lifted her face with a finger beneath her chin. "Willa, you're so pretty and sweet. My heart gallops like a runaway horse everytime I look at you."

His voice was low and persuasive. She couldn't resist him and stood perfectly still when he moved closer to her and put his arms around her. She had thought she would never be able to bear a man's body close to hers again after what happened in Vincennes. It had been so degrading, so humiliating to lie helplessly beneath the rutting boar who took her. All of that was out of her mind now.

Colby's lips gently touched hers. He held her loosely, giving her the choice of staying close or pulling away. His mouth was soft against hers, and such a lovely feeling unfolded in her midsection and traveled slowly throughout her body. Warm, moist lips left hers and traced the line of her brow and delicately touched her closed eyelids. His lips worked downward, touched her cheek and the tip of her nose, then settled gently on her mouth again where they moved sweetly, gently.

Colby trembled with the effort it took not to hold her tightly to him. Every nerve in his body cried out for her. He yearned to unlock the mystery of why she enchanted him. He had known girls more beautiful, better schooled, knowledgeable in the arts of pleasing a man, but this little waif had captured his heart.

"Colby—"

"Don't talk, my love. This is all so new to you. Just let me hold you." He gathered her closer and her arms went about his waist.

She pressed her face against his shirt, not wanting him to see the tears that sprang to her eyes at his tender words. She listened to the heavy beat of his heart and moved her cheek against it. His lips were in her hair, and she moved her face until her lips found the pulse that beat at the base of his throat. A feeling of faintness swept over her. She wanted to cling to him, to give him love. More than anything she wanted to believe that there was someone in all the vast world who truly loved her.

His arms tightened around her and he cuddled her against him. They stood like that for a long while, and he stroked her hair. Finally Willa stirred and moved away from him. He let his arms drop away from her.

"We'd better go back."

Colby took a deep shuddering breath, held her hand to his lips and kissed her palm, her slender fingers, her wrist. His gentleness brought immeasurable tenderness to her breast and tears to her eyes.

"You'll be mine, my beloved," he whispered. "Someday I'll take you home to Carrolltown as my bride."

The import of his words reached into her mind, and she held herself away from him.

"Oh, no. . . ."

"Oh, yes! I'm sure of it."

There was a deep silence between them. Presently, with his arm encircling her waist, they began to walk back along the creek bed toward the darkened cabin.

Chapter
Nineteen

D ays rolled into weeks and weeks into a month without any word from or news of Elija or Stith Lenning. Summer laid its hot hand along the Wabash. Wild bees buzzed around flowers to swab out precious pollen. Young birds left the nest for the first time to explore the world. Blossoms that had been so beautiful in the spring had turned into succulent fruit an army of birds were feeding upon. Within the bounds of the limit Farr had set for them, Liberty, Willa and Amy had stripped the area of choke-cherry, wild plum and grape. They fought with the birds for the bounty in the garden as well as the fruits they spread in the sun to dry.

Liberty asked Mr. Washington if he would bring Sugar Tree to the station for a visit, because with the children to look after and cooking for the men, even with the help of Mr. Thompson's man, it was impossible for her to take the time to travel down to the ferry.

One morning he came striding up the lane shortly after dawn. A tall full-bodied Indian woman kept stride with him. Her loose dress of brightly woven material fell to mid-calf. On her feet were brightly beaded moccasins that came up to cover her stout legs. Her face was strong and plain. She wore silver loops in her ears, but not as large as those of her husband.

"Mrs. Quill, I'm pleased to present my wife, Mrs. Washington." Mr. Washington made a formal bow by crossing one arm behind him, one in front and bending from the waist.

"How do you do? How are you? I am fine." Sugar Tree grasped the sides of her skirt and curtsied. Liberty did the same.

"How do you do, Mrs. Washington? I'm so glad you came to call and so pleased you speak such good English. Won't you come in?"

"Sugar Tree, you go on home when the sun is—" Mr. Washington pointed his forefinger straight up.

"Oh, Mr. Washington, can't she spend the day?"

Sugar Tree gave her husband a cool stare. "I stay the day," she said flatly, turned her back, and walked into the cabin.

Liberty smiled sweetly at Mr. Washington, waved, and followed Sugar Tree into the house.

The Indian woman went directly to the clock on the mantel. She was fascinated by the swinging pendulum and the constant ticking sound. She smiled broadly when the clock chimed.

"Mr. Washington say me someday get clock." She sat down in the rocking chair and rocked so hard Liberty was afraid she would tip over backward. "Fine chair." She got up from the chair and roamed around the room. She looked, stroked, touched and marveled at everything in the cabin.

Mercy stirred and let out her usual cry. "Pee, pee."

Sugar Tree went to the bunk and knelt down. "Fine girl. Fine boy."

Liberty was afraid Mercy would be frightened. But the child looked at Sugar Tree's smiling face and held up her arms. Sugar Tree picked her up and held her carefully.

"Fine girl, fine girl," she said over and over.

"Pee, pee," Mercy said again.

Liberty didn't know if Sugar Tree understood or if it was merely instinct, but she took Mercy outside, lifted the shirt she used as a nightgown and let her hunker down just outside the door. Mercy let water and Sugar Tree picked her up again. Amy and Willa looked at Liberty and grinned. They had been trying to get Mercy to use the outhouse and to break her of the habit of squatting in the yard whenever she had the urge.

Sugar Tree carried Mercy on her hip throughout most of the day. Liberty remembered that Mr. Washington loved children too. She wondered why they did not have any of their own.

Although their ways were strange to each other, an easy companionship developed between the women at Quill's Station and the Indian wife of Mr. Washington. Liberty showed Sugar Tree how to make switchel and to fashion buttons from the shells along the river. Sugar Tree watched Willa make plum pudding and shook her head as if to say it was too much trouble. She showed Liberty and Willa where to find the prairie turnip, cow parsnip, wild potato and onion. They found wild rhubarb to roast over hot coals and black root for coughs, and grape root to stop bleeding. She taught them to take the pulp of the cottonwood tree and boil it. They were surprised because it was not unlike maple syrup in flavor.

The day passed amazingly fast.

While the sun was setting, Sugar Tree departed. She took with her the plum pudding from Willa, brass buckles from a pair of Amy's outgrown shoes, and a pair of scissors from Liberty. She waved good-bye and went through the trees to the sawyer camp to walk back home with Mr. Washington.

That day a friendship had been forged that would last throughout the years.

The work force had swelled to twenty men and boys. The barracks walls were up, and shingles for the roof were being shaped at the camp. The crew was divided now. Half of the men worked on the buildings and setting the posts for the stockade; the other half felled, shaped and brought the logs to the building site. It seemed to Liberty that almost overnight a drastic change had taken place in Quill's Station. During these weeks she saw Farr only from a distance during the day, but the nights were hers. After a dip in the creek he came to the wagon where they still slept and crawled in beside her. This was her time with him. Here in the wagon he was wholly hers, and she welcomed him with open arms.

"The men are going to take a week off starting Sunday," he said one night. "They've been working steadily and want to get home to see how the crops are coming."

"How long do you think it will take to finish the buildings?"

"A month. It's gone faster than I thought it would. I'm sure we can finish before time to cut grass for the winter feed. Most of the homesteaders depend on that grass to keep their stock alive in case of a heavy snow."

"I miss Rain," she said sleepily. "I hope he's all right."

"I miss him too, but he's got to make his own life. I suspect he'll go cross the big river and go west. Missouri is opening up."

"Farr? Do you long to cross rivers that haven't been crossed and climb mountains that haven't been climbed?"

"Right now all I long to do is kiss you, Mrs. Quill." He turned to her and pressed his cheek to hers. She could feel the movement of his jaw when he whispered, "Take off that gown so I can love you properly."

The men left for home before daybreak, all except Mr. Thompson's Negro slave. Mr. Thompson had told him to stay until he came for him, and he didn't dare do anything else. Farr persuaded him to go home with Mr. Washington for a couple of days and then return to help him build a large open fireplace with a cobblestone chimney. The women would need a place to cook if the settlers all had to gather inside the stockade and stay for any length of time.

Liberty liked having the homestead to themselves again. It was peaceful after weeks of being among so many people. She worried too, because if Stith was going to do anything to even his score with Farr, it would be while the men were away. She didn't believe for a moment that he would forget the humiliation of her rejection and the beating he took from Farr. His pride would not allow it.

During the months Liberty had been at Quill's Station, there had been only a few occasions when Indians had come within sight of the cabin. They usually used the river for travel. Late one afternoon, when a large group with women and children passed by on the road, Farr went out to speak to them and later gave them a side of deer meat from the smokehouse as a token of friendship. Occasionally a small group of mounted Indians passed through the woods, and Liberty learned of it only through conversation between Farr, Colby and Juicy.

Shortly after sunrise on Sunday, Liberty walked to the doorway of the cabin and was startled to see a group of mounted Indians come out of the woods to the west and head toward the house.

"They're coming in, Farr," Colby said in a conversational tone from the bench beside the door.

Farr was working on an axe handle and didn't look up. "How many?"

"Dozen."

The leader of the party was fully dressed, the others naked to the waist. His shirt was light, soft doeskin; long, fringed, and belted at the waist. His trousers were darker buckskin, also fringed, and on his feet were elaborately beaded moccasins. His midnight black hair hung down over his shoulders. Small blue feathers were tied to thin braids on either side of his face. He was an arresting figure, but it was the horse he was leading that caught Liberty's attention.

"Isn't that . . . that . . ." Liberty stumbled over the words and a cold fear settled in her stomach.

"Yessiree. It's the horse Rain rode away on, and that gent leading the mare is Tecumseh. Be gracious, Libby. Tecumseh is king among his people." Colby's voice was a low murmur. He got up and walked out toward Farr.

"Amy, Willa, bring the children and come out. We have company," Liberty said before she stepped out into the yard.

She prayed that Amy wouldn't run up to the horse and demand to know what had happened to Rain.

Farr stood and raised his hand in greeting.

Tecumseh slid from the horse and held out his hand.

"It is good to see my friend, Farrway Quill."

"It is good to see my friend, Tecumseh."

Colby and Juicy went forward and shook hands and exchanged a greeting with the Indian chief. Then Juicy acknowledged the remainder of the still-mounted party.

"Yo're welcome," he said in English, then repeated a similar greeting in the tongue of the Shawnee. The Indians nodded solemnly and slid from their ponies. They stood beside them until Juicy took his pipe out of his pocket and sat down under the oak tree. They sat down in a semi-circle around him.

"Fetch my bag of tobaccy, Amy," Juicy called.

"Willa, make up a batch of that switchel for our friends," Colby said, and sat down in the circle.

Farr and Tecumseh walked toward the cabin.

"You and Colby Carroll have taken wives since we last met."

"Only I have taken a wife."

"You have been long without a woman. Does this one fill your heart with joy?"

"She is all a woman should be. Liberty, come and greet my friend, Tecumseh," Farr called and held out his hand to her. He watched proudly as she came toward them, her head held high, her lips smiling. The Indian chief also watched, his expression hidden behind his unreadable face.

Liberty thought Tecumseh a magnificent figure of a man. He was tall, erect, muscular, light copper in complexion instead of the reddish brown of his people. He had a quiet dignity that would have set him apart from his men even without his fine dress. His mouth was firm and strong, his nose straight and narrow, his eyes a clear transparent hazel that showed a mild expression of interest.

"My wife, Liberty," Farr said when she reached them.

Liberty held out her hand. "I'm pleased to meet you."

His handshake was strong. "You are as fair to behold as my sister said. You have chosen well, Farrway." His eyes remained on her face while he spoke.

"She is a good wife," Farr said simply.

"And brave. My sister told me of her bravery. She sends greetings and a gift to the White Dove on the Wabash." He went back to his horse, returned with a bundle and held it out flat in both hands. "It is a token, for there is no way to pay for the life of a loved one."

"Thank you." Liberty took the bundle from his hands and unfolded a beautifully beaded, white doeskin dress and matching white knee-high moccasins. "Oh, thank you!" she exclaimed. "They're beautiful." Her eyes, sparkling with pleasure, went from one tall man to the other. She held the dress up in front of her.

"It is fitting for the White Dove," Tecumseh said solemnly, and looked at her with such an inexpressible intensity that when he smiled and a glimmer of humor shone from his dark eyes, she was the one to stare, because he was an extraordinarily handsome man. "My sister said she worried all through one night before she decided White Dove would be a more suitable name for you than Silver Fish."

Liberty's laugh rang out. "I'd much rather be a dove than a... smelly fish. Please thank Tecumapese for me."

"It will please my sister that you like her gift."

"Then she and Rain Tallman arrived safely?" Liberty's eyes went past Tecumseh to the mare and then back to his face.

"The White Dove has a fondness for the son of John Spotted Elk?" he spoke to Farr while still looking at Liberty.

"Yes. The horse Rain rode to Prophetstown is one my wife brought from her home in far away New York State."

"He asked me to return the horse and tell you to give Colby Carroll his pay. He also sent his promise to return when there is peace once again in the land."

"Then he's all right?" Liberty asked anxiously.

"He has gone to the land beyond the big water where he

will become a man. He talked of your sister and her marriage to Old Wolf. Rain Tallman will come for her one day."

"Did he say that?" Liberty asked, thinking it would be something she could tell Amy.

"He did not say the words, but he spoke much of her to his father, John Spotted Elk."

Tecumseh's head turned slowly until his eyes had viewed the entire compound. "We learned of the fort you build for the soldiers even before Rain Tallman came with my sister." It was a statement, and there was not a trace of accusation in his voice.

"Let us talk, Tecumseh, for it may be long before we can speak together again."

"Yes, Farrway Quill. It will be long before we may speak again like this."

Farr stepped inside the cabin and took from the mantle the ceremonial pipe given to him by Tecumseh years before. With a bag of tobacco and a burning sliver from the fireplace, he returned to the yard. He and Tecumseh walked toward the barracks that would temporarily house the patrols. They sat on the ground in front of the door and smoked in silence for several minutes before Tecumseh spoke.

"I am leaving this country to visit the tribes to the south and to ask them to become a part of our Indian union. I carry with me a message to all tribes, the Cherokee, Seminole, Choctaw, Chickasaw, and the smaller and more scattered tribes, the Santee and Cayuga, Catawba, and Biloxi, that they must pledge themselves to join the Shawnee to keep the white man from taking over our land."

"I cannot say that I blame you or that I wish you success. Because if you are successful in uniting the tribes in war against the whites, many of your people and my people will die."

"It is true," he said sadly. "But what are we to do, Farrway Quill? I cannot say what will become of us, as the Great Spirit has the management of us all at his will. I can only try to save our land and our people."

"I would do the same. I'm building the fort not for war, but to protect my family and friends should war parties come down from the north. The Sioux and the Fox are aligning themselves with the British in Canada, and I look for them to raid along the Wabash."

"This is true. I would hope the southern tribes will not do this. The Indian tribes should unite and become one nation, living in peace with the whites. Why are the whites alarmed at this? Has not the United States itself set the example by establishing a union of Seventeen Fires?"

"I don't know the answer, Tecumseh."

"I have instructed my brother, Tenskwatawa, that he should continue to preach our doctrine and that he should maintain the peace. It is extremely important now. Within another five moons the amalgamation will be powerful enough to stand by itself and make its demands. A great sign will be given to them and it will be a turning point in the fortunes of all the Indians of this great land. I believe this." Tecumseh stood. "I will bid farewell to the White Dove of the Wabash. You have nothing to fear from my people, Farrway Quill. I wish I could say the same for the Sioux and the Fox."

Liberty, dressed in the beautiful white soft dress and moccasins, stood in the doorway of the cabin and waited for Farr and Tecumseh to approach. She had brushed and braided her white-blond hair in two long ropes, and they hung down over her breasts. Her face was radiant, her eyes shining, her lips red and smiling. Farr's eyes clung to her. He was sure he had never seen a more beautiful woman. She was also lovely on the inside, where it counted the most. He was also sure that Tecumseh sensed as much.

Tecumseh saw the pleasure on Farr's face when he looked at his wife and felt a pang of regret for his lost love. Three years had passed since he had said good-bye to Rebecca Galloway, the blond, blue-eyed girl who had taught him to speak the white man's tongue so fluently and read the white man's words. He had loved her dearly. But as much as he loved her he could not forsake his people and adopt the white man's way of life and mode of dress, for to do as she required, he would lose the respect and leadership of his people.

Tecumseh untied the blue feathers from his own braids and retied them to the ends of Liberty's. He did this slowly, as if it were a ceremony. Something in the sad expression on his face made Liberty want to weep. When he looked into her face her eyes were filled with tears and shone like bright stars.

"Do come back," she whispered.

"Only the Great Spirit knows if we will meet again, for death is but an instant away from us all." His voice was heavy with regret.

Tecumseh shook hands with Farr and went quickly to his horse. He leaped to its back, turned and raised his hand in farewell. And then, followed by his party, he rode back into the woods.

Later that day Farr and Liberty walked toward the river, and Farr told her about the love affair between Tecumseh and Rebecca Galloway.

"I think you reminded him of Rebecca, Libby. She was blond and blue-eyed like you, or so I've been told. Her father was an Ohio farmer. Tecumseh spent time visiting with the family, and they became attached to him and he to them."

"Her father didn't mind Tecumseh courting his daughter?"

"Evidently not. He and Rebecca spent a lot of time together. She taught him the Bible, Shakespeare, and world and American history. He learned of Alexander the Great, Caesar, and other empire builders, and certainly during this time he pondered the efforts of Pontiac and King Phillip and the reasons they had failed. Eventually he asked Rebecca to marry him, and she consented on the condition that he abandon his Indian ways. Tecumseh thought it over for a month, then refused and bade her farewell, telling her that he could never leave his people."

"Oh, how could she? If she loved him and he loved her, couldn't they have found a compromise?" Liberty slipped her hand in Farr's and he held it tightly. Without her being aware of it, they had reached the river. Farr turned north toward the place where Fawnella was buried.

"Tecumseh feels strongly that his mission in life is to unite the tribes, and if all the tribes stand together, they will be a force to reckon with. He believes that it's the only way they can receive a fair share of the land and the say in governing it. He also believes that someday soon there will be a sign, an omen so obvious that all who believe in him and in the future of the Indian nation will take up their weapons and follow him."

"Oh, why must there be wars? Why can't they set aside so much land and let the Indians have it?"

"Because the land was theirs in the first place. Why don't the Indians set aside so much land and let the white people have it?"

Farr saw the worried look on her face, and wishing to make her smile again said, "You look mighty pretty in that white dress, little White Dove of the Wabash."

"Thank you." She could feel the rosy flush that covered her cheeks and looked quickly away. "Do you have an Indian name?"

"Tecumseh gave it to me a long time ago when Juicy and I first came here. It's *Wahbah-comeshi*."

"Meaning?"

"I don't know if I should tell you," he laughed down at her. They had reached the clearing where Fawnella was buried, and now they stood on the bank overlooking the river.

"Why not?"

"Because then I'll have to tell you how I came to get the name."

"I promise not to laugh."

Farr was holding both her hands in his. He brought them up to his chest and held them there. He almost lost himself in the radiance of her smile.

"I'll hold you to that promise. It happened shortly after we came here to the bend in the river. Juicy and I made a make-shift camp, and one day Juicy wandered away, leaving me here alone. When the Indians came out of the woods, I was sure they were going to scalp me. The only thing I knew to do was to climb the tree. I dropped everything and shimmied up the tree as high as I could get. I thought they hadn't seen me, but now I know I had left a trail a blind man could follow. The Indians stood under the tree and looked up at me. The big fellow began to laugh, and the others yelled taunts that I didn't understand, but they made me angry. I thought as long as I was going to die, I'd go down fighting. I started down the tree and when I got to the lower branches, I lost my hold and fell, landing right on my backside. The Indians doubled up laughing, and I jumped up ready to fight. I don't know what would have happened if Juicy hadn't come loping into camp."

"Then what happened?"

"Nothing. Juicy and Tecumseh had been friends for a long while."

"So what does your Indian name mean?"

"Oak Tree."

"Oak Tree?" Liberty let out a peal of laughter. "I'm married to . . . Oak Tree! Am I to be called, Mrs. Tree?"

"You promised you'd not laugh," he growled menacingly, grabbed her and held her close. "I'll have to punish you." He held her laughing eyes with his and lowered his lips to hers.

Unembarrassed and unintimidated, she eased her mouth up to his. Her lips parted softly as they touched his chiseled mouth. She felt the hand on her back slide down to her hips and press her upward. She kissed him lingeringly, sweetly, then turned her mouth away and laughed up at him.

"This is punishment?" Her arms encircled his neck and she pressed her mouth to his again.

It was hotly exciting, the familiar sweetness she had only known during the darkness of night. Her mouth opened under his and she sensed his growing hunger. The power of it goaded her to kiss him with a fiery hunger of her own. Her tongue darted through his parted lips to taste him.

It was so maddeningly good to have him hold her in broad

daylight. She was riding the crest of the wildest, sweetest abandon, her body moving slowly and sensuously against his, her hair coming loose around her face. His kisses became wetly passionate. The need for air forced her to turn her lips away.

"Oh, God! You sweet woman, you!" His voice was a breath in her ear. She could feel his heart racing against hers. "I haven't quite figured out what it is about you that draws me to you. I only know I want to be with you all the time. I'm jealous as hell of anything that looks at you or touches you."

Keep talking, darling, she thought.

"I was proud today." Farr's words came now in an agonized whisper. "You were beautiful and gracious. But I saw the way you looked at Tecumseh. And I thought you might have wished . . . you hadn't been so hasty to marry."

"No! Oh, no! How could you have thought that, my sweet man, when I love you so? You're my darling, my love, my life." Her arms tightened about his neck and his about her until she was lifted off her feet.

"You mean it? Am I your love?" It was a quivering whisper.

"Yes! Oh, yes. I've tried to show you . . . without saying it."

"Say it. Please say it again."

"I love you, my husband. I love you—"

"And I love you, my sweet White Dove." His arms loosened until her feet were once again on the ground and he could look into her upturned face. "I was afraid to love you, but I couldn't help myself. You bewitched me with your beauty, your goodness, your independent spirit. I wanted to tell you here in this place where I buried Fawnella so that you know the ghost of that time in my life is at rest. I love you with the love a man gives to the woman who stands beside him, who is truly his mate. It's a giving, taking, and a lasting love, sweetheart. The feeling I had for Fawnella was the awakening love a young boy feels for a young girl."

"I prayed that you'd really love me, the person inside me,

and not just...want my body in the night." She raised gold-tipped lashes and immediately became lost in the clear green pools of his eyes.

"Ah, honey..." His arms tightened lovingly. "I was loving you with my body and now I know with all my heart. I can't tell you what a wonderful change you've brought to my life."

"And mine. Oh, Farr, I've never had anyone to depend on, but that isn't why I love you. I love the man that you are: strong, loving, caring. That first night I saw the way you were with Mercy, and I think I fell a little in love right then. I love everything about you."

He laughed a little huskily and lowered his mouth to hers. His lips were soft and gentle.

"Everything about you pleases me. This little upper lip of yours, this little crease beside your mouth that shows when you're angry and press your lips together." He licked it with his tongue. "Open your eyes, Liberty Bell, and look at me."

Her lids fluttered open and she leaned back to look up at him. Now she was free to express her love for this big frontiersman who was her husband. All the love in her heart was reflected in her eyes.

"Does it please you when I butt into men's business, refuse to stay in a woman's place, insist on having my say?" Her eyes sparkled devilishly and there was laughter in her voice.

He smiled down into her radiant face. "It may not please me all the time, and I admit there are times when I want to spank your butt, but I'll fight for your right to say your piece." He placed a quick kiss on her nose. "Come and help me pull the weeds from around the flowers you planted around Fawnella's headboard."

"You were so busy...I had marigold seed—"

"I have been busy, but not much that you do escapes me."

The twilight was deepening when they walked, arms around each other, down the path toward the homestead.

Chapter
Twenty

It had been easy to find out the information that Hammond Perry believed would discredit Farrway Quill. The barmaid at the tavern was a wench looking for the main chance, and for a few shillings she had told him every word that had passed Norman Cooley's lips within her hearing. Most of it made little sense to her, but not to Hammond, who, by putting bits of information together, pieced out the story of Willa Carrathers' life and that of her former master. He began to form a plan, using the information the Thompsons gave him of how Quill had wrested the indentured woman from their control.

Captain Heald had written a report on his return to Vincennes stating that perhaps Lieutenant Hammond Perry was not the right person to be in charge of the defense of the southern half of the Illinois Territory. He had filed it with Major Taylor, the fort commander, and Hammond had been called to task. During the questioning he had conducted himself in a professional yet humble manner. He apologized for any mistakes he may have made and convinced the major of his sincerity to do his job to the best of his ability for God and country. There were no specific charges made against him, and due to the shortage of officers, Captain Heald's report had been filed away without Governor Harrison's having been made aware of it.

A month after his fight with Farr and a few weeks after Hammond had sent inquiries to Cairo and to Saint Louis trying to locate Norman Cooley, Stith arrived in Vincennes. At a back table in the tavern, over tankards of ale, Hammond swore Stith to secrecy and told him what he had learned about Willa Carrathers and how they could use the information against Farrway Quill.

Stith's usually flat eyes lit up. "Treason?"

"Treason." Hammond wiped the foam from his lips and smiled smugly.

"I can add fuel to that fire. I've been letting a half-wit Indian hang round my place, giving him a tot or two of rum now and then. He's good at sneaking around and seeing what's going on at Quill's. He told me Tecumseh paid a visit to Quill's Station. Quill showed him the barracks building he built for the patrols. Tecumseh looked it over, then he and Quill had a long talk."

Stith waited to see what effect this news had on Hammond. He was pleased to see a shine appear in his eyes and a smug, satisfied look settle on his dish-shaped face.

"Good, good," Hammond chortled, rubbing his hands with glee.

"If that Indian sucker is planning a war, what's he doing at Quill's? Is Quill going to open the gates and let those red devils in to massacre soldiers in their beds?" Stith lowered his voice to make his words more menacing.

"Tecumseh is out stirring up as much trouble as he can, and his brother Prophet is running amuck up on the Tippecanoe, talking about his crazy prophecies. It's a point we can add to the list against Quill. He was consorting with the enemy. If Harrison doesn't have him shot on the spot, he'll run him out of the territory. If that happens, he's as good as dead. I'll be waiting for him."

"You'll have to fight me for your chance at him." Stith took a large sip of the bitter ale. "When this is over, I'm taking over that station. I'm going to build a town around it and call it Lenningtown. I'll be the most man in the southern territory. The settlers will trade with me or starve. That blond bitch will come crawling to me when her belly's empty. When she does, I'll spit in her face and take that sister of hers right before her eyes. I always did like that young stuff that ain't been busted. That old man hasn't had her. He's too damned old."

Hammond wasn't interested in Stith's plans for Quill's Station. But he listened and pretended he did.

"After I settle with Quill, I'll concentrate on the bitch." Hammond's eyes swung around the empty barroom to be sure they were not being overheard by the nosy barmaid. "I figure it'll take about a month or six weeks for Cooley to get here. I offered him money, enough to bring the bastard running. As greedy as he is, he'll fight his way through the whole goddamn Indian nation to get here. I'll present my evidence at the right time and with luck we can try that bastard and have him shot before Taylor and Harrison know it."

"How'll you do that?"

"Because the officers sitting in judgment will be so goddamn worked up about Prophetstown, they'll believe anything I tell them about a traitor."

"What if the servant girl won't admit who she is?"

"I know ways to make that slut tell anything I want her to tell. It's your job to get her before Quill learns that we know about her."

Stith looked at the small man coolly. He didn't like him. He hated to admit it, but Liberty Carroll was right. He was a weasel and a piddly, low-caliber crook. In his opinion Hammond Perry was not fit to command a herd of cows, much less a platoon of men. But that was not his concern. He would use him.

"I said I'd have her here."

"All right. It'll be best if we're not seen together too often." Hammond stood. He felt more confident when he was on his feet looking down on the large man than he did sitting across the table from him. "When Cooley gets here I'll take the patrol south and arrest Quill. You just be sure that girl doesn't run off somewhere."

"Yeah," Stith grunted and raised his tankard to his lips. He heard the tapping sound of Hammond's boot heels on the plank floor as he left the tavern. "Cocky little bastard," he snarled. He emptied his tankard, banged it on the table, and yelled to the barmaid to bring more ale.

By late October the pumpkins had been gathered, the corn picked, and hay had been cut and stored in the loft of the barn. Liberty, Willa and Amy were busy making hominy, grinding corn into meal, and storing the turnips, potatoes and cabbages in the cellar. Colby located a bee tree. He and Farr brought home two deerskin bags of honey and enough honeycomb to make a good supply of candles.

After the stockade and barracks were finished, Farr offered fifty cents a day to any man who would stay and help add an extra room to his cabin and make a sleeping place in the loft for his growing family. Most of the men stayed on, and in three days' time the work was finished, with a double bed built into the wall of the extra room and three single beds in the loft. Willa and Amy sewed skins to fill with cornshucks for mattresses, and Liberty made pillows by stuffing the legs of worn buckskin britches with down feathers.

In the evening either Willa or Amy sat at the spinning wheel working the wool into thread to be knitted into warm stockings, caps and mittens. The nights now were cold, but warmth from the two fireplaces kept the cabin toasty warm. Farr, Colby and Juicy used every spare minute to saw the big tree trunks into manageable lengths so they could be split for use in the fireplace.

Liberty had heard nothing from Stith or her father. She seldom thought of Elija, and when she did, it was with a little guilty pang because it was so easy not to think about him. She went about her tasks with a smile on her face and a thankful heart. She had found a place to call her own. She had Farr's love, Amy was safe, Mercy and Daniel were healthy and happy, Willa and Colby spent more and more time together, and the stockade was there to give protection should they need it. Had she stopped to think about it, she would have realized that such a Utopian existence couldn't go on forever.

Early one morning in November the signal came. Three short blasts on the horn at three intervals. Liberty was on her way to the barn to gather eggs. At first she wasn't sure what it was. Then it came to her like a bolt. At the first sign of Indian trouble, the homesteader would blow on the horn. The signal would be picked up and passed on from homestead to homestead until everyone in the Wabash Valley was notified. Three short blasts, three times meant an Indian raid by a sizeable party.

Farr and Colby came running toward the barn, their rifles in their hands, powder horn and shotbags hanging from their shoulders. Juicy was already in the yard with the horn relaying the message to the homesteaders to the south.

"You know what to do, Libby," Farr said. "Keep the children and Amy in the house. You and Willa stay close to Juicy and do exactly as he says. The guns, the powder and shot are ready if you need them. Colby and I will ride out and see what's going on."

"Farr, darling—"

"Mind what Juicy says, Liberty Bell. He's in charge here until I get back."

"I will, darling. Don't worry about us. Please be careful, my love."

Colby rode out of the barn leading Farr's horse. Farr kissed Liberty hard on the lips, sprang up onto the bare back of the horse and followed Colby out the gate. Liberty stood looking after them, dazed by the sudden turn of events. In the space of a couple of minutes her ideal world had changed drastically.

Juicy shouted orders. "Tell Dan'l ta keep Mercy in the house, Amy. Ya 'n Willa stake the cows close ta the barn, then start carryin' water. The barrels is full, but the buckets ain't. Libby, close the shutters, then get yoreself up on the walk by the barracks 'n watch ta the south. I'm agoin' up on the roof 'n see what I can see."

"I can do that, Juicy."

"Do what I tell ya," he roared. "I ain't so gawddamn ole I can't climb a ladder."

Farr and Colby bypassed Lenning's place and went through the woods toward Luscomb's. They heard shots as they neared and saw Luscomb beside the wagon. He was fighting off two Indians while his wife and brother carried the children back into the house. From the looks of it, Farr concluded he had been loading his family in the wagon when the Indians attacked. Four more Indians came running out of the timber that lined the river, the black paint of war on their faces.

Farr jumped from the horse, knelt and took aim. His shot struck the first Indian, flinging him back. Colby's shot took the next one. While they were reloading, they heard an anguished scream and saw Dorrie Luscomb come running from the cabin. She swung the butt of the rifle at the Indian who was lifting her husband's hair. The blow never landed. A painted savage grabbed her, smashed her skull with his tomahawk and snatched the rifle from her hand. Seconds later he died from a bullet fired from Farr's rifle. The rest of the Indians broke and ran toward the river.

At a signal from Farr, Colby slipped into the woods to the north. Running lightly, Farr circled the south side of the homestead. They met at the river in time to see an Indian canoe riding swiftly on the downriver current and pulling to the far bank where half a dozen canoes were beached.

Satisfied that the raiding party had left the homestead, Farr and Colby hurried back to the capsuled horror of Luscomb's and his wife's murdered bodies lying in the yard. The bodies of four of their attackers were also there. Luscomb had killed one and Farr and Colby had accounted for three.

"Delaware." Farr leaned down and pulled an amulet from around the neck of the dead warrior who lay beside the wagon. "More than likely they've broken loose from

Tenskwatawa up at Prophetstown and have struck out on their own. It's a large party to require six canoes."

Farr could hear the children crying inside the cabin. The door opened and Peewee, Luscomb's young brother, stuck his head out.

"Keep the kids inside for a while," Farr called. He stooped and lifted the lifeless body of Dorrie Luscomb and placed her gently in the wagon. Colby laid Donald Luscomb beside his wife. Farr took a blanket from the hastily gathered belongings the family had piled in the wagon and covered the dead couple before he called out to Peewee. "Bring the kids out, and hurry it up."

With tears streaming down his face, the young boy came out of the cabin, cradling a crying infant in one arm and leading a three-year-old girl by the hand. His mother and two young boys followed. The elderly woman appeared to be in shock. Farr helped her up onto the wagon seat, put the infant in her arms and set the small girl on the seat beside her. There was nothing to do but put the two small boys in the back of the wagon with their dead parents. Colby gathered up the rifles from the dead Indians and put them in the wagon as well.

"Whip up the team, son, and head for the stockade," Farr said. "Colby will be with you."

Scattered shots were coming from the north. Farr turned his horse into the woods, and running him as fast as the tangled brush would permit, he cut west and then north so he would come out onto the road again. When he reached the place where he could see for any distance, he saw two wagons about a hundred feet apart coming on at full speed trying to outrun a group of mounted, yipping Indians. George Thompson's Negro man was whipping up the team. George was in the back firing his weapon. Farr could see the ashen faces of Mrs. Thompson and Harriet as they hung onto the sides of the wagon.

In the second wagon Maude Perkins sat beside the driver. She was holding onto the seat with one hand, and with the other she was stinging the backs of the sweating team with the whip. Her four boys were in the back, two on each side, firing when they thought the Indians were close enough to hit.

The first thing to cross Farr's mind was that the raiding party had split, some taking to the stolen horses, the rest going on downriver in the canoes.

Farr rode back into the woods, dismounted, ran to the edge of the timber, knelt and waited. When the Indians were within firing distance, he fired his weapon. A warrior was flung from his horse and the others pulled up suddenly. Farr reloaded in a matter of seconds, took aim and fired again. His bullet struck a rider, but didn't knock him from the horse. The Indians, mounted on mules and plow horses they had stolen, wheeled their clumsy mounts and looked for the unseen attacker. After a moment of confusion, they rode into the woods to the east.

Farr waited. When the Indians failed to reappear, he mounted and rode north for several miles. Seeing nothing and hearing no more shots being fired, he turned back toward home.

From the platform where she could see over the stockade, Liberty saw movement on the river. Keeping to the far bank and under the cover of the hanging willows, three canoes moved steadily. She shouted the news to Juicy, then shaded her eyes with her hand and looked south. Coming along the road were five black-clad, white-aproned and capped women of the Sufferite community. With them were three times that number of children, ranging in age from babes-in-arms to a girl not quite Amy's age.

Liberty's breath almost left her when she looked again to the river and saw that the canoes had come out from beneath the willows. Each canoe carried three painted warriors. They were paddling strongly against the current as they crossed to the Illinois side of the river. She looked again at the approaching women and children and realized that if they didn't run, they would never make it to the stockade before the Indians saw them. Without stopping to consider the risk, she climbed down from the platform.

"Indians! They're coming from the river!" she shouted. "Amy! Stay by the gate and let me back in." She heard Juicy shout for her to stay inside, even as she tugged open the gate. Ignoring his order, she squeezed out one side and ran down the road.

The women saw her coming and responded to her excited shouts for them to hurry. Each picked up a child and began to run, urging the other children to move as fast as their little legs would allow them. Liberty continued to yell for them to hurry, sped past them and grabbed up a small girl who was lagging behind, grasped the hand of another child and pulled her along. As they neared the gate they heard the yipping of the Indians and then a volley of shots from Juicy and Willa's guns. Amy ran out, grabbed an exhausted child up in her arms and raced back inside, where she set her down and pushed on the heavy gate to swing it shut as soon as the last of the women and children were safely inside.

"Take the children to the house," Liberty told the panting women. Then, "Can any of you shoot a gun?" They looked at her blankly. "Never mind," she said.

Shots came from the north and Juicy yelled, "Libby! Amy! Stay by the gates. Wagons comin'! Hee, hee, hee! Let 'em have it, Colby, boy! Shoot the bastards!" Juicy fired again. "Run, ya blasted, dog-eatin' varmints," he shouted. "Open the gate, Libby. They're acomin' in!"

Liberty and Amy pulled back the heavy double gate and the Luscomb wagon thundered through. Colby's mount danced nervously as he pulled him up to wait for another wagon. The Thompson wagon came through, closely followed by another. Colby swung his horse in a circle so he could scan the road to the north and then to the south. Seeing no one else approaching, he gigged his mount and rode through the gateway.

"Shut the gate!" He jumped from his horse and started up the ladder to the platform.

"But Farr—"

"Shut the gate! Farr'll be along."

"Libby, that was Papa in that wagon with Mrs. Perkins."

Liberty scarcely heard her sister. Her heart was pounding with fear. Farr! Farr! She couldn't think of anything else except that Farr was out there with those yipping savages. She climbed to the platform and squatted beside Colby.

"Where is Farr?"

"He'll be along. Don't worry." Colby lifted his head and peered cautiously over the barricade.

"Don't worry? Damn you! What happened to—"

"Calm down." Colby turned, grinned at her and stood his rifle butt end down on the platform so that the muzzle rested between the points of the logs that formed the stockade. Juicy did the same. "They're gone, for now at least. Farr's nosing around. It would take more than a flea-bitten Delaware to catch him."

"Delaware?" Juicy spat over the side. "Ain't ne'er had no use for Delaware."

"Luscomb and his wife were killed," Colby said sorrowfully. "The bodies are in the back of the wagon."

"Oh, my God! Those poor children." Liberty pressed her palms to her mouth.

"You and Willa better go on down and do what you can."

"Oh, and the baby. Oh, my goodness, Willa. What will we do about the baby?"

Colby caught Willa's hand when she passed him to follow Liberty. "Are you doin' all right, honey-girl?"

Willa tugged on her hand and glanced at Juicy. "Colby!"

"Don't be embarrassed, honey-girl." He brought her hand up to his lips and kissed her knuckles. "Juicy knows you're my honey-girl. Don't you, Juicy?"

"Well, I ain't blind, y'know."

"See there? Everybody knows. Kiss me before you go."

"I'll do no such thing! Colby!"

Colby laughed. "I love to tease you, darlin'. But I guess I'll have to watch my step from now on. I didn't know you could shoot. Or was Juicy doing all the shooting?"

"Hee, hee, hee," Juicy laughed. "T'warn't all my doin'. She was ashootin'. That gun'd knocked her tail over teakettle if'n she'd a had a full load in." The old man looked at her fondly. "Ya got ya a good woman, son. She's got a passel a grit. Scared hell outta one a the bastards without even aimin' at 'em."

"Good girl!"

The praise brought a rosy glow to Willa's cheeks, and when she dared to look at Colby, her heart fluttered at the warm proud look in his eyes. He placed a light kiss on the back of her hand before he released it, and she climbed down the ladder with a prayer in her heart that this wonderful feeling of belonging would last.

The Sufferite women had gathered their children into the far corner of the stockade. They huddled around them as if shielding them from the others. There was not a sound from the children or the women. They stood passively, waiting, when Liberty approached them to invite them into the barracks building to sit down. They shook their heads and turned away, then back to peek from under the stiff brims of their bonnets at her uncovered head, the red fringe on her blue shawl, and the beaded moccasins on her feet. As Liberty walked away, she could hear them whispering among themselves. How could they be so stupid? she thought. They would stand there like dumb beasts until that old man came and told them to move.

The Luscomb baby had cried fretfully for a half hour. It was hungry and could not be satisfied by the spoonsful of milk being put to its mouth. Amy tried everything she could think of to hush the baby's cries. Willa made a sugar tit that pacified it for a while; then it started up again. Finally, in desperation, Amy picked up the child and carried it across the side yard to where the Sufferite women stood with their children. They never turned as she approached, so she nudged one of them in the back with her elbow.

"I saw you nurse your baby." The woman turned and she raised her voice so she could be heard over the cries of the infant in her arms, and repeated, "I saw you nurse your baby. If you've got any heart at all, nurse this one. Its mother lies in that wagon yonder, dead." She shoved the child into the woman's arms, turned and walked back toward the house. Before she'd gone a dozen steps the baby's cries became muffled and then stopped.

Neither Liberty nor Amy made any move to speak to their father. They were busy with the Luscomb children and the grandmother, who had finally realized the enormity of what had happened to her family and was sobbing uncontrollably. The Browns arrived and Liberty went to greet them. The Palmers came in with several other families she hadn't met.

The one acre inside the stockade that had seemed large when they were building it now seemed to Liberty to be full and overflowing with people, wagons and animals. The quiet homestead was a beehive of activity, but so lonely without Farr. Every time the massive gate opened and he didn't come in, Liberty had to fight down the fear that he wouldn't return.

Maude Perkins began issuing orders with the precision of a drill sergeant as soon as they arrived.

"Elija, take the horses to the barn and rub them down. Mind that you do a good job, dear, or they'll catch a chill and won't be worth a flitter. The boys will do the shootin' if there's any to be done. John taught them good. Elija, move now. Stop lagging and holding onto your back. There's nothing wrong with it." She went close to him and dug her elbow into his ribs. "You didn't let it bother you last night," she whispered.

"But, Maudy—"

"Don't Maudy me, Elija Carroll. When you finish with the horses get that box of food out of the wagon and take powder and shot up to the boys. Mercy me, you're slow as molasses." She slipped her neat bonnet from her head and let it hang by the strings. "My, but Mr. Quill's done a fine job. Just imagine doing all this since we were here. We must do our part of the work, Elija. We'll need a fire out here so we women can have a cook spot. You do that and I'll take the shot and powder to the boys."

Maude hurried across the yard and met Liberty, who was headed for the Luscomb wagon.

"Mrs. Quill?"

"Hello, Mrs. Perkins."

"I was surprised to hear that you and Mr. Quill married. My, but that put a crimp in Harriet Thompson's plans."

"Harriet's loss was my gain. Not that I think Mr. Quill had serious intentions toward her."

"Dear, there's something I want to tell you before someone else does. Your father and I . . . ah, we jumped the broomstick. I'm Mrs. Carroll now." She tilted her head and smiled sweetly. "I hope you don't mind, dear. I've been lonely since John died, and I know Elija has."

"Of course I don't mind. I hope . . . you'll be happy together."

"I want you to know too, dear, that Amy is welcome to come and make her home with me and Elija."

Liberty's quick mind grasped the fact that her father hadn't told Maude that Amy had married Juicy. He was probably ashamed he had forced her into it.

"Amy has always been with me, Mrs. . . . . Maude."

"We'd be glad for her to come for a visit then. I've never had a girl to fuss over."

"I'll tell Amy."

"Maudy," Elija called. "Cain't one a the boys come tote this box?"

"No," she called over her shoulder. "You can do it. Hurry now, take the box inside, and come right back and start a fire for Liberty." She looked back at Liberty and smiled sweetly. "He just needs someone to tell him what to do. He's really a good hand at plowing, and I never saw a better hand at grubbing out stumps. He cleared out an acre of stumps this summer. We'll plant it next year in tobacco. Now isn't that grand?"

"Papa cleared an acre of stumps? Well, my, it sure is

grand. It's plumb . . . grand." It was grand, she thought, it was so grand she was dumbfounded.

"What can I do, dear?"

"Everyone will need a hot meal. Stew would be best and we can cook it out here. There's milk for the children and I have a big batch of bread, but probably not enough to go around. We're lucky it's not cold today."

"Leave it to me and Elija. We'll get a pot boiling and everyone can throw something into it. Don't worry, dear. I'll take care of it."

"Thank you. There's a big iron kettle in the barn. I'll get it."

"It's too heavy for you, dear. Elija can do it."

The small, neat woman smiled so sweetly it was hard for Liberty to believe she had the iron will to get any work out of her father. But there he was carrying the box into the house and coming back out just as she had told him to do.

"Elija," Maude called. "Go to the barn and get the big kettle."

Liberty excused herself and went to join the women gathered around the Luscomb wagon. All the women were there with the exception of the Sufferite women, who were still in the corner, and Florence and Harriet Thompson. The Thompson women sat huddled together on a bench beside the house, not speaking to anyone.

The women who clustered about the wagon were stunned by the tragedy. They were thinking how easily it could have happened to them. They talked, but not about the massacre. It was too new, the shock too fresh in her minds. Mrs. Brown was passing around her pewter snuff box and each lady took a pinch, sniffing it from between her fingers or placing it on the back of the hand to inhale. She offered the box to Liberty who shook her head.

"Ain't ya a snuffer, dearie?" Mrs. Palmer asked and then, not waiting for the obvious answer, continued, "I tried chewin' tobaccy once, but it made me sick." She chattered nervously. "Mrs. Quill, seems you'd use snuff. Landsakes, if'n half a what I hear is so, you do most things good as a man."

"Ain't it just a shame about Dorrie and her man? My, my, what'll happen to them younguns?" A woman spoke in a hushed tone as if the couple in the wagon would hear.

"It's terrible is what it is. Has anyone seen to the younguns?"

"They're inside," Liberty said quietly. She looked at the blanketed body of Dorrie Luscomb and tears welled in her eyes.

She heard a shout from the platform for someone to open the gate. It creaked open and Farr rode in. Relief made Liberty's shoulders slump. She blinked back the tears and went to meet him.

Chapter
Twenty-One

The men gathered around Farr to hear what he had to say. The women hung back, all except Liberty. She stood by her man, her hand held tightly in his.

"The raiding party was a group of renegade Delaware acting strictly on their own. They were not Shawnee. They—"

Mr. Palmer interrupted. "What difference does that make? They was Injuns, warn't they? An Injun's an Injun. They's all dog-eatin', murderin' bastards!" He looked around seeking approval and several of the men voiced the same opinion.

"I disagree," Farr said firmly. "All Indians are not the same, just as all whites are not the same. We've been here eight years. The Shawnee have been peaceable."

There was a murmur of disgruntled comments which encouraged Palmer to speak again.

"Tell that ta Luscomb over thar, and his woman, and that passel a orphant younguns. They ain't acarin' if'n the Shawnee's been *peaceable*."

"If you don't want to hear what I have to say, Palmer, back off, and I'll tell the rest of the men." There was an icy tone to Farr's voice that clearly said he was losing his patience.

"Go ahead. Speak yore piece." Palmer hitched up his britches, leaned over and spit out a chew of tobacco.

"Mr. Washington and I have been scouting north and south. As I said before, the Indians were a group of renegade Delaware. They've gone downriver, at least for now. I don't think they knew about the stockade or the signal horns. Some of you may have lost stock, but we didn't see any smoke, so you didn't get burned out."

"We ort a not hightailed it in here like we done. We ort a fought off the bastards like that Lenning feller done. Him 'n the nigger at the ferry didn't come in. Bet *they* didn't lose nothin'." The bearded homesteader who spoke looked around at the others to verify what he said. There was a murmur of agreement.

Farr took a long slow breath to steady himself. He was tired and hungry and irritated. When he spoke it was in a quiet, controlled voice. Every word came out clearly and struck the homesteaders like sharp stones.

"While Mr. Washington and I were scouting north of here, they axed his ferry. The Indiana side will have to be completely rebuilt. The ropes were cut and the ferry is now a couple of miles downstream. Mr. Washington should have stayed and protected his property instead of making sure it would be safe for you folks to return to yours."

There was an instant of quiet and shuffling of feet. Mr. Brown, who Liberty thought was one of the more reasonable of the homesteaders, broke the silence.

"The Sufferite men didn't come in. They sent their womenfolk, but they stayed to see they didn't get burnt out. Maybe it's what we should a done. If we hadn't had this place to come to, we'd a stayed and fought. Maybe we won't be so lucky next time."

"Hell! Quill don't have ta worry none. His woman's already here." Palmer's beady eyes settled on Liberty.

"Hush up that talk!" George Thompson spoke for the first time. "The damn savages would've had us, and the Perkins too if Quill and Colby Carroll hadn't came out and saved our hides. No one forced you to help build this place, Palmer. None of you had to come here, and none of you have to stay."

"We can come if we want 'n stay if we want. We put work in this place—"

"Quill put in more than any of us."

"I jist get riled, him a excusin' them Shawnee—"

The banging on a pan turned everyone's head. Maude and Elija stood by the fire. Elija banged on the skillet again, and Maude smiled sweetly.

"Come and eat. Bring your own bowls and spoons."

The meeting broke up. The women went to their wagons to get eating utensils, the men wandered away in groups, talking to each other in low voices. Liberty stood beside Farr. It had been hard for her to keep still, but she was learning the ways of the frontier. If she had spoken, Mr. Palmer would have been pleased to try to hush her up, and it would have caused more problems for Farr.

"What's the matter with them, Farr? They're the most ungrateful bunch I ever met."

"They're scared, Libby. When a man's scared he has to blame someone."

"But you've done so much, worked so hard—"

"They work hard trying to improve their homesteads. Some of them think that what they helped us do here is an improvement on my land. The truth is, I hate it. I don't like looking out my door and seeing nothing but that blasted stockade."

"I don't like it either, darling. When this is all over and there's peace again, we'll tear it down."

"I love you, Mrs. Quill." He smiled down into her face. The noisy din around them faded away and there were just the two of them, cocooned in the warmth of their love.

"I love you, Mr. Quill."

His hands came up and gripped her shoulders and then slid caressingly up and down her arms.

"I think your pa's met his match." His mouth twitched and humor came into his eyes.

"I think so too." She giggled softly. "Maude said they'd jumped the broomstick. I guess that makes them married until they get to a preacher to make it proper. She said Papa cleared out an acre of stumps this summer."

"And that's strange?"

"Strange? You'd have to know Papa better to know how strange. Amy won't talk to him, and he seems to be avoiding me."

"Give it a little time, honey. He may be different now that he's out from under Lenning's influence."

"Open the gate," Juicy called from the platform.

Liberty walked with Farr to the gate. He swung it open. Preacher Ellefson stood there. The Sufferite leader didn't speak or step inside the stockade. He raised his hand and beckoned. The Sufferite women, herding their children in front of them, filed out the gate. The one carrying the Luscomb baby thrust the sleeping child into Liberty's arms as she passed.

Farr propped the gate open. He and Liberty watched the procession file down the road, the preacher leading the way. Liberty looked up and met his twinkling eyes.

"I think maybe the old boy has the right idea," he said teasingly. "He sure knows how to control his women."

"Farr Quill, those poor women don't have minds of their own any more. They didn't talk to anyone or let the children play. That old man beckons and they follow. You'd not want me to be like that. Your life would be too easy. You'd not have anyone to argue with, or insist on having their say."

"You're right, sweetheart. I wouldn't change but *one* thing about you." He looked down at the babe in her arms and then into her eyes, his glinting devilishly.

"One thing?"

He bent his head to whisper in a voice he used only when they made love, "I'm waiting to see you get as round as a watermelon."

"Well!" She gave him a sassy grin. "You're just going to have to work harder at getting that job done, Mr. Quill. Looks like you've got your work cut out for you."

Night came early. It was clear and cold. A large red moon came up over the treetops. Although eager to get home, the settlers decided to stay the night and see the Luscombs decently buried in the morning.

Guards were posted, even though Farr was reasonably sure the danger had passed. The women and children were settled for the night in the house, three or four to a bed, and on pallets spread on the floor. The men and older boys bedded down in the empty barracks building where a fire had been going all day in the fireplace. It was not as warm as the house, but it was reasonably comfortable.

Florence and Harriet Thompson took their blankets into Colby and Juicy's room, getting as far away from the others as they could. Mrs. Thompson was still smarting from the beating her pride had taken the last time they were there.

As far as Willa knew they had not spoken to anyone. They watched her with hate-filled eyes. It had made her extremely nervous for the first hour or so after they arrived. But then she became so busy she almost forgot about them. She had given all her attention to the three older Luscomb children and their grandmother. Amy had solved the problem of feeding the baby for the day, but the Sufferite woman had left the stockade, and some other arrangement would have to be made.

When the house was quiet, Willa lay on her pallet, wide-eyed and awake. The infant was beside her. She wondered what she would do to keep it quiet if it awakened and wanted to eat again. The last of the milk had been doled out to the children before anyone thought to save some for the baby.

An idea that she wanted to talk over with Liberty had been in the back of her mind all evening. She remembered from her childhood in London that many babies were raised on goat's milk. Sugar Tree loved children. She and Mr. Washington had a couple of goats—if Sugar Tree hadn't butchered them. Willa thought now that that was a likely possibility. She hated the thought of the Sufferites taking the Luscomb baby. She hoped there would be some way the children could stay together, but that too was a remote possibility.

The immediate problem was feeding the baby. She decided she would get up early, really early, go to the barn and milk. Perhaps the infant would sleep until then.

In the wee hours of the morning the baby began to whimper. Willa woke instantly and put the sugar tit in its mouth. It sucked noisily and drifted back to sleep. She got up and knelt beside Amy's pallet.

"Amy," she whispered. "Wake up."

"Huh?"

"I'm going out to milk. Move over by the baby and keep the sugar tit in its mouth."

Amy grunted and shuffled sleepily over to the other pallet.

Willa pulled a sliver of wood from the coals in the fireplace, blew on it until it blazed, then lit the lantern. She took Colby's coat from the peg on the wall, threw it around her shoulders and went out into the cold darkness. The stars were bright. The moon, having nearly completed its journey across the sky, shone faintly through the trees to the west. It was good to be out of the stuffy cabin. Nothing stirred. Usually when she came out to milk the geese waddled out to meet her. But not that morning. They were in a pen down by the springhouse to keep them out from underfoot.

Willa reached the barn, pulled open the heavy door, and slipped inside. She heard the lowing of the milch cow, raised the lantern and saw her at the end of the barn, tied to a rail. There were six stalls in the barn, three on each side, and a long narrow aisle between. Loose hay was piled at the end and the cow was chewing contentedly. Willa took a bucket from the nail on the post, hung her lantern on the nail, and hunkered down beside the cow.

"Bossy, bossy," she crooned, her head snug against the side of the cow. "We got to have milk for the babe."

Her strong, experienced fingers pressed the cow's udder, then she grasped a teat in each hand. The stream of milk from first one teat and then the other hit the bottom of the bucket with a familiar swishing sound.

"Bossy, bossy, good bossy," she continued to murmur to the cow as she milked. Willa liked to milk, liked the smell of the cow, the warm milk. Bossy was such a calm, contented animal.

One of the horses moved restlessly in its stall. Willa looked over her shoulder and thought that perhaps it was the colt, or maybe the mare was coming in heat which would make the stallion restless. She continued to milk until she heard a scraping sound, then a muffled curse. Fear brought her to her feet and turned her around. She gasped.

Stith Lenning stepped out into the aisle from one side and another man came from the other. The man stepped back, and Stith Lenning walked down the aisle ahead of him.

"I tole ya she'd come out. Didn't I tell ya? Didn't I, Mr. Lenning? The Injun said she'd come afore daylight. She ain't a bad looker fer a bond gal."

"What do you want?" Willa backed against the cow. The words came out in a choked whisper.

She had never seen Stith Lenning up close. Looking at him now she could see why Liberty feared and hated him. His eyes were such a light gray they barely had any color to them at all. His face was broad, his mouth and nose big, and his hands—the one that came up and clamped over her mouth before she could scream was big too.

Fear made Willa almost crazy. She lashed out with her hands and feet, her blows landing on his chest and chin, but her puny strength only irritated him. He held her away from him. With one hand over her mouth and the other at the back of her head, he lifted her by the head until she stood on tiptoe.

"Be still," he snarled, "or I'll break your damn neck. Get a rag to stuff in her mouth."

Willa was more frightened than she'd ever been in her life. Oh, Colby! Farr! Somebody! Please come, she thought. In desperation she began to struggle again. Stith swung her roughly about. His hand left her mouth, but the instant it did, the other man filled it with a dirty rag. Willa gagged as the rag was tied securely in place. Her hands were pulled behind her back and bound tightly.

Now that she was silenced, the other man moved close and ran his hand down over her breast. She struck out at him with her foot and he grinned, showing stubs of broken teeth. He was fairly young, but his face was scarred from many fights and his eyes were bloodshot and watery. He wore a knit cap on his head and a heavy wool coat. It was the clothing of a riverman.

Stith looked at her closely, and when the man lifted his hand to her breast again, Stith knocked it away.

"We got what we come for. Let's go."

"I ain't had me nothin' like this fer a long time. I'd shore like ta see what's under them skirts."

"It's the same as under any skirt. You can have all you want of it as soon as we get her down to my place. Now get up in the loft and drop down. I'll get her up there and lower her down to you."

Willa's eyes went wide with fear. She hadn't known there was a place to get out of the barn from the back. The barn was built out of upright logs, the same as the stockade, and they had used the barn as a section.

"Ya want that I tip that lantern in the hay?" The weasel-faced man was already on the rungs leading to the loft.

"No, you fool. It'd draw attention and we need to be long gone from here before she's missed. Get on up there."

Stith yanked on Willa's arm and shoved her toward the ladder. She shook her head. There was no way she could climb it with her hands tied behind her back. Stith seemed to realize that. He picked her up and flung her over his shoulder. Jackknifed, she had the wind knocked out of her. Her head swam and she thought she would throw up. She knew if she did she'd choke to death.

Stith went up the ladder to the loft. Bending low because there wasn't room in the loft for him to stand erect, he felt his way along the wall to the end of the barn. He set Willa on her feet and with one hand clamped to her arm, he stuck his head out through an opening and looked down.

"Psst! Are you there?"

"Yeah."

"I'll drop her down."

Willa began to struggle again, her fear giving her strength.

"Goddamnit! Be still!" Stith jerked her to him and slapped her so hard her head struck the wall. Stunned, she sagged against him. He picked her up and pushed her feet and legs through the opening. Then, with his hands beneath her arms, he lowered her.

Willa vaguely realized the man below had grasped her around the legs and heard him say: "I got her. Ya can let go."

The full length of her slid down the man's body. Her skirts came up to her thighs, and she felt a rough hand between her legs. The shock of it brought her to full awareness, and she threw herself away from him, stumbled and fell. Seconds later Stith dropped down beside her.

"Damn you to hell! I said leave her be for now." Stith bent over and yanked Willa to her feet. "Let's get out of here."

"I was jist afeelin' her twat," the man whined.

Stith's hand on her upper arm was like a vice. It propelled Willa's feet forward. They had gone only a few stumbling steps when they heard a dull thud. Stith stopped and swung halfway around. The man beside them dropped like a stone. Willa was grabbed from behind and yanked out of Stith's grasp with such force that she was thrown to the ground.

"Get out of the way, Willa!" Farr's voice came out of the darkness. Willa rolled and rolled until she came up against the back of the barn.

"Gawddamn you, Quill!" Stith bellowed with rage.

"You stupid, raping, son of a bitch!"

"Is talkin' all you can do?"

"No, by God! I'm going to kill you!"

"Have a go at it then," Stith snarled.

Farr saw the gleam of the knife blade and drew his from his belt. Both men knew this fight was to the finish, that one of them would die. Farr was determined it wouldn't be him. He knew better than to get in close to a man Lenning's size when he had a knife in his hand. He backed off and waited. Stith moved to the side, then back, waiting for a chance to move in. Farr knew these tactics and turned slightly to the side, giving him the chance. Stith lunged. Farr's move was lightning fast. He drew back his arm and threw his knife with the speed of a well-aimed bullet. Momentum kept Stith coming even after the knife pierced his heart to the hilt. Farr stepped out of the way. Stith passed him and fell.

Farr stood over him for a moment, then turned him over and pulled the knife from his chest. He had been a man and now he was nothing. Farr felt not an ounce of pity for him, for what he was doing to Willa was a vile, treacherous thing.

"Willa," he called softly. "It's me, Farr. You'll be all right now."

"Mmmm. . . ."

He found her, lifted her into a sitting position and took the dirty rag from her mouth. Willa gagged and gagged, and when she stopped gagging, she began to cry. Farr untied her hands and helped her to her feet.

"Is he . . ."

"He's dead." Farr put his arm around her and she leaned against his shoulder. "He wasn't a knife fighter, but he chose the weapon. It was him or me."

"There's a hole in the back of the barn."

"I found it. I saw the light and came out to see if you were all right. I heard a noise in the loft. When I got up there, they had already dropped you down and Lenning was going out the opening."

"They were going to take me to his place and he was going to let that other man—" Willa was shivering from the cold and from nerves.

"Don't think about it." He patted her on the shoulder. "Are you all right? I've got to tie up the one I knocked out. Then we'll go around to the gate."

The shock of being taken by force and seeing a man killed had shaken Willa so much that her weak knees could scarcely hold her. When Farr awakened Colby, she fell sobbing in his arms. Farr left her with him, went to Liberty's pallet and touched her cheek with his fingertips. She was instantly awake.

"Come," he whispered. He wrapped the blanket around her and they went out into the crisp morning air.

"What's happened?"

"I just killed Stith Lenning."

"Oh, my goodness! Are you all right?" She wrapped her arms about his waist. "What in the world was he doing here in the middle of the night?"

He told her about Willa. "She's with Colby now. Poor girl, she was scared half out of her wits. Colby loves her, you know."

"I know. But not like I love you. Darling, I'll be so glad when all the people leave and we're alone again. But you don't need me to tell you that now. What do you want me to do?"

Stith Lenning's body was brought in and laid out some distance from where the Luscombs lay in their hastily built coffins. The men wandered over to look at him.

"Don't look like it was much of a fight." Amos Palmer stroked his chin thoughtfully.

"He daid, ain't he?" Juicy snorted.

"Ain't no marks on Quill, is they?"

"'Course they ain't. Farr's as good with a blade as anybody I ever did see. He can pin a fly ta the wall if'n he takes the notion."

"I just said there ain't no marks on Quill."

"I heared what ya said, dadblameit! Are ya sayin' Farr didn't give 'em a chance at 'em?" There was a threatening edge to Juicy's voice.

"I ain't asayin' nothin'. I ain't the big muckity-muck 'roun' here."

"Ya be a whisker away a bein' nothin' a'tall." Juicy spoke slowly and his hand moved down to the knife in his belt.

"Now simmer down." Edward Brown stepped in between the two men. "We're all jumpy. We can't be fightin' amongst ourselves. We got these folks to bury. Think of those poor younguns without no ma and pa."

The men gathered around the breakfast fire. The talk was of nothing but the attempt to kidnap Willa and the killing of Stith Lenning.

"Women what go flauntin' themselves is trouble sure

enuff. It was untimely early fer her ta be out thar in the barn. Seems like somethin' ain't right somehow." Amos Palmer, stung at backing off from an old man, continued to voice his opinion.

"What do you mean? Do you think the girl wanted to be dragged away by those men?" Maude was turning meat in the big spider skillet and whipped the smoke away from her face with the end of her apron.

Palmer ignored Maude and turned to the man beside him. "Lenning minded his own business far as I know. Right well set up too. What'd he be draggin' off a bond gal fer? 'Pears like he coulda bought her if'n he'd wanted her. It don't make no sense a'tall."

"There wasn't any milk and the Luscomb baby was hungry. That's what Willa was doing in the barn." Maude spoke with exaggerated patience as if she were talking to a child. "More meat, Mr. Palmer?" She looked pointedly at the big piece on his plate.

"I don't recollec' that I was atalkin' to ya."

"Elija, dear," Maude said with her usual sweet smile, "put more meat in the skillet. If we keep Mr. Palmer's mouth full he'll not be able to *blab* so much."

"Why . . . why," Amos Palmer sputtered. "Ain't nobody ever goin' to hear my woman backsassin' like that. If'n was mine I'd learn ya yore place."

A long forgotten manhood made itself known to Elija. He bristled with indignation. Before he stopped to think of the possible repercussions, he faced Palmer squarely and spoke sternly.

"Watch yore mouth if'n ya ain't awantin' a real plaguey hobble. Nobody's talkin' such ta my woman!"

Palmer's mouth dropped open. He started to say something, thought better of it, then turned and elbowed his way to the back of the crowd.

"You're such a sweet man, Elija," Maude whispered. She smiled proudly up at him and squeezed his arm.

"Naw, I ain't," he said with a new dignity, but somewhat stunned that Palmer hadn't hauled off and hit him.

*   *   *

Juicy and Colby stood over the riverman who sat slumped against the wall of the barracks, his hands and feet tied. Through the blur of pain in his head, he had told them his name was Hoffman.

"I ain't done nothin'," he whined. "I was scared a that big feller 'n done what he tole me." He looked fearfully at the tall, light-haired man they had pulled off him when they first brought him into the stockade.

"Bullshit!" Colby snorted. "I ought to put a bullet right between your eyes!"

"He ain't worth the waste a one." Juicy let go a stream of tobacco juice that landed dangerously close to the man.

Farr came toward them with a shovel on his shoulder. He and some of the men had dug the graves on a grassy knoll on a slight rise across the road from the homestead. He had asked Peewee Luscomb if he wished to take his kin back to their homestead and he had shaken his head numbly and asked Farr to pick a place.

A grave for Stith Lenning had been dug some distance from that of the Luscombs.

"What are we going to do with this piece of horseshit, Farr? I'm for hanging him." Colby glared down at the terrified riverman.

"Naw, Colby boy." Juicy cut off another chew of tobacco and stuck it in his jaw. "That be over in a wink. What say we burn 'em?"

"No!" Hoffman screeched. "I ain't done nothin'. I tole ya I warn't goin' to hurt the gal!" The man was livid with fear and Farr decided to let him suffer for a while.

"Let's get the burying over, then we'll vote on hanging or burning."

Chapter
Twenty-Two

B y mid-morning the burials were over, and the settlers began to pack their wagons for the return trips home. The boy, Peewee, would take his family, except for the baby, back to the homestead. Farr had talked to him and to the grandmother and told them he was sure that one of Mr. Washington's goats was giving milk. He asked them if they had any objections to Sugar Tree taking care of the baby if she were willing. The grandmother had said they would be grateful for her help.

The Thompsons and the Palmers pulled out ahead of the rest and headed north. A half hour later the other wagons were ready to go. The children had been bundled up against the cold late November wind, and the adults stood in the yard beside their wagons, visiting. Unless there was more trouble, it would be spring before they saw their neighbors again. Liberty and Farr stood among them, saying their good-byes.

"Patrol comin'! Patrol comin'!" The call came from one of the men who had led his team outside the gate.

There was instant excitement among those waiting to leave. Some people walked, some ran to the gate and waited for the soldiers, hoping against hope that they were not bringing news of another raiding party. They stood silently and watched the procession as it approached.

Sitting ramrod straight, Hammond Perry led a platoon of twelve men down the road and into the stockade. With a clatter of hooves, the disciplined soldiers rode into the area, turned and formed a single line behind the sergeant and the lieutenant.

In his colorful uniform of blue and red, Hammond Perry stood out from his buckskin-clad troops like a small peacock in a barnyard, Liberty thought, and a wave of apprehension seized her. He walked his horse to the center of the compound. There was hardly any sound at all except for the creak of saddle leather, the stamping of hooves, and the sharp chatter of a squirrel high in the oak tree. His eyes settled on her face, then on Farr's. He sat his horse and carefully scrutinized every nook and corner inside the stockade.

When he spoke, it was to make a crisp announcement.

"Go on back to your homes. The danger is over for now. The Delaware have gone downriver."

Hammond walked his horse back to the troops and spoke in low tones to the sergeant. A wary look came over the sergeant's face, then he frowned.

"Sir? I'm beggin' yore pardon, sir—"

"It isn't your job to question my orders. Do it!"

"Yes, sir." He turned to the troops and shouted, "Dismount." The men swung from their horses and stood at their heads.

Hammond looked down the line of troops, then nodded to the sergeant. He moved his horse to the side and turned to face the crowd.

"Rifles at the ready!" the sergeant shouted.

The men responded instantly. They dropped to one knee, lifted their rifles and aimed them at the group standing in the yard.

"My God! They be agoin' ta shoot!" someone shouted, and the crowd began to scramble for cover.

A woman screamed, a man cursed, and frightened children began to cry. Some of the people ran behind their wagons, some ran inside the barracks, some stood as if rooted to the ground.

"What the hell are you up to, Perry?" Farr strode forward with Colby and Juicy beside him.

"I'm placing you under arrest, Quill. Seize him!" he ordered sharply.

Farr made no move to struggle when the two burly troopers

pounced on him, knocked him to the ground, then hauled him to his feet. Liberty came running across the yard, wormed her way between the soldiers, and grasped Farr's arm.

"What's happening?"

"Stay back out of the way, sweetheart. We'll find out soon enough."

"Farr! Oh, darling—"

"Remove the wench from the prisoner," Hammond ordered crisply.

The sergeant took Liberty's arm. "Come away, ma'am," he said gently. "It ain't goin' to help none to make him mad," he murmured for her ears alone.

Liberty was in no mood to heed his warning. Anger, like a living thing, rose up from the very core of her being. It jarred and then shook every reasonable thought from her mind. She jerked her arm from the sergeant's grasp.

"You vile, stupid, feather-headed, jackass!" she shouted. "You slimy toad! You're a *little* man, Hammond Perry, trying to make up for your lack of size—"

"Libby, hush." Her father's voice only goaded her to say more.

"You'll never be half the man Farr Quill is if you live a hundred years. I'm glad your brother didn't live to see you again. He thought you were so grand, but you're nothing! Nothing! He was ten times the man you are. You're hateful and spiteful and ugly—"

"Enough!" Hammond roared. His face was beet red. He gripped the ends of the reins as if he intended to strike her. "I'll not take insults from such as you!"

"You've no right to arrest Farr!" Liberty was not the least bit daunted by his anger.

"I have been authorized to arrest him for treason. Now it's treason and *murder*. I was told by Amos Palmer that he killed Stith Lenning this morning."

A murmur rose from the people who had come out from behind the wagons and gathered in a small knot. Mrs. Brown stepped forward.

"T'wasn't murder, Lieutenant. Lenning was takin' off one of the women here—"

"Were you there? Were you a witness to the killing?"

"Well, no, but—"

"I suggest you take your family and go on home. This is no concern of yours."

The sergeant gently pulled Liberty back. "Why is he doing this?" she whispered frantically.

"He's showin' us who's boss, ma'am. Don't worry 'bout your man. He'll get a trial. I'll see nothin' happens 'tween here 'n Vincennes."

"He killed him, guvner. I saw him do it. Cold blood, it was!" the riverman yelled. "They be goin' to kill me too. Burn me, they said."

Hammond turned cold eyes on the riverman. He studied him for a moment before he spoke. "Untie that man and bring him here."

"That bastard was helping Lenning." Colby's voice rolled out over the murmur of disapproval from the crowd.

Hoffman's feet were untied. He stumbled in his haste to get to Hammond's horse. "I warn't doin' nothin', guvner. The wench was awantin' ta go with us. She be sweet on Lenning 'n—"

Colby turned suddenly and struck the riverman across the mouth. It was a wicked, powerful blow, and the man staggered and fell in a heap. He lay on the ground with blood trickling from a smashed lip. Colby heard the click of metal and found himself looking down the barrel of Hammond Perry's rifle.

"Get back or I'll shoot you where you stand for interfering with government business," he snarled. "This man is witness to a murder."

"He's a goddamn liar!"

"That's for the court to decide." Hammond raised his voice. "Sergeant, get the woman, Willa Carrathers, out here."

"What's she got to do with it?"

"I don't have to explain my orders to you, Carroll. Back

off! Get a mount for Quill and one for the woman, sergeant, unless you want to ride double."

"Lieutenant? Can I speak to you privately?"

"No, you may not. Do as you're told or face charges yourself when we get back to Fort Knox."

"Yes, sir. Johnson! Slane! Saddle up a couple horses."

"You rotten son of a bitch! You're not taking Willa!" Colby shouted and would have dived at Hammond if Juicy had not grabbed him.

"Hush, boy. Look at Farr. He knows the odds is piled agin us. Our time'll come."

Liberty had never felt so helpless in all her life. She had no doubt Hammond would order Farr shot if he resisted. Farr knew that, too. He stood perfectly still. She went to him and put her arms around his waist. The soldiers holding his arms made no move to stop her.

"What does it mean, darling? How can you be charged with treason and murder?"

"I don't know, sweetheart. He's got something in mind. Don't rile him anymore. He's just stupid enough to open fire."

"Where will he take you?"

"Vincennes. It's the only place he can take me. It'll be all right. I have friends there. Go talk to Willa and tell her not to worry. The sergeant is a decent sort. He'll see that nothing happens to her."

"Why is Hammond taking her?"

"He'll try to use her as a witness against me."

"But . . . treason?"

"There's no way he can prove I've betrayed my country."

"I love you. Oh, I love you."

"I love you too, sweetheart."

Colby was with Willa and she was crying. He had put her in his heavy wool coat and tied a shawl over her head.

"Don't worry, darlin'. I'm coming too. I'll follow you all the way, and when we get to Vincennes we'll get this thing straightened out."

"What have I done?"

"You haven't done anything. He's using you to get to Farr. All you'll have to do is tell what happened, and we'll be back home in no time at all. You're not alone anymore, sweetheart. You've got me and Farr and Liberty. Come on, smile for me, pretty girl."

"I'm scared, Colby."

"Don't be scared. I'll not be far away. He can't keep me from following. If anyone lays a hand on you I'll kill him. I swear it."

"Come on, ma'am, mount up." The sergeant turned his back to Hammond and mouthed to Colby. "She'll be all right."

Liberty brought Farr's heavy coat and he slipped it on before they tied his hands behind his back. She only had time to kiss his cheek before the troopers shoved him toward the horse and helped him mount.

"Stay close to Juicy and listen to what he tells you," Farr said. "I'll be back soon. Juicy," he called, "get word to Mr. Washington."

"I'll do it, son."

The sergeant allowed Colby to help Willa mount and then led her horse and Farr's to the middle of the procession. The riverman was boosted up behind one of the troopers and the sergeant gave the order to move out.

Hammond Perry rode past Liberty. He tilted his stiff neck to look down at her. The gloating look on his face made her sick to her stomach.

"You don't have much luck with your husbands... Liberty. Perhaps you'll do better next time."

The deliberate use of her given name was an insult that Liberty ignored. She ran to the gate, and when Farr passed by his eyes clung to hers even as he turned in the saddle to look at her for as long as possible. She could scarcely see him for the tears, yet she stood there until he was out of sight.

Liberty wanted to scream, to rant and rage at the injustice being done to Farr. She turned and went back inside the stockade. If Colby was going to Vincennes, she was going too.

The settlers were gathered in bunches, all talking at once.

This was the most exciting thing that had happened in a long while.

Elija stepped out away from the Perkins' wagon as Liberty ran toward the cabin.

"Libby . . . I be plumb sorry—"

She didn't stop or look at him. "It's too late to be sorry," she said angrily. "I'll never forgive you for telling Stith we were coming here."

Colby was in the room he shared with Juicy. A blanket was spread on the bed and on it was a shirt and a bag of coins.

"I'm going with you."

He looked up. "All right. Take an extra dress for you and for Willa, underthings, and bonnets. Something that looks nice. We don't want to look like a bunch of ne'er-do-wells."

"Oh, thank you, Colby. I was afraid you'd argue."

He continued to throw things on the blanket. "It wouldn't have done any good," he muttered.

Amy, with the Luscomb baby in her arms and Daniel and Mercy hanging onto her skirts, came to the doorway of the new room Liberty and Farr had shared for such a short time.

"Are you going, Libby?"

"I've got to." She went to her sister and hugged her. "Please understand."

"I do, Libby."

"Thank you, honey. Oh, you've grown up so much this summer. Juicy will send word to Mr. Washington and Sugar Tree. They'll come and stay until we get back. You're not afraid, are you?"

"No. Don't worry, Libby. We'll be all right."

"I know you will." Liberty took a dress and a bonnet out of her trunk.

"I like that woman Papa married, but I don't want to go live with them."

"I'm glad. I don't know what Daniel and Mercy and I would do without you."

"Libby? Are you comin' back?" Daniel's eyes were big and round and full of tears.

"Of course I'm coming back." Liberty dropped to her knees beside him and hugged him and Mercy to her. "You help Amy with Mercy."

"Yes'm. Why'd they do that to Farr?"

"It's all a mistake, Daniel. I'm going to Vincennes and help to get it all straightened out."

"Can . . . can me 'n Mercy call you mama?"

"Of course you can. I'd be proud if you called me mama." She kissed his cheek and then Mercy's. "I've got to hurry so Colby and I can catch up to the patrol. Be good children, and mind Amy. I'll be back soon."

Colby led the horses from the barn and boosted Liberty into the saddle.

"Git right in 'n see Harrison, soon's ya get thar," Juicy said. "That little cock is got somethin' or he'd not a come actin' like he done. He was too sure a hisself. Ya got bribe money if 'n ya need it?"

"I got it. Got Farr's rifle and mine, plenty of powder and shot. Libby, did you get bread and meat? It's nearly fifty miles to Vincennes."

"I got it." She echoed what he'd said to Juicy without realizing it. "Juicy, do you think Sugar Tree will come?" Libby tried not to look at the anxious little group that stood in the doorway of the cabin.

"'Course she will. I sent word a'ready. Yo're not to worry none 'bout us. Jist get on up thar 'n do what ya can fer my boy."

When Liberty saw the tears in the old man's eyes, hers filled. She leaned over and with her hands on his shoulders to support her, placed her cheek against his.

"Oh, Juicy. I love you. We'll bring him back."

"We be waitin' . . . daughter."

It took an hour of hard riding before they sighted the patrol up ahead. Then they slowed the horses down to a fast walk.

"There's a connection between Lenning and Perry," Colby

said suddenly. "There's some reason why Lenning risked so much to try and get Willa. Willa remembered Lenning saying, 'we've got what we came for' and the other man saying, 'the Indian said she'd come out early to milk.' They were waiting for Willa, not just a woman, as we at first believed."

"What will they do with Farr when they get to Vincennes?"

"If Perry has proof to substantiate his charge, they'll put him in the guardhouse at Fort Knox. He's probably filed something with his superior officer. Perry doesn't have the authority to do something like this on his own."

"You mean Captain Heald?"

"Captain Heald was going back to Fort Dearborn. It's more than likely Captain Sinclair. He would be the senior officer if Major Taylor is away."

"What's the captain like?"

"Typical West Pointer—all rules and regulations. Hates Indians. He feels he was demoted when he was sent out here."

They lapsed into silence that lasted for a long time. Liberty wasn't used to riding. Soon she was gritting her teeth and concentrating on staying in the saddle. The insides of her thighs were rubbed raw, her back felt as if it would break in two, and her bottom felt as if it were being pricked by a thousand needles.

The patrol didn't stop until it was almost dark. Colby and Liberty moved in a little closer, and Colby found them a suitable place to stop for the night. He helped Liberty off the horse. She could barely stand.

"Keep moving," he said. "Don't stop or you'll stiffen up. I'll water the horses. Walk until I get back."

Liberty counted as she walked. Twenty paces and turn, twenty paces and turn. She was sore, tired and hungry, yet her bodily discomforts were nothing compared to the turmoil in her mind. Would Farr and Willa have blankets? Would they be fed? What awaited them in Vincennes?

Colby returned, unsaddled and staked out the horses. He brought the pouch that hung from Liberty's saddle and they sat down on a blanket and leaned back against the trunk of a giant oak tree.

"It'll be cold tonight. God, I hope it doesn't snow." Colby handed Liberty the food bag. "I don't want to risk a fire."

"They'll have one, won't they?"

"Yeah, but I don't want to take the chance someone will slip up on us."

Colby took a bite of the bread and meat Liberty handed to him and chewed slowly. They ate in silence, listening to the sound of the horses cropping the grass nearby and the whisper of dry leaves stirred by the wind. Each was thinking of someone not too far away, hoping they were warm, being fed. When they finished eating, Colby moved over closer to her.

"Lean against my shoulder, Libby, and I'll cover us with both blankets."

Grateful for the warmth, Liberty snuggled against Colby and wondered if she would be able to get on the horse in the morning. Finally she dozed.

Sometime later she became aware that Colby had tensed, and the rifle across their laps had moved. She lifted her head and listened.

"Psst! It's me, Sergeant Callaway." The voice came from behind the tree. A shadowy figure moved around from behind them and squatted down. Colby's finger eased off the trigger of his rifle.

"I could've blown your head off, Sergeant."

"I know it. Why do you think I was huggin' that tree? I just want to let you know the little lady is all right. Two of my best men are keepin' an eye on her. Both of them got girls not yet grown. They'll do right by your woman."

"How is Farr? Does he have a blanket?" Liberty asked.

"He's all right too."

"My husband isn't a traitor, Sergeant. I don't know what Lieutenant Perry thinks he could have done."

"He thinks he's done something. He's got the order from Captain Sinclair to come arrest him."

"Is Governor Harrison in Vincennes?" Colby asked.

"He left about a week ago for Fort Wayne. He's all fired

up about winning up on the Tippecanoe. Did you hear about that?"

"We haven't heard any news."

"We whipped the fire out a them Indians up at Prophetstown and scattered 'em to hell and back. Tecumseh'll have a hell of a time uniting the tribes now."

"When will Harrison be back?"

"I don't know, son. I'm just a sergeant."

"Then Perry's doing this while Harrison's away."

"'Pears like it. But Major Zack Taylor is commander at the fort. He be in Fort Harrison for a while. I don't know when he's due back. He's a fair man 'n his say overrides Sinclair's. Could be he don't know 'bout this yet. Tell ya what, Carroll, take Mrs. Quill to Moll Glover's house when ya get to Vincennes. It's down a ways from the Council House. It's got a sign. She'll have a room. Then what ya've got to do is try 'n delay things until Harrison or Zack Taylor gets back."

"Thanks, Sergeant," Liberty said.

"Yo're welcome, Mrs. Quill. Little Bandyass—'scuse me, ma'am, but that's what the troops call him—will hang hisself one day soon. I've gone through a half dozen lieutenants like him. I've been tempted to shoot him more than once myself. He'll push too hard one day 'n somebody's gun'll go off, accidental-like. We'll be pulling out at dawn. Should be in Vincennes by the middle of the morning. I'll see you at Moll's."

The sergeant moved around behind the tree and was gone without a sound.

Chapter
Twenty-Three

Liberty had expected Vincennes to be a raw, wilderness village of several hundred people. Instead it was a town, a real town with churches, taverns, mercantile and the Territory Capitol Building. When she expressed her surprise to Colby, he told her there had been a town there for eighty years. It had been settled as a French outpost in 1732.

A light snow was falling as they rode into town and down a rutted street. The houses were hewn timber set upright in the ground and chinked with stone and mortar. None were more than one story high. The roofs were slightly pitched and all had porches on one or two sides. All the houses, except for a few, Colby told Liberty, were patterned after the French houses in New Orleans.

As they approached the center of town, Colby pointed out the two-storied Legislative Hall, and Grouseland, the home of Governor Harrison. The mansion was the finest home Liberty had ever seen. It was big and square, two-storied, with a high pitched roof. A half dozen tall brick chimneys soared above the roof, and smoke was coming from all of them. The double porch roofs were supported by massive round columns.

"My, it's grand," Liberty said. "But I'd not trade my home at the station for it."

"Jefferson Academy is a few streets down, and this building is the newspaper office. It's the only newspaper in the terri— By God! That bastard's taking Willa out to the fort!"

They had been following along behind the patrol, keeping it in sight. Now Colby gigged his mount into a trot.

"Where's the fort?"

"A couple of miles above town. I'm going out there to see Captain Taylor."

"I'm going too."

A grin spread over Colby's tired face. "I thought you would."

Fort Knox was a well-established fort. The neat rows of barracks and officers' quarters had the look of permanency that more than twenty years gave to buildings. The timbers were weathered, the shingles peeling, the porch roofs sagging. Snow was now sticking to the ground and forming white patches. It stung Liberty's cheeks as she and Colby followed the patrol through the gates. Just inside they were stopped by a sentry.

"The lieutenant said you're not to come any farther, sir. I'm sorry." The soldier was young. Not even old enough to shave. His nose was red from the cold. The hand that held the rifle was rough and chapped. He stood with his shoulders hunched against the wind.

"You've told me," Colby said. "We're going in, are you going to try and stop us?"

"No, sir. I ain't never heard of no order like that before."

"Perry is a shithead. You know that, don't you?"

"Yes, sir." The soldier grinned.

Colby pressed a shilling in his hand. "Get a hot brandy when you go off duty."

"Thank you, sir."

The troops had been dismissed except for a small detail that surrounded Farr and Willa. They were dismounting in front of the headquarters building when Colby and Liberty arrived. Farr dismounted by himself, but the sergeant had to lift Willa from the saddle and hold onto her to keep her from falling. By the time Colby and Liberty dismounted and tied their horses to the rail, the group had gone inside.

"Come on." Colby urged Liberty toward the door. "Be careful what you say, Libby. You'll get more with sweet words and smiles than you'll get flying into a temper."

"I've been thinking about that, Colby. Don't worry. I can act like a lady when I want to."

To Liberty's surprise there was only an aide in the room, but she heard voices coming through the thin partition.

"We wish to see Major Zachary Taylor," Colby said.

"Major Taylor took a detail up to Fort Harrison. We don't expect him back until next week."

"Who is the officer in charge?"

"Captain Sinclair."

"We wish to see him."

"He's busy. You'll have to come back later."

Liberty let her shawl slip off her head and hang onto her shoulders. Her hand fluttered to her hair and brushed startling blond ringlets back from her forehead.

"We know the captain is busy, Sergeant." She smiled up into the young soldier's face.

"Private Simpson, ma'am."

"Private? Well, for goodness sake. What's the matter with these officers? I'm going to talk to my Uncle George about this. Have you met my uncle, Private Simpson?"

"No, ma'am."

"I thought everyone knew George Rogers Clark."

"I've not . . . met General Clark."

"Never mind. We must see the captain. My indentured girl is in there and she's terribly ill. Oh, dear me!" Liberty's hands went to her cheeks and her eyes went from the aide to Colby. "I hope it isn't something catching."

"Well, in that case, I'm sure the captain won't mind being interrupted."

"Thank you." Liberty pushed ahead of him and flung open the door to the inner room.

Hammond Perry was standing in front of a desk. Farr and Willa were to one side, and the guard stood beside the door. The man at the desk jumped to his feet.

"Private! I said we were not to be disturbed," he roared. "Who are these people?"

"Don't be angry at the young man, Major. I just had to know if Mistress Carrathers was all right. You see, she's been so terribly ill with fever and . . . spots." Liberty looked at the officer, then away. She jerked her head back to look at him again with surprise and recognition on her face. "Ohhh . . . Major! Didn't I meet you a few years ago at a ball at West Point?"

"You may have, ma'am. But I don't—"

"You don't remember me? I was Liberty Carroll then." She smiled, pouted prettily and leaned over the desk to extend her hand. "But why would you remember me? You were surrounded by the prettiest girls in New York State."

Captain Sinclair held her hand while his eyes devoured her face. She was the most beautiful woman he'd seen since he'd come to this godforsaken place. Her eyes were bright and full of admiration. Her cheeks rosy and her lips red and smiling. Good God! he thought. How long had it been since he'd seen hair like that?

Hammond was infuriated by the openmouthed admiration displayed by Captain Sinclair. It was something he hadn't counted on. In fact, he hadn't counted on *her* being here.

"This woman is Quill's wife, Captain."

"I was the widow of Lieutenant Perry's brother when I wed Mr. Quill," Liberty explained, her eyes still holding those of the captain. "The Perrys are *all* such fine people. Your Lieutenant Perry comes from some of the best stock in New York State, Major. I bet you know that, so I'll stop bragging. Now, about Willa. Oh, how are you feeling, dear?" Liberty let her eyes pass over Farr as she went to Willa and put her arms around her. "Act sick," she whispered. Then aloud, "Have you vomited anymore? Is there still blood in it?"

"I . . . I'm not feeling good." Willa sagged against her.

"There, there. Can't she sit down, Major?"

"Of course, she can. Get a chair," he said to the guard.

"Be sick," Liberty breathed in her ear. "Be real sick."

When Willa was seated, she leaned over and rested her face in her hands. Liberty stood beside her and patted her shoulder. During the commotion of getting the chair, she had dared a look at Farr. She saw that he was watching her. He stood straight, towering over the other men in the room, his face unreadable. But she knew him so well, and the twitch at the corner of his mouth told her he was flaming with angry impatience.

"I'm sorry for interrupting, Major." Liberty's voice was low and filled with regret.

"It's all right, ma'am. I understand your concern."

Hammond threw Liberty a look of pure hatred. He noticed Captain Sinclair hadn't corrected her when she called him major. The fool liked the sound of it! The twit was playing on his vanity and he was falling for it. He even refused to be seated while she was standing. Hammond felt the disadvantage of having to look up at every man in the room.

"I have arranged for the prisoners—"

"Prisoners? Oh, dear," Liberty wailed.

"Just a moment, ma'am," Captain Sinclair said gently. "Let the lieutenant finish."

"We'll hold Quill in the guardhouse. The woman can be locked in the laundry room, if that's all right with you, sir. I'll have one of the women keep an eye on her." Hammond clicked his heels together and stood at attention. "Is that all, sir?"

"Major?" Liberty said in a timid voice. "What are the charges against Mr. Quill and Willa?"

"The charges against your husband are serious, ma'am. Treason. And now murder, or so the lieutenant tells me."

"Who is accusing my husband? Besides Lieutenant Perry?"

"There is a reliable witness. The case will be heard the day after tomorrow. Your husband will have a chance to defend himself."

"Who will hear the case?" Liberty allowed her voice to get fainter.

"I will, ma'am. I'll appoint two of the junior officers to sit with me on the court. I'm the senior officer here at the fort. The commander is away."

"I'm sure you'll be fair, Major. Will one of the junior officers be Lieutenant Perry?"

"No. He will serve as the prosecutor."

"Who will defend my husband?"

"He can defend himself, or I can appoint someone to defend him."

"I'll defend myself." Farr spoke for the first time.

Captain Sinclair shrugged.

"Please, sir." Liberty's voice trembled and her eyes were large with bewilderment. "Do you mind telling me why you are holding Willa?"

"According to the charges Lieutenant Perry has filed, she has a definite connection to the treason charge. It's essential we have her as a witness," he said gently.

"Oh, dear. If she can help clear my husband's name I want to nurse her back to health so she can testify. She's been so ill lately. I fear for her after that long cold ride, and if she's in the hot, moist air of the laundry room she might —her lungs are poorly. Please, sir. Let me take her back to a clean, airy room in town. I promise I'll have her here and on her feet when you're ready for her."

"The girl stays here!" Hammond roared. He stuck out his arm and pointed his finger in Liberty's face.

She feigned shock, gasped, and leaned back away from him. It took all her willpower to keep from slapping his face.

Hammond realized his mistake the instant he saw the crimson tide of anger rise up to flood Captain Sinclair's face.

"I'm sorry, sir. The woman is important to the case. I think we should keep her here."

"I make the decisions here, Lieutenant!" Captain Sinclair snapped.

"Well, for goodness sake, Hammond. You forgot yourself again." Liberty clicked her tongue against her teeth. "That's why he's a major and you're just a lieutenant."

"You can take the woman with you, Mrs. Quill," Captain Sinclair said, and stroked his long mustache with a thumb and forefinger. "I'll send my aide along to see that you get settled."

"Thank you. See there, Hammond? You should remember

your rank and ask the major before flying off the handle and making plans on your own. Even *I* know majors are far higher up than lieutenants."

Hammond was livid with fury. His mouth worked and the chin that was sunk into his neck quivered. He would have liked nothing more than to cut the bitch's throat. With jerky strides he went to the door and held it open for Captain Sinclair. He hurried after him.

"Sir, may I have a word with you in private?"

"Yes, what is it?"

They walked to the far corner of the room. Hammond turned his back to the aide and spoke in low tones.

"Sir, I have a witness that will testify the woman is a spy for the British."

"Well, for God's sake, man, why didn't you say so?"

"I just found out."

"Does she know she's suspected?"

"No, sir. I thought to spring it suddenly, during the trial."

"Hmmm . . ." Sinclair stroked his mustache once again. He envisioned himself a hero for having convicted not one, but two spies. After it was over, perhaps the blond beauty would need comforting . . . "I'm sure that Mrs. Quill knows nothing about any of this. It's more important than ever that the woman get on her feet so she can stand trial. We can't drag a sick woman to trial, even if she is a spy. Too many would feel sorry for her."

"But she's not sick, sir. She's playacting."

"Did you tend her on the trip from Quill's Station?"

"No, sir. The sergeant did."

Captain Sinclair bellowed to the aide. "Get Sergeant Callaway."

Liberty lingered behind when Colby came to help Willa. She leaned heavily on him, much to Liberty's relief. At the door, she called to the captain.

"Major Sinclair, may I speak to Mr. Quill? I'll be just a moment." She laughed lightly. "I can't get him out through the cracks in the wall, but I warn you, I may try."

"I'm taking the prisoner to—" Hammond was shut off by a glare from the captain.

"You may have five minutes, ma'am."

"Thank you." Liberty closed the door as soon as the words left her mouth, turned and threw her arms around Farr. "Are you all right, darling?" She stood on tiptoe and kissed his mouth, his chin.

"That was some show you put on, Mrs. Quill." He bent to kiss her nose. His hands were bound behind his back so she did the hugging. "Where did you learn all those woman's wiles?"

"Colby told me before we came in that I could get more with sweet smiles than I could by losing my temper. I hate all that deceit, but I'll do anything if it will help you. It worked on the aide so I thought I'd try it on Captain Sinclair. Did you see how he preened? I wanted to laugh in his face." She rubbed her fingers over the stubble on his cheeks. "Let's not waste time on that pompous ass. Governor Harrison is in Fort Wayne, and Major Taylor went to Fort Harrison. We've got to delay things until they get back. Hammond seems to think Willa is important to his case. If she's too sick to leave her bed, they'll have to delay the trial, won't they?"

"I've been trying to figure out what I've done that could in any way be called treason. Not to mention what connection Willa would have to it. Delay things as long as you can, sweetheart. Have Colby snoop around and see what he can find out about when Harrison will be back. Whatever Perry has cooked up could be cleared up if Harrison were here."

"We're staying at Moll Glover's. The sergeant came to see us last night. He'll help us if he can. I love you. Oh, I love you. I don't like it here, darling. I want us to go back home." Her blue eyes, filled with tears, shone like stars.

"We will. I worried about you making that long ride. The troops were full of praise for you, but they didn't dare let Perry hear any of it. Stay close to Colby, hear?"

"I will. I love you so much. I guess I was just too happy for it to last."

"Hush that talk, Mrs. Quill. Give me a big smile. I was half mad when I saw all those pretty smiles you were giving the captain. Mad . . . and proud," he teased. "You're mine, my sweet Liberty Bell. All mine."

"I'm yours forever and always. The captain is an egotistical horse's ass!"

Farr laughed. "That's more like my girl!"

The door swung open. The captain's aide and two guards came in and hustled Farr out. Liberty went to the outer room as the sergeant came in from the outside. Willa was leaning heavily on Colby's arm.

"Sergeant Callaway, were you aware that this woman was sick?"

"She didn't complain, sir."

"That isn't what I asked you."

"Well, sir, I knew she wasn't in too good a shape. I had to lift her from the horse 'n hold her up."

"Thank you, that is all."

After the door closed behind the sergeant, Liberty clicked her tongue again at Hammond.

"Shame on you, Hammond Perry, for doubting me. If your mother were alive, God bless her soul, she'd give you a good hiding for making Willa take that long ride, sick as she is. If this poor girl passes on it will be all your fault. Come feel her head. She's burning up with a fever. Come on, but be careful of the spots."

Hammond almost choked on the anger he dared not show.

"Private Simpson will go with you, Mrs. Quill, and see that you and the woman are settled in." Captain Sinclair bowed over the hand she extended.

"Thank you, Major. It's so refreshing to meet a gentleman here in the wilderness." Liberty smiled into his eyes before gently pulling her hand away and going to the door the aide was opening for her. "Major," she said, smiling up at the aide. "Can't you find it in your heart to make this nice young man a sergeant?"

Moll Glover's house was one of the few in town that had a porch that wrapped around three sides. It was squat and square and sat amazingly close to the street with just a path between it and the traffic that passed. A sign, faded and crudely lettered, was suspended from the porch roof. It read: ROOMS AND EATS.

Moll Glover was a buxom woman with flaming red hair. Her huge pendulous breasts hung down over the band of the long, white apron tied about her waist. She greeted them with a friendly smile.

"Do you have room for these folks, Moll?" Private Simpson asked. He regarded the woman with a definite air of superiority.

"I reckon. Who's payin'?"

"We've money to pay," Colby said quickly.

"I thought you might be guests of that *grand* Captain Sinclair the *private* serves. Thanks for bringing them, Simpson. Good-bye." Mrs. Glover firmly pushed him out the door and slammed it shut.

Liberty, Willa and Colby stood in the entry that ran the full length of the house. When the door closed behind the aide, Mrs. Glover turned and dusted her hands as if they were dirty.

"I'm careful of Private Simpson," she said, shaking her head. "He tells Captain Sinclair every word that's said in this house. Need a place to bed for a while, do you?"

"Sergeant Callaway told me to bring the ladies here." Colby still had his arm about Willa. "This one isn't feeling well."

Moll bent her head and peered into Willa's face. "What's ailing you, dearie?"

"She's tired and needs to lie down," Liberty said.

Moll looked at her. She had taken the shawl off her head

and was holding it. Moll reached for the wet shawl and hung it on a hook in the wall beside the door.

"My, ain't you a pretty one. I bet Sinclair 'bout wet his drawers when he saw you. Regular ladies' man, he is."

Liberty smiled. She decided that she liked Moll Glover and that the outspoken redhead didn't have much use for the officers at the fort. She wondered what Moll thought of Hammond Perry. She found out when Moll spoke again.

"At least he's a man, even if most of his brains are atween his legs. It's more than I can say for Hammond Perry. If he don't squat to pee I'll miss my guess."

"Ma'am, do you have two rooms?" Colby asked quickly, not knowing how Liberty and Willa would take the brash woman's vulgarities.

"I got one the ladies can have. I'll make you down a pallet in my traveler's room."

"You can put his pallet in our room, Mrs. Glover." Liberty glanced at Colby and then smiled at the woman. "He's my brother. We're all family. It'll give you another space to rent out."

"It's fine with me, honey, and I ain't caring if he's your brother or not." Moll laughed. Her face was fat and wrinkle free, her eyes bright and twinkling, her teeth small, even and white. Liberty laughed with her, not caring a bit that Moll knew she had lied.

"Now I know why the sergeant sent us here." Laughter was still in Liberty's voice when she spoke.

Moll lifted her eyebrows. "The sergeant will be around tonight, I suspect. Let's get this young lady to bed, then your 'brother' can take the horses to the livery." She laughed again as she led the way down the passageway.

The room was small, the walls mud plastered and sized with lime until they were dingy gray. There was one window, high up and covered with deerskin like many of the others in town. It let in a weak light. The bed was a frame nailed to the wall. A cracked pitcher and basin sat on a shelf.

"Not fancy," Moll said, "but it's clean. I can bring in a hod of coals. It'll take off the chill."

"It's fine." Liberty went to Willa after Colby eased her down on the bed. "I'll take care of her, Colby."

"I'll take the horses to the livery and come back."

"Do you suppose we could have some tea, Mrs. Glover?"

Moll's sharp eyes went from one to the other. "Come on out when you've settled in. I'll put on the kettle. I don't know what you folks is up to, but I ain't blind. The 'sick' young lady straightened up considerable when the private left."

Willa's fearful eyes went to Liberty's face. Liberty was studying the big woman. Knowing they needed her help, she made a quick decision.

"You're too smart for us, Mrs. Glover. Willa isn't sick. Oh, she's worn out, but that's all. We're just pretending she is so we could bring her here. Lieutenant Perry wanted to lock her in the laundry room. He's accused my husband of treason and thinks Willa will be a witness against him."

"What's little Bandyass up to now? Treason, is it? Shitfire! I'll swear, that little fool is always stirring up something. Treason! He probably thinks it'll make him a big man if he convicts someone of treason. How sick do you want Willa to be? I can give her a dose that'll make her throw up all over the little turd."

Liberty sighed with relief. "I think I love the sergeant for sending us here," she said weakly.

"Well, don't get to loving him too much," Moll said pertly. "He's my man and I'd not stand a chance against you."

"You don't have anything to worry about there, Moll. Even if I didn't love my husband to distraction, I'm probably too skinny for the sergeant's taste."

Moll laughed. "He do like to bounce on my soft belly." She dropped her eyelid in a knowing wink and left the room.

Willa and Liberty took off their wet coats and hung them on the pegs to dry. The room was cold and damp. They sat down close together on the bed and pulled the blanket up around them.

"What in the world is happening, Libby? Farr didn't murder Stith Lenning. It was dark, but I saw him with a knife in his hand, and *he* ran at Farr. Why did Lieutenant Perry say what he did to the captain about treason? What does it mean?"

"I don't know. But Farr says if Governor Harrison were here he could straighten this whole thing out. He wants Colby to snoop around and find out when he's expected back. Meanwhile, we've got to keep you so sick you can't go to the fort to testify."

Colby returned. The three of them talked it over and decided to confide in Moll Glover. They went to the kitchen and stood before the warm fire until the chill left their bodies. Then they sat at the table over cups of hot tea and told her the full story.

"I realize now that I made a mistake when I lost my temper at Hammond the first time we met," Liberty said regretfully. "He lost face in front of Captain Heald and he'll never forget it. He hated Farr even before that, and I didn't help matters any."

Moll had been looking at Willa with a puzzled look on her face. "Dearie, I'd swear I've seen you someplace. But pretty as you are it'd seem like I'd know where it was."

Willa looked frightened and Colby reached over and took her hand in his. "Willa lived here in Vincennes for about six months with some people by the name of Cooley," he said. "She and her mother came from England. Her mother was bonded out to pay the passage, and when she died, the bond was passed on to Willa. Cooley inherited the bond, took her to Detroit, then down the Ohio to Louisville, and then on to Vincennes. He ran out of money and sold the bond to some people by the name of Thompson. Mr. Thompson gave the bond to Farr Quill, who freed Willa of the obligation. She's going to be my wife just as soon as I can arrange it."

"Well, for God's sake. I remember now. I only saw you a time or two. You was skinny and scared looking. That fat

Bella Cooley was a bitch! I can't blame her much, married to a gambling, mean bastard like Norman Cooley. Why honey, you just look so pretty now, and you got this young gent to look out for you. I'd not a known you was the same girl."

"Sometimes I can't believe how good things have gone for me. I feel different inside too. Like I'm . . . worth something," Willa murmured and held tightly to Colby's hand.

"Them Cooleys are back. I saw him the other day going in the tavern."

Willa's face turned white. "He's back . . . *here?*"

"Big as life. Strutting around like he had the world by the tail. Wearing a new hat and a fur collar on his coat."

"That means he's got money again. He was always like that when he had money."

"Don't worry about him." Colby held her hand in both of his. "As soon as this is over we'll go back to Farr's. Next spring I'm taking you home to Carrolltown."

"Moll, do you think Sergeant Callaway will be in tonight?" Liberty asked.

"I'll be plumb put out if he ain't. It'll take more than a little old snowfall to keep him away," she said confidently.

"I'm anxious about my husband. Hammond Perry is so damn mean! I'd not put it past him to lock him up somewhere without heat or blankets or anything to eat." There was a quiver in Liberty's voice.

"What you got to worry about is your man trying to get out. Perry'd have a excuse to shoot him. Then he'd not have to prove he's a spy. Callaway knows that. He knows everything that goes on out there, dearie. He likes your man or he'd not have sent you here. He'll see to him. He knows where to put a shilling so it'll do the most good."

Chapter
Twenty-Four

As the afternoon wore on, Liberty became nervous and weepy. She paced the floor restlessly. She felt caged in town and longed to be back home with Farr. She thought of Amy and Mercy and Daniel with his serious little face. She thought of how her life had changed in the last year. A year before she had only Stith Lenning to worry about. Now he was dead. He had finally met a man who refused to be pushed around and bullied, and she didn't have to worry about him any longer. Moll's voice intruded into her thoughts, and she stopped pacing to listen.

"We'll have to be careful. Bandyass'll send his spies around. Sarge will be in tonight and tell us what's going on. He'll know if that crackpot doctor got back from Fort Harrison. If he did, you can bet your buttons he'll be here in the morning before he goes to the tavern."

"Doctor? I hadn't thought about them having a doctor at the fort," Colby said.

"He ain't much a one. You're stretching the word acalling him that. Looking at him is enough to make you puke," Moll said with disgust.

"What in the world will we do, Moll, if he comes to look at Willa?"

"Don't worry 'bout that. I can fix up a dose that'll fool that drunken old fool. It'll make you sicker than a dog, hon," she said to Willa. "You'll be hating my guts while you're throwing up yours."

"I'll not hate you, Moll," Willa said. "I don't know what we would have done without you and Sergeant Callaway."

* * *

It was late when Sergeant Callaway arrived at Moll's door. He was cold and tired. But before he and Moll disappeared into her room, he told Liberty that Farr was in an unheated room, but that he had fur robes and a thick stack of hay for a bed. He had had a hot meal and later a mug of hot buttered rum had been smuggled in to him.

Farr had sent a message. He wanted Liberty and Colby to go to Grouseland and speak with Mrs. Harrison. If the governor was not expected back soon, perhaps she could get a message to Zachary Taylor.

The sergeant also brought the news that the doctor would be calling on Willa in the morning.

It was a long, cold night for the three who huddled in Moll Glover's small room. Around midnight Colby got up off the floor, spread his robes over the women on the bed and crawled in beside them.

"To hell with propriety. I'm freezing!"

They lay spoon fashion with Willa between Liberty and Colby. He wrapped his arms around them. Warmth seeped into their bodies and they slept.

Morning came. They hurried down the passageway to the warm kitchen. It had stopped snowing during the night, but the sky was still gray. Moll told them over cups of hot tea not to worry about the doctor's visit.

"If you're willing, hon, I'll give you a dose of melted lard, snuff, and jimsonweed that'll make you so sick you'll want to die. It won't hurt you none except to give you the trots."

Willa avoided looking at Colby. "I'll take it."

"The old quack won't be here until the middle of the morning, so eat a good bait of breakfast. You'll need something in your belly to throw up."

"I'm sorry you've got to do this, Willa," Liberty said.

"Are you sure it won't hurt her?" Colby's young face was showing the signs of strain.

"Hell yes, it'll hurt, but it ain't nothing she can't stand." Moll forked thick slabs of meat into the spider skillet.

"After the doctor comes, Colby and I will go call on Mrs. Harrison."

"Mrs. Harrison's a fine lady," Moll said. "I ain't in her sewing circle and she don't invite me to tea, but what the hell, she's still a fine lady."

Colby carried an iron pot filled with hot coals from the kitchen fireplace to their room to take off the chill. He paced restlessly in the kitchen while Willa was put to bed and given the vile dose. She gagged repeatedly, and Moll spooned molasses into her mouth to keep the concoction down so it could reach her stomach.

By the time the doctor arrived she had already vomited twice and the chamber pot beside the bed reeked with a foul odor. Her stomach cramped and sweat beaded her forehead. The sound of her moans were more than Colby could stand. He put on his coat and left the house.

The doctor was everything Moll said he was. His clothes were dirty, his eyes watery, and his hands shook. The smell of stale ale was on his breath. His examination of the patient consisted of lifting her eyelids, looking in her mouth, peering into the chamber pot and sloshing its contents.

"Her intestines are wrapped around her liver." He announced his decision, yanked off his eyeglasses and put them in the wooden case he carried under his arm.

"That's just what I thought was wrong, Doc." Moll shook her head regretfully. When the doctor looked away she winked at Liberty.

"Give her a spoonful of mutton tallow and soda every two hours and feed her molasses mixed in flour twice a day. Keep her bowels moving. If she ain't dead in four days she'll get better."

Liberty walked with him to the door and pressed a couple of shillings in his hand when he held it out.

"Thank you for coming, Doctor. Be sure and make your report to Captain Sinclair. If we need you again, we'll send for you."

She watched the doctor slosh through the snow to the tavern and then went back down the passageway to the room.

Moll was holding Willa's head over the chamber pot.

"There, there, lovey. I'll get some milk to settle your stomach. You done good, real good. The old fool don't know his ass from a hole in the ground."

"What a terrible old man! He probably kills more of those poor men than he cures. He was filthy!" Liberty mopped Willa's head with a damp cloth. "Oh, Willa! I'm so sorry you had to do this."

"Old Doc ain't so bad with gunshots and boils, but he don't know doodlely 'bout anything else. He'll go back and tell Sinclair she's sick all right, and he'll tell it in the tavern and to anybody else that'll listen. He'll be back in four days so he'll get another shilling."

"Willa can't go through this again. Isn't there something else we can do?"

"We'll paint some spots on her next time. He'll think the poison's coming out. A week is the most you can get out of this, hon, if that long. After that you'll have to think of something else."

Liberty took care with her toilet and dressed in the best she'd brought with her, blessing Colby for telling her to bring something so she and Willa would look presentable. She piled her light colored hair on the top of her head and perched her bonnet on it. With Colby's hand firmly on her arm, they walked to the mansion to call on Mrs. Harrison. The house was even more impressive when they were near it. They rang the bell beside the door.

A Negro servant answered the bell, bowed formally, and ushered them into a foyer.

"Mrs. Farrway Quill and Mr. Colby Carroll wish to see Mrs. Harrison."

Liberty looked at Colby in surprise. His manner was that

of a gentleman who was not accustomed to taking no for an answer.

"Wait here, suh."

The servant went down the hall and through a set of double doors. While they waited, Liberty glanced at the beautiful chandelier that hung from the ceiling, the gleaming floors, the carved oak staircase and the Queen Anne chairs with complete disinterest. Her thoughts were so taken up with what was happening to Farr that there was no room for anything else.

The servant returned. "I is ta show yo in, suh."

The servant took their coats and hung them on a hall tree. Liberty knew it was proper to leave on her bonnet, but she removed it. Snow had fallen from a tree branch as they passed, and it was wet. She patted her hair in place and followed the servant down the hall.

Mrs. Harrison stood to greet them. She was a plump, gracious lady in her late thirties. She came forward with outstretched hands.

"Mrs. Quill, I'm delighted to meet you. We hadn't heard that Farrway had taken a wife."

"I'm delighted to meet you, Mrs. Harrison. Farr and I were married rather suddenly. I understand it's not uncommon here on the frontier to meet, fall in love, and marry within a few weeks' time."

"I'm beginning to believe that there is nothing uncommon here on the frontier. We're fond of your husband. I hope you'll be very happy." She offered her hand to Colby. "It's good to see you again, Colby." He bowed over her hand, placing a kiss on her fingers. "Always the gallant gentleman," Mrs. Harrison laughed. "I said that to your mother once, and she had an answer that I don't think you'd quite appreciate. Come sit down. I've ordered tea."

Mrs. Harrison made polite conversation with Colby about his parents until the tea cart arrived. After they were served, she leaned back in her chair with lifted brows and waited. Liberty had decided to leave most of the talking to Colby.

He told her the facts as they had happened and asked her when her husband was expected to return.

"Oh, dear! This is the most ridiculous thing I've ever heard. Farrway Quill a traitor! What possible evidence could they have to try to prove such a thing? The governor will be furious and will most certainly straighten this out when he returns."

"When do you expect him, Mrs. Harrison?"

"I'm not sure, my dear." She sat quietly while several seconds ticked by. "If I could get word to Zachary," she murmured as if talking to herself. "Zachary would know what to do."

"Mrs. Harrison," Colby said urgently, "Captain Sinclair's aide said the fort commander wouldn't be back until next week. That's five or six days away. I don't know if we can delay that long. Lieutenant Perry is bursting to get started with the trial."

"Of course he is. With Farrway convicted and executed, it'll not matter in the least if the governor or the fort commander likes it or not. He would be rid of an enemy." Mrs. Harrison spoke irritably.

"They wouldn't do that!" Liberty's hands flew to her cheeks and her eyes went round with shock. "Oh, heavens! I hadn't thought they'd go that far on their own without the governor or the commander's approval."

"It's hard to tell what ambitious men will do, my dear. I have seen some pretty stupid things done in the name of justice. I'll send for Zachary Taylor. He's a levelheaded man. If he can't stop this altogether, he can delay it until Will gets back."

"Thank you, Mrs. Harrison." Liberty stood and smoothed her skirt down over her thighs. "We'll be going. I want to see my husband today if they will permit it."

"My dear, it wouldn't do any good for me to tell you not to worry, so I won't say that. I know that I'd be worried sick if this were happening to Will. Be assured that I'll do everything I can to help Farrway."

"Thank you again."

"I hope sometime we can meet under different circumstances, my dear. Take heart. We women can accomplish a lot when we set our minds to it."

The air outside was cold and damp. Liberty shivered and held on to Colby's arm.

"Does she know your mother?"

"Yes. My parents were here a couple of years ago and spent several days. The governor wanted my father to take a position in the government, but he refused."

"Colby Carroll, you're an aristocrat."

"I'm no such thing. I'm my own man, cut my own trails." He looked grim, as if he were displeased with what she said.

"I was joking," Liberty said quickly.

"I know. It's just that I'm not in the mood for it."

By the time Liberty and Colby got back to Moll Glover's Willa was feeling better. She was pale but smiled weakly at Colby. Moll had brought her into the kitchen, and she sat close to the fire with a blanket about her shoulders.

Colby squatted down beside her. "I'm going to the tavern. Tell me what Cooley looks like."

"You're not going to—"

"Knock his teeth down his throat? No, not now, at least. He doesn't know me and I might learn something if I hang around him a bit."

"He's not very tall, has black hair, and is kind of round. I don't know how else to describe him."

"I do," Moll said, pulling a meat pie out of the oven built into the side of the fireplace. "If you see an asshole swilling ale, it's him." She laughed uproariously. "He'll be wearing green velvet britches and a long black coat with fur on the collar."

"I want to go out to the fort, Colby." Liberty had taken off her shoes and stockings and set them beside the fire to dry.

"I don't think they'd let you see him, Libby," Colby said gently. "I thought I'd snoop around the tavern, then ride out and see if I can bribe one of the guards into letting me see him. I'd have a much better chance than you."

"He's right, dearie," Moll said, and as much as Liberty wanted to see her husband, she had to agree.

The days dragged by slowly. The weather cleared, the sun came out and melted the snow. The streets were a slush of mud. Colby had met Norman Cooley and learned from his bragging that he was due to come into some money.

"He'll do anything for a shilling," Willa said dejectedly. "He'll say just what the lieutenant wants him to say."

"I've seriously thought of killing him," Colby confessed.

"Oh, no!"

"Sweetheart, I'm only talking. God knows I want him dead, but I'll not kill him unless it's my life or his."

"Have you seen the riverman?" Liberty asked.

"He's here. He dives into the first hole he finds when he spots me. He's got a better coat and is spending money in the tavern. Perry must be paying him to stick around."

"I know it's hard for you to believe, but Jubal, Hammond's brother, was a sweet and gentle man. He was nothing like Hammond. I can't help but be glad he didn't find out how his brother turned out."

Colby saw Farr each day for a few minutes and reported back to Liberty that he was being treated fairly well. Sergeant Callaway, like Moll said, knew the ins and outs of the fort, whom to trust, and whom not to. He saw to it that Farr had extra food and a warm bed.

On Sunday evening Private Simpson came to the rooming house to tell them the trial would start the following morning. Captain Sinclair refused to delay any longer. He said he would come with a wagon to take Mrs. Quill and Willa Carrathers to the fort. When he departed, Colby hurried over to the mansion to learn if Mrs. Harrison had heard from either Zachary Taylor or her husband.

He returned with a worried look on his face. "She hasn't heard," he said as soon as he came into the kitchen.

"What did she say?" Liberty never felt more like crying in her life.

"She sent an urgent message to Major Taylor telling him to return at once and to call on her before he went out to Fort Knox. She's sure he'll come as soon as he can."

"It may not be soon enough."

"She said she sent for Captain Sinclair and asked him to delay the hearing until Major Taylor or her husband returned. She said he told her they had conclusive evidence that Farr was a traitor and that he was aided by Willa. He explained that the reason for the hasty trial was so that the chief witness could testify before he left town on important business."

"Important business, my foot," Moll snorted. "The only important business Norman Cooley ever had was going to the pot after a dose of croton oil."

"This is like a nightmare." Liberty sat down heavily in the chair. "It's hard to believe that one man could cause all this. If anything happens to Farr, I swear I'll kill Hammond Perry."

Chapter
Twenty-Five

The morning was cold and clear. The guard brought in a basin of hot water, soap, a towel, and even a razor. Apparently Hammond Perry did not wish his prisoner to appear in public as one who had been persecuted or ill-used. And Farr had no wish to pose as Perry's victim. He cleaned up, shaved, and made himself as presentable as he could under the circumstances.

The two militiamen who came for him gripped him by the arms, even after his hands were tied behind his back as if they fully expected him to make a sudden dash for freedom. They conducted him to what was most assuredly the largest room at the fort. It was packed with people. Liberty and Colby were there, sitting in chairs on one side. Willa sat alone on the other side of the room with a soldier acting as guard beside her. Hoffman, the riverman who was present when Farr killed Stith Lenning, and a portly man in green velvet britches and a fur collar on his coat were in the corner talking to Hammond Perry. Off-duty soldiers stood along the walls.

Liberty's eyes clung to Farr's for the short time it took for him to pass her. Then he was shoved down onto a chair and the guard stood behind him. Captain Sinclair, splendidly dressed in his best uniform, his mustache waxed, his hair puffed on top and clubbed in back, stood behind the table at which the officers of the court-martial were seated. He was as much the center of attention as the prisoner.

Farr glanced at Hammond Perry and could almost read his thoughts in the gloating expression on his dish-shaped face. He would expose his enemy as a villain, prove him a traitor, and personally see to it that he was shot. And afterward he would most certainly be a hero and commissioned a captain in Governor Harrison's army.

Farr glanced at the other two officers sitting with the captain on the court. Not one of them was known to him. They looked honest, sensible, but they had been chosen, he was sure, because their judgment would reflect that of Perry and Sinclair.

Captain Sinclair seated himself and slammed his hand down on the table for quiet.

"This court is in session. Lieutenant Pringle, as secretary to this court, you may begin to set this down so there will be a record of these proceedings: The court accuses Farrway Quill and Willa Carrathers of consorting with the enemies of the Northwest Territories and passing information that resulted in the deaths of soldiers during the battle at Prophetstown."

An angry murmur came from the men that lined the wall of the room. This was more serious than they had at first believed.

"Farrway Quill, do you have anything to say before we start?"

"No."

"Willa Carrathers?"

"No." Willa spoke so softly she was barely heard by the men at the desk and not at all by the crowd.

"Proceed, Lieutenant Perry."

Hammond stood and faced the room. "I'll question Farrway Quill. Stand and be sworn in." Farr stood. "Do you swear the statements you are about to make are the truth, the whole truth, and nothing but the truth, so help you God?"

"I do."

"Sit down." Hammond took several steps away from Farr, then returned to stand before him. He rocked back on his heels, clearly enjoying his role as prosecutor. "Did you, in the spring of this year, come to a conference called by Governor Harrison to discuss the possibility of an Indian uprising led by Tecumseh and his brother, known as Prophet?"

"You know I did. You were there."

"Immediately after you left Vincennes, did you go south

into the states of Kentucky and Tennessee and visit a chief known as John Spotted Elk?"

"I did. He's a friend of mine."

"Did you also visit Tecumseh at that time?"

"I did. He's a friend of mine too."

Hammond teetered back and forth on his heels. "Spotted Elk's son has been living with you. Is that true?"

"His adopted son. Rain Tallman is white."

"White? We all know about whites who turn Indian. Blue Jacket, for example, is a white man who took up savage ways. He was made a chief and murders his own race."

"You don't know that," Farr said quietly. "Besides, that has nothing to do with what's going on here."

Hammond's face reddened at the calm rebuke. He resumed his questioning with vigor.

"Did not Tecumseh's sister spend several weeks at your homestead on the Wabash this summer?"

"No. She stayed with Mr. Washington and his wife. She had an injured foot and was waiting for it to heal."

"She was never at your homestead?" There was a sneer in Hammond's voice. He looked over Farr's head to the men who stood quietly listening to his every word.

"I didn't say that."

"Rain Tallman, the son of Spotted Elk, left your homestead and made a beeline for Prophetstown. Is this true?"

"Yes."

"He left rather suddenly, I'm told. Wasn't it just after two boat loads of powder and lead arrived at your, ah, so-called *fort?*"

"Yes. Your spies did a good job. Did you pay them well?"

"I'll ask the questions. I—"

The door at the end of the room was thrust open so hard it bounced off one of the men lining the wall. He let out a string of curses that were cut off abruptly when he saw the man standing in the doorway. The tall man stood there for a moment surveying the room. Then he closed the door and took off his coat and hat.

Captain Sinclair began to rise out of his chair.

"Don't let me interrupt your proceedings, Captain Sinclair. Carry on." The man's authoritative voice boomed in the suddenly quiet room. The man handed his wet coat and hat to a soldier, crossed his arms over his chest, and leaned back against the wall.

Hammond glanced at his witnesses. Hoffman and Norman Cooley had begun to squirm. They whispered to each other and glanced toward the back of the room. Sweat broke out on Cooley's face. His composure shaken, Hammond cleared his throat before he resumed his questioning.

"Shortly after that . . . Tecumseh came to your homestead with a horse. Wasn't the horse payment for information passed on to him by Rain Tallman about the powder and shot?"

An angry growl came from the crowd. Hammond smiled, pleased with the response. Liberty jumped to her feet and was quickly pulled down by Colby.

"No," Farr said simply. There was an expectant quiet, but he said no more.

Hammond stuck his tongue in his cheek and tilted his head as he looked at the paper in his hand. "Did you show Tecumseh the barracks and the shot tower you built on your property when he came to your homestead?"

"I didn't have to show it to him. He's not blind."

Hammond reared back and pointed his finger in Farr's face. "You murdered Stith Lenning because he knew you were planning to turn that powder and shot over to the Shawnee, didn't you?"

"I killed Stith Lenning because he was coming at me with a knife," Farr said evenly.

"You killed him over that woman." Hammond pointed his finger at Willa. "You killed him because he knew she was a spy for the British and he knew you sympathized with the Indians." He waved several papers in Farr's face. "I have letters here from homesteaders who say you have often expressed sympathy for the 'poor Indian' who is being crowded out by the whites." Hammond wheeled away from Farr without giving him a chance to answer. He went to the table and spoke to Captain Sinclair. "Here are letters from

Amos Palmer, Florence Thompson and Stith Lenning, the man Quill murdered. I will question Willa Carrathers before I call my witnesses."

"Swear her in."

Hammond stood over Willa. "Do you swear to tell the truth, the whole truth and nothing but the truth, so help you God? I suppose you British do take an oath the same as we Americans do."

"I do."

"Speak up, woman."

"Her name is Miss Carrathers," Captain Sinclair said sharply.

Hammond glanced quickly toward the back of the room, then shuffled his papers.

"Is it true you lived here in Vincennes as the indentured servant of Norman Cooley?"

"Yes, sir."

"Are you English?"

"Yes, sir."

"Were you in Detroit approximately three years ago?"

"Yes, sir."

"Did Mr. Cooley have to chastise you more than a dozen times for consorting with British militiamen?"

"No!"

"I must remind you that you are under oath. Did you sneak away and meet militiamen a half dozen times?"

"No! I didn't meet anyone."

Hammond laughed. "Never mind the number of times. While here in Vincennes, did you not sneak out several times and meet a man who had come downriver and pass to that man information you had learned about activities here at the fort?"

"No!"

"Your former master said that you did. He said his decision to leave Vincennes was because he feared he'd get in trouble because of you."

"No! He was out of money—"

"Don't lie!" Hammond shouted and pounded his fist against his palm.

"I'm not lying!" Tears were streaming down Willa's cheeks.

"I'll kill that little weasel!" Colby's voice reached into every corner of the room.

"Another word from you, Mr. Carroll, and you'll leave the room," Captain Sinclair said sternly.

"Is Carrathers your *real* name?" Hammond asked.

"Yes."

"You don't know a lie from the truth. In your veins runs the blood of the vilest traitor this country has ever known!" Hammond turned and strode to the desk, looked toward the back of the room, then went back to stand looking down on Willa's bent head. "Look up," he shouted. "Look up and tell his court that you are *not* the daughter of Benedict Arnold!"

Colby jumped to his feet and was immediately seized by the guard. "Goddamn you, Perry," he shouted.

"Sit down or you'll be placed under arrest," Sinclair said.

Willa's face was as white as a sheet.

"Answer me," Hammond shouted.

"I was told that I was."

"Told by whom?"

"Mrs. Coulter, the lady who paid our passage."

"You are the acknowledged, bastard daughter of Benedict Arnold?"

"Yes."

"Does your father live in London?"

"Yes."

"What message did you bring to the British from your father, Miss Arnold? What message?"

"I didn't even know him."

"Ha! Likely story. You have been meeting Quill and passing information to him from the British. You arranged for him to wrest your papers from Mr. George Thompson so it would be more convenient for the two of you to work together."

Farr got to his feet. He towered over Hammond. "Perry, you can badger me all you want, but I'll be goddamned if you're going to badger that poor girl. Sinclair, hasn't this farce gone on long enough?"

"Sit down, Quill. You haven't denied any of the charges against you. Prophet was ready for our men when we got to Prophetstown. You could have alerted them through Rain Tallman. You have taken the enemy, Tecumseh, into your home and showed him the supplies sent to protect the settlers in the Wabash Valley. Then you killed the only man that had proof this woman was a spy."

"Not the only man, Captain Sinclair. I want to question Mr. Norman Cooley, who was this woman's—"

"Just a moment." The tall man who had been standing at the back of the room came forward. "I have a question for the young lady before you call your so-called witnesses. Miss, how old were you when you came to America?"

"I was six years old, sir."

"When did you begin your indenture with Mr. Cooley?"

"When I was eleven."

"At eleven years you had to work to pay the cost of passage for you and your mother to come to America. It seems unlikely to me that Benedict Arnold would send a six-year-old, or even an eleven-year-old to deliver a message—and not even pay her passage. Arnold may be a traitor to his country, but he's not a fool."

"But Major Taylor, I have a witness." Hammond moved back away from the tall man so he could look up at him.

"I'll question Mr. Cooley myself. If he's lying about this child, so help me God I'll hang him before the day is out!" The major's voice rose and quivered angrily.

"If you would only let me continue, sir. Mr. Hoffman was present when Quill killed his friend, and his friend confided—" Hammond's words were cut off when the door slammed shut. "Mr. Cooley?"

"I think your Mr. Cooley flew the coop, Lieutenant. He just high-tailed it out of here so fast his coattail was standing out straight behind him. The rat-faced riverman was having a hell of a time keepin' up." A murmur of laughter erupted. Hammond's face turned a brick red and his chin quivered with anger.

"You . . . you frightened off my witnesses, Major Taylor."

"It was my intention. If they had been honest, they would have had nothing to fear. Rats usually desert a sinking ship, Perry. Remember that." Zachary Taylor grabbed up the papers the court recorder had been writing on. "Untie Farr," he commanded gruffly.

When Farr was free, Liberty rushed to him. "Is it over, darling?" She wrapped her arms about him and buried her face against his chest. "Oh, I hope it's over."

Zachary Taylor turned and faced the men in the room who were enjoying Hammond's discomfort so much they could scarcely keep the grins off their faces.

"If one word of what has happened here today is spread in town, I'll see to it that each of you is transferred to Fort Dearborn immediately. Do you understand? Now get out of here. I want a private word with my officers."

The men filed out quickly and quietly. The threat of being sent to *Eschicagau*, the Lonely Station, was enough to subdue the rowdiest among them.

Colby was on his knees beside Willa, drying her tears. She was crying softly and trying to keep her face turned away from him.

"It's over. It's going to be all right now, sweetheart."

"It'll never be all right."

"Of course it will. Now we can go home. But before we go we're going to pay a call on the preacher here in town."

"No. I couldn't—"

"You will be my wife before this day is over," Colby said firmly.

Zachary Taylor stood looking at the four officers. "What have you got to do with this?" he asked the lieutenant who was acting as court recorder.

"Captain Sinclair asked me to sit in, sir."

"And you?"

"The same, sir," the other lieutenant said.

"I believe you. You have my permission to leave. What I said to the men goes for you. Understand?"

"Yes, sir."

When the door closed behind them, Zachary Taylor turned to Hammond and CaptainSinclair.

"I want to know what the goddamn hell you're trying to pull off here! This is undoubtedly the worst example of ethics I've ever heard of. Did you think to conduct this trial without my knowledge or that of the governor, and have Farrway Quill shot before we knew about it? What was in it for you, Sinclair? Did you hope to make major? No," he said sharply and held up his hand when Captain Sinclair would have spoken. "Farrway Quill has the complete trust and support of both Governor Harrison and myself. He turned down a commission to be commander of this fort. He's worth *ten* of you!" the major shouted. "It's due to his efforts that there have been no uprisings to speak of in the Northwest Territories for the last several years."

"But sir, Tecumseh—" Hammond's face was rigid, his back ramrod straight.

"Quill is a friend of Tecumseh, and of John Spotted Elk. That friendship is what makes him a valuable messenger for the governor of this territory."

"I did not know, sir."

"I'm disappointed in you, Captain Sinclair," the major said. "How could you allow an upstart lieutenant to talk you into doing something so stupid?"

"But—the murder—" Hammond's voice had suddenly dried up.

"Yes, the murder. What about that, Farr?"

"Stith Lenning had Willa tied and gagged, and was carrying her off into the woods. I grabbed her away from him and he came at me with a knife. I killed him."

"Was he wanting a woman, or this one in particular?"

"He wanted Willa, but I don't know why."

"Do you know, young lady?"

"No, sir. Unless it had something to do with Mr. Cooley."

"What do you know about this, Perry?"

"Nothing, sir." Hammond looked straight ahead, his eyes ocused on the wall.

"Was it Cooley who told you the young lady was the aughter of Benedict Arnold?"

"Yes, he did. He was convinced that she was a spy."

"After you crossed his palm with a shilling or two, eh, erry?"

"Sir!"

"I have my spies, too. It was a mean and cruel thing he id to you, young lady, blurting out that your father was a aitor."

"I didn't know it for a long time, sir. Even when I learned f it, I didn't think much about it. But when I got to know ho he was," Willa's voice trembled, but she was deter-ained to continue. "Mum worked for Mr. Arnold's wife, ien she and Mr. Arnold—Mum said Mr. Arnold sent her to is friend, but Mrs. Arnold took the passage money."

"We don't care about any of that, Willa," Liberty said efore turning on Hammond. "Hammond Perry, your mother as as crazy as a loon, and you've got a mean streak up our back a mile wide. I don't care if Willa's father was the evil himself. She is a sweet, good, kind girl, and I'm proud iat she's my friend."

"And I'll be proud to make her my wife," Colby said as e pulled Willa to her feet.

"I want to apologize, ma'am, for the insensitivity of my fficers." Zachary Taylor took Willa's hand. "Your father iade a terrible mistake in judgment, and no doubt he will iy for it the rest of his life. Let that in no way affect you id your happiness with young Colby Carroll." He raised Villa's hand to his lips.

"Farr, I owe you an apology. Heald brought back your eport and your recommendation to put someone other than erry in charge of the patrols. With the shortage of officers, put your suggestion aside to consider another time. I'm orry now that I did."

"I'm thankful you got back, Zack. My patience was getting pretty thin, and I was worried about my wife. I never know what she'll do. If this thing had gone on much longer she might have gotten a gun and stormed the fort." Farr hugged Liberty close to his side.

Captain Sinclair stood at attention. "Is that all, sir?"

"No, it is not all. You and Perry stay here while I see my friends out. I have several more things to say to you."

As soon as the door closed behind the major, Captain Sinclair turned on Hammond with such fury Hammond was sure he was going to strike him.

"Goddamn you, Perry! You blithering idiot! You've fixed things now. What happened to your star witness? And that fool, Hoffman? Taylor won't stop until he has our hides tacked to the wall."

"How the hell was I to know they'd run or that Taylor would be back a week early? Don't put all the blame on me. You wanted to be a hero," Hammond sneered.

"You said it was all worked out. You said Lenning would testify. Why did you go through with it after he was killed?"

"Because it had gone too far to back down."

"We'll be sent to Dearborn, damn you!"

Hammond walked to the window, looked out, then turned to face Captain Sinclair with such a look of hatred on his face he reminded the captain of a small poisonous viper.

"I'm not through with Quill or that bitch. Someday, somewhere, sometime, they'll pay. I'll settle the score if it takes me the rest of my life. If I can't get him, I'll get that goddamn white Indian kid he thinks so much of, or that sister of hers, or those damn kids they took in."

"All you're concerned with is revenge. I'll think of that later. Good God, man! Do you realize we could be demoted? If that happens—" Sinclair's mouth clamped shut on the words.

Hammond's chin began to tremble. His head jerked back several times before he turned his neck stiffly to glare up at Sinclair. Spit trickled down from the corner of his mouth and his eyes took on a glassy stare.

"Someday, somewhere, sometime. . . ."

* * *

In the outer room Zachary Taylor ordered an aide to bring a wagon to take the ladies back to town.

"I came as soon as I got Anna's message, Farr. My God! I don't want to think about what would have happened if I hadn't received it. And by the way, before I left the mansion Anna told me to invite you and Mrs. Quill, Colby Carroll and his young lady to come to dinner and spend the night. She was taken with your wife and would like to get to know her better."

"I'm *taken* with her too, Zack." Farr's arm tightened across Liberty's shoulders. His green eyes were alight with love as he smiled down at her. "We'll be happy to accept Anna's invitation."

"And before I forget, Nathan Heald also sent a message. Hull Dexter, the man you're looking for, is at Rock Island."

"That means he's out of my reach for now. But he'll be back." Farr held out his hand. "Thank you, Major. If you get down the Wabash, pay us a visit."

"I'll be busy for a while seeing to some transfers to Fort Dearborn. But who knows? Maybe in the spring."

"Farr, isn't this a grand bed? Wasn't it nice of Mrs. Harrison to ask us to spend the night?" Liberty wedged her nose beneath his chin and nipped his neck with her teeth.

"Grand," he agreed. They had just come languidly out of nowhere into a reality where thought was again possible. He had not left her body. Her arms encircled him to hold him there.

"I wonder how Willa and Colby are doing?"

"I notice you didn't say *what* they were doing."

"I know what they're doing, you silly, sweet, wonderful man. This is their wedding night and they're loving each other like we're doing."

"We didn't on our wedding night."

"Didn't you want to?"

"Hell, yes!"

"Why didn't you then?"

"I was afraid you'd . . . not want me to."

"I'll not believe that for a moment. You didn't like me then."

"You talk too much," he said and took the smile off her lips with a kiss.

As soon as he released her, she said, "Willa was dumb-founded when Colby stopped at the preacher's house. When he makes up his mind, it's made up."

"He gets that from his father. Stop talking about them. Talk about me."

"Farr Quill, you're a spoiled, rotten little boy!"

"Uh huh." He shifted his body as if to leave her. She tightened her arms and legs. He chuckled and kissed her lips softly, almost gaily, while his glorious strength filled her.

"Farr, darling, what would we have done if the major hadn't come back? Oh, it scares me to think about it."

"I was going to escape," he said simply and continued his kissing.

"I'm glad you didn't try that! Hammond would have had an excuse to shoot you then."

"I'd have picked my time. Mmmm . . . you feel so good." His hand stroked her hips. "I like your strong body. You're soft only in the right places—like here, and here." His hand moved up over her belly to her breasts, his lips traveled and teased. "I had a few spies, and I knew which ones were Perry's. I thought I'd give him enough rope to hang himself, and we'd be rid of him."

"Stop talking about him. Talk about me."

He drew back his head. Moonlight coming through the clear glass window lighted the room. She could see the grin on his face. Then he kissed her, a kiss like the ones he'd given her before, only somehow different. His mouth was tender on hers, almost reverent, giving, yet taking.

"Don't get used to all this luxury, Mrs. Quill. Tomorrow I'm taking you home, and taking some of the sass out of you."

"That's tomorrow. What are you going to do about to-night?"

"I'm going to love you until you're so tired you'll have trouble staying in the saddle tomorrow."

"I doubt that, but try anyway. I'm ready to go home. I miss Amy, Daniel and Mercy and Juicy and Rain. Oh, I hope Rain's all right." She placed kisses all along the side of his jaw. "Farrway . . . I miss my house."

"Oh, Libby, my Libby, I missed *you*, I missed this," Farr whispered. "The hardest part was not being with you. I thought about you every day and every night as I lay on the straw bed. It's been a week since I held you like this. Did you miss me, Libby? Tell me."

He turned her over and pressed her slim body into the soft mattress, driving deep, while she held her breath at the wonder of it.

"Oh, yes, yes, I missed you."

He lay on her, a dead weight, an infinitely dear weight, one she held tightly to her. Her hand moved through his hair, down his neck, and over his back in soft caresses. She studied his face staring down at her, aglow with love and desire, felt his hands possessing her, and his brawny torso between her knees. Happiness surged through her being.

"You're my love, my life," he whispered. "I'm going to hold you in my arms every night for the rest of our lives."

Her eyes, her mind and her body were filled with him. There was nothing hurried or demanding about the way they loved each other. Their passion swelled, rocked them, enveloped them in a swirling, translucent world where nothing existed but the two of them. He made love to her until she was sweetly exhausted.

"Sleep. Tomorrow I'm taking my White Dove home," he whispered and cradled her in his arms.

"No, *Wahbah-comeshi*," she murmured sleepily. "You're taking Mrs. Oak Tree home."

Author's Note

Quill's Station, the Sufferite community, and all the people in this story are characters from my imagination, except for the following who were in the area at the time of the story and may have acted as I have portrayed them.

Tecumseh, Chief of the Shawnee

Tenskwatawa, (the Prophet) Tecumseh's brother

Tecumapese, their sister

Chiksika, Tecumapese's son

Sugar Tree, Shawnee maiden

Governor William Harrison, who later became the ninth president of the United States

Anna Harrison, his wife

Zachary Taylor, known to his soldiers as "Old Rough and Ready," who later became the twelfth president of the United States

Captain Nathan Heald, Commander of Fort Dearborn

After the bitter defeat at Tippecanoe, Tecumseh was unable to unite the tribes and push for the right to their land. He went over to the British during the War of 1812 and was killed during a battle with Governor Harrison's army, August 5, 1813.

Among the Shawnee there are many traditions, but none so sacred as the one which was born the night Tecumseh died.

Tecumseh will come again! In that hour of the second coming, there will be nakude-fanwi undawa, "one town of towns." It will mark the end of strife, wars and contentions among all Indian tribes. Then the celebration will consummate all the Great Spirit intends for His red children. It will

begin in the spring and continue without ceasing, from tribe to tribe, until the season closes.

The sign of this second coming will be a star appearing and passing across the sky, as it did at the time of Tecumseh's birth, and Tecumseh will again be born under the same circumstances, to lead his people to this "one town of towns" for all Indians.

Tecumseh will come again!

Dorothy Garlock

Dear Reader,

LONESOME RIVER is the first book of the Wabash River Trilogy. At the present time I am working on DREAM RIVER, the second book, to be released in the spring of 1988. It is Rain Tallman's story and takes place several years later. In DREAM RIVER you will meet once again the characters you met in LONESOME RIVER. The third book, RIVER OF TOMORROW, will be the story of Daniel and Mercy, the orphan children found by Farrway Quill.

I am grateful for the acceptance my Colorado Trilogy received from you, the final critic. Through your letters I have made lasting friendships. To my new readers: if I have entertained you for a few hours, I would be pleased to hear from you and add your name to my mailing list so that you will be notified when my next book is released.

You can write to me, Dorothy Garlock, % Warner Books, Inc., 666 Fifth Avenue, New York, N.Y. 10103. Your letters will be forwarded to me immediately. I will answer each letter as quickly as possible.

Dorothy Garlock
Clear Lake, Iowa